Bruce Merewether was born in Hokitika, New Zealand. His family moved to Christchurch where his first job was in the Bank of New South Wales. He soon moved on and began working at Claude and Associates Advertising on print and TV advertising and design, and later writing headlines and copy. He also organised and directed photo shoots for several large clients over the North and South Is. Ten years ago, Bruce left the company to write fiction. After several false starts, he revisited advertising disciplines and created his own briefing paper. Bruce is married to Mary with two sons.

I would have to single out my wife, Mary. We were watching a TV news item about a couple whose careers involved writing and editing. They both began writing e-books to relieve money problems. The outcome was the success of one of their efforts. Mary asked, 'When are you starting your book?' I didn't start that night… but I started quite early the next day.

The other person I credit for inspiring my work would be the writer of 'stretched fantasies' of post-war espionage: Ian Fleming, creator of my boyhood (and adulthood) hero, James Bond. I read and reread the opening pages of *Dr No* and *Casino Royale* and of the 'neat little officials' – Turkish customs staff welcoming Bond to Turkey in his seminal novel *From Russia With Love* – featuring Head of Station T and likeable rogue Darko Kerim. A master class of character creation.

Bruce Merewether

The Two Little Birds

A story of love, life and war

AUSTIN MACAULEY PUBLISHERS®
LONDON * CAMBRIDGE * NEW YORK * SHARJAH

Copyright © Bruce Merewether 2024

The right of Bruce Merewether to be identified as author of this work has been asserted by the author in accordance with sections 77 and 78 of the Copyright, Designs and Patents Act 1988.

All rights reserved. No part of this publication may be reproduced, stored in a retrieval system, or transmitted in any form or by any means, electronic, mechanical, photocopying, recording, or otherwise, without the prior permission of the publishers.

Any person who commits any unauthorised act in relation to this publication may be liable to criminal prosecution and civil claims for damages.

This is a work of fiction. Names, characters, businesses, places, events, locales, and incidents are either the products of the author's imagination or used in a fictitious manner. Any resemblance to actual persons, living or dead, or actual events is purely coincidental.

A CIP catalogue record for this title is available from the British Library.

ISBN 9781528912709 (Paperback)
ISBN 9781528913003 (Hardback)
ISBN 9781528916691 (ePub-e-book)
ISBN 9781528916684 (Audiobook)

www.austinmacauley.com

First Published 2024
Austin Macauley Publishers Ltd®
1 Canada Square
Canary Wharf
London
E14 5AA

A warm thank you to the many friends who supported and encouraged me on the journey. In no particular order, I thank the following for checking and vetting. Stella Edgar, Christchurch, Jenny Clark, Timaru, Steve and Shirley Perriton, Christchurch. Keith Diedrichs Christchurch, Susan Jacobs Auckland, Sally Ewart Christchurch and the many others who lent an ear or an opinion and offered constructive criticism. I also mention my wife's book club members who read, reread and proofread along with encouraging comments.

Chapter 1

The cooling breeze off the sea gently moved the curtains and caressed the naked back of Marion Springfield as she lay in that most delicious state – drifting in and out of sleep and resampling vague memories of the previous night.

Half dreaming, she brought back the scene of a 'girl's night out' at the last pub and last round of drinks. Assorted males appeared with the usual lines. One, Jon Simpson, had made some standard pickup compliments that Marion parried away for a minute or so until she realised she was talking to an ordinary looking guy but with an extraordinary presence.

She shivered, shifted restlessly as she recalled feelings not usually experienced with the average male. With a growing sense of excitement tinged with a little fear, she recalled standing outside the pub calling a taxi on her mobile, a warm breath in her ear followed by a whispered voice told her that she wouldn't need the taxi home. Jon Simpson stood beside her, dangling the keys to his car.

Marion hesitated, then, defying a lifetime of precautionary advice, accepted his offer. It dawned on her she had seen him before around the small country town and telling herself to trust her instincts and gut feelings she climbed into a battered Falcon wagon. What Marion didn't know was that not all of her 'friends' had gone. One, Sonia Watson, was standing concealed in the shadow of the pub doorway with a small smile on her face.

"I live out on the beach," she said, breaking an uncomfortable silence.

"I know, I've done my research."

"Oh, so you've been observing me from afar," she replied.

"Yeah, I know what I like when I see it," he said.

"Better not get too keen. I'm already booked to my fiancé, James Barclay."

"Yeah, I know him too. You can do a hell of a lot better," he said scornfully.

"You're very confident, aren't you?" she said with a little smile.

They drove on in awkward silence, both knowing there was more to come, but when and how? They soon pulled up beside the long drive that wound its way to her little beach cottage.

"Looks nice, I'll drive you down," he said.

"Don't worry, I need the walk in the fresh air," she said, turning to face him.

Suddenly he reached over and pulled her towards him. "I've always wanted you since the moment I saw you," he said. He kissed her hard on her lips. Marion thrilled to the new sensations and the different feel of a different man caressing her. It was as if she had never experienced sensual pleasure before. It was different and it was something she instinctively knew she could never, ever give up.

"My God, what am I doing? I'm engaged and not to you!" she suddenly exclaimed. "God, I've got to get out of here." She wrenched free of his grasp and, exchanging one last look, turned and ran up the drive, leaving him deflated and slouched back in the seat.

"I'll call you…I've got your number," he shouted at her rapidly retreating back.

#

Marion spent double her normal fifteen minutes in the shower, hoping that somehow it would awaken her from what she felt was both a nightmare and a beautiful dream that had visited her life at the same time. Eventually the water ran cold, so she walked onto a small deck looking out over a sparkling azure blue sea. It was totally private so she stood naked in the now warm breeze and strong sun, watching gulls effortlessly swooping and hovering in the updraught over the sand dunes, while she dried her near black medium length hair.

When dry, she lay back on the lounger, soaking up the sun in this idyllic little piece of paradise and wondered how her life could suddenly turn so complicated. To her friends there wouldn't be a problem – give the cheeky interloper who arrived uninvited into her life the flick and make sure everything is fine with James Barclay, her fiancé, son of a prominent horse breeder and the most eligible bachelor in town, easy as that. Except Marion knew in her heart of hearts that 'most eligible' or not, for her there was something missing in James that she hadn't noticed before – until Jon Simpson turned up.

One thing that hadn't changed in her life was the cottage, a legacy from a favourite aunt she had spent many weeks staying with as a young girl. It was hers now and it had brought stability to a life that had seen several dead-end jobs and a couple of non-event relationships. The property transaction process had also awoken an interest in a career path of property valuation and she was several months into an extramural degree course that would give her a valuable qualification.

Add to this her engagement to a local prominent horse breeder's son and until last night, everything was looking sweet.

#

A full moon had appeared from behind the clouds as Jon Simpson sat watching her walk the white crushed shell drive. It had taken on an unreal luminosity in the moonlight and was a surreal image that would remain with him for the rest of his life. Soon she had disappeared from sight. Expelling a lung full of air together with a mild expletive, he reached for the starter, found the gears and swerved the big car out onto the main road, firing a spray of shingle onto the grass verge.

In a few minutes he was at his rental, the headlights sweeping the old overgrown macrocarpa hedge as he swung into the driveway. Banging the door open, he flicked the switch on the jug and grabbed the safest food he could find from the fridge. A restless night of little sleep saw him lying awake waiting for the sun to hit his bedroom window at six am in the morning.

Where to go from here? Staring morosely into a cup of lukewarm coffee, he suddenly stood up, ditched the dregs in the sink, grabbed a threadbare Swanni, car keys and beanie and headed out the door to his wagon. Checking the tool box was in the back, he jumped in and headed off out of town. He had things to get on with: a five-kilometre fencing contract for a local farmer that was running behind and another eight kilometres waiting in the wings from his next door neighbour.

Jon Simpson, twenty-eight years old, had done some yards at university but tiring quickly of that, decided to get back to fresh air and hard work for a few years as an itinerant fencing contractor. His farm upbringing in New Zealand's South Island had given him the skills and toughness to handle the work and the hard men and women he worked for.

He headed south driving through rolling hill country with flats fenced off for deer farming.

Deer fencing was his core business and he was about to turn into the property he was currently working on. He pulled up at the entrance and sat for a while looking over the project and composing himself for the meeting with the often testy, difficult client.

Gerald Brown did not impress Jon Simpson. The son of a successful and wealthy property developer, Gerald was ill-suited to the family business and had been 'settled' on a deer farm that took his fancy – an expedient way of moving him on from involvement in property development. However, Gerald's father wasn't about to throw good money after bad and engaged the services of a farm manager to unobtrusively 'help' steer his investment in deer and offspring.

He drove on through the new, impressive and excessive stone entrance and up the lengthy drive, pulling up in front of an outbuilding serving as an office. Sam White, farm manager, came out and leant against the car.

"Gidday Jon. Gerald will be down in a minute – reckon you'll have that last stretch done by Friday week?"

"He bloody better. He knows the timetable. Three hundred and fifty hinds will be here on Saturday week from True Blue Stud!" Gerald Brown had appeared at the door of the office.

"Still got the old Ford 'coon I see. The money I'm paying you I would have thought you would be driving something better. You're lowering the tone around here, hey, I'm putting my wife's three-year-old Audi allroad on the market. I can just see you in that, should take a look." He was taking the mickey now and Jon knew full well. He let this sort of stuff go over his head. What goes around comes around.

"By the way, you got a minute in my office?" Gerald said, adding, "By yourself."

Jon and Sam exchanged questioning glances as Jon followed Gerald Brown into the office, closing the door behind him. The rough humour had gone and Brown was sitting scowling behind an oversized desk.

"Don't bother sitting down, because this won't take long," he said with a false smile. "Four words…Don't go near Marion!" he said, repeating with the false smile.

"Marion who?"

"What you and Marion didn't know is that someone saw you and her leave the pub last night," said Gerald.

"And what's that mean to you?" Jon said evenly.

"I won't tell you what it means to me, but I will tell you what it means to you. You won't get another fencing contract for a hundred kilometres around and you might like to check out a good tent because you won't be living in your little shack any longer. I know of a certain property developer who's interested in that land. The district needs a new supermarket and he thinks where you are is just right. Of course it wasn't going to happen for a few more years, but we can always hurry things up a bit."

Jon Simpson stood returning Gerald Brown's hard stare while thinking furiously about how to outmanoeuvre him. Finally, he had to admit to himself that he had no quick answer.

"Well, it looks like you've got me stuffed," he said.

"Yeah, I thought so too," he replied.

Jon turned and walked through the door, got in his car and headed out to the fencing site. Gerald Brown would keep. And he might just get some use out of an almost finished law degree.

Jon had to admit he didn't have much wriggle room on this one. He needed the money that Gerald paid and he needed a roof over his head, although the bit about the supermarket was probably more puff than anything else. He'd just have to keep his head down and get the work done. But he couldn't put Marion out of his mind and while working he carried thoughts of the encounter in his car, that sustained him through the tedium of a hard day of digging post holes and stapling and straining a deer fence. That night he drove back to town towards a low sun washing pink and mauve colours through rolling hills.

It was a stunning final curtain to a hard day at the office, but he felt confident that before too many days would end he would get what he was looking for, Gerald Brown or no Gerald Brown.

Sonia Watson hadn't stopped smiling since that night she instinctively hid herself in the shadow of the pub doorway. Why she hadn't stopped smiling is that she knew she now had all she needed to return James Barclay to her side.

The first thing to do was to create a meeting with James at a place where a frank and full discussion could happen away from nosy townspeople. She also had to give him a compelling reason for the meeting, which was something she knew he would be wary of. She would pick her time to call him and that time was now. She knew that every Thursday he drove a short distance out of town to a point overlooking the sea and sat parked up looking towards a small offshore island, eating a takeout lunch and coffee.

As a child, his father often took him fishing near the island and it held a place in his memory of simpler, happier times. For James Barclay was a troubled man. Sonia Watson was his childhood sweetheart and it had not been in his plans for him to drift away from her during her short OE and end up engaged to Marion Springfield.

She picked up her phone and dialled his mobile.

"James speaking."

"It's Sonia. I need to talk to you, James…"

"Sonia, I'm not interested, I—"

"You will when you hear what I've going to tell you, I'm coming up to the point now. Don't go away."

She snapped the lid shut on her phone, grabbed the keys to her small Toyota and headed off to the point, driving quickly along the twisting road before he could change his mind. He was still there, the front door open and with one long leg stretched out. He was drinking his coffee and smoking a cigarette – the one a day he had managed to cut back to.

He didn't move or acknowledge her when she let herself into the front passenger seat. Eventually, taking one last drag on the cigarette, he stubbed it out and turned to face her.

"Well?" he said flatly.

"I want you back."

"You know I'm engaged. We asked you to the party and you didn't turn up."

"What did you expect? We were dating for five years and knew each other for ten."

"You had to do the big OE. If you'd waited eighteen months, we'd have both gone together."

"It's all old history now, James, but what it's not is this. Ask me who ended up taking Marion home from the pub last night."

"And who was that?" replied James.

"A guy from out of town doing a fencing contract for Gerald Brown," she replied. "And if you have any other doubts about where your future lies I'd give serious thought to your connection with the five thousand dollars that went missing from the polo club. You know I know and your father knows who caused that to disappear and your father ended up having to make it reappear to balance the books. Remember, it's a small place we live in and people have long memories."

Sonia and James both sat in silence staring out across the sea. Finally, she opened the door and walked over to her car. She pulled up beside him, cracked the window and gave him one last message.

"Think carefully, James, your future depends on it. Call me." One thirty am. He checked his watch once more to make sure. The full moon sent its soft message of light, forming the shadow of a plus symbol from the nearby window frame. Jon watched it creep slowly over the floor, reminding him of coming up with a minus on Marion.

He lay there another five minutes gathering courage. Emotional need met physical desire: he vaulted out of bed, brushed his teeth, threw on a pair of jeans and a dark thermal top, a pair of old running shoes and he was out the door with a small Maglite torch in his hand. He was not sure how she would greet him in the early hours of the morning, but he won't worry about that until he had to. It was only a few kilometres to her place but he took a longer route through the sand hills to avoid nocturnal spies with big mouths.

The friendly moon was providing light for sure footing and fast progress and soon the outline of her cottage appeared. There was a low power light over the back entrance, a 'landing light' left on just for him, he told himself, smiling wickedly. Padding softly up the steps, he approached the French doors and peered cautiously inside. He could make out her sleeping form in a bed only a few feet away. Taking a deep breath, he tapped softly on the window. Praying she won't scream and call the neighbours, he tapped again with a slightly more insistent touch.

Marion shifted in her sleep and settled back to her dreams. Cursing softly, he started tapping louder. This time she woke up and looked fearfully in the direction of the noise. He was sure she can see him now and stood under the light so she could identify him.

Her face lit up with recognition and she leapt out of bed and opened the door. "You shouldn't be here, but I'm glad you are. Wow! I can't believe it," she exclaimed.

"Last time you ran away," he protested.

"Yeah I know. Maybe I should have stayed. I knew that when I got to bed later; I didn't sleep more than an hour."

"Me neither," he replied.

He wrapped her in his arms and pulled her tightly to him. She was only wearing a thin nightgown and could feel him pressing hard against her stomach. She was gulping deep lungfuls of air as she fought two tides of passion, one that threatened to take out into an unknown sea, the other pulling her back onto the beach of familiar territory.

He freed his hand from around her back and slowly started massaging her breasts. This returned her to their first encounter a few nights ago but it also brought back the anxiety she felt when waking up the next morning.

"Please, please go," she said unconvincingly as she pushed him towards the door.

"I'm going. But you know that I'll be back for you one day soon," he said, his voice suddenly hard and tight with emotion. He turned and pausing under the light for a few seconds, looked at her, then stepped off the porch and vanished into the night.

Chapter 2

Sonia Watson woke up alone, but in the warm glow of knowing that she was on course to regain her first love, James Barclay. She was never more convinced of the truth in the old saying: "Knowledge is Power." She was now confident she had all the ammunition she needed to take back what she regarded as rightfully hers. She hadn't looked for another man since the breakup, but with strong sexual needs she continually hungered for the hard muscle and male scent that a mature man would bring to her bedroom.

Cameron Barclay had rashly conducted a secret, clandestine affair with Sonia Watson for six years. Sonia, being no fool, realised this serious and illegal indiscretion by her future father-in-law was as good as money in the bank, her bank. Cameron Barclay was a wealthy man. He owned and ran one of New Zealand's leading stud farms. He also made the crafty decision to marry into money as well. His wife, Helen Barclay, was the sole benefactor of her deceased parents' large holding of prime land one hundred kilometres south.

Sonia's mother had died when she was young and her father, a farm labourer, only just managed to provide a meagre living for them both. He never remarried or took another partner so she spent her childhood growing up in a lonely, bleak home. But she grew up quickly and with a realistic sense of pragmatism. Sure, Cameron Barclay took advantage of a young girl, but she was not so young in attitude and had quickly moved on from the day she lost her innocence. In her early teens, one of her few emotional releases was to ride and care for the several horses that her father's employer, Todd Baxter, kept on the farm for his wife and children. They were a warm generous couple, who saw in Sonia a raw need for connection and happily provided the horses and facilities for Sonia to enjoy. Under Todd's tutelage she rapidly learnt the skills of riding and developed a feel for her charges, pouring much of her unexpressed love into their care. It was during one of her frequent visits that she came across a large luxury car parked in the driveway. The car belonged to prominent horse breeder, Cameron Barclay, who was leaning against the car talking to her father's boss. As she walked past the pair Todd called her over and introduced her to Cameron, briefly explaining about Cameron's horse breeding enterprise. Sonia felt an immediate attraction to the older man and Cameron felt an affinity for a girl with an obvious talent with horses.

Sonia drifted off to a place of sleep where worries and anxieties are left at the door. She woke, refreshed, made coffee and then decided to confront her first possible problem. She called Cameron on his mobile. Cameron had taken the precaution of running a separate mobile for her calls only. He kept it in a safe place only he knew of and took it with him when alone. He was alone in his car this day and picked up the call after only a brief delay.

"Cameron Barclay speaking," he said with the guarded voice that is the preserve of people from all walks of life with something to hide.

"It's Sonia here," she replied quietly.

The bald truth of the matter is that there wasn't an excess of love or emotion in their relationship.

He needed an itch scratched that his cultured and cool wife couldn't reach, and she was filling some need from a childhood short on warmth and love. As well, she was extremely highly sexed and was addicted to something that so far in her life she could only get from Cameron Barclay.

"I've spoken to James," she said matter-of-factly.

"I know, he's been in a shirty mood all day. He hates feeling like he's being pushed around," he added.

"We just need to make sure the fencer guy keeps hanging around Marion," she replied. "Gerald Brown is stuffing things up," she added, "he's told me that he gave Jon Simpson – the fencer guy – a big serve about chasing Marion."

"Shit!" he exclaimed. "Why did you tell him?"

"James is very impressed by Gerald Brown and I wanted him to think that everyone knew about him and Marion, in case he decided to forgive her and take her back," she replied. "But you've got some pull with Gerald, give him a call and tell him we're onto it and to back off. The guy needs the work to keep him here. With a bit of help behind the scenes, like more work, and say a bank loan for a house, we'll get him to stay here. And…" She was now on a roll. "Why don't you put him in your senior team? You were moaning you were short of good flankers. He's as hard as nails and fit as from all the fencing."

Cameron, as a release from the big stakes and big ego world of the international bloodstock industry, coached the local senior rugby team, the other passion he'd maintained from his days as an exceptional, and aspiring young rugby player. His career virtually ended before it had started by a knee injury in an All Black trial match, an injury that would never be right again. He found the involvement coaching the team took him back to his grassroots and maintained contact with the down-to-earth people of modest means.

Before Sonia met Cameron, she made it her business to know about everything and everyone. It naturally followed that she came to know all aspects of the game of rugby and the guys that played it, because rugby was still the all-consuming interest in small communities and the main topic of conversation – after horses and farming – in this part of rural New Zealand.

"When am I going to see you again?" he said, changing the subject.

"You call Gerald Brown and calm him down first and then we'll talk about when you will be seeing me, and where," she added.

"OK, OK," he said impatiently.

Sonia Watson was the only person on the planet that could talk to Cameron Barclay the way she did. But she still feared that it might only be a matter of time before he tired of her like he had with his wife. She had to plan her parachute very carefully. And although she loved James in her own peculiar way, her survival instincts, honed through a tough upbringing, told her that he wasn't a stayer either.

#

He was driving back from town and he pulled over and picked up his other phone. Gerald Brown's number came up and he hit the appropriate button.

"Gerald Brown here," the voice with the affected accent came through the hands-free car phone.

"Cameron Barclay here, Gerald," he said mouthing bloody wanker to himself.

"What can I do for you, Cam?" Using the short version of his name, got right up Cameron Barclay's nose. It was a familiarity that had to be earned by people that he respected and it had nothing to do with money, power or position. They could be a player that had turned out through thick and thin, season after season for the senior rugby team he coached or they could be a farm labourer or a wealthy bloodstock owner. He stifled any reaction and moved on to the purpose of his call.

"Yeah, gidday, I just want to talk to you about a young fella that's doing some fencing for you."

"I thought you might call about him. I gave him a short, sharp message about who he was seeing."

"I know, I just want you to lay off him and regarding that issue it suits me that he is seeing the Marion girl," he said carefully.

"OK," he replied, wondering what the hell Cameron Barclay was up to now. "How's the bloodstock business?" Gerald asked moving on to less testy ground.

"Can't complain. Well, I'll be off but I'd appreciate if you can see that young fella right – give him more work if you've got it – I want to nail him for my openside flanker for what's left of the season, so anything you can do to keep him around would be good. Thanks, bye."

Cameron Barclay couldn't wait to get off the phone and sat staring ahead to the hills in the distance. He turned his thoughts to Sonia and when he could get his hands on her again.

#

Helen Barclay lay back in the claw foot bath looking up at the ceiling and wondering if she had got it right with the bathroom colour. She had just spent the previous eighteen months gradually restoring the once beautiful, centuries-old homestead. She fell in love with the house quicker then she had fallen for Cameron when he showed her around on the open day all those years ago. It was the ultimate manoeuvre that had her walking down the aisle to her waiting groom. And three weeks later after returning from her honeymoon in Italy, he carried her over the doorstep of their new home.

She ran some more hot water and using an expensive body lotion bought on a return trip to Italy, began massaging her breasts and stomach. Cameron's attention now seemed to be taken up so much by the farm and stock that she wished she could have stayed on in Italy with him forever.

Her daily bath had become a ritual and a reward to compensate for the reduced interest from Cameron.

Before meeting Cameron, Helen lived on a large holding where her parents ran sheep and cattle and were prominent members of the local farming community. Helen's mother was university educated, with a degree in art history. She was a skilled water colourist and encouraged local artists with her deep resources of wealth and her own talent. It was a short step for Helen to follow her example and she took a fine arts degree majoring in painting and sculpture. Her current passion for sculpture was evidenced around the grounds with many of her highly original pieces. Her other dream that was taking more and more of her attention was her ambition to travel to Italy and stay as an Artist in Residence.

As she dried herself, she reflected on the way her life had panned out. She had the all-absorbing passion of her art and it largely replaced what she didn't get from Cameron. When she did think about him and measured his commitment to the farm, she felt in a vague way that it didn't add up.

She considered another woman in his life but couldn't come up with any likely candidates. If she thought outside the square, she might have seen it staring her in the face. But in her limited experience of life she would never in a million years come up with her son's one-time girlfriend, Sonia Watson, in her early twenties, as the 'other woman'.

She pulled on an Italian bathrobe and walked out through bi-folding doors onto the flagstone terrace. She was indeed an 'Italiano' and admired the design flair and passion for things of beauty she absorbed like a suntan while in Italy. So inspired by the stunning house and garden landscapes she saw on her honeymoon, she was now working on a formal topiary garden in front of the terrace – her own piece of Italian inspiration – imported to rural New Zealand.

She sat down on the recliner chair and thought about her Italian dreams and about her Italian friend Arianna who she met while they were doing a degree in fine arts at university in Wellington. Arianna had been encouraged to come to New Zealand to study by her uncle, a successful restaurant owner prominent in the local Italian community.

She dwelled on these thoughts and made a mental note to contact Arianna to tell her of her plans. Helen settled back and let the late afternoon sun warm her and infuse her with its energy. She was suddenly woken from her reverie by the hall phone. She slowly stood up and half asleep headed inside to pick it up. It was Cameron.

"Don't worry about dinner for me…I've got a meeting with a bloodstock agent from Hong Kong…it could drag on for a while…just leave it on the bench with a plate over it."

"Ok…fine…" she said blandly.

Another typical end to another day with Cameron Barclay.

#

The bloodstock agent from Hong Kong that Cameron Barclay was leaving his dinner on the bench for was, of course, the 'other woman', Sonia Watson. He picked up his special 'hotline' phone and hit the number for Sonia.

"Hello, Sonia speaking."

"I need to see you…like very soon," he said.

"Yeah I know, where?"

"I'll meet you at the small house with the red roof by the bridge on Lost Valley Road. It's the only house along that stretch. Drive in and park in the garage, I'll leave the door open…I'll be there waiting for you," he replied quietly, as if worried he might somehow be overheard.

He drove along the main road until he reached the Lost Valley Road turnoff. Looking furtively in the rearview mirror he turned and drove quickly until he reached the house with the red roof. He looked up and down the road, then turned up the drive and pulled into the large double garage at the end.

Leaving the door unlocked he went into the house and stood in the kitchen. He took off his shirt and dropped it on the floor, then went a few paces into the hall and took off his moleskin trousers, dropping them in view of the kitchen and leaving the adjoining door open. He then opened the first door in the hallway into the main bedroom. There was a large king-size bed and he threw his shorts off and lay back on the bed and waited for Sonia, now totally naked.

If ever there was a couple that hungered for each other with the intensity of advanced stages of starvation, it was Cameron and Sonia. He lay back and contemplated the house he conveniently had the use of for as long as he liked. It was provided by a grateful school mate from the past. A mate who was being bled dry by a lowlife con – come blackmailer who had a bit of dirt on him. Cameron listened to his friend's story, told him he didn't want the details of his private life then went to see the bastard that was picking on an old friend. He was big enough and tough enough to get the small-time crim to come to his senses without even laying a hand on him. Job done and he now had a convenient little bolthole.

The sound of a car approaching reminded him why he was here. He heard the car door slam and the sound of her shoes on the gravel drive. The door opened and slammed shut and a few minutes elapsed before Sonia walked through the door.

Sonia had something he couldn't resist and she was the only person who could exert that sort of control over him. Cameron lived for his ambitions and their fulfilment which meant controlling everything he possibly could in his life. The responsibility weighed on him and Sonia's strong hand was a welcome relief to a person who always had to be right.

Chapter 3

Jon Simpson lay back on the bed beside Marion, having just finished a great home-cooked meal with the bemused, uncertain smile that 'seemingly' good news brings. Leaving Gerald Brown's deer farm after a day's work, he had found Cameron Barclay leaning against his car apparently waiting for someone – that someone was him.

Cameron Barclay stepped forward and Jon pulled up beside him. "Got a minute?" he said.

"Sure," Jon replied warily.

"Cameron Barclay," he said stretching out a hand…"Jon Simpson, isn't it?"

"That's right," Jon replied.

"I understand there's been a bit of a problem with Gerald. Am I right?" Jon nodded in reply.

"I think you'll find things are sweet now." he said raising his eyebrows.

"Yeah…no worries…now," Jon said guardedly.

"Great…Because I want to talk to you about something if you've got a couple of minutes. Here jump in my car…" he said opening the door of a big black BMW M5.

Jon slid into an interior of unfamiliar plushness and luxury. He was temporarily transfixed by the array of lights, LEDs, and the pièce de résistance for a guy with a 20-year-old Ford Falcon, the onboard GPS.

"Right…let's get down to business…" he said as he swung his large frame smoothly into the driver's seat. Jon noted the ease of movement for a big man and reflected that he could probably look after himself.

"OK then…" he started off…"I've done some digging and from my contacts in town I'm told you are a bloody good openside flanker. That you played a couple of seasons for a 'varsity' team that took out the senior competition two years in a row. They said you were one of the main reasons for their success…"

he finished and looked at him accusingly from under his eyebrows as if challenging him to disagree.

"Ah…yeah…I won't turn down a compliment," he replied wondering what was coming next.

"Right…well, cutting to the chase…I want you to play the rest of the season for our local team that I coach. We've got five games left and have a chance of winning the competition cup. Well, what do you think?"

"What about Gerald Brown's deer fence? I need to put weekends and twelve-hour days into it otherwise it's not going to get finished. Gerald will have my nuts."

"Don't worry about that. I'm getting you another hand. A good, experienced fencer that I'm paying for. It will be finished right on the nail. I want you on that team and I've covered it off with Gerald. Not that I could give a toss what he thinks," he finished and looked at him expectantly.

#

Jon arrived home and after a peck on the cheek, told Marion of his conversation with Cameron.

"Well, what are you going to do?" Marion asked after hearing him out.

"I've got nothing to lose and I've missed playing. I'll call him tomorrow and tell him yes."

#

Since Marion's first night with Jon she had been living with a feeling she couldn't describe. She felt that suddenly her life had relevance and meaning she never realised she was missing. The thought occurred to her that she was simply right for him and he was right for her. She went through her part-time occupation merchandising and promoting a natural skincare range around the region with a quiet smile as if she had a secret only she would ever know.

She felt a stab of guilt for what was inevitably going to happen to her engagement to James, but the feeling of 'rightness' about her relationship with Jon, added strength to her conviction that change was necessary and inevitable.

Stopping for a coffee at a place she regularly visited while travelling for her work she found herself sitting near Sonia Watson. She was naturally wary about her since Sonia finally arrived home from her overseas trip to find that James hadn't 'stayed put' as she had expected and was engaged to the new girl in town, Marion Springfield.

Marion was therefore surprised by her warmth and friendliness and couldn't believe Sonia would accept defeat so easily. It seemed more than a coincidence that Sonia was there when Marion came in at her regular time and she felt there was an agenda she didn't understand. She turned it over in her mind while travelling to her next retailer.

#

Helen sat and watched the Arts channel on Sky TV and retiring at 12.30 am, was almost asleep when Cameron came home at 1 am. She feigned sleep so she wouldn't have to ask how the meeting went and then spend the rest of the night wondering if his response was genuine or not. He dropped his gear on the floor and slid quietly into bed and within what seemed like only seconds, was fast asleep, snoring lightly.

Of course she was anything but asleep and lay dwelling on her thoughts. After thirty minutes, she could stand it no longer and rising, put on a dressing gown and joined the thousands of other insomniacs, fixing a meal, drinking hot chocolate, reading, making love, watching television, or surfing the net. Helen chose the latter and sat in the dark, with the screen lighting her face as she sat and planned her future.

She googled Italy – Artists in Residence, and sat browsing through the wide range of options. Helen was often not very happy, but she was happy now pursuing a dream she never realised she had, having lived for so long under the shadow of Cameron's dynamic and powerful personality.

She scrolled down through the Artist in Residence opportunities smiling to herself at the exciting array of options. Her eyes sparkled with an enthusiasm she had not felt since she was a Fine Arts student at university.

The problem of course was how to tell Cameron. It occurred to her that he may secretly like the idea of her going to Italy but she knew his controlling instinct would kick in and there would be issues. She closed the computer down and headed for bed. She knew she would sleep easily now and that during the night her unconscious mind would sort the information and create a broad picture of her future plans.

James drove back from his meeting with Sonia at the point overlooking the sea, deep in thought on developments.

His father had seemed strangely unconcerned when he heard about Jon Simpson and the engagement of Sonia and himself being history. James himself felt relieved if the truth be known. He had taken up with Marion on a whim and sometimes asked himself if she was his sort of girl. He now felt back in his comfort zone. Sonia was smart and looked after the details, something that didn't hold much appeal to him.

James took after his mother – creative, sensitive and not that interested in the stud farm as a career option. This was something he could never tell his father who was desperately hoping James would suddenly develop enthusiasm for a career in the training and breeding of thoroughbred horses. He may not be the answer to his father's prayers, but back with Sonia, he felt re-anchored in life, if not yet in the right place.

It was difficult to put a finger on what James's function was in the Barclay farming operation.

If James was put on the spot, he probably wouldn't know either. Cameron would say that he was here to learn. His lack of aptitude was surpassed only by Cameron's dogged determination that James would, through some osmotic process take on the skills, knowledge and inclination to become a genuine partner in the business.

Where there should be stacks of bloodstock journals, there were expensive, imported, interior design magazines and sophisticated lifestyle publications like Wallpaper and Urbis. James and his mother pored over these and discussed the contents at length.

#

Cameron kept his head in the sand regarding the truth about James and instead occupied himself with his bloodstock business, Sonia, and the local senior rugby team. The latter now temporarily grabbing the lion's share of his attention. It was coming up to finals time. Jon had been with the team for the past three games and had repaid in volumes Cameron's well-informed gamble. He was athletic and talented, but most of all he played with almost total disregard for his own health and safety. He was a proverbial Clark Kent – mild, easy going off the field – ferocious and fearless on it – exactly the requirement for his position of openside flanker.

He also fitted in well with the team, with the exception of one player, Wayne Mason. In fact, there were two problems. One was that Jon's on-field performance was soon to overshadow Wayne, who played blind side flanker – a comparable position to Jon. Cameron, ever the bush psychologist, worked to minimise the problem by taking Wayne aside and emphasising the value of every individual to the team. He also made him vice-captain which seemed to be the answer to issues on the rugby field.

However, one issue that couldn't be sorted on the rugby field was Wayne's attraction to Marion. Wayne had tried several times to start something with Marion before she met James. He was never successful and he brooded over this blunt lesson in life and love, until the match up of James and Marion. This seemed to be the end of the issue. James was part of the 'landed gentry' while he was only a worker at a local sawmill, who left school at fifteen. Cameron, his rugby coach since he was five years old, was his mentor and a man he most admired and looked up to.

Rules were rules and Marion was now James's girl and that was that. All of this changed when Jon came onto the scene and turned life in the small rural town of a thousand or so people upside down. Wayne's modest education, his rural rawness and his lack of prospects were suddenly brought back into sharp focus for him to stew over. However, these problems were soon to be relegated to life's back page with the rapidly approaching rugby finals.

#

Cameron Barclay, with final day tension written all over his face, stalked into the senior team changing room of the Waihi Rugby Football Club. The players were going through their own individual preparations – some were reading, others sat with notebooks going over moves and strategies, while others lay on the wooden benches chilling out and listening to their music on headphones. He walked the floor, looking into each player's face. As a successful coach he had an intuitive feel who to kick in the butt and who to give a supportive word of encouragement to. He had coached teams to be a team first and a group of individuals of widely varying talents, second. He knew from his playing days that successful teams were the ones that played for each other.

It is only a rural district derby, but in this country where rugby is king and the feelings so intense to the local players, such a final is every bit as important as an international test match is to top players. And many an international player has run out on the hallowed turf of huge overseas stadiums and have started their careers at such a humble level. The referee poked his head in the door. Cameron looked up and said to everyone, "Right…it's your time now. Whatever you've got in you, leave it out on that field. Now go out and do it for yourselves and the team…and Waihi!"

#

Marion sat looking out at the modest gardens of Waihi Community Hospital. She was red-eyed from lack of sleep. The sound of the blood pressure pump squeezing Jon's arm was the only sound in the room. She looked over to him, closing her eyes against the memory of the freak tackle that left Jon prone on the turf. He didn't move for several seconds and the St John's Ambulance came quickly to attend to him.

The prognosis was serious but hopeful. Jon had sustained a neck injury that had left him paralysed from the waist down. The doctors were optimistic that the injury was not permanent. He had some feeling in his feet, an encouraging sign that he could expect a good recovery. Just how good, only time would tell.

Cameron was shattered. The game was played out for the twenty minutes left and Waihi won the final for the first time in fifteen years. Celebrations were muted and a very sober and concerned Cameron and a couple of senior players stood by Jon's hospital bed telling him they would take care of everything, including the remaining deer fencing for Gerald Brown. Jon nodded and Marion, still looking ashen faced, gave Cameron a wan smile of thanks.

It was now different days, and different ways. Marion drove slowly with exaggerated care away from the hospital. Everything suddenly seemed so fragile. She feared for herself almost as much as she worried about Jon. The brutal force with which fate could plunge into her life like a home invasion and walk off with health and happiness, caused fear to ripple through her.

She was of course suffering from delayed shock and finally turned into her driveway with a huge feeling of relief.

Marion was now on the treadmill well known by all people with loved ones in critical medical care; the continual rotation of running a house, earning a living and visiting the hospital. In her prayers, she hoped it would all turn out to be a temporary test of character and her loyalty to Jon, and that soon they would be back to normal. Jon fit, healthy and back to his teasing, lovemaking ways, having a laugh at her expense and generally not taking life too seriously.

#

Cameron immersed himself in his world of breeding horses, Sonia, and keeping Gerald Brown happy with his deer fencing. He never forgot Jon and he regularly visited the hospital. The prognosis was good, supporting the initial opinion that Jon would make a good recovery. How good, everyone would just have to wait and see.

Chapter 4

The additional distractions gave welcome space to Helen to continue with her Italian Artist in Residence project. She kept putting off the day she would tell Cameron her intentions, hoping that once confirmed and finalised it would have a momentum of its own and sweep any objections from Cameron aside. In the meantime, there was plenty to do.

Returning to her computer she uncovered several residences that held appeal. But one stood out from all others and she fell for La Macina di San Cresci, located, as described on the home page, near Greve, in di Chianti, the heart of Tuscany and between the two great cities of the Renaissance – Florence and Sienna.

She was enchanted by the fact that the residential building Pieve di San Cresci was already in existence in 948 AD, before Leonardo da Vinci and when Florence was just a small town.

Helen's mind swam with the thoughts of living in such a place. While she loved the raw beauty of New Zealand, she dreamed of a life in a world with such an ancient pedigree and couldn't wait to put her feet on the streets and paths trod by histories past.

Cameron announced he was going to a horse sale at Wainui, a day's drive away and that he would stay a couple of days as he had 'other business' to attend to. Helen was now able to proceed with her plans unfettered by Cameron's presence. She downloaded the application form and set about compiling an up-to-date curriculum vitae. This process took the rest of the day and she went to bed that night her head buzzing with thoughts of her future.

She awoke the next morning and with a long day ahead prepared an unusually large and hearty breakfast. Helen usually didn't have much enthusiasm for breakfast. In fact, she never felt that interested in food or ever hungered that much for anything, until now. The project had injected purpose into her life and she finished a large coffee and she set about her next task compiling a collection of photographs of recent work and considering what project she would commit to during her stay. The photographic record was straightforward but coming up with a project to work on while in residence was going to be more testing.

Helen decided now was the time to contact Maria. She scrolled down through her sent file and finding her last email sent off her message and closed down the computer and went off to bed with a smile on her face.

Cameron was, as usual, being economical with the truth. Yes, he was going to Wainui, and yes there was a stock sale, but he was no more than mildly interested. The 'other business' is that he was looking at a veteran car, a side interest like rugby he'd never had time to pursue. The main reason of course was a few days of R & R with Sonia, who covered her absence to James with a fictitious 'friend' in Wellington. James's reaction was neutral and Sonia was reminded of vague questions she had asked herself about just how hot James was for her. As far as sex was concerned, he was barely lukewarm when compared to Cameron. Feeling uncomfortable with these thoughts, she quickly put the whole issue of her dual relationship with father and son out of her mind, moving swiftly into her favoured 'functioning pragmatism' mode.

Being forever cautious, Cameron arranged to meet Sonia at the house on Lost Valley Road. She would leave her car in the garage and they would continue to Wainui in his car.

He had booked for three nights at The Railway Hotel which was substantially better than it sounded. It was a beautifully restored two-storey building from the early 1900s and Cameron had reserved a room – the best they had – on the top floor.

They checked in, with the reception clerk doing a quickly disguised double-take at the man in his mid-40s and a woman who looked no more than 25. Cameron, tired and distracted failed to notice the name 'Barry Mason' on the reception clerk's name badge. Sonia took the lift with the porter and their two small cases while Cameron used the stairs. Having a younger woman in his life was a less than gentle reminder that he wasn't young anymore and a bit of exercise would be a good idea.

They showered and discussed what came next. Sonia would take his secret credit card – with a generous limit for these occasions – and do the shops while Cameron would look-up the guy with the veteran cars. They would meet back at the hotel at about 6 pm and dine at an exclusive restaurant in a discreet location that Cameron occasionally visited while travelling.

Sonia departed smiling. She could shop on her own without Cameron hanging around asking if she really wanted or needed this or that and Cameron could spend time talking cars and kicking tyres. He took the torn, folded page from a veteran and vintage car magazine and finding the small advert set off, while Sonia headed up town to the inner city renewal project recently completed.

Weaving her way through a tangle of brick-walled lanes and alleyways she found herself in a maze of small boutiques and designer shops created by owner-operators. She felt a pang of envy, while talking to motivated and passionate retailers, selling stunningly original clothing, imported euro-design furniture, and ethnic pottery and glassware. At a small boutique, she tried on several articles of clothing, settling for a stylish, subtly embroidered little black evening jacket with shocking pink buttons she would wear to dinner that night.

She wandered through the 'previously loved' shops with collections of old and not so old that in this context took on an added value and charm she would not have recognised before. While she enjoyed herself, she felt strangely unsettled and felt that something was missing in her life. Needing a little more 'retail therapy' she visited a small up-market perfume and cosmetic shop. Sonia had never purchased Chanel before and she decided today was the day. She picked up a bottle of Chanel's new offer, Chanel Noir, that as you would expect, came in beautiful black packaging – a pleasing reminder of her new jacket.

An immaculate shop assistant appeared and sprayed a series of sample cards with the Chanel range. Sonia simply couldn't resist the one that caught her eye first, the Chanel Noir and happily paid the asking price of two hundred and fifty dollars. Cameron will complain, but will be secretly pleased that his woman judges him able to afford the luxury of expensive perfume. With men, she knew it was all about egos and reminded herself of this as she left a beaming assistant who'd just closed the single biggest sale of the day, only a minute before closing time.

At a cafe, she ordered a cappuccino and a complicated compilation of fruit and pastry that was delicious. She picked up a magazine and leafed through it. She checked her watch, drank the rest of the coffee, then stepping onto the footpath walked briskly and headed back towards the hotel. She would be late, but not too late for Cameron, and what she imagined would be a beautiful meal later that night.

Freshly showered and wearing her stunning new jacket, Sonia checked herself in the full length mirror for the third time. She hesitated while holding the just purchased bottle of Chanel. Less is more she decided and placed it carefully back on the antique marble washstand. It would keep until later. She closed the door and swept down the stairs like Scarlet O'Hara in Gone With The Wind to join her 'Rhett Butler' in his BMW M5 idling patiently at the front door of the hotel. Sonia, unusually for one so young, had a fascination for old movies, that, quaint and restrained, contrasted with today's fare and seemed to search out and find a responsive chord from her childhood.

As she sat in the seat and buckled up she reminded herself that in spite of her indifferent mood earlier, life was good – she was going out in her new jacket, to an exclusive restaurant, in a luxurious BMW driven by a wealthy man brimming with natural charm and rugged self-confidence.

#

"How did you go with the car," she asked breaking the silence more than out of genuine interest.

"Well…the one I am interested in is beautiful," he replied distantly. "I think I'll buy it…we just need to agree on the price…It's a six cylinder MG convertible, painted in a beautiful British racing green, built during the war in 1938."

Sonia couldn't understand the preoccupation of men with cars. She understood the attraction of a near-new luxury BMW, but the mysterious attraction of old cars puzzled her. It was similar to their attachment to old clothes and especially those used for fishing, complete with fishy odour. She smiled at the 'jokey' phrase often quoted, that men 'loved their cars more than them'…there was possibly more than an ounce of truth in it.

The restaurant was a converted house at least eighty years old, tucked up in a little valley and named Frederich's after the owner and head chef. They were greeted by the man himself who recognised Cameron and led them both with great ceremony to the best table looking out over a cottage garden. Cameron could see beyond a trellis a well-tended vegetable garden with herbs. This impressed Sonia and Cameron as it meant 'just picked' freshness for the vegetable part of the meal. Their coats were taken and they sank into two easy chairs beside an open fire with an aperitif each – compliments of the house.

They could have been on Mars, they felt so remote from their normal life.

Finishing the aperitif they sat up at the table to order their meal. The waiter came and left them the menus to consider.

Cameron decided on the Herb-encrusted New Zealand Rack of Lamb and Sonia chose Pan-fried Market Fish. The wine waiter recommended a 2009 Burnt Spur Pinot Noir Martinborough for the lamb and a 2008 Trinity Hill Pinot Gris by John Hancock for the fish. Both agreed and sat back and relaxed. Sonia had one glass of Pinot Gris and sat on the second for the rest of the night. The meal and wine arrived and in this secret little restaurant and after several glasses of the smooth drinking Pinot Noir, Cameron had eased off the weighty cloak of Jon's injury, running his bloodstock farm and the stress and strain of maintaining the false frontage of marriage and mistress.

With the easy sense of well-being a great meal with two superbly matched wines brings, Cameron and Sonia strolled arm in arm along the curved brick path to the restaurant car park. There, the black BMW M5 sat potent and powerful, awaiting his presence. The leather upholstery, the state of the art electronics and expensive sound system assured Cameron, mellowed by one of the best reds he'd ever tasted, that he'd 'arrived' and it had all been worthwhile.

They belted up and Cameron guided the car out and onto the short shingle road leading onto the main state highway. Once there he sat back and let the car have its head. The five litre V10 urged the big car forward with only the barest resonance of the Pirelli tyres and the muted howl of the V10 engine reaching their ears. The dark shapes of trees and farm buildings loomed up and flashed by with the powerful headlights of the car lighting up the road for two to three kilometres, although not quite far enough to pick out a car parked under some trees. It was a highway patrol with a bored but not too bored officer about to call it a night. Cameron's headlights found him soon enough in his fluoro vest, waving a torch.

"Christ…" plus several other similar words was all Cameron could say. He pulled over and lowered the window.

"Good evening sir. Any reason for the hurry?" enquired the officer. "Look, I'm very sorry I just didn't realise I was over the limit."

"Well, you were considerably over the limit – in fact fifty five kilometres/hour over the limit sir," he replied bending forward and looking into the car.

"Have you been drinking tonight sir?"

"Yes…" Cameron replied quietly.

The night that had promised so much ended up delivering a blunt lesson with no compromise. With Sonia driving, they continued into town where Cameron was required to submit to a blood test. He was over the limit, but not hugely and would appear in court in three months.

He would almost certainly lose his licence for six months and receive a one thousand dollar fine. The real problem though was the publicity that had potential to blow the whole story all over the region. If there wasn't much else going on around the country then the weekend papers might consider it a tempting piece of dirt to titillate readers with.

Cameron was permitted to drive until the court case. They signed out of the hotel in the morning and drove back home, cutting the stay by two days. The trip home was completed in almost total silence, each lost in their thoughts and after several hours driving arrived at the Lost Valley house for Sonia to pick up her car. A perfunctory farewell with a peck on the cheek and Sonia was in her car and gone. Although they both knew there would be no soft landing to a relationship like theirs and that sheer magnetic physicality would have them back at the Lost Valley House at the earliest opportunity. The problem facing Cameron was dealing with the court case and his affair with Sonia being caught in the glare of the spotlight particularly worried him. What he didn't know was that a partial solution was already unwittingly being prepared by the subject of his greatest concern.

#

Helen hardly slept the night she received the email confirming her acceptance of her Artist in Residence application. She got up bleary-eyed and was surprised to find Cameron's car in the driveway. He had stayed over at the Lost Valley house and drove the short distance home in the morning. She entered the kitchen to find him sitting up to a plate of bacon and eggs and a large coffee.

"Well, hi…you're home early," she said greeting him in a sunnier mood than she would normally. "Yeah…the veteran car didn't work out and the sale was a waste of time," he replied flatly.

"Oh well…never mind." She was thinking furiously about whether now was a good time to break the news about Italy. He was meant to have been away another two days and she was counting on having that time to work out how she would approach him. He looked at her closely. She was different, bright, positive and cheery, not her usual demeanour. There was something on her mind and Cameron, ever the cynic, and of harder stock than Helen, sensed it.

Well, here goes nothing, she thought to herself.

"Cameron…I want to discuss something very important to me," she said quietly.

"Yes…?" he replied.

"I'm going to Italy."

"Holy Hell! Really?" he exclaimed.

"Yes…I'm going to be an Artist in Residence," she said gaining in confidence and conviction.

"Well…best of luck!" he said expansively, waving both arms in the air and smiling.

She was puzzled. She couldn't figure his reaction. She poured a coffee and wandered through the kitchen and out the bi-folding doors onto the patio, where she sat and reflected on the previous twenty minutes. She closed her eyes and it suddenly dawned on her. He wants me to go, but that wasn't the surprise – what did surprise her was not encountering his controlling instinct…making a line in the sand just for the sake of it.

There was something else to it all but Helen with her naïve, unsuspecting nature didn't join all the dots until much later and then only with a little help from the outside.

#

Marion had spent the last three weeks since Jon's injury working her part-time merchandising rep job for the skincare range, visiting Jon and catching up on assignments for her correspondence course for her property valuation qualification.

Her phone rang and she answered a call from the hospital requesting a meeting to discuss Jon's progress. Marion drove off to the hospital with the conflicting twins of optimism and anxiety pulling at her emotions. When she arrived, she was shown into an isolation room. Jon was already there and greeted her with a big grin and a passionate hug.

"God…I'm going bloody crazy in here with all these gorgeous nurses running around."

"Yeah, but you won't be much use to any of them or me until you get better," she fired back with a one-finger salute.

She sat in the visitor's chair beside Jon and waited for the orthopaedic surgeon who suddenly swept into the room with an entourage of eager young medical students, keen to learn.

"Right!" he said dramatically. He was very large, with a stage-like presence, a full-on ginger beard and deep, booming voice that exuded boundless confidence.

"Get 'em up," he said, waving one large hand at the light boxes on the wall where one of the students began clipping several large X-rays.

Marion immediately felt buoyed and positive along with him.

"Well, we've got some very good news," he said looking around the room with large bushy eyebrows raised as if expecting a round of applause.

"This young fellow," looking in Jon's direction, "is doing great. He is on the road to a full recovery and with his fitness and attitude I would put one hundred dollars on him walking out of here within three months. Except it won't be here. He'll walk out and be off to a spinal unit in Christchurch for the full physio expertise only they can provide." He stood and beamed around the room until he reached Marion, whose face had dropped at the last bit of news.

"Oh dear, I should have put that better…shouldn't I?" he said lamely.

"Oh no don't worry…It's what's best for Jon," she said quietly, thinking of Jon being half the length of the country away. She sat glumly holding Jon's hand and digesting this latest news while the specialist launched into a lengthy discussion with his team of students.

#

In her mind, Helen was flying to Italy already. She had taken a crash course in Italian and checked at least five times that her passport was current. Now that La Macina di San Cresi had accepted her application she sent a further email to Arianna confirming two possible dates that she could start.

She then went online to book airline tickets with House of Travel. Helen had decided to fly out from Christchurch so she could stay a couple of nights with her favourite aunt.

Aunty Sue had come to the rescue, when Helen in her early twenties decided to do a fine arts degree. Returns on the farm were going through a cyclical low and cash flow was tight for Helen's parents. Aunt Sue had another agenda for her generosity. She had wanted to do the same degree course that her sister, Helen's mother had done, but her parents were not having a bar of it and insisted she do an accountancy degree instead. Sue flew through the degree she didn't want to do and worked for a small one-man firm until she married.

She had a child before her husband of five years departed for Egypt in August 1940, arriving in Egypt 29 September as part of the third echelon destined to eventually take on General Erwin Rommel's forces brought in to shore up the less than enthusiastic Italian troops. He was never to return or Sue remarry. She brought up their son while returning to work for the small accountancy firm two days a week to help make ends meet. The owner, a widower himself, reached the age where enough was enough and with no dependents to consider, he made Sue a generous offer. She would take over the firm with her safe pair of hands and pay him a modest lump sum plus a monthly percentage of the gross income.

This arrangement left the financially prudent Sue in a more than comfortable situation and easily able to help out with fees and living expenses for Helen. She never felt it a burden and through Helen got to live some part of her original dream.

Knowing Sue's unfulfilled passion for art, Helen had kept her updated on all of her projects since she graduated. It was now the least Helen could do, spending the last two days in New Zealand filling Sue in on the details of her Artist in Residence adventure and answering the many penetrating questions her aging but sharp-minded aunt would have lined up for her.

#

Within a few days, Helen had Maria's reply to her email. Maria suggested that Helen take the later date for her Artist in Residency as she had an exciting add-on to offer Helen. Maria and her young brother Martino would meet Helen in London and take her on a short whistle stop tour of Italy, starting with a few days in London.

Maria and her brother had inherited their father's business of trading in antiques, collectables, objects d'art, as well as the art and craftwork that flowed steadily from the small villages and cottage industries speckled throughout Italy. With Martino's background of involvement in modest, low- to medium-budget Italian films, they quickly morphed the antique business into a thriving operation, supplying all manner of the odd, quirky and unusual that is required by the propping departments of the Italian and wider film industry.

This could range from sourcing rare cars or used clothing, old tools and agricultural equipment from the forgotten wardrobes, sheds and garages of deceased estates. This resource saves filmmakers time and money and adds to the elusive authenticity they were always looking for.

Maria and Martino had contacts in London, and travelling in a large van with purpose-built trailer, were to spend a few days going around the traps in greater London. The van had three berths which could be used at a pinch if required. The prospect of this intrigued and excited Helen and she felt like a 'twenty something' young thing again, about to embark on her big OE that she had never got around to.

The rest of the trip was to go through Italy and was described in vague detail that Helen decided would become clear when she hit London.

Chapter 5

A shadow of suspicious doubt crossed James's mind when Sonia announced she was off to see an old friend in Wellington. The name she mentioned didn't ring a bell. But things more important to James had popped up recently. An old school friend had made contact and wanted him to stay in Wainui a few days to discuss a business proposal. James had a faint idea what it might be, as the two had been close friends at school and had talked about a wide range of ideas for business start-ups.

He told Helen and Cameron of his plans, packed a case and left that morning in his little British racing green Mazda convertible that Cameron had bought him when he graduated top of his class at boarding school in his final year. Helen and Cameron, being immersed in their plans and challenges, gave it a few minutes thought, then moved on, relieved that it seemed James might be choosing a path in life.

#

As James drove down the immaculate, white-fenced drive and past the BARCLAY FARMS sign at the gate he had a feeling that he was on the way out of a jail that was soft, easy, and nice, but a jail nevertheless. He also felt a surge of boundless optimism that he was on the way to discovering a new life. He put on an early Beatles track and sat back and enjoyed the way the sharp-handling little car ate up the hills and corners. He took his time on the boring straights and stopped off wherever he fancied.

By the time he was approaching the outer suburbs of Wainui, he had the passenger space packed with bags of fruit, craft bakery loaves and a couple of pieces of funky pottery that caught his eye. He checked out his GPS and followed directions to 38 Baker Street, pulling up in front of a beautiful cottage with a veranda across the front. He was in the middle of unloading when he got a big slap on the back. He turned to find his old school friend, Geoff Lander who had seen him pull up outside. They exchanged enthusiastic greetings and between them lugged the contents of the car inside the house where they eventually phone ordered a Thai takeaway and killed the twenty minute wait quaffing back a good Australian red and catching up on the past five years.

Geoff had completed a diploma in interior design and after working for a local retailer for a couple of years, resigned, and started his own small company. A healthy savings account plus a little help from a doting Grandmother enabled him to make the move and survive the first year, but the enterprise still lacked capital and human resources. Geoff needed an extra pair of hands, but not just anyone. He needed a person who would have the same dedication and passion that he had.

The person, he realised was the same person he shared dreams and aspirations with back in their school days and that person was James. Geoff recalled that James was never the farming type and he knew it was only a matter of time before his feet would begin to itch. He also recalled that at the age of twenty-five James would receive a sum of money from his father. He wouldn't need to bring that fact up as he intended offering James a partnership. If he was interested, James would naturally count on using the money.

The time had come for Geoff to pitch the idea to James. They finished the Thai and sat back with the last of the red.

"I think you should move here and join the company," said Geoff, never one to beat around the bush.

"Company…what company?" said James, with a laugh.

"Yeah, yeah…I know…but there's heaps of potential down here. I took a couple of big clients with me when I left the old job. They followed me. I didn't have to twist their arms. Oh, and the local dairy farmers have had a great year, they've got money burning holes in their pockets."

"Their wives' pockets more likely," James threw in.

"Yeah…you'd be right there." Laughed Geoff. "They love coming into the shop and looking around. If I had more good top-end stuff I could sell it all, no worries."

"I'd take you on as a 50/50 partner. I'll get my accountant to come up with a figure and you can get yours to check it out. It's small beer at this stage but if you want on board, we need to do it right, right from the start," said Geoff suddenly getting serious.

"Hey, don't worry, I'm interested. …Let me sleep on it and I'll let you know tomorrow."

"No problem, we'll go down to the shop tomorrow. Its Saturday so we don't open 'till 10 am. We'll do breakfast in town and get back to the shop about 9.30. You can have a look around which won't take you long. As I say it's early days, but tons of potential."

The mellowing effect of the red and the long drive was taking its toll on James. He gave a couple of huge yawns and told Geoff he was all for calling it a night.

He fell on to the bed, pulled up the covers and after a few minutes of mulling over the evening slipped into an easy sleep with the lingering thoughts that things were heading in a direction that finally felt right for him…at last.

#

The team had gradually come to terms with the injury to Jon, and with the Finals Cup sitting proudly in the trophy cabinet, got into the spirit of the end of season night with even more cheers and beers than previous seasons.

Before the formal part of the team speeches, there was a brief tribute to Jon including a report on the positive news of his rapidly improving condition. Mention was made of his big contribution to the success of the team given the short time he played for them. Cameron had insisted that Marion come along to accept 'Player of the Final' award on behalf of Jon who was now working hard at rehabilitation at the Burwood Spinal Unit in Christchurch.

When the time came, she approached the stage to a few whistles and ribald remarks, shook the club captain's hand, thanked him very much and returned to her seat where she sat with the other girlfriends and wives drinking white wine and enjoying the friendly chat of a small town. Her glass was soon empty so she headed off to the bar. On returning, she had to pass close by a very drunk Wayne Mason who was making a lot of noise with some equally drunk mates.

"Whoa…wait a minute…where are you goin' Marion babe?" He said as he grabbed her arm and pulled her onto his knee, spilling half her wine.

"Wayne!" she said in her sternest voice. "Behave yourself and let me go please!"

"Not 'till I get a nice big kiss," he slurred back.

Marion leant over and gave him a token peck and then wriggled partially free.

"Hey…that wasn't a big kiss,"…he said loudly, "Jon's not here so why don't you just come and sit with me ehh?" he said still keeping a vice like grip on the sleeve of her jacket.

Suddenly pulling as hard as she could she slipped free of the jacket. Surrendering it to Wayne, she gave him a final glare and made her way quickly back to the comparative safety of her friends, leaving a very drunk Wayne with the jacket over his head, much to the amusement of his mates.

Cameron had been outside, but returned in time to see the last bit of action. He made a mental note to keep an eye on the situation and particularly Wayne Mason, as he knew he could get a bit aggressive with a few beers on board.

As the evening wore on, many felt they'd had their fun and left to get on with the rest of their lives. Some of those remaining, like the last half glass left in a bottle of wine, were worse for wear. Marion was not one of those as she had kept to a solitary glass plus half the one Wayne had managed to spill. She was driving and as she had an early start for her area rep job she made ready to leave. Observing this from across the room was her hot suitor – Wayne. He slumped sullenly back in his chair watching her with an eye half closed. A mate had connected with a weak drunken swing during a slurred exchange of insults and expletives earlier in the car park.

Wayne was still holding her jacket, so with what he regarded as a bona fide reason to remind her he was still around, got unsteadily to his feet and lurched towards the door she had just exited, grabbing one of the few remaining full bottles of wine as he went by.

"Hey…Marion!" he yelled out to the back of the lone figure of Marion heading towards her car at the end of the now deserted car park.

#

Cameron's mobile woke him at 3 am. At that time of the morning, there would be nothing but trouble on the line. Helen woke briefly, yawned and went back to sleep, assuming it was a call from a Japanese buyer not taking the trouble to check time zones. Cameron picked up and walked quickly through the bedroom and into his office, grabbing a dressing gown on the way.

"Cameron…Cameron…it's me, Marion!" her highly stressed voice came over the phone.

Cameron felt a chill go through him, and somehow he knew instinctively what he was about to hear.

He got his car and headed at speed down the drive and out onto the main highway. It was a 25 minute drive to the bridge over the Waipu River and he did it in double quick time. He found her leaning back against the bridge sign with her hands behind her head staring at the ground. He pulled up and got out with the car rug over one arm. There was blood over her face and bruising. Cameron wrapped the blanket around her and she got in the car. She sat very quietly as they drove slowly back towards Cameron's house where small pieces of the story gradually came out. She was accosted by Wayne at the club car park and quickly forced into his car, parked surprisingly, right next to Marion's. Cameron reflected that there may have even been a bit of forward planning to all this.

Then the whole sad story that is played out in courts every week around the country was rolled out to Cameron's ears, sitting at his breakfast bar with a strong coffee. Sophie was reasonably composed. Wayne had driven them to a back country road and tried the softly, softly approach. When that didn't work, reverting to type, he tried force and that's when the wheels fell off Wayne's life. He got as far as a low-grade indecent assault, then suddenly realising he could be in a heap of trouble, he pushed her out of the car…gave her a heap of verbal abuse, then gunned the engine and with tyres screeching, raced off down the road.

Cameron showed her to the spare bed and sat with the remainder of the coffee pondering the question of what to do now. He considered taking her to the police but she was adamant she didn't want that and he started thinking he could handle it in a way that would be better for all. In the end, he realised that he needed sleep as much as Marion and he put the thoughts and worries off for tomorrow and turned in.

In the morning after a good breakfast, he drove Marion out to pick up her car, then headed off to see Wayne. As he drove, he ran through his approach. He had several cards he could use and he rehearsed the sequence and the emphasis he would give. He pulled up in front of a surprisingly well-kept house. When Wayne came to the door, his face turned white when he found who had knocked.

"I think you and I need to go for a short ride?" he said quietly. Wayne didn't reply but simply followed Cameron out to the car.

"Here's what's going to happen Wayne. You'll be leaving the rugby club, your job and this locality. I'll jack you up with a job down in a mill in Waipu with a guy I know and you never show your face around here, or contact Marion again. If you don't comply, I'll be taking Marion down to the police. You'll be on probation at the job and I suggest you watch how much booze you put away in the future."

They pulled up back at Wayne's house. Cameron handed Wayne an envelope with a letter for the job and a one hundred dollar note. Wayne got out of the car and headed for the door.

"Don't test me on this Wayne!" he said as he walked away.

Wayne turned and looked back at Cameron and Cameron knew from the look on his face that he was now history in these parts.

Wayne took Cameron's advice and threw his kit in the back of his ute and headed off. But before he did, he had one last thing he decided he had to do. He, like Sonia knew of James's habit of having a cigarette and coffee at the point overlooking the coast. Like Sonia he knew the day and time that he went there. He pulled up beside James, got out and tapped on the window, James lowered the window and Wayne leant in and said, "G'day James, there's something you need to know about your old man."

Chapter 6

James left Geoff's place without giving him a final decision on the offer. He told Geoff he was interested but wanted to give it some more thought at home. Geoff knew what he really meant was that he was going to check out the lie of the land with his father. Without quizzing him on it Geoff was sure James probably needed to resolve the question of money and Cameron may not be that fussed on his money going to something other than farming. Geoff sensed that James needed to do some careful groundwork and he was mostly right. For James though, the ground had changed dramatically since his encounter with Wayne.

The trouble was James didn't know what to do with the information that Wayne had given him. The truth was that he simply wasn't that devastated about Sonia, as he had to admit that he had tended to go along with the relationship with her rather than being passionately committed. He couldn't decide what to think about his father other than that he wanted to be as far away from him as possible.

James agonised over the issue and finally decided on a course of action. Instinct told him that Sonia would somehow be the answer and he went and confronted her with all he knew. He also told her he was very attracted to the business offer from Geoff but was unsure how his father would handle it. Sonia's feeling of guilt over her relationship with Cameron assured him that she would use her influence to get James the money he needed to close Geoff's deal.

A few days later Cameron was away on business and Sonia called to tell him that she had a cheque for him, as Cameron was too embarrassed to see his son for some time after the disclosure.

James made the decision and called Geoff to tell him yes.

#

Marion was still a bit shaken from her ordeal with Wayne so decided to pay a surprise visit to Jon in Christchurch. Without telling him, she contacted the spinal unit and booked into the flat he was living at. She got a timetable of Jon's day and planned to arrive at the flat when he was clear of physiotherapy sessions.

As her plane lifted into a clear blue sky she settled down for a short but beautiful flight taking her away from the strife and trouble that had arrived in her life. The small plane flew south in ideal conditions and descended over the spectacular Southern Alps to make a perfect landing on time at 1 pm. She collected a rental car, put her suitcase in the back and headed off towards the hospital. As she drove she was getting excited at the prospect of being with him again but was unsure as to what he would be able to do physically. Previous information had been vague about what she could expect and because it was three months since she had slept with Jon, sex was high on her list of priorities. He was due back at his flat at 2.30 pm so she cruised slowly along to the disconnected monotone of the GPS. With another thirty minutes to fill, she pulled into a promising looking coffee shop.

A young couple sat closely together planning their weekend in hushed conspiratorial tones, occasionally looking around guiltily and reminding her of the times when she and Jon were together, talking the same way. She was suddenly struck with overwhelming feelings of loss without him and got up quickly and left the café and its love-struck couple. Now she drove with more urgency. She was soon pulling into the entrance to Burwood Hospital. The receptionist showed her Jon's flat on a site plan and an orderly with a bunch of keys took her over and let her in.

The flat was a little untidy and she could smell Jon's presence. This and being away from everything she had endured gave her the first sense of peace since the Wayne episode. Air travel always exhausted her no matter how short and she lay on the bed and drifted into the best sleep she'd had since Jon moved to Christchurch. A man vaguely resembling Jon was slowly and gently caressing her. Warm dry hands began to massage her legs. By now, Marion was wise to what was going on but feigned sleep and played along with Jon's little game.

Eventually she couldn't stand it any longer and opened her eyes to the man in her life she hadn't seen for three months. Jon was sitting in a wheelchair with a big, stupid smile.

"Hello…had a good sleep?" he asked.

"That was the best dream I've ever had. But does it qualify as a dream if one of the participants is wide awake?" she asked, eyes gleaming.

"I'm not answering that…I'm totally innocent," he said resuming his slow, smooth massage.

"So what have you been doing to yourself without me around," she said with a hint of a smile.

"Oh you know…a bit of this and that."

Three weeks later Marion was back home and took a call from Jon. He was up and about and flying back tomorrow. "Could she please be at the airport for flight 98 arriving at 3 pm Thursday?" She was there an hour early and stood flicking impatiently through the magazines at the little bookshop. Eventually the plane landed on time and Marion watched it taxi up to park beside the terminal. Its twin props wound down to a slow idle and then stopped. Jon was first out and after negotiating the boarding steps walked with growing confidence across the tarmac. One stride through the automatic doors and they were suddenly together. Marion wrapped her arms around him – Jon dropped his case and did the same. They clung to each other for several minutes until Marion pulled one arm free to wipe a tear from her eye. Jon released an arm and picked up his case. They turned and with his free arm around her shoulder walked her out to her car. They got in, buckled up and headed along the short drive and out onto the main road.

"Hey…I've got something pretty big and exciting to tell you, but let's wait until we get home." Marion loved surprises, but hated having to wait for them, so put her foot down and in 15 minutes they were pulling into the driveway of the flat. He grabbed his one piece of luggage and followed her inside. Stifling her impatience, she made 2 cups of coffee, threw a packet of biscuits at him and took the coffees over to sit beside him on the couch.

"Ok, so what's happening?" She asked, her eyes bright with anticipation.

"Remember the guy I said hello to the last day you were there?" Marion nodded.

"After you left he caught up with me again. His name's Frank Brewster. He's a partner in a law firm in Christchurch and came from a high country station near Lake Tekapo in South Canterbury. He did law, his brother did agriculture, so the brother took over when their parents retired. Frank got a bit of the action money-wise, but could never get farming out of his head, so as a small project he bought 150 acres with an old cottage on it, 35 minutes from Christchurch. And guess what…he wants to start up a deer farm, and he wants me to set it up and run it. He knew I came off a farm that ran a small deer herd. Long term there could be a shareholding or an opportunity to buy into it. In 5 years when I turn 35, I will get a bit of family money from a rich old Aunt with a big heart….which could come in handy. I'll need to do a bit of catchup on deer farming. Lincoln College will have something….What do you think?"

"We're going to have to leave here, but It's getting a bit boring anyway. I could transfer my little sideline down there while it all gets going."

"In the short term Frank's paying me out of the tax right-off he gets, but you probably need something to do," he thought for a moment…. "But you need to keep away from the deer. The stags can get a bit stroppy….they're not slow and stupid like sheep."

And so they talked into the night until both agreed to shut-up and get some sleep.

After several marathon phone calls with Frank, the stage was set for their departure. Frank put a 'kick start' sum of $10,000 in their joint bank account for expenses, with more if they needed it. They both drew up a list of friends, work mates and old mates for the 'goodbye' party and Jon turned his local clients over to a keen young buck from the footy team who'd been working for him. They shook hands, with plenty of hugs all round and with both nursing hang-overs, boarded the small plane that headed off for Harewood International Airport at Christchurch.

Jon and Marion fitted into the rural community like a well-worn glove. Marion morphed skin care merchandising into direct selling at 'party plan' get togethers around the small communities. She and Jon were happy, Frank was happy and the local Rugby Club was happy, because although Jon declined to add his weight to their senior team, he took over coaching the under 35kgs, a team their first born son was soon to become a member of.

#

The day finally arrived when Helen was to board the short domestic flight to Christchurch for her two-night stay with her Aunty Sue prior to boarding the two and a half hour flight to Sydney and then on to the twenty-three hour long-haul flight to London, stopping briefly in Dubai. She'd seen little of Cameron and the contact was civil and verging on friendly. He told her of Marion's experience with Wayne. She offered a sympathetic word for Marion, then put it under 'life in Wahi' knowing that Cameron would soon sort it out.

They were both conscious they would be out of each other's lives for a period and this created a relaxed and easy truce. Cameron still had a licence, the imminent loss of which was successfully hidden from Helen. He cheerfully heaved the suitcase into the BMW, opened the door for Helen, then backed out of the garage and accelerated down the long drive, lined by the classic white painted fences of a prosperous bloodstock farm.

Cameron always felt a swell of pride whenever he drove the three hundred metres of curving private road to the highway. The scene reminded him how far he'd come in a short time.

Helen climbed the boarding steps onto the small plane and paused at the door before turning towards Cameron who was leaning his big frame against the observer deck railing, talking to an acquaintance. Just before Helen had given up on him and taken the last step onboard he looked around and waved enthusiastically. I loved you once, Helen thought as she waved back and went through the door into the compact cabin.

#

The two nights in Christchurch with Sue flew by with Helen sensing that Sue was feeling her life had not been lived as she would have liked. Even approaching middle age Helen felt an obligation to make the best of the adventure ahead, repayment for the investment Sue had made in her.

A little after midday the shuttle gave one polite toot and the driver appeared at the door to pick up her luggage. Helen was in a quiet daze as they covered the short distance to Christchurch International Airport. She woke from her daydream at the drop-off, paid the driver and manoeuvred her case towards international departures. Within a few minutes, she had checked in and headed to the departure lounge. At the duty free shop, she bought a cheap camera and soon found the perfume counter where she lingered over Chanel's latest offer, Chanel Noir. She tried a sample and experienced a feeling of déjà vu. What was puzzling was that the perfume reminded her of Cameron and his BMW. She put it out of her mind, made her purchase and moved onto more browsing, noting as she went that there was still London and Italy to absorb her shopping instincts.

She soon boarded the aircraft, swallowed a sleeping pill and slept through the short flight to Sydney. Another brief stopover and she was now boarding the seriously large Airbus A380. There was no turning back now. She was on her way and ready for anything fate had up its sleeve.

A merging sea of browns and dirty yellows gradually replaced evidence of human land use that lay far beneath the turned up wing tips of the Airbus as they inched slowly across Australia, the largest and strangest island in the world. She pondered the disappearance of ancient land bridges that ring fenced for millions of years a unique and individually different range of animals and plants, and at a later period, humans. The flat plains of smudgy colours eventually gave way to endless wave formations of burnt brown hills, a sort of smaller, less tidy version of classic dune formation as per the Sahara desert.

Considering they were covering the ground at about ten miles a minute, the length of time it took to finally pass over the north west coast of Australia, where blue waves of the Indian Ocean replaced brown waves of the desert, dramatized the immense scale of Australia compared to New Zealand's skinny size zero. Tiring of her self-imposed geography lesson Helen turned off the screen, pulled the eye mask down, lay back and let the sleeping pills do their work.

An hour or so later she awoke groggily and needed to visit the bathroom. While standing in line, she overheard a comment relating to 'Baghdad' and took a turn at the tiny viewing window. Sure enough, on either side of the aircraft was a spray of millions of lights like fairy-dust spread across the near black landscape. She spotted what was surely a military compound with a large blank area, bordered with powerful lights and a brightly lit central area that together with the dramatic effect of dozens of oil well flares, provided a sinister punctuation to an otherwise magic scene.

It was a reminder that her home, now getting further away every minute, was situated in a very innocent part of the world where no recent wars nor any likely to come, provided a safe haven, a paradise compared to the countries she was now flying over. Her mission to be an Artist in Residence suddenly seemed a ridiculous and self-indulgent pursuit when compared to the daily life and death struggle of ordinary people, thirty-nine thousand feet below – dodging suicide bombers, Jihadists and waring religious factions.

Another glimpse of life in the real world came when she returned to her seat, switched on her video screen and selected the flight tracking mode. Showing clearly on the simple map was their course performing a recognisable dogleg around the northern most point of Syria. Helen was relieved to realise that airlines carefully plotted courses that avoided the airspace of countries in turmoil where there might be a bored or angry, trigger-happy individual in command of a missile launcher and nothing to fire at.

She settled back, thankful that her slim frame gave her a reasonably comfortable and roomy flight and popped another sleeping pill, pulled down the eye mask and vowed to sleep until London appeared on her horizon.

Chapter 7

James now had all he needed to change his life. He no longer felt the subtle, implied and undeclared obligation to his father and the career path plan that he hadn't asked for. He was now free from Sonia, a relationship that had fitted a little too comfortably. His mother was in Italy, so he felt no tug of loyalty or duty to her. He was now free to act as he wished. He took the envelope containing Cameron's cheque, folded it and put it carefully in his wallet. He packed a couple of suitcases, collected a few personal treasures, then boxed up the rest and dropped it all off at the Salvation Army shop.

He wrote, Thanks for the cheque. Regards, James and left it on the kitchen bench for Cameron. He would contact his mother in Italy and tell her about his new venture in business with Geoff, but was unsure whether to tell her about Sonia and Cameron. There would be time to think that through very carefully when he was settled in at Geoff's business.

He then loaded the sum total of his material life to date into his car, drove down the beautiful tree-lined drive bordered by immaculate white fences and onto the main road without looking back. The top was down on the little sports car and he enjoyed the buffeting of the wind that he felt was blowing him free of any last vestiges of his previous life – just like his trip south a few months ago, except now he had moved on – and was staying moved on.

#

Helen woke with a start to find a smiling air hostess with coffee ready to serve. There had never been a more welcome dose of caffeine and she swallowed it quickly over her parched air-travel dry throat. It meant Heathrow was now a mere two and a half hours away, a short time compared to the marathon scale of the whole flight. An animal program set in Africa kept her distracted for the last few hours of the flight to find they were now within twenty minutes of Heathrow.

She sensed a subtle downward sensation as the big plane reduced power, gradually beginning its descent from thirty-nine thousand feet and easing into a left turn explained casually by the captain as necessary to clear air traffic currently taking off.

The bump and whine of the massive landing gear being activated was followed by the equally high-pitched whine of hydraulics operating the wing flaps. This signalled the plane was within a couple of hundred feet of Heathrow real estate. With a loud bump earth met plane and they raced along the runway before the full force of the reverse thrust dumped a hundred kilometres/hour from their landing speed within a few hundred metres. They came to a stop and Helen sat drained from the long flight, choosing to let early movers haul luggage from overhead storage and clog the aisles.

Soon enough she was heading along the air bridge and onto the customs and immigration people. Clearing these she found her suitcase and looked through to the public area for Maria and Martino.

Hey Kiwi Girl! Said the sign in big purple letters with pink hearts and cupids that could only be for her. Sure enough, standing grinning under the sign with racy graphics was Maria and Martino, Maria's brother that Helen had only seen before in a family photograph. Helen blushed under the gaze of amused bystanders.

Maria saw Helen five years ago on a family visit to New Zealand but it could have been five decades given the passion of Maria's greeting. Martino held back a little, but in a gap in the action Helen sneaked a look at a classic modern-day Adonis, tall, runway-model lean and astonishingly good looking. She'd convinced herself he would just have to be arrogant and conceited.

That was not the case. Martino was quiet, self-effacing and modest, a reflection of the hard work and discipline expected by careful and prudent parents. Martino predated Helen by fifteen years but that didn't stop her from having thoughts better entertained here than at home in New Zealand. He reminded Helen of a male model at her life drawing classes twenty years ago that she found quite a unique experience. Helen the quiet one, although brought up in the birth, life, death environment of a farm, had led a cloistered life where men were concerned.

"Follow me," said Maria and with that turned and walked briskly towards the exit and a taxi cab she had grabbed ten minutes earlier. Helen returned from her daydreams to the present. Martino had wrested the case off Helen and was following up the rear.

They raced along in the taxi at great speed until they came to a stop behind a line-up stretching at least half a kilometre. This process continued for another thirty minutes until the start of Earls Court Road and eventually turning into Barkston Road, where Maria and Martino had three rooms in a comfortable hotel they always used on business trips to London.

#

Helen left her case in the secure room of the hotel and unable to access her room until it had been serviced, the best move was to head to the nearest café for the first food in twenty five hours that wasn't on a plastic tray, balanced on a pull-down table and eaten with a plastic knife, fork and spoon.

They all ordered the classic English fry up – eggs, bacon, sausages, tomatoes and baked beans that to Maria and Martino was a change from their normal fare and something Helen wouldn't have touched in a dozen years. As Cameron would say, "That's a breakfast that puts lead in your pencil." The heavy, energy-dense food with a strong coffee hit the spot and she felt ready for a day where sleep, that her body demanded, had to be rejected to get her body clock in sync with local time.

Maria finished her coffee and gave a quick rundown on the program for the next three days – she had several contacts to catch-up with where she didn't need Martino, so she proposed that if Helen could stand his company for a while he would give her a tour of London, a city he was totally familiar with, having visited at least two dozen times from when, as a young boy, he accompanied his father on combination business/holiday trips, learning the family's trade. Helen was left with a little smile on her face at that announcement and couldn't think of a better way of getting through a day when she would rather be sleeping.

"Where would you like to go first Helen?" he said looking towards her with sleepy dark eyes.

"Harrods!" she replied without hesitation.

"And then?"

"Let's think about that, when we've done Harrods," she replied with a smile.

"Ok—Harrods it is. I think we'll take a taxi rather than walking. I also think you need all your energies for shopping…eh? Wherever in the world they come from, all women I know love shopping."

Helen wondered how many women Martino 'knew' a thought that only served to pique an already aroused interest. After the twenty years of sleepy rural New Zealand with a steady but preoccupied Cameron – Helen, now in bustling, cosmopolitan London felt she was absorbing a kind of ethereal 'urban energy' from the several million people she'd suddenly ended up in the middle of. Young again but with a sensual awareness that lay untapped in her twenties.

She now revised her summation of Martino as quiet and self-effacing, thinking there is more to him than meets the eye. Martino and his lazy Dean Martin drawl was having an effect that was beyond good looks and a trim body. She delivered a stern warning to herself to not get carried away like a schoolgirl just out of a convent.

Helen put it all back in a box and closed the lid, for now, and turned to catch the fleeting images of London; the shops, the brands, the people flicking past as the taxi sped towards Harrods, weaving through more traffic in five hundred metres then she would see in Waihi, New Zealand in a year. She watched the driver weaving in and out of the traffic while he quizzed her in a strong cockney accent on New Zealand, the All Blacks and Tauranga – where a smart younger brother was living and according to him, doing very well.

Helen couldn't give him anything he didn't already know on the All Blacks but filled him in on Tauranga just as they pulled up in front of Harrods.

Entering Harrods was to roll back the years to when as a five year-old from the country, she was taken by her parents to a large department store in Auckland, three days before Christmas. The skills of some of the best display artists in New Zealand bedazzled her young eyes, not used to big city glitz and glamour. Thirty-seven years on, standing in the entrance to Harrods of London, she was for a few seconds stunned, recalling the magical experience that was part of her dreams as a child.

"You alright?" asked Martino aware Helen seemed to have been standing in a daze for several seconds.

"Yes, no problem," she replied quickly returning to the present.

Together they walked past the tall, imperious security staff, pausing before a shrine to Lady Di and Dodi. The memory of that fateful day returned. She turned and pushed painful images away and within a few paces entered the jewellery department where Helen's eyes widened at the largest and most amazing display of jewellery that she could ever imagine. She walked in silence between numerous glass towers that appeared like miniature high-rise buildings with each containing a number of exquisite pieces.

They moved on through to the produce hall containing the largest and most comprehensive range of food products she had ever seen. All manner of fish, game, preserves, and processed meats sourced from the UK, Europe and hundreds of countries worldwide. Helen found it all very impressive but a little overwhelming and was pleased to move onto fashion and footwear.

If she was impressed by the jewellery and produce department, she was blown away by the plethora of famous brands in fashion and footwear. Gucci, Visage, Louis Vuitton, Jimmy Choo, Christian Dior and at least a dozen or so more world-famous brands and prominent international designers passed her eyes as she wandered through a fashion paradise.

Martino was a mute passenger in this journey, slightly amused by the delight obvious in Helen's eyes. He stopped by her side when she paused by a beautiful Louis Vuitton handbag she had always admired. As always the design was simple with impeccable attention to detail and quality and featured a pale brown panel either side, starting wide at the top and tapering towards the base.

Either side of the matt black handles and forming each end was the iconic trade mark livery of Louis Vuitton, a dark brown area of material with tone on tone renditions of the legendary overlapping letters of the LV logo sharing the space with positive and negative fleur-de-lis and circles within circles. Helen was looking for a price tag just as an assistant approached her.

"Three and a half thousand Euros if Madam was wondering," he said casually.

"Thank you, I'll take it," Helen heard her voice say as she glanced up as if looking for moral support from Martino. His reply was a simple shrug of his shoulders, as if to say, well you are a woman, it's your money. There is nothing more to say.

Slightly numb, she handed over her credit card, waited then entered the pin number as the sales person intoned the usual, "Excellent choice Madam." Helen wondered how many sales he made a day at this level.

There was a sharp reality check for Helen when a few minutes later, while clutching her new purchase and feeling as if she'd just stolen it, she casually eavesdropped on another shopper making a purchase for 20, 000 Euros. This instantly adjusted Helen's guilt level downwards and she reminded herself that the farm, with her stake holding, had enjoyed three highly lucrative years on the trot and this was after all the only really extravagant purchase she'd made in years.

Helen had one more purchase to make and she now headed towards the fashion area with its exciting array of world famous brands.

She went straight for the Jimmy Choo counter and its spectacular display of high fashion shoes. In one instant, she saw exactly what she wanted; a pair of Saoni 100 embellished suede pumps. She fell instantly for the pale suede with a caged T-bar silhouette, a scattering of black, silver and gold pearls and crystals made the shoe irresistible.

"I think it is time for coffee and food?" asked Martino as they found themselves wandering aimlessly with Helen having exhausted all shopping desires.

"Show me to it. I am totally spent," she said.

"I believe you. Follow me," he said as he changed direction, towards, she prayed, some caffeine and carbs. Sure enough, Martino had them at an area cordoned off and containing a few customers and a posse of immaculately turned out waiters.

The star of the show, however, was the maître d' dressed in a tuxedo and white cotton gloves who, with dancing feet pirouetted, swooped and swerved his way around the customers and their tables. Enquiring here, checking there and summoning with a complex array of gestures – both beckoning and directing – waiting staff to satisfy without the slightest of delays, every whim a customer could entertain. It was a performance that deserved an Oscar and an endorsement that here was a man who made every aspect of his job satisfying and enjoyable.

Each ordered an espresso and croissant then sat back and observed the action. Helen was happy being entertained by the maître d' until she indulged in a little discreet eavesdropping on the adjacent table. Two ladies were discussing their purchases that made Helen's look like petty cash. The conversation turned to what they could possibly do this coming Winter, that wasn't too dreadfully boring. Both agreed they might just have to settle for skiing in Switzerland again, only this time vowing to avoid that awful place where two seasons ago they'd spent ten hideous days.

Given the strained accents and heavy name dropping, Helen felt she was an extra in the middle of a 'rich bitch' television soap and exchanged conspiratorial smirks and winks with Martino.

She suddenly felt close to him, the restraint from a distracted Cameron over the last three years left her hungry for intimacy and she glanced down to find she'd unwittingly placed her hand on his arm. She was about to move it away, but before she did, Martino had clasped his right hand over hers – it was warm and dry and held her captured hand strongly against his arm. A tingling and thrilling warmth flowed from him up her arm and through her entire body. She blushed at the unexpected intimacy that although quite tame, meant they had stepped onto new, unchartered ground. In so doing, they'd set a mark in the sand that would always be there. Both knew this and as they looked warily into each other's eyes they both knew there was no rewind of what had just passed between them.

#

In an awkward silence that followed, the bill came. So on that cue they paid, picked up their bags and headed off.

"Exercise is best for a good night's sleep after a long flight and jet lag," said Martino, quietly adding, "Lets walk back to the hotel."

"I'm happy with that," she replied.

They set off lost in their own thoughts after the small intimacy over lunch. With nearly three thousand New Zealand dollars of fashion wear tucked into the Harrods bag carried by Martino and her Louis Vuitton bag swinging jauntily from her hand, Helen was perfectly happy to spend the walk window shopping. Streetwise Martino positioned himself slightly behind and to her right in case any opportunistic bag snatcher might be tempted. He was aware that tourists standout like beacons to the people that make their living on the streets picking pockets and grabbing whatever they can.

"We'll go this way," he said pointing down Old Brompton Road. "It's slightly longer but there is something I think you should see and I think with your art and design background you will appreciate it very much."

Within a few hundred metres, Helen found herself in front of London Lamborghini. It was now Martino's turn to gaze in awe. Most Italians never lose their pride and enthusiasm for their own country's superb range of high-performance cars. Helen too found herself more than slightly stunned by the collective power of five 'out of this world' super cars in colours from a strident yellow, that was like a screech of chalk on a black board, to a blue, that plunged into the deepest waters of the Caribbean.

Her eyes swept over sensual shapes with lines and creases, both audacious and outrageous. While she was not greatly interested in cars, her art and design background stirred a response by such a visual symphony of seemingly limitless power, extravagantly wild colours and the unquestionable promise of fighter jet performance.

"You can now see how we came up with David," he said referring to Michelangelo's classic work.

She gave a concurring hmm…exactly, and started to contemplate the thought of Martino as David, a live version, but standing motionless for her eyes to feast on as long as she wished.

"For God's sake grow up and start acting your age," she admonished herself. But the words she knew in her heart were just hollow posturing, and she also knew there was no point denying her real thoughts and feelings, and carrying a false belief she was going to somehow contrive to swerve around a conclusion that was inevitable.

"Right Martino, enough fantasising. I'm off back to the hotel. Which way is it?"

"Just follow me," he said waking from his dreams of beautiful cars with beautiful bodies, and turning on his heel, strode off with Helen in his wake. Luckily she was fit from the exercise she got on the farm and kept up with him all the way to Barkston Road. At reception, she picked up her room key and inquired about any good restaurants nearby. The receptionist recommended The Little French Restaurant, just five minutes walk around the corner.

Helen rang and booked, telling Martino that the meal and wine were all on her as a thank you for being such a brick about showing her around Harrods. Martino was a little puzzled over being called a brick but decided it would be a good conversation piece later. Maria rang to say sorry, but she was being wined and dined by one of her favourite customers and that she couldn't get out of it and did she mind if Martino looked after her tonight as well. She promised to make it up to her when she wasn't so busy. It was the second time today for Helen to smile at some 'bad news' from Maria about having to put up with Martino.

Helen retired to her room and stripping off lay on the bed and with the warmth of the sun shining through the partly closed drapes, fell immediately into a deep but fitful sleep, packed with a strange montage of aircraft, flaming oil wells in Iraq and an over-the-top maître d'. Looming out of it all was Martino sitting as you would expect in a bright yellow Lamborghini, sporting the most beguiling of smiles that slowly dissolved into a hideous leer, followed by a look of terror as the car transformed into an aircraft that took a direct hit from a missile and trailing smoke and flames, spiralled downwards towards an oil well, already alight. Seconds before it hit, Helen woke abruptly with sweat glistening all over her body and her pulse racing. She stared vacantly at the ceiling for a few minutes, gathering her breath.

Her limbs were on a go-slow as her body fought to stay in home time when she would normally be sleeping. She rolled off the bed and examined herself in a full-length mirror. Her opinion favoured positive while she contemplated Martino lying bronzed and chiselled on white sheets like a model in an expensive perfume advertisement. Would he look at her the same way he looked at the Lamborghini with a direct and intense gaze, with his tongue playing unconsciously over his perfect white teeth or would he feel uncomfortable and look away, comparing her with his last conquest, likely a stunning Italian or maybe some other damn gorgeous European female with beautiful long hair and a twenty-five year old – no children yet, body.

Who cares, I'm not marrying him, he's my free tour guide through London and Italy. Enjoy the moment, the days and weeks I'm here with him, not Cameron. She wandered into the modestly appointed bathroom, turned on the hot tap and unscrewing a bottle of expensive bath gel, dumped the entire contents into the bath and slowly slid her body under the hot scented water. She lay back looking at the ornate ceiling, then closed her eyes and pictured Martino, lying back on white sheets again, with that quiet, enigmatic smile, just like Mona Lisa.

After a ten minute nap, Helen opened her eyes in a bath now only lukewarm. She felt better, and fit enough to last an evening with Martino at The Little French Restaurant. She climbed out and went through to the bedroom, dried herself, then took from the wardrobe the beautiful mauve Gucci wraparound dress just purchased at Harrods.

Let's see what this handsome bastard makes of this? He's a man, so I know he'll be a bastard at some point, she said to herself as she twirled around, doing a quick evaluation in the mirror. She found her makeup bag and the Channel Noir and went to work. The effect was outstanding and she knew this from his body language and his eyes – even before he told her in a few words, how stunning she looked when she opened the door to his polite tap. She made one last adjustment to her new dress and stepped into the small lift that took them down to the foyer.

His reaction, from a man 15 years her junior, told her she had turned a sharp corner in her life. In fact, by going on her adventure/expedition, she had done more than just, 'gone around a corner,' she had selected a path taking her away from her old life. The evidence had stared back from the full-length mirror, wearing the faintest of quiet smiles. Not a smug, rather, a self-confident smile, saying, "I'm here to have what I deserve and what I need."

Now she'd made sure she wasn't letting her side down with short-cut preparation, she took the chance to appraise the man of the moment, and rather than goofily looking him up and down, she grabbed occasional glances of his reflection in shop windows as they walked past.

Understated and immaculate, was the understatement of the year to describe Martino. Helen had no idea what fashion designer he was wearing but he carried it all with a fluent ease.

They continued the short walk and turned right into Hogarth Road. Although The Little French Restaurant was listed at number 18, the best access was from Hogarth Place, a tiny lane, speckled with dozens of small businesses, clinging tenaciously to precious footprints of expensive London real estate like marine life on a rocky foreshore. Each of their signs and sandwich boards tested and searched for customers in the passing current of humanity, otherwise known as foot traffic. It occurred to Helen that the greater the value of the resource, in this case real estate, the smarter and more creative the user had to be. Each business seemed to have muscled themselves onto their own patch. None more so than 'Mobile Corner' a small mobile phone retailer that occupied a sharp triangle of space created by the intersection of the lane and Hogarth Road. The effect was as if a beautiful old tram, with narrow, arched windows and an unfortunate orange/blue livery, had morphed into a triangle shape that best suited the space available. Again, space that was just too valuable to be fallowed.

Chapter 8

They soon found themselves standing in front of The Little French Restaurant, resplendent in an exuberant purple. The name however was more restrained and understated and set on a curved line, in a light serif typeface and completed with the inevitable cockerel. A quick glance at the sandwich board touting for business outside, also conveyed a story of lightness and restraint in the prices quoted. This held instant appeal for Helen, still feeling a pang of guilt over her Harrod's expedition and also won approval from Martino, with the legacy of his prudent parents still living on through him. Encouraged by the impression of a relaxed and informal atmosphere, they entered and were shown to their table.

It was soon apparent this was no 'faux French' attempt at an eating establishment when they silently explored the impressive range of a bona fide French menu and it was going to be more than a few minutes before polite conversation was ventured into. In the meantime they both decided on starters. Helen ordered a L' onion au Gratin, a traditional homemade soup baked in an oven and Martino, Poulet Fume 'Paysanne', a dish of smoked chicken, fresh herbs and mushrooms, wrapped in thin leaves of filo pastry served with green mayonnaise.

The wine waiter came and Martino, in deference to Helen, ordered a New Zealand Oyster Bay Pinot Gris. The waiter opened the bottle and poured the half glass taster for Martino. He nodded approval and they clinked glasses in a toast to the next three weeks. They had almost finished their first glass by the time the starter course arrived. Helen put this down to both being a little nervous. It was one thing to be 'doing London' with a handsome young Italian but this had now escalated into a first date, and good Helen's nagging voice was asking if she knew what she was doing. It was certainly Helen's first ever step towards a potential affair no matter how tentative.

They ate in silence and after the waitress had taken their plates both agreed that if the rest of the food was the same quality as the starters then they were in for a good evening. Helen was becoming more and more curious about Martino's origins and was being reminded every hour of the differences between countries of the 'New World', New Zealand and Australia and that of the 'Old World' of Europe and the UK.

"Tell me about your family and where they lived?" she asked.

He turned and stared out the window for a few seconds then began.

"My grandparents were good simple farmers with a vineyard, an olive grove and fifteen cows that provided milk for a small amount of cheese for the household. They grew all the food they needed and produced a small surplus that paid for extras. When he was young, my father had plenty of what I think you call 'entrepreneurial instinct' and developed branding for the cheeses and olive oil. With the money he made and a loan from the bank he purchased the property next to them and steadily increased their production and sales. One day an exporter contacted my father and put a deal together that sent my family's cheeses and olives to the rest of Europe. I even think they reached New Zealand and Australia. There are plenty of Italians in Australia.

"My grandparents had never seen so much money and yet still refused to own a car or even travel in one. With the money my father made they could have driven around in a Ferrari if they wanted to. My father stayed in the house until he married and then built another house nearby for himself, his new wife and Maria and me, when we came along. By the time I was fifteen, I knew growing olives and making cheese wasn't for me so I went to acting school and got some small parts in movies, then I landed some modelling work in Italy and London. My father had no one to take over, our grandparents had both died, so he put the whole thing on the market and sold up. He made enough money to buy a small antique business that had accommodation attached in Roma. You can probably guess the rest of the story."

"Wow, I don't know if I can beat that. My parents were farmers and I was their only child. I had a nice happy life, but a little dull, compared to yours I think. Both my parents have died so I'm all alone," she said in a self-mocking way.

"Well, you're not alone now. You're with Martino and I'm here to show you Italy, and I know the best bits by far. Hey! and I want to go to New Zealand one day. Maria has told me a lot from the time she was there and then you can show me your New Zealand," he said enthusiastically.

Although Helen thought what a great idea that would be, she had to acknowledge that she still had a marriage albeit damaged and shaky. It made her think of her home and Cameron, which right now wasn't something she wanted reminding of, and quickly changed the subject.

"Where are we off to tomorrow?" she asked.

"Covent Garden," he replied as the waitress appeared with her notebook and pen.

"I'll have Supreme de Volaille 'Farci Duxelloise'," he said grandly, which as the menu explained was a breast of chicken, with a wild mushroom duxelle stuffing, served with mild Dijon mustard sauce. The waitress turned to Helen.

"And I'll have Canard Josephine," she said, reading to herself from the menu that it was tender breast of duck, marinated in Asian spices, grilled and served with sauce bigarade.

"We both like birds," said Martino.

"Well, I prefer blokes actually," she replied.

Martino looked a little puzzled so Helen explained what a bloke was and Martino smiled at the little joke.

Martino poured another wine for them both and relaxed back in his seat. "Now tell me about yourself and your journey to be an Artist in Residence, at the um…La Macina di San Cresci. Do you want to become a famous Italian artist like Leonardo or Michelangelo?" he said jokingly.

"No no…I just wanted to get my life out of a rut, shake my cage or, more like break the lock and escape and be free!" she added when she realised that Martino was looking more than slightly puzzled.

"Oh…I think I understand. What is your style of painting?"

"Oh dear…the hard ones first. Well I'm evolving my style from representational to abstract. I have moved from canvas to using thin MDF board that I mount on inch square rails that create a canvas like effect and can be mounted on a wall like a standard canvas."

"But why do you want to paint on board and not canvas?" he asked.

"I like the speed of the brush stroke I can get on a smooth board. I can be more explosive and spontaneous with colour. I take a simpler approach to painting now. My only interest is in expressing myself and I no longer spend hours navel gazing and overanalysing things. I want to learn to paint like a child again, which is what Picasso spent his life doing. Like him I am inspired by the art of primitive people with its strong symbolism and bold use of bright colours and exciting shapes. I also love the cave wall drawings of prehistoric man using limited materials and implements."

Helen's eyes were lit with energy and super chilled Martino was a little surprised at the passion she showed.

"Wow!" was all he said and reached for his wine that had sat untouched while Helen shared her personal views on art and her art in particular.

"I did a fine arts degree so I am not oblivious to the work of all the great artists but now after twenty years doing same old, same old, I am really much more into expressing my feelings and emotions. I also wasted some of my early years living in the shadows of my heroes: Picasso, Vincent Van Gough and particularly Paul Klee, who I see is featured at the Tate Gallery at the moment. We must go," she said, and then quickly returning to her subject about living in other people's shadows, "You become, as we say in New Zealand 'like a possum in the headlights'. You are so infatuated with your heroes that all you can do is pale imitations of their work or worse, nothing at all. I had to stop obsessing about them and set about doing my thing."

"We all have a shadow or two we have to move out of," replied Martino.

Helen looked at him and guessed he was referring to his dynamic, high achieving father.

After Helen's lengthy dissertation, they sat in subdued silence and focused on their meals that had arrived shortly before she finished talking. Like many reserved people who don't often hold centre stage, Helen suddenly felt self-conscious in the glare of the spotlight and worried she might have gone on too long with a wine fuelled exposure of her inner thoughts on art and life. She needn't have worried as Martino soon confided that he was impressed by her candour.

They finished their meal and decided to end with a small selection of cheeses and coffee. The jet lag was catching up with her and when the bill arrived she resisted Martino's protests, paid it and stifling a yawn, made to leave. They walked back in silence, swerving around a noisy group bursting onto the footpath from a brightly lit pub. They were soon in the foyer of their own hotel and saying good night to the night staff at reception, headed up the stairs to their rooms.

Helen sat on the bed and although very tired she had a sudden and strong desire to make contact with home. She pulled her laptop from the case and went to her emails. There was only one and she opened James's short and precise account of Cameron's secret life. The reaction she had surprised her, because she felt only relief that at last she was now fully up to speed on what was really going on in her marriage. Although she didn't like the thought of this disclosure producing a sort of pay back, 'tit for tat' reaction to immediately open herself to Martino, she couldn't fool herself that there was now less reason for any agonising and lengthy guilt trip. In fact, the remainder of her stay with Martino escorting her around London and through Italy, minus the elephant in the room, was suddenly a lot simpler and therefore more attractive and exciting. Helen stifled the negative thoughts and fears of a divorce and drifted off to sleep preferring the fantasy that – dare she think that it might become a reality – a short-term fling, no guilt and no strings attached.

She woke at eight o'clock to the sounds that a neighbourhood in a city of eight million makes as it wakes to the new day. She lay quiet and still, as if hiding out in a wildlife blind and listened to the abbreviated snatches of workday conversations, instructions shouted, meetings arranged, appointments made for a beer at five and truck doors banging shut along with the occasional curse.

But there was something more, another sensation that made her feel she possessed a sensory organ other than for hearing, that picked up the subtle, less obvious signs of eight million metabolic rates ramping up, heart beats increasing, toasters banging down, kettles whistling and hair slicked back or brushed, a distant but distinct background 'thrum', like a big stereo system on full volume but not playing anything. It was slightly scary but very thrilling to someone from a district of about five hundred people, coming to the similar size space filled with eight million. She lay back and enjoyed the tiny tremors of excitement that rippled through her.

A long shower under a rose as large as a bread and butter plate and plenty of body lotion had her ready for the day which started with a breakfast she only just got to. Martino and Maria were already well through their coffees. Helen made do with cereal, toast and coffee so she wouldn't hold the day up. Martino and Helen exchanged glances they thought were discreet, but Maria knew what she was looking at and upon hearing the gist of James's email decided her best friend should be cut some slack in the area of love and romance. She also decided that she wouldn't be doing her any favours by rejoining the team and invented a reason to leave her in her brother's care. Another important client needed urgent attention only she could give. She bade them farewell and agreed they should meet at the local wine bar at five that night. Martino and Helen managed to hide most of their pleasure and both of them blew her a kiss as she departed the dining room.

"OK, so what now Mr Martino?" she said with eyes now alive and interested after a good night's sleep.

"Well, I suggest we do Covent Garden first. Then I think we should have a menage a' trois with Mr Klee seeing you were so infatuated with the man."

"Well, he was my first love. The young farmers I grew up with couldn't hold a candle to him, or a paint brush for that matter," she added smiling.

"Well, I need to see what I'm up against so it's The Tate Gallery in the afternoon, agreed?" he said as he stood up and turned to go.

"Agreed," she replied, picking up her bag and sunglasses and following Martino out of the dining room.

The taxi driver this time was a West Indian but with the same cockney accent as their first driver. His parents had come to London fifty years ago. He talked proudly about his two lads, one sports mad with a chance to play for Chelsea, the other a budding academic who was lining his sights on a career in medicine. Helen envied the way all the pieces of their lives appeared to be falling into place and she thought of James and his past inability to find his niche and wondered if the moneyed background had robbed him of the incentive and killer instinct to find his place in life earlier. Still, he seemed to be getting somewhere now, she thought, as the taxi was adding its small contribution to the already great distance from home and family. Another day with Martino and another day of experiences and surroundings that took her further than just a mere distance expressed in kilometres. She was changing and it worried her for a few minutes until she once more mentally closed, but didn't lock the door on her life back in New Zealand.

The taxi pulled up on King Street, near the Covent Garden Metro. They paid, told the driver they'd keep a lookout for his footballing son in the media, wished him and his family well and wandered off towards Covent Garden.

As they approached they were pulled towards the beautiful clear sound of one of Helen's favourite Puccini operas. She was drawn to it like a moth to a flame, towing Martino in her wake. They came to a balcony and looked down on singers from the Covent Garden Opera House performing to an audience of diners.

They stood for an entrancing ten minutes and eventually headed off. Helen had a mission in mind and that was to visit the only outlet of Carat, the maker of jewellery featuring manufactured diamonds – affordable, but still at a price that one takes seriously. The interior of the shop was cross-hatched by the narrow beams of piercingly bright lights that generated like responses from the many pieces of beautiful jewellery arranged under the counter and in the cases.

Also arranged and on display were the equally beautiful shop assistants, each one a black-suited model of impeccable taste and grooming, that included the irresistible allure of the softly and carefully crafted vowels of Europeans speaking English as a second language. Helen decided that Carat's offering suited her and tried a pair of pearl drop earrings with a matching pendant. After a short period of indecision, she bought the whole set.

She could have happily stayed but sensing Martino was getting restless decided to put him out of his misery and they set off for coffee and food. They found it at an 'island' set up and boasting the endorsement of the Naked Chef, Jamie Oliver. Helen smiled at a warning sign to parents of noisy, out of control children that any child caught running around would be given a puppy and an espresso.

They finished their lunch and headed off on a meandering course taking in the potpourri of retail on offer. Looking ahead Helen spotted an image and a word she thought her eyes would never see again. The word was 'Moominland', and it was the name of a shop devoted to a series of books written by a Norwegian lady, Tove Janssen. The books featured a collection of simple line drawings of quirky and lovable characters some vaguely modelled on hippopotami and other animals. Helen had the book as a seven year-old and read it and reread it until she could tell the whole story to her mother, often word perfect.

It is testament to the fact that many children vault from one obsession to another that when Helen's mind turned to other things the book gradually disappeared from sight and was eventually irretrievably lost. Helen, as she grew, sometimes wondered if it had all been a figment of her imagination. She had none of the other books written by Janssen and as the period predated the internet there was no ready resource to use to find the other books in the series. It was all part of her childhood past in which memory often merges fact with fantasy. It stunned Helen to so abruptly confront a whole trove of books, children's stuffed toys, wall friezes and a range of other merchandise. It also surprised her that to her knowledge all this was not evident in New Zealand.

She made one purchase of 'Comet in Moominland' the original book that so captivated her 40 years ago. They left the shop of enchanting memories and headed off with the intention of walking most or all of the way back to the hotel, taking in the sights and sounds on the way.

#

A brief phone call on route from Maria to Martino organised the delayed dinner date for all three. Martino pushed for a return to The Little French Restaurant. Close to the hotel, excellent food and a combination of low prices and low-key charm was all that was needed to convince Maria. She hinted strongly to Martino that she had a surprise announcement for them so they decided they had walked far enough and grabbed the next taxi back to the hotel. A further call from Maria arranged that Martino and Helen would head to the restaurant early to secure a good table, for four. Martino raised his eyebrows at this news, but unable to shake any information as to who the extra person was from his obstinate sister, he accepted that he and Helen would have to wait and see. Martino was happy to spend the hour or so reading a car magazine but Helen's mind was racing over all the possible answers with a frustratingly small information base.

They sat down and Martino, looking to taste a New Zealand red, were soon into their second glass of Oyster Bay Pinot Noir. Inhibitions were disappearing along with the red wine as they shared intimacies and dawdled through the appetisers. They were about to look further down the menu when Maria, with a flushed face from rushing and not a small amount of embarrassment, suddenly turned up with her mystery companion.

After introductions, Helen and Martino were able to take stock of the new addition to their group. His name was Aloisio Branco and he owed his surname to a Portuguese father and rebellious young upper-class Englishwoman who, defying her parents and her snobby friends, married the tall, dark, handsome and charismatic man from the little country with the grim North Atlantic washing its shoreline and big neighbour Spain, grabbing the front row seats looking out over the Mediterranean.

Their son didn't share his father's height but inherited his strong personality and charisma. He sat and charmed the table with a mix of self-deprecating humour and funnier observations. They had met in London through a mutual business interest, as Maria explained when the dust had settled over introductions and apologies for arriving late. In fact, the 'mutual business interest' was a slight understatement as Maria went on to say that she and Aloisio were looking to merge two businesses. Aloisio had a retail business in interior design employing a daughter from a previous marriage as a design consultant and sales rep. His contact with Maria on sourcing and supplying some of her requirements had led to a discussion on the merits of enlarging the shop floor space and creating a studio-like facility that would stock some of the weird and wonderful objects d'art and off-beat items that Maria frequently came across.

These would typically apply to top end, 'out there' apartments and houses of the rich, famous, and infamous. They both knew that if you were flavour of the month, then you could just about name your price. In fact, the more grandiose or off the wall the commission, the bigger the invoice and in turn, the bigger the ego boost for the client. There were plenty of rich or nearly rich clients who saw value in adding to their fame or notoriety. Interior design magazines and TV design programmes would clamour for edgy and exciting things to fill their pages and airtime and for many of their clients there had never been such a thing as bad publicity.

Where this left Martino was not clear to him, but Maria hastily assured him of the position of operating the Italian part of what had just doubled into an exciting and dynamic business. She also mentioned connections that Aloisio had in Australia and New Zealand and made sure he saw the potential for travel to those parts and further. Martino's eyes lit up as if he was standing beside a brand-new Lamborghini with the key in his hand.

Maria further explained that she was staying in London to see through and sign off the sea change that she had part authored for her and Martino's lives.

"I'm sure you won't mind me not tagging along on the rest of your trip," she said, winking at Helen and noticing she and Martino's hands were often under the table.

"Well…I honestly can't think how I'll get along without you," she replied hamming it up. "Oh, and by the way I just love your sexy new top, especially the plunging neckline. I've never seen you wear anything quite like that before, Maria," pausing to look meaningfully across the table at Aloisio and let the good-humoured retort find its mark.

"Hey, good things take time," she replied, smiling back.

The immediate future for each of the four people sitting at the table had been decided and agreed on. There was now only one thing to do and that was to get better acquainted with The Little French Restaurant's wine cellar.

It was in the early hours of the morning that they all decided enough was enough and that along with the sun, tomorrow was only just over the horizon. Maria and Aloisio grabbed a taxi and headed off into the night and Helen and Martino set off on the short walk to the hotel hand in hand.

"Tomorrow, Venice, I can't wait to show you," Martino said as they shared a boozy kiss at her door. She reached for the handle, gave him one last peck on the cheek, and then firmly pushed him away with her forefinger on his prominent Roman nose. "What do they say about the size of a man's nose?" she asked herself.

"Not just yet." Her words followed Martino as he reluctantly headed to his room. You'll keep, he mumbled to himself, only just managing to shed his shoes before he fell onto the bed. His last thought before he fell into deep, heavy sleep, was how much the Portuguese guy could drink.

Chapter 9

The rain thrashed out of the black night and railed against the windows of the quaint 1940s style launch or as they are called it in Italy—'Vaporetto', as it skirted past the coloured navigation lights and on towards the canals of Venice. Helen concentrated on holding her stomach in as the little launch surged forward on the swells and slid into the troughs between the waves. She wasn't fearful as she had regularly boated on Lake Taupo with her parents, but while she might have been a seasoned sailor, she wasn't a seasoned drinker and was now paying for last night.

They finally pulled up at the wharf and she was able to take in her surroundings. With the rain showing no signs of easing, they were quickly more interested in making it to their hotel. Fortunately, Martino knew exactly where it was and they were soon in the foyer and being shown their rooms. A reasonable meal was available and with both suffering from the previous night they ate a small amount in glum silence and it wasn't long before they were both in their own beds.

Non-stop rain is a great leveller of famous destinations and after checking the forecast Helen and Martino decided they would cut their losses and head off to Florence the next day with the intention of revisiting Venice at a later date. Travel arrangements were changed and the booking of the hotel in Florence changed to a day earlier.

Breakfast was a standard tourist offering, prosciutto ham, boiled eggs, croissants and coffee. The rain still drifted in voluminous squalls across Venice, which by design was already the world's wettest city. They went back to their rooms, collected their luggage, bade farewell to the concierge and headed to the wharf. The same quaint retro launch or Vaporetto was ready waiting and with its engine burbling took them slowly along the canal towards open water.

"Venice, you owe me," said Helen.

"We'll be back," said Martino," doing his best Arnie impersonation.

"Hey that's pretty good, but it should be, you are after all a famous movie star," she teased, snuggling up to him against the cold and wet.

The little launch had now exited the canal system and increasing its speed soon had them on the wharf and heading to the railway station. They climbed on board the sleek stainless steel tube with other wet-faced tourists looking forward to drier climes. It was Helen's third fast train trip ever. She looked out at the jumbled urban mix of industry, small businesses and homes, passing slowly at first but soon gathering speed as the view gradually changed to an open countryside of farm buildings and fields, all now flicking past at two hundred kilometres per hour plus. They were still a bit down on spirit and energy from wine and weather, so dozed on and off as the fastest mass transport on wheels sped them on a giant arc across northern Italy.

Suddenly all went black as a tunnel swallowed them, then spat them out again, followed by another and another. Several towns and small settlements later Helen opened her eyes and sensed a gradual slowing. Martino, who was already awake announced that Florence would be along soon.

The speed dropped little by little until they finally drifted gently and silently into their mooring, Florence Railway Station.

Towing luggage against a tide of faces, all intent on going in the opposite direction, they looked for the nearest taxi stand. Helen spotted a free taxi with a young driver leaning back smoking a cigarette, looking like a student putting himself through university. Martino exchanged a few words in Italian and the driver put their luggage in the trunk while they climbed into a Fiat station wagon and fell gratefully back on shabby people-worn seats. It was no matter, they were here now, speeding down the streets of the city of the renaissance. Helen watched the inspired madness of Italian traffic that resembled a Formula One Grand Prix start, on a narrow track with an early hairpin and every driver desperate to be first through.

The intensity and passion inherited by most Italians means there is passion and intensity everywhere, even for the mundane task of driving in traffic. She smiled to herself at the hilarious thought of reincarnations of Leonardo Da Vinci or Michelangelo standing on a corner gobsmacked and wide-eyed at what now passed over the streets of their beloved city. Another ten minutes and they were outside their hotel, a convincing restoration of a three hundred year old building with a view of the Arno River. They negotiated check-in then took the lift to their rooms. Helen went straight to the window and pulled back the heavy, plush drapes.

On the opposite bank lay quintessential Florence. A jumble of terracotta buildings sat aglow in the afternoon light. Cypress trees stood as pencil straight sentinels. Deep shadows, contrasting with a late burst of sunshine, created for just a few moments the rich colours of an old master's landscape.

To her right she could just see one of the world's historic treasures, the Ponte Vecchio Bridge – the only bridge that Adolf Hitler had ruled to remain undamaged during the retreat of German forces, now jammed with buildings and businesses like toadstools on a log. Helen dragged herself away from the window, opened her luggage, then lay back on the bed and watched as across the river lights flickered on one by one. She soon decided this to have been the best of all sights on her trip so far.

She dropped off into a light sleep and woke twenty minutes later to a soft tap from Martino. She opened the door and he greeted her with a jacket slung over his shoulder.

"Hungry?" he asked.

"You bet," she said and retreated into the room to tidy herself up.

Martino knew the area and when she was ready he led her out of the hotel to a long narrow restaurant that did honest meals at a reasonable price. This was proven by their cliental, a slightly rowdy and boisterous crowd of young 'Brits' on some sort of tertiary break.

They finished their meal and wine and wandered through the network of tiny, cobbled streets that led them past narrow fronted shops and businesses. One such shop sold leatherwear from a frontage no wider than two–three metres. The owner who looked more like a portly doorman for a dingy backstreet cabaret in Cairo quickly stood on his cigarette and smiling followed them inside.

He stood guard a few metres away over a shop full of the most beautiful leather garments Helen had ever seen. Helen and Martino ignored the standover style and after several minutes Helen found one she couldn't resist. A jacket of the supplest suede with tiny perforations in two panels on the front and one on the back that created a texture and effect that Helen had never seen before. Impractical, prone to soiling, ridiculously expensive and extremely desirable. Helen watched as the owner packed the jacket into a plain unbranded bag and entered twelve hundred euros. Helen pressed the credit button and put the card back in her wallet. They both walked outside with the owner smiling at their retreating backs. Making up for time lost to the past she thought to herself. Today's time was moving on and they decided to head back to their hotel. In the foyer, Helen noticed a poster for excerpts from a range of operas to be performed by the Japanese Soprano, Hiroko Saito at Chiesa di Santa Monaca, a smallish church dating back to the fifteenth century.

"I want to go to that," she said looking at Martino.

"Agreed," as any Italian would say.

Martino checked out the address of the venue and was deep in thought for a while. "Right…we'll go on our last night and we'll eat at a great restaurant I went to plenty of times while I was working here and I think a new outfit is needed to go to the opera. Wouldn't you agree? I know just the place."

"Well?" Helen said expectantly.

"His name is Gian Francesco Giofre and he is a brilliant young designer, unique, exclusive and unmistakeable. You'll love him. We should go there tomorrow so you've got plenty of time to get what you really want. He works in the shop while you look around. He graduated in Scenography and worked in the tailoring sections of various theatres in Florence."

"What on earth is scenography."

"Dressing windows," he said simply.

That night Helen lay awake like an excited schoolgirl the night before her first prom. She eventually drifted off, to dreams of Italian designers, beautiful clothes and opera.

#

The next day Helen and Martino arrived at Giofre's studio, paid the taxi and walked inside. Helen didn't know where to look first. She walked along a line of evening wear and stopped at a unique, one-off design cut on the cross to flatter any figure. Gian swooped up and plucking it off the rack, held it in front of her, drawing attention to how the colours complemented her skin tones and emphasised the blueness of her eyes. He led her towards a changing room and handed it to her with a flourish.

"Wow, this I really like. I'm not looking at anything else," she said pulling the curtain back to show the two men.

Martino held the door of their taxi open as Helen in her new outfit stepped onto the footpath beside the fifteenth-century church. The outside was deceiving, it was verging on plain and restrained when compared to most other buildings in Florence. It revealed its hidden charms as they went through an entrance as ordinary as the interior wasn't. They sat quietly for a few moments with a few others observing a silence that was implied more than required. An usher approached and politely asked if they and others seated would please remain outside. This was a request made by the soprano herself.

Helen and Martino leant back against a convenient railing and made small talk. The request by the singer for the audience to leave the auditorium secretly impressed Helen. The soprano had the style and gravitas to insist on something some people might call petty. Obviously the soprano took her art very seriously and would not have arrived where she was now if she hadn't – a short experience that Helen clasped to her own artistic self. An usher eventually came out and gave the all-clear. They both took their seats and waited.

A low level of sound came from the audience as the remainder of the seats gradually filled up. There were whispered greetings between friends, the rustle of movement and shifting of bodies. Finally the doors were closed to latecomers and the audience settled into the evening. Helen admittedly was not an opera aficionado, but like people not 'into art' – but liking what they liked – she liked most of what she'd heard thus far. She couldn't translate the lyrics but what she could understand and appreciate, was the immense power, passion and beauty that often seemed to be an exaltation of life in all its joyful and tragic moments. Helen entered into a quiet, wide-eyed state when the soprano herself finally took the stage.

After an eternity of silence the soprano began the evening. Martino was of course familiar with the content with Helen recognising some arias she'd heard before. However, the aria chosen for the finale made the whole evening one to remember. It was the soprano aria – 'O mio babbino caro' from the opera 'Gianni Schicchi', by Giacomo Puccini – a heartrending and passionate love story of tensions reaching breaking point between a girl named Lauretta and her father Gianni Schicchi. Her father had forbidden her to pursue the love of a boy whose family did not meet the societal status necessary for her father's approval. During the aria the soprano moved to be only metres away from Helen and Martino. The effect on Helen was as if the power of her voice had entered every cell in her body. She could not believe the immensity of the moment.

Chapter 10

Martino certainly knew what he was doing when he agreed to run with the hot little Fiat Abarth with its twin exhausts, seventeen-inch alloy wheels and one hundred and twenty three kilowatts under his right foot. The hire company told him it was just the car they needed for a long-haul drive and the tight, windy roads ahead of them. And it was more than just nippy, it was a midget missile on wheels. The road around the Amalfi Coast was no surprise to Martino, but Helen had never in her life encountered a more narrow road on which to fit two cars.

Just grabbing hold of the wheel of the tiny, thinly disguised racing machine woke Martino from his easygoing, sleepy-eyed state and transformed him into road rage on wheels. Fortunately the combination of the narrow girth of the car and Martino's natural ability behind the black, thick-rimmed wheel meant they avoided head-on collisions with the equally insane and aggressive on-coming traffic. Headlights loomed towards them and whipped past centimetres away only to be replaced by one coming around the next corner going even faster.

They were making good progress towards the hotel and they needed to as they were running well behind their expected arrival time, it was now dark and they were desperate for a meal. A prudent phone call ahead had let the hotel know they were on the way.

The little car raced into and through a tunnel with the throaty sound of the exhausts reverberating off the walls. Martino's eyes were gleaming while Helen just thought it was too loud. Nevertheless she had to admit that it did all add to the excitement of the night.

"It's just a few corners past the tunnel, we're nearly there," he said glancing quickly at Helen.

"Thank God for that," she replied.

"We're here." Martino said triumphantly as the beautiful white clifftop hotel overlooking the sea that was one of civilisation's cradles suddenly appeared ahead. He turned left onto the rooftop car park. Two attendants appeared, put their cases on a trolley and headed in the direction of the lift. Helen and Martino descended a short staircase to the foyer and began the check-in process.

To underscore that she now had a new life, Helen had made the reservation for her suite in her maiden name. They both handed over their passports and waited for the reception desk to complete the processing. It was while waiting that a door opened behind them and Helen turned to see an elderly Italian woman emerge, take a few paces towards them and stare unabashedly at her. She was not much more than five feet tall and after taking a couple more steps, paused and looked intently into Helen's face. She then turned her attention to Martino who was conversing in Italian with the receptionist. Finally she smiled faintly and nodded. Helen smiled back and the old lady returned to her room. Reception in the meantime had processed their booking and they followed the porter to their rooms with Helen slightly puzzled over the old lady's appearance.

As they had arrived late she only had a few minutes to splash some water on her face and run a comb through her hair and while Helen repaired her lipstick Martino stood outside tapping his feet.

To celebrate their arrival at the coast they both chose fish of the day and followed their waiter's suggestion of a local white.

The effects of the long drive, plus the wine meant they were outside the door of their rooms soon after the meal was finished. Martino had disappeared into his as Helen approached hers. Partly visible under the door was a heavy cartridge envelope. Helen opened the door and picked it up. Her name was written in a beautiful script across the front. She went inside and reached for an envelope opener from a wooden writing desk. Slitting it open, she extracted a letter on matching paper. The same elegant script conveyed a short message that included an invitation for Helen and her partner to join the writer for tomorrow's evening meal, compliments of the house. In the corner of the letter was a tiny and exquisitely rendered illustration of two birds on a leafy branch. The signature read Ersilia Abelli.

A PS instructed her to take the letter to reception for further instructions.

Helen had absolutely no idea what was behind this and an explanation of it being a simple act of kindness didn't add up. She placed it on the bedside table and after washing off her make up, climbed gratefully into bed and in minutes was asleep without looking at the moon sitting over the second most famous sea in the world, or giving any more thought to the letter with its illustration of two little birds on a branch.

Helen woke to the sound of a passable imitation of Dean Martin softly crooning 'Volare'. She lay back, performed a feline stretch that lasted at least a minute, rolled on her side and then onto her feet. She drew the curtains back revealing the blue expanse of the Tyrrhenian Sea. The sun was awake also, throwing a spray of highlights across to the smudgy hills in the distance. On the left and right, near vertical cliffs rose from the sea covered with a pastiche of buildings, both old and new. Aromatic plants and small shrubs threaded their way amongst the rocks giving sensual aromas to the gentlest of warm breezes Helen had ever felt. She was naked so reaching for a robe stepped onto the balcony and leaned over the railing. Below was a pool at near sea level. The pool man, far too young to know more than one Dean Martin song was now whistling and vacuuming the bottom.

"Hi you." Martino's sleepy drawl came from over the low wall from the neighbouring balcony, reminding her of where she was and who she was with.

"Hi back," was her sleepy reply with a long yawn.

"I think you should have saved your money and booked just one suite."

"Hey, don't you worry yourself about all that. Just remember what your big sister said, good things take time. See you at breakfast at nine o'clock," she said looking at her watch.

"I'll be there," he replied.

Helen went back into the room and drew the curtains. Still feeling tired from the travel she lay back on the bed and drifted into a half-sleep mode from where she often reviewed her life and where it was going. She acknowledged that her physical desire for Martino was building but Helen knew that if she was anything, she was patient and careful.

She reminded herself of her childhood and exciting trips to town with her aunty and her two daughters. They'd go to the pictures where she and her cousins were treated to an ice-cream each. At the end of the movie, her aunty would buy them each a small bag of sweets. Her cousins would have eaten all of theirs before they were halfway home. Helen's parents forbade sweets so Helen would carefully time the eating of hers to finish the last one as they headed up her drive. Helen's moral to the story, spin out the eating of forbidden fruit.

Helen had decided days ago that she would pick the time and place for what Martino was hinting not very subtly about. The place she knew was right here overlooking the Tyrrhenian Sea and the time just might be right for tonight. The letter's few words had somehow communicated a feeling of an ageless love and tenderness. Helen sensed this and felt an affinity to this place and its people.

While holding onto this feeling of warmth, she reached for a small bottle of massage oil that smelt of vanilla and hazel nuts. She breathed out in one long sigh and gradually drifted off to sleep.

Twenty minutes later she woke to the sound of a small fishing boat setting a steady beat as it entered the bay. The motor slowed and finally stopped, followed by the sound of voices and the rattle of an anchor chain. Voices started again and then silence only interrupted by the occasional knock of an oar. A seagull hovered around interested in a quick snack. It occurred to Helen that take away the motor and the modern fishing tackle and this process would have been happening for a thousand years or more, simple boats built the same way by generations of people living off the sea.

She ran the shower as hot as she could stand, vanquishing most of the aches of the long-distance travel. Another body audit in front of the multi-wall mirrors, where nothing is hidden from close examination, fired her to race through a quick set of squats, push-ups on the bath and high leg raises followed by a range of Pilates stretches. Admonishing herself for being so neglectful, she grabbed a huge white towel and dried off. She had fifteen minutes to meet her self-imposed deadline for breakfast and given her obsession for controlling life's finest details she took all the shortcuts she knew to be out the door, up the lift and sitting down to breakfast on the balcony overlooking the pool and ocean by the time Martino arrived.

"What on earth can we do today?" they both said in unison. "Ok, I'm going for a swim after breakfast has gone down."

"Agreed, and then we'll walk to town," replied Martino.

"Right, see you in the pool in thirty minutes. Oh…by the way we'll be eating compliments of the house tonight."

"How is that happening?"

"I'll tell you down at the pool."

Martino was cruising lazy, languid laps of the pool when Helen finally arrived delayed by a bout of indecision over the swimsuit, one piece or bikini? She finally plumped for the bikini. It was daringly miniscule, but after all she was in Italy now and knew Martino and any other man would mark the yes box with a big tick. The 'Dean Martin' pool guy certainly did and he made the most of it while Martino was blissfully knocking off the laps. Helen, aware of this, made sure he got his money's worth. This was not the Helen of old. She was now on the other side of the world from Cameron, making up for lost time.

Smart bastard, trust him to be good at everything she thought as she lay back on a recliner watching Martino's effortless style through her new Gucci sunglasses. Suddenly, on a very un-Helen impulse she jumped up, whipped off the Guccis and did a bomb right beside him. He emerged coughing and spluttering and it was all on. She swam for all she was worth but Martino was better, diving like a playful seal under her he came up a few metres ahead and promptly ducked her head under the water. She surfaced coughing and spluttering, and furious. A wrestling match ensued but her red face quickly became one of embarrassment when standing up at the shallow end she found her bikini top had ended up around her waist during the playfight. She quickly restored her modesty but it was definitely the young pool guy's day.

Frolicking around like two adolescents had served to break the thin layer of ice in their relationship and after drying her hair she lay beside him and put her head on his chest. Her eyes closed and her breathing matched his. Her long slim fingers played unconsciously with his dark chest hair and for the first time in more than a decade, she felt intimacy, peace and trust. Of course as she quickly cautioned herself, her man of the moment was bound to be just a short-term fling but the big difference now with her failed marriage was that at least she was under no illusions.

Live for today, she thought again as the sun warmed her face and she drifted in and out of a light sleep.

Martino stirred and Helen woke from her short nap. They sat up and looked around. Time had moved on, the fun and games were over so the pool guy had given up on them and was now sponging water off the steps leading down to the sea.

"Hey, you were going to tell me about how we're eating free tonight," Martino suddenly remembered.

"I can't tell you anything now, you'll just have to wait until tonight like me," she teased.

Helen decided she would go to reception without Martino, get the mystery instructions and then wait with anticipation for whatever was to unfold. They made their way back to their rooms agreeing to meet in reception in an hour and then stroll into Amalfi. Helen waited a few moments and then retrieving the letter headed off to the foyer She approached the receptionist, a young Italian male. He read the brief letter nodding slowly.

"Madam, you have been invited by Signora Ersilia Abelli to dine with her in her private suite. The letter says that she would be honoured if you and your partner would give her the pleasure of your company at seven pm. You are to inform reception by twelve noon if you accept the invitation."

"Oh yes, absolutely, we'd love to accept the invitation. I can't imagine what it's all about, perhaps you might know?" Helen asked hopefully.

"I have no idea what her reasons are. Madam Ersilia is a very private person and lives in the hotel under special circumstances, indeed you must also be someone special as invitations from Signora Ersilia are rare." He paused then went on, "As you have accepted I will notify Signora Ersilia and give you the security card that will allow you onto her floor. Simply take the lift to the third floor, swipe the card and you will have access to her floor. Enjoy."

There was obviously no more to be gained from reception so Helen, barely able to contain herself, skipped the lift and bounded up the stairs to tell Martino. She stopped at his door, went to knock then changed her mind. She knew little more than Martino but decided she would keep what little she did know to herself. After all the letter was addressed to her.

Helen's mind was occupied with things other than their little sojourn around Amalfi. She ate a cooling gelato and purchased a bottle of 'fermented sunshine' as she called limoncello, the liqueur made locally from the abundance of lemons growing along a coastline tilted by God's hand at just the right angle. A giant solar panel capturing sunshine in a bottle.

They'd soon had their fill of the crowds of people at Amalfi and headed back up the winding road with scores of 'Sunday Grand Prix drivers' flying at them. They were to take their cue from the locals and quickly developed a sidestep to match any Spanish bullfighter.

"Let's meet at the bar at six thirty and I guess we should dress semi formal," Helen said while waiting for the lift.

"How do you know where to go?" he said.

"Don't worry, it's all organised."

The lift closed and they rode up, each thinking their own thoughts.

Helen opened her door, picked unerringly the right clothes for the evening and hung them up to air. She then sprawled on the bed in her underwear and after all the fresh air and lusty exercise slipped into deep, dream-rich sleep. She woke forty minutes later with a start, experiencing a short panic attack that she had somehow overslept and ruined the whole evening. Helen's self-awareness told her she was an obsessive high achiever, where everything she did had to be just right. As such she carried through her life a fear of failure verging on the pathological and along with that of its nasty twin sister – a deep-seated dread of letting other people down.

Of course with a mindset like that, she rarely let others down, though that fact went unrecognised by her and was therefore no comfort. The thing she did recognise is that you don't turn up late for an evening with an aging matriarch living in the top floor apartment of a five-star hotel overlooking the Tyrrhenian Sea. She checked her watch and took several deep breaths to calm her elevated pulse. She then stripped to the buff and wandered into the bathroom where she performed a series of Pilate stretches. Helen's new status meant that the body for which she always cared, had stepped up a level or two in importance. She was now putting a higher price tag on it and it therefore had to look worth it. One last turn for the 'see every angle' mirrors and she had scooped up the letter from the bedside table and headed up the lift to her rendezvous with Martino.

"God he's gorgeous," she whispered quietly to herself as she swerved between the tables to where Martino was sitting with a tall glass of limoncello, loaded with chunky blocks of ice and looking over the Tyrrhenian Sea towards the last rays of a dying sun. "Thank God he doesn't know it," she added. Like swimming, walking or just sitting around, as he was doing now, everything happened with an economy of effort and a languid ease. He was one of those rare men who without knowing it, made everyone else look as if they were trying too hard. Natural talent, that most infuriating gift when held by others, giving the impression of not having a care in the world. She searched through her holiday slackened brain for the one right word. It came to her later, insouciance.

"Nice jacket," she said, admiring the drape and easy fit of what was probably from an Italian designer made possibly from the finest micron Merino wool grown in the New Zealand high country.

Martino raised an eyebrow to the waiter who appeared beside them. He raised another eyebrow in Helen's direction and she responded with her order.

"Thank you Signora," and he was off to the bar, picking up another order on the way.

They were both content to sit back in silence and enjoy. One niggle, though not unpleasant, was the one big question nagging her. What was this evening all about? She put it aside and relaxed with her drink, finishing the last of it as the sun vanished over the horizon.

"Right, we need to move on," she said with finality.

They pushed level three and rode up in silence. When the lift stopped, Helen swiped the security card as instructed. The doors opened without delay to deliver them into the small foyer of the penthouse suite. Automatic lighting flicked on revealing a door and a brass name plate engraved with Ersilia Abelli and a small red button. They were where they were meant to be.

Martino leaned forward and pressed the button. Thirty seconds that felt like thirty minutes to Helen went by before the door was opened by a suited, middle-aged man with a fine head of steely grey hair, carefully brushed and giving the impression of a playboy gambler from Monaco. His cultured voice with a trace of a southern French accent matched the image. He greeted them with a warm smile and politely asked if they would mind waiting. The door was ajar and they heard him announcing that the guests had arrived. He returned and led them through to a large dining room. A door went through to a state-of-the-art kitchen with a server sealed off by a larger version of a roller slated blind as commonly used on period writing desks.

Ersilia Abelli stood up from her chair by the window and taking a few steady paces, shook Martino's hand and then reached towards Helen. She gripped her offered hand in both of hers with a warm dry grip and a strength that belied her age.

"Thank you dearly for accepting my invitation. I have waited an eternity for this moment," she said looking directly into Helen's face.

Helen didn't ask why. She understood the purpose of tonight was to look and listen. Signora Ersilia directed them to two large and comfortable chairs, placing Helen nearest to her. Helen guessed one of the few failings of her age would be a degree of deafness. Helen was obviously a guest of some honour, the reasons she imagined, would be revealed during the evening, in Ersilia Abelli's own good time.

The suited man servant turned out to be jack of all trades. He appeared from the kitchen holding a tray of drinks.

"I'm so sorry, I should have asked you what you wanted to drink. As you would probably guess I do not entertain very often and I also must make amends and introduce my good friend, gourmet cook and man about the house, Alain Marceau."

The tray was put down and another round of handshakes ensued followed by the dispensing of the drinks to all.

"This is absolutely fine," Helen said sampling her drink. Martino merely nodded.

"Now as for our meal tonight, Alain is able to produce most of what is on the standard menu in the hotel dining room and anything that is not able to be produced here he will order from the main kitchen and have it brought up. Believe me it is not an issue," she added.

"And I suggest we get the food ordering out of our way and we can get on with the rest of the evening."

Alain produced three hotel menus and a wine list. The room went quiet while these were studied. As it transpired all meals chosen were required to be prepared in the hotel kitchen, giving Alain the night off. However, he busied himself finishing the partly prepared tray of hors d'oeuvre which he duly brought forth.

The group were now well supplied with drinks and snacks so Signora Ersilia drank a healthy measure of her wine and set the empty glass carefully and emphatically on the table. She cleared her throat and turned towards Helen who sensed the moment had come.

"My dearest daughter. " She paused, looked upwards and took a long breath. "I am so pleased to at last welcome you into my home and what little is left of my life," Signora Ersilia said looking intently into Helen's suntanned face that was now quite pale.

"My God. What are you saying?" gasped Helen, sounding cornered and desperately looking for an escape route.

"I know, it's difficult to believe, but it is the truth as I am sitting here."

She reached over to a small table and without saying a word picked up a large aged, scruffy envelope and passed it to Helen. Helen's face was still white and her hands shook as she took the envelope which she promptly dropped on the floor. She was now scarlet and hyperventilating and after taking several deep breaths slowly regained her composure.

"My dear child. I knew there would be no easy way so I decided to be as bold as your gallant father, Alan Marshall, seventy five years ago."

It was like an eternity as Helen, feeling as if she was moving in slow motion, reached down and picked up the fallen envelope. With her hands trembling, she opened it carefully and removed three battered photographs which she laid on the envelope resting on her knees. Two of the images showed her father clearly recognisable with a couple of soldier mates enjoying a cigarette by a road sign in the middle of the desert in North Africa. Helen recalled seeing photos like these at home when she was a young girl. The third picture she had never seen before and was of her father in front of a house most likely in Italy. Beside him was a woman with long dark hair. Helen's father had his arm around her. She was young, beautiful and unmistakably Ersilia Abelli.

Chapter 11

Alan Marshall waited to disembark along with the other men retreating from one of the more heroic stuff-ups in modern warfare. As in rugby, their favoured sport in New Zealand, the old hands always say it is a lot tougher to go backwards than it is to go forward. They also say that if it's a stuff-up, it's because you've been outnumbered, out thought and outmanoeuvred, or your supply lines were too long and you have inferior weaponry or intelligence compared to your enemy in some, or all of the above.

If you follow all the correct theories in rugby's defence strategies and make no mistakes, theoretically no opposition can score against you, but score they do, which is a varying combination of a stuff-up on your part and exceptional ability or rare genius on theirs. The people responsible for the stuff-ups in warfare are comparatively small in number and take their life's work in the study and practice of warfare very seriously. They also more often than not, take the lives of the men and women they command just as seriously. However, they are as human as the lowest ranking soldier under them and fail and show poor judgement just as they do. The differences lie simply in the size and the cost of the failures, but ironically failures have a habit of producing heroes.

The old hand he'd just spent the last hour sitting and listening to and adding in the occasional comment on the deck of HMS Glengyle stood up, cadged another cigarette, slapped him on the back and wishing him luck headed off to his assembly point nursing a bad limp. Alan looked at his companions, two NZ Army escorts; Nicolas, a full-blooded inhabitant from a tiny village in the White Mountains of Crete and a NZ Army medical officer he'd buddied up with called Evan. The group stood up stretched and joined the thinning ranks of allied soldiers disembarking.

Twenty-four hours earlier Lieutenant Alan Marshall and the remaining members of his platoon had spent two frustrating days scraping out a trench overlooking the Maleme Airfield. The only tools available were their own infantry helmets, indicative of the lack of supplies and equipment that were discarded when pursued by German troops during an ill-conceived venture of allied forces into Greece. His platoon were part of the 22nd Battalion and were first landed in Egypt to add to the British and Australian forces sent into the ring with Mussolini's armies. For a more political than military reason, a large proportion of this force crossed the Mediterranean to Greece to honour a British commitment of support.

The operation was a total disaster culminating in a madcap exodus of soldiers and what little equipment that could be salvaged back to Egypt. Alan Marshall and his platoon's misfortune was to be at the end of the line and miss the boat to Egypt. The only option was to divert the stragglers to Crete. These troops became known as Creforce and ended up in a desperate situation with critical shortages of field artillery, trenching tools, tents and boots, and chronic shortages of the most essential items for the task at hand working rifles, and machine guns, and something to fire through them.

Alan's platoon was one of many charged with defending the airfield and destroying whatever the Germans drove over it or landed on it, but on the twentieth of May 1941 the biggest surprise of their war so far was not an invasion from the sea but an invasion that landed right in front and around them. Large, slow Junker transport aircraft flying across from Athens appeared with one followed by another, and another, and another, each plodding slowly overhead, spilling out uncountable numbers of white and coloured parachutes while Stuka dive-bombers provided aircover for troops that were already on the ground.

Most paratroopers landed on the airfield and the surrounding area, but with parachutes equipped with only one strap many were unable to guide themselves to a convenient landing of their choice. As a result some ended up in the sea and drowned and others on buildings or trees where they became easy targets, while others landed on rough, rocky ground, injuring or breaking ankles or legs.

Following the paras came troop transporters landing crack mountain troops and gliders also full of troops, the latter easy targets until they lowered the altitude of their approach. Ill equipped as they were, the Anzacs were able to shoot paratroopers at will during the vulnerable drop stage and the airfield was soon covered with the dead, nearly dead, or seriously wounded young Germans. As deeply as the Germans were in trouble with heavy losses the Allies were soon to be in far more.

Short as they were of the tools necessary to win a battle let alone a war, a campaign that hinted early at success, soon went bad and quickly turned into a major military disaster. Paratroopers were still landing like locusts on a ripe cornfield and kept coming in never-ending waves. Stuka dive-bombers made strafing and bombing runs over the defensive positions creating vast clouds of dust that jammed the few Bren guns in use and provided cover for the German attacks.

If it were not for the ferocity of the 28th Māori Battalion, more than matched by determination of the local partisans and the resilience of the average allied and ANZAC soldier, defeat and retreat would have happened much earlier. Faced with the continual backup of a seemingly unlimited number of well-armed and equipped infantry, the 20th and 22nd Battalions had become isolated and had eventually ceded all control of the area to the German troops.

The Luftwaffe owned the skies and the gliders kept unloading troops. For Creforce, the end was coming. An order to retreat went out to all allied troops carried by brave, fleet-footed runners with a short life expectancy. The message passed on was that they were to make their way east to the village of Galatas and on to the port of Sfakia on the southern coast where they would be picked up by an assortment of craft including Royal Navy destroyers.

When Alan Marshall got the news, he gathered his depleted platoon around him and confirmed what they already knew. They were to leave as soon as it was dark, conserving ammunition so they could defend their position long enough to escape under the cover of night. As Alan commented, "We're not going to win this bloody war by dying in a battle already lost." They took turns at keeping a lookout over the open ground between them and the nearest German troops. Alan reasoned that the Germans, although suffering huge losses and being stung by the ferocious resistance from Crete civilians and the ANZACS, would now be aware they had the upper hand and could therefore afford to wait them out rather than adding unnecessarily to their already heavy casualties.

Nighttime eventually dropped its welcome cloak and they made ready to depart the meagre protection of their barely adequate trench. When Alan was satisfied it was dark enough, he gave the order to quietly but quickly withdraw and head to Galatas.

For speed they used the road but were ready to dive for cover in the event of sighting any German patrols. Alan was still convinced the likelihood of this was low as he was sure the Germans would be lying low, licking their wounds. Using the road would also likely bring them quickly in contact with other retreating allied troops. From there, they would plan the rest of the trek to the embarkation point at Sfakia with the benefit of whatever information was picked up in the meantime.

Alan trudged along nervously checking every shadow, the way lit by a weak moon partly masked by cloud. He knew the moon was a mixed blessing. The vision it gave him was also given to the enemy. He quashed his anxious thoughts by reminding himself they would surely still be keeping their heads down. A youth spent deer stalking in the rugged bush-covered interior of New Zealand's North Island equipped him well for fast, soundless travel through rugged country.

The platoon was making reasonable progress considering their lack of food and water and their numerous injuries. Many had contracted dysentery from contaminated drinking water which added to the struggle. Alan's platoon had now joined a small tributary to a larger stream and in turn to an even larger river as more and more troops streamed forth from other defensive positions. The word from the rest of the exhausted and hungry soldiers was that if you wanted to get off this island from hell you needed to pull your finger out and get to Sfakia Bay on the southern coast as soon as possible. To get there on time daylight travel was going to be necessary. But it carried the risk of aerial attacks from Stukas and Me 109's and dead bodies of soldiers lying on the road was warning enough to the unwary.

Other troops told them that Galatas was just up the road and they'd best get there soon if they wanted to get some food and water. It would only be a matter of time before the small village would be overrun by German troops and there would be no food or water from them, but you would get a long slow trip to Germany with free board and lodgings for the rest of the war. The road sign for Galatas appeared and they soon came to the small town with a church full of wounded Kiwi soldiers.

As they had no serious injuries they were told to get some food and get on their way to Sfakia. They were given food and some wine in a goat skin by local women who risked harsh reprisals to themselves and their families for helping soldiers from the other side of the world.

One of the men broke some bread into pieces and dealt it out with olives and goat's milk cheese to eager hands that hadn't seen food for two days. The wine was passed from man to man and each took a swig as they hid in a small outbuilding used for making goats' milk cheeses. Wine was foreign to most of them and they would rather have had a beer in their hand like they would have back in New Zealand.

"We'll get used to it," was the only thing anyone said and Alan wondered if they were pondering the likelihood of this modest repast being their 'Last Supper'.

"Right, once everyone's had something to eat we'll head off. We're going to have to cut across country a bit to avoid German troops and keep your eyes and ears open unless you want to be the next body lying on the road." The urgency in Alan's voice came through in a low hoarse whisper.

He leaned back looking at his men wolfing down the first food they'd had in two days. Alan knew that being on the footy field on training night is one thing but playing a real game with big buggers coming at you at a hundred miles an hour is totally different. Similarly, he knew that to date his experience in warfare-for-real, was short, sharp and shocking and no amount of training could have fully prepared him for it. He also knew there was a whole lot more to come and that he was going to have to dig really deep if he was going to hang together and get the job done without his name ending up on a headstone on a barren hillside in Crete, even if the view was great.

Shaking off the stomach knotting feelings of self-doubt he stood up and looked cautiously around. The short rest for him and the men was worth having to freshen up and restore alert eyes and ears. They all knew they had to get moving if they were going to make the embarkation point.

Avoiding chance encounters with German troops by cutting across country made travel with only the early hints of the dawn light touching the hills behind them, made the going slow, difficult and treacherous. After another twenty minutes and steadily increasing light they could make out Suda Bay and the dark reassuring shape of a destroyer of the Royal Navy. They also knew that the new day would bring the Luftwaffe pilots in their Stukas to attack whatever allied ships they could find, including any unwary allied soldiers making their way along the road. This knowledge added an extra measure of urgency to their stride.

Progress over the rough ground in low light was proving more difficult by the minute as their way was littered with rocks, boulders and other hazards. The donkeys local people used for transport were born and bred for this terrain, but not men with injuries and dysentery from the other side of the world, in Crete less than a week. With daylight getting stronger by the minute, they were able to detect a road several hundred yards away.

Alan had a hard decision to make. Stay where they were and risk spraining or breaking ankles or get themselves on the road and make faster progress. He decided on the latter and they set off across country to access it. They were making steady progress, but so was the sun and along with the increasing sunlight came the threat of air strikes. As if to answer his darker thoughts Alan could hear the faint and distant drone of aircraft. The others had heard it as well and lengthened their stride. Alan heard a string of curses behind him and turned to find one of the men who was nursing a turned ankle had come to a stop.

"I've turned my bloody ankle again." It was Mark Stringer the youngest in what remained of Alan's platoon.

"Stop here and I'll bandage it up, you others keep going. Take that narrow gully near those trees."

They headed off and while Alan wrapped the tight pressure bandage he heard the sound of fast approaching aircraft. A tight formation of six Stukas were flying at high altitude with the sun behind them on a heading towards the destroyer. One by one they peeled off, diving out of the sun with their banshee wail increasing to a high-pitched scream. The anti-aircraft guns on the destroyer opened up and immediately scored a hit.

A stricken Stuka broke away and with smoke trailing was trying to make it to Maleme. The plane was too sick for that and slowly and inexorably began its descent towards the ocean. It hit at speed, cartwheeling three times before it amazingly ended right way up and miraculously intact with clouds of steam and smoke billowing into the sky.

Alan watched as the small figure of the pilot slid the canopy back and climbed onto the wing. For a reason, he couldn't explain he felt a huge sense of relief. He had seen enough dead young men in his short experience of this war that he couldn't help but welcome the sight of the young German pilot's survival of such a catastrophic ditching. Although within the next few moments, he was to have his attitude slightly modified.

One Stuka had been delayed and turned up late and in so doing broke with the predictable pattern of German operations. Alan heard it coming as he stood beside the injured soldier. It was approximately fifteen hundred yards away descending from a height of four thousand feet and positioning itself to make a shallow dive through the valley behind them. Alan knew what the pilot was thinking and knew he was as powerless as a swimmer in water with a shark. He stood up and started futilely firing shots at the approaching aircraft and shouting at his men. They didn't hear above the noise and it was only as the Stuka got closer that they heard what he was shouting about.

It was a half reasonable prize from a very accurate bomb placement. The handy depression concentrated the blast and removed the remnants of Alan's platoon from any further responsibility for the war or its outcome. The pilot waved his wings and flew off after his comrades, happy to claim a strike and avoid copping a ribbing for being late.

Alan stood staring vacantly at the gully where a few minutes earlier his men were walking through. For twenty seconds he stood, his head frozen in some other place, facing down the hill towards the still smoking demolition of the gully and four men. Three days ago, half his platoon of raw recruits was separated in a brief skirmish then promptly captured by a chance encounter with a German patrol.

Now the first black thoughts of stark reality that roared into his brain was the realisation he was instrumental in their loss. Mark Stringer was standing, stunned into numb silence contemplating the abrupt extinction of mates he had known for only a few days.

This was Alan's first experience of losing men he was responsible for and in the minute or so it took to recover he was no better than the raw recruits just killed. At last reality kicked in. With a racing pulse and a dry mouth, he broke into a reckless madcap dash down the hill towards the road. It was as if he thought he could somehow save them – after the event.

Ten yards from the little gully and the remnants of his men he slowed to a walk and regained his composure. Mark Stringer caught up and together made a rapid search for personal belongings and ID tags. Hearing the not too distant crackle of small arms' fire they quickly stuffed the few things they could find in their pockets. They stood up and Alan took one last look at the scattered remains. He closed his eyes to the sight and his mind to the thoughts crowding in on him. After taking several deep breaths, he opened his eyes and looked at Mark, then carried on down the hill towards the road leading to Sfakia and the rescue ships. He didn't look back.

Alan and Mark, the oldest and youngest surviving members of a platoon that for the purposes of the war no longer existed, set off to put as much distance between them and Galatas as possible. They were quickly absorbed by other troops as increasing numbers joined the exodus south. They soon adopted a slow plod as the debilitating effects of dysentery and lack of food and clean water took effect on the strength of even the fittest of soldiers.

Their journey eventually reached into the steep flanks of the White Mountains with one torturous and draining climb after another on a road that twisted and turned, first forward and then backward on itself as it lifted them higher and higher into the mountains.

One of the hazards was the constant threat of strafing runs from the Luftwaffe and they all had to be ready to dive off the road and take any likely looking cover. Experienced hands always looked ahead for any rocks or gullies that might provide some protection. Alan having just experienced losing all but one of his platoon was now very alert to the threat of approaching aircraft.

Water was the next biggest survival issue after dodging air attacks. Lack of food was just tolerable but thirst could not be lived with for more than a couple of days given the daytime temperature and the continual steep, hard climbs they all faced. Wells were few and far between and when any number got to them it was every man for himself. The level of desperation was so great that fights frequently broke out as thirsty men competed for water.

Alan was becoming aware that Mark was struggling. He was only nineteen and a physically young nineteen at that. He was becoming seriously dehydrated and needed water badly. Alan decided he might have to provide a bit of aggressive defence of his young charge next chance they got to refill their already empty water bottles. He was confident he could more than hold his own with the competition. He was tall and lean with big hands and a strong back from two years clearing scrub with his brother on the family farm. They were about to take the farm over before they decided the needs of their country and the people of Europe being dealt to by German aggression were greater.

The main problem was a big loud mouth who liked to bully his way to the front of any queue and Alan had a natural aversion to bullies whether they lived at home or Berlin. His name was Sam and he'd spent what was to Allen a wasted youth riding around on motorbikes and sitting in milk bars until he was old enough to go to the pub. He always had too much to say for himself and hadn't done a hard day's work in his life. He was a big noise in a small town and he came from the same area of New Zealand as Alan. Alan knew of him and also knew he was the sort of big soft prick who would back down when confronted.

They marched on trying to forget how thirsty they were and trying to stay alert to the threat of aircraft. The word was that the next well was another three miles away which isn't a great distance on the flat but was a different story on the steep hills they faced. Alan had a small reserve of water in a flask normally holding rum or whiskey. He gave Mark a short swig, screwed the cap back on and stuck it back in his pocket.

As they trudged on Alan gave some thought to the man management issue he saw looming. He was accustomed to giving orders from his stints in the territorial army he and his brother had spent time in before the war. They had both received call-up papers as part of the national ballot. It seemed it was going to be a pain in the arse at the time but they settled into life in the army for the three month stints and both made the most of it to the point where their natural leadership skills were recognised with commissions. Alan's style was not to be a bombastic parade ground tyrant with an overemphasis on rant but rather to set an example using plenty of common sense and firm restraint. If that didn't work, he could always crank the volume up a bit if needed. He mulled these thoughts over while they walked which helped prepare himself for the possibility of a 'friendly fire' conflict.

He could see the well coming up ahead and some of the stronger of the troops increased their pace and moved ahead of the pack. Sam had come into the army in poor condition so he was never up front through natural speed or stamina, instead he relied on pushing into someone else's place when he finally pulled up red-faced and blowing.

They got to the well and Mark took his turn filling his water bottle. Sam came puffing up and stood behind Mark telling him to pull his finger out. He decided he'd waited long enough and grabbed Mark by his shoulder. Alan was ready for this and clasped a big left hand on Sam's wrist and squeezed with all he had. He'd found out in his youth that he had a freakishly powerful grip and that in the occasional pub scrap in the past he often only had to exercise this strength to convince aggressive and overexcited protagonists to forget it and have another beer. Sam turned and looked at Alan and decided to forget it.

"Thanks for that," Mark said after he'd drunk a good measure of his canteen.

Daylight was on the way out and Alan and Mark decided to lay up near the well and set off again early in the morning. They slept on the bare ground as only the totally exhausted could and at four thirty am they refilled their water bottles, ate some of a piece of three-day old bread Alan was carefully measuring out and set off with the rest of the early risers.

Alan and other officers gathered the men ready to leave and found they had a dozen who were still carrying the standard 303 calibre army issue rifle. The instruction was that if any aircraft decided to have a go at them they would all fire a concentrated volley and hope to hit the engine or a fuel line or with a bit of luck, fuel tank. It was also agreed to share the load of carrying a rifle. Each one would be passed onto someone else to take their turn.

Another agreement made was that if an enemy aircraft turned up the person holding the rifle at the time would fire at the plane. All this gave them something to think about other than food, water and rest.

Alan was a crack shot from deer stalking back home. What he didn't know was that Mark was even better and had scored top of his intake on the rifle range at both prone and standing. He had just handed his rifle onto Mark when he heard the sound of aircraft approaching. His first thought was to grab the rifle back but a newly confident and assertive Mark refused. It was a pair of ME 109s. They were scouting for allied soldiers heading to Sfakia to harass. They sighted Alan and the fifty or so troops and swept over at low altitude, then pulled up into a steep climb and at the top dropped off into a long right hand turn that would bring them back in line with their target. But the targets were now ready and those with rifles propped themselves behind handy rocks.

Mark got behind his rock and adjusted the sights. He had a full magazine and decided to fire early to give himself the best chance of a fatal hit. The rest of the armed troops would be shooting as well, so while Alan had to admit it was long odds to bring an aircraft down it was better than doing nothing and it may work to discourage further attacks.

Mark was to make their day and himself a hero. His first shot from long range at the leading aircraft appeared to have struck gold. A few seconds after he fired, a thin stream of smoke that was increasing rapidly started pouring from the engine and was soon followed by flames. The aircraft pulled out of its high-speed dive and the troops could see the flames now in the cockpit. They saw the pilot slide back the canopy and make a leap for his life. What the troops saw as he plummeted towards the unforgiving White Mountains was that a flame from the cockpit had also caught hold on his chute.

The pilot soon spotted what the troops had already seen and he now had less than thirty seconds to be at peace with his maker. Some troops cheered wildly as he raced downwards with the impotent and redundant parachute trailing a plume of smoke and spinning pointlessly behind him.

He hit a steep White Mountain slope bouncing over and over several times before he came to a rest that was surely permanent. He lay motionless, facedown against a large friendly rock with his arms and legs splayed out as if he was making love to it. The stray thought of the words 'earth to earth' suddenly entered Alan's brain. He turned away, looked at Mark and hoarsely whispered, 'Good shot mate. The other pilot decided that firing expensive cannon rounds at half-starved soldiers who were probably going to die of thirst or dysentery anyway, wasn't worth the risk of ending up on the same mountainside as his fellow pilot. He pulled out of his dive and peeled off, followed by a hail of 303 bullets.

Alan reflected how surprisingly vulnerable these sophisticated killing machines could be when a well-directed bullet smashes a fuel line and pours high octane Avgas onto damaged electric wires or the red-hot exhausts of a V12 engine. Several soldiers came up and clapped him on the back, including, to his credit, a slightly embarrassed Sam who not only clapped him on the back but also shook his hand. For all its destruction, war sometimes brings out a person's better side Alan reflected.

All but one man climbed out from behind their cover positions and returned to the task at hand, getting to Sfakia within the next thirty-six hours. They each had a slight but discernible lift in their step from the victory over the enemy air attack.

"I'll give you this back, I don't think I'll have any trouble getting another one," Mark said to Alan as he handed him the prize rifle.

The man who didn't get to his feet was suffering from dysentery on top of shrapnel wounds to his shoulder and stomach. Alan had another tough decision to make. Leave him here with a supply of water to wait for assistance or send the others ahead and wait and see if he would respond to a longer rest. He decided to go with the latter. Ironically the White Mountain range – presenting a formidable barrier that made the escape from Crete that much more difficult also provided a source of better quality water coming as it did from such a remote source. Another irony was that the stricken soldier was a medic who had just finished his medical degree when he decided the war was more important.

There was something about this bloke that made Alan decide to give his all to get him through. He knew that the toughest part of the trans-alpine trek was behind them. It wasn't exactly all downhill from here but there were more downhills than uphill and Alan was confident he could get them through in time to catch the boat back to North Africa. His name was Evan Jefferies and he perked up a bit after taking another swig of water and told Alan to get a bottle of tablets to treat his dysentery out of a small pack he was carrying. Alan gave him a tablet with some water, then with him providing support, they both staggered off forty or so minutes behind the others.

"If I get out…of this…I'm coming back…when this bloody mess…is finished," Evan gasped between the effort of moving each leg forward.

"Yeah. Why the hell would you do that?" Alan replied minutes later. "I love the scenery," was all he said.

Obviously he wasn't going to let on right now why he would want to come back to a place he was more likely to die in than return to. Alan wondered if Evan was lapsing into delirium and he had to admit that the effects of limited water, no food and the ravages of dysentery were probably having an effect on his head as well. The mountains, the road and the rocks and rough scrub all seemed to merge and change, swimming around in a kaleidoscope of shapes and forms.

Chapter 12

As the road passed slowly beneath his feet and a fierce sun beat down on his head and shimmered off the road into his face Alan slowly realised a small group of even smaller buildings were two to three hundred yards ahead of them. Alan squinted through half-closed eyes and could make out a village of no more than half a dozen cottages. In his state of mind he seriously considered it was more likely a mirage, an oasis of cool water, shade and kind, giving people who weren't trying to blast them into oblivion. They would provide care, a little food and most of all, clean water for their cracked lips and parched throats and even some to fill their water bottles.

A small group of children who were outside stopped the game they were playing and ran into one of the houses. They were replaced by a large and formidable looking woman dressed in the garments of the people that lived in the remote and desolate White Mountains. Arms folded, she stood her ground in the doorway of her house. Alan decided it was now too real to be something created by his feverish imagination and looked with cautious optimism towards her as they slowly drew closer. When they were nearly opposite, she abruptly and decisively stepped out onto the road and putting out a large left arm that almost went around them both, guided them quickly into the house without saying a word. Even if they hadn't wanted to it's unlikely they could have resisted given their depleted strength and her comparative size.

They found themselves in a simple tidy room with an earthen floor, a large heavy wooden table and a wood burning stove at one end of the room. Two of the children previously seen outside materialised from nowhere to cling to their mother and gaze with large eyes as black as coal at the two strangers from the other side of the world.

She moved them away and gesturing to Alan and Mark to sit down at the table she went to the stove where she filled two bowls with a stew like mix. She then issued a rapid-fire instruction in her own language to the eldest child who disappeared out a door to return ten minutes later. She spoke briefly to her mother who merely nodded.

In the meantime, Alan and Mark had made short work of the delicious stew with tastes and flavours they'd never encountered before, pushing the two empty bowls away and wiping their mouths on the back of their hands. It had only taken a few weeks in the army to erode years of strict table etiquette of sharp-eyed mothers. This mother however, took it as a compliment and promptly gave each a refill. They were halfway through the second helping when a short, powerfully built young man entered the room. He exchanged a few brief words Alan again couldn't understand, with the woman, presumably his mother, then turned slowly and sat down at the table opposite the two soldiers.

Alan knew they all belonged to a tribe of fiercely independent mountain people living mostly concealed lives, occasionally outside the law in the wild, inaccessible mountain area of Crete. The same coal black eyes that belonged to what Alan assumed were his younger siblings continued their close examination of them both. Alan was feeling under a little pressure. He seemed to come to some sort of conclusion and astonished them both by introducing himself as Nikolas…in near perfect English without mentioning a surname. He reached across the table and shook their hands. Alan knew he and Evan had just passed a close examination which the strong handshake underlined.

The woman filled a small earthenware pitcher with water and put it on the table with a couple of glasses. The young man's steady gaze never left them as they drank the pitcher dry. When they had finished, he asked them their names and where they had come from. Being told they both came from New Zealand seemed to soften his demeanour and he asked where they were heading for. Alan told him and thought that his reply only confirmed what he already knew.

"You must get to Sfakia by tonight if you wish to catch the destroyer that will be in port soon," he stated emphatically.

He was silent for a moment then announced suddenly. "I will take you to Sfakia by a donkey cart, we will leave when it is dusk and by taking a route only my people know I will get you to Sfakia before the destroyer departs."

Reading Alan's concerned face he went on. "I know that the destroyer will not be leaving until at least midnight as it will take them all that time to get all the soldiers that are waiting on board."

Alan was left wondering where does he get his information from, but his next thought was not to waste time and energy worrying about it. It was obvious

Nikolas was the sort of person who would keep what he knew to himself and only release it when he was ready.

"Why are you doing this?" Alan asked.

"My mother has a special ability to see into the hearts of people, she tells me you both have good in your hearts and can be trusted."

He looked over to his mother and directed a few short sentences to her. She replied and he turned back to Alan.

"She also told me she can see that your friend will come back to Crete when this foolish war is no longer and do great things for our people. She can tell he is a man with great powers of healing."

His mother approached them sitting at the table then turned and spoke quickly to her son. "My mother says you both need urgent treatment for dysentery. She will prepare an old but reliable remedy that will reduce the symptoms dramatically. In the meantime, I suggest you rest in preparation for the final part of your journey. I will go and make ready the cart. I warn you it will not be a very comfortable ride but still much better then walking."

His mother had disappeared into an adjourning room and reappeared with a small bottle of dark liquid. She poured a measure into two glasses which she placed in front of them and stood over them with arms folded until they had each drunk their fill.

"God knows what was in it, but whatever it was it has done something for me," Alan whispered to Evan who nodded weakly but still looked like death. They both lay back on a cot, each determined to get what respite they could from their situation.

"The effects of the treatment will not be lasting, you must only drink the water I will supply you with for the trip and you must get treatment when you get back to North Africa," Nikolas told them adding, "I will give you one small bottle each to get you through the next twenty-four hours."

Evan had drifted off into a deep sound sleep but Alan couldn't let go. There was too much here he wanted to know about and too many question marks in his thoughts. Nikolas came in and sat down placing a bottle of wine and two glasses on the table in front of him. Alan didn't need a stronger hint that he was here to talk and got off the cot and sat down opposite. They looked at each other for a half minute or so, wondering where to start.

A twenty-five year old from the other side of the world sitting opposite a young Cretan man who spoke near-perfect English, yet could when the occasion arose, change into a virtual outlaw. It didn't add up and made Alan all the more curious. Wine was a rare novelty in New Zealand but Alan never the less quaffed his like it was the first beer after a hot day on the farm. He put the glass back on the table. In the four weeks or so the New Zealanders had been in Greece and Crete, they had grown accustomed to a drink so different to their usual draught beer from the local pub.

"So you want to know how someone who has lived the life I have, could have learnt to speak English as well as I do." He stated this confidently and leaning back on his chair, waited for a reaction. "Ok, I will tell you. An anthropologist came through here when I was eight years old. He was interested in the people of Crete and particularly people like us who lived in the highlands. He was doing the same thing in other countries around the world and wanted to see what things highland people had in common. He planned to write a book on it all. He ended up staying here with us for two to three months which was unusual because in those days we didn't encourage strangers to stay for long, if at all. He noticed I was taking a lot of interest in his work and he began teaching me English. It seems he was quite impressed, so much so that he strongly urged my mother and father that I be permitted to go and live in Athens and go to school there and that he knew a wealthy sponsor he was confident could be persuaded to provide all funding required. He told my parents I was very intelligent and to not waste the opportunity. My parents were a little different to the others here and often took an independent line of thinking. He convinced them that sadly the old ways would not last forever and it would be an advantage to them and the rest of the family to have an English speaker in their midst. So I went and lived in Athens until I graduated in Anthropology, which you might have already guessed."

They spent another hour talking with Alan telling him about New Zealand and the farm he was in the process of taking over. Nikolas's eyes widened at what Alan was telling him. Cretans were hugely proud of their country, its heritage and history of generations of Cretans who paid with their blood and lives to defend their birthplace from invaders over thousands of years. What Nikolas was hearing sounded to him like a paradise on earth, remotely situated deep in the South Pacific away from jealous, acquisitive neighbours and ambitious power-seeking politicians. He couldn't believe there were only two million people living there and that a man or woman could by working hard get to own a farm the size of which he could only dream of. Alan was beginning to view home through new eyes now as well and wished that he was back there climbing the hills with his brother to tackle that last bit of gorse and blackberry and finishing the day having a cold beer with his mates.

What amazed Alan who like most Kiwis at that time hadn't been further than Australia, was that aside from language there wasn't much difference between people from the other side of the world as he would expect. Nikolas abruptly stood and looked out the small window.

"The sun is no longer, we must get ready to leave soon. I suggest you wake up your friend and get him mentally prepared for a tough night."

Alan nodded and gave Evan a shake. He groaned and eventually dragged himself out of bed like a reluctant teenager on a school day.

The woman filled their drink bottles and wrapped some cheese and bread in a small muslin bag. She then gripped each in turn by their shoulders with a fierce strength that no longer surprised Alan. As she did this she looked with intensity into their eyes giving them a strong message that they were not permitted to even think of dying at the hands of an enemy she detested. Without doing anything else she turned and went back to mending a garment by the light of a couple of small squat candles.

As they headed for the door Alan paused at a photo of a large man with a heavy moustache. He looked back at the woman and knew instantly he was looking at her husband, a husband that was yet to make an appearance. She looked up and noted his interest. Dropping the sewing she made a pistol out of her right fist and pointed her forefinger at the side of her head. She cocked her thumb and closed it on an imaginary firing pin. Her head slumped forward on her chest. The message was clear. Alan looked one last time at this large, impressive woman of strength and resilience then followed Evan outside.

Nikolas was standing waiting with a small cart harnessed to what Alan hoped would be a cooperative donkey. He had thrown a bed of straw on the tray and a rough blanket on that. They tossed their meagre kit on, along with the army issue rifle that in Mark's hands had made him famous and a hero in one shot. Alan watched Nikolas kit up and was surprised to see a lethal army issue throwing knife and what appeared to be a cosh as well as a small automatic pistol. He pocketed the last item and noticed Alan watching.

"Beretta. Italian, small, easy to hide and lethal enough within four to five metres. I haven't mentioned it before but I was put through a short, concentrated course on running an insurgency operation. It seems I attracted the attention of the Greek Military when they found I came from the highlands and spoke good

English. They had placed people in the university to identify anyone with the talent and background they were looking for. I believe the British had a hand in it."

He peered at an ancient timepiece he'd taken from a purpose-built pocket and then he climbed up onto the cart. Alan and Evan followed suit. They left with a half-moon at their backs, heading away from the rear of the cottage onto an even rougher road than they used to get here. Alan thought that the timepiece may have been handed down, just recently.

"We're taking a route few outsiders know and it's best we leave without anyone in the village realising you were here. If they are questioned by the Germans then they won't have to lie. You don't know who might crumble with some of the tricks and techniques they use."

Alan was aware of the high pain tolerance people often have who live hard lives on a hard land, but he knew there was more than one way of getting information, especially from those with relatives and children. It is one thing to take pain inflicted on yourself but it is different to see it applied to a child by an enemy quite prepared to go to any lengths. I might find out a bit more about this mountain man before the night's over, Alan thought.

The donkey cart made slow but steady progress over a track that reminded Alan of some at home that with heavy rain were transformed into mini rivers with the water ripping away the top surface to expose bedrock. They bumped and bashed their way along the rough road knowing that every bump was getting them closer to their ship and North Africa.

Alan and Evan lay back on the straw bed wondering if it would have been easier to walk. They soon put such thoughts aside when Nikolas mentioned that they were now less than four hours from Sfakia. The little cart was entering a narrow gorge. It was quiet and windless which combined with the soft, low light of the moon and the debilitating effects of dysentery caused Alan to drift into a sleep filled with dreams of home, and an attractive local girl who had decided he was getting too long in the tooth to stay footloose and fancy free. His dreams then moved to deerstalking in the hill country behind the family farm and he was about to pull the trigger on a prize stag when a shot fired to his left only twenty feet away jolted him out of his dreams. The sounds of heavy hobnailed boots scrambling over rocks and men shouting orders in German wrenched Alan away from a place halfway between Crete and home.

A second shot sounded above them and a ricocheting bullet blew chips and dust off a rock a few feet away and whined off into the night. Powerful torches splashed a pool of light around the cart and its occupants. Don't do anything to give them an excuse to shoot us, Alan said to himself. As his eyes adjusted to the strong light he found they were surrounded by four soldiers with rifles plus an officer with a Luger machine pistol. A sixth person appearing to be wearing Cretan clothes stayed back out of the light and soon melted away into the darkness. Nikolas spotted him and as he turned and watched him go he drew his thumb across his own throat, a gesture that only Alan and the man saw. The officer said something in German to his men then approached Alan.

"I assume you are going to Sfakia," he said politely.

"My name is Alan Marshall, I'm a lieutenant in the New Zealand Army and my serial number is 18366556."

"A beautiful country, a cousin of mine moved there ten years ago. I wish I had joined him but it is too late now. You and your fellow soldier will both be taken prisoner and eventually end up in Germany. Unfortunately your Cretan friend showed poor judgement ignoring our ample warnings about aiding allied soldiers and will now meet a different fate."

The officer issued a brief order in German and two soldiers pressed the muzzles of their rifles into Nikolas's back and marched him towards a large rock. They were now twenty yards away.

"This man is innocent of wrongdoing and you know full well it is against the Geneva Convention to commit a summary execution without due trial," Alan protested with all the power and conviction he could muster.

"Save the sentiments, I know this man is responsible for the killing of at least twenty uniformed German soldiers."

Just as he was to give the order to proceed with the execution, two dark figures moved silently and swiftly from the shadows behind the rock. Simultaneously, three large calibre rifles aimed at the officer and his two men boomed out from above. In the narrow gorge, the deafening sound crashed back and forth off the rock walls. Using this distraction, the two men in well-rehearsed symmetry, grabbed each rifle and taking advantage of leverage, spun their holders around so they were held briefly against their attackers' chests. The soldiers' natural reaction was to hold on for dear life to their long unwieldy weapons which gave their attackers time and space to inflict a lethal knife stroke across their throats. The soldiers dropped their rifles and grabbed desperately at wounds now leaking their lives over Cretan soil.

The attackers seized a firearm each and dropped onto one knee to cover the other three Germans. Nikolas moved quickly from the large rock which was to have been his place of execution, that instead hid the two dark figures who saved him. He stood briefly over the two wounded soldiers then quickly dispatched them with his Beretta. He then walked to where the two other soldiers and the officer lay dead or dying. Their unknown saviours were now carefully picking their way down the steep slope from their vantage point where they'd rescued Nikolas from certain death and Alan and Evan from spending the rest of the war in a German prison camp.

The German officer had a serious chest wound and was still alive but only just. He turned his head and looked at Nikolas with the dull eyes of the dying. Nikolas returned his gaze then carefully aiming the Beretta, fired one shot into the temple of the man who'd ordered his death only minutes earlier. Alan, watching, was left with the feeling that the officer who'd been part of so much death and suffering may have even welcomed the natural justice of his end. Nikolas then spoke quickly in Cretan mountain dialect to the group who had arrived in the nick of time. He then turned to Alan and Evan.

"These men have saved our lives. They did this because they want to rid Crete of all Germans as they hate them for what they have done to our people and our way of life. I will not tell you where they are from, which lessens the danger to them. They are now going to deal with the traitor who disclosed our whereabouts to the enemy," he said to as he holstered the little Beretta.

He held a rapid fire conversation with their rescuers then turned to Alan and Evan.

"This unfortunate incident has cost us time, we must press on in order to make the sailing. I am told by our friends that we will find a gift ahead of us that will help us on our journey."

He turned to the donkey that had waited patiently while men sorted out their differences. He stroked its muzzle and said something in Cretan and then gesturing to Alan and Evan climbed onto the cart. Alan thought it fortunate that it hadn't occurred to the patrol to also execute the donkey and disable the cart.

Alan didn't know what he'd said to the donkey but they seemed to be making faster progress than before.

"Those men hold you both in very high regard, they cannot believe you left a paradise to come and fight in our war," he said to Alan who was amazed at the composure of a man who had just cheated certain death by a few seconds.

Around the next corner they found the gift, a German vehicle that the patrol had arrived in to set their ambush. They approached it cautiously but needn't have worried for the driver was nowhere to be seen. Alan looked over the edge of the gorge and could only imagine his fate. Nikolas untethered his donkey from the cart and told them to climb on board the vehicle. He went round the front and lifted the bonnet. A few minutes later, he slammed it down and climbed into the driver's seat.

"The Germans have a disabling device. If you want to steal one of their vehicles you have to know where it is." He started the engine and they headed off up the steep and narrow road running alongside the bottomless blackness of the gorge.

"The donkey will find his own way home or be picked up by our people. They are too valuable to be left behind," he said reading the unspoken question in Alan's mind.

The German troop carrier ground away in a low gear as they climbed higher and higher out of the gorge. They soon realised the river was now getting ever closer to the road and reducing in size. Alan knew this meant they were nearing the top of a pass. He also knew by the distance travelled so far they should soon be in sight of the port and the ships. As if reading his mind Nikolas offered the information that within half a mile they would be in line of sight with Sfakia. Alan shivered with the anticipation of getting off this island, intriguing but inhospitable in its present situation. He was also going through delayed shock from the close escape Nikolas had from certain death, and Evan and himself had from capture and an uncertain future in Germany, if they'd ever got there.

Alan wondered if he was ever going to get used to killing fellow humans and he thought of the holiday job on the killing chain of a local freezing works. Even as a country boy the first seven hours turned his stomach. By the end of seven days, he was totally blasé. Maybe a survival mechanism kicks in when death is around, the mojo that makes the difference between one soldier surviving and another soldier dying. But then you still have to make allowance for that fickle bitch, Lady Luck, to have you in the right place, at just the right time.

They were now struggling up the steepest section of any road Alan had ever seen. Nikolas found the extra low ratio gear and deftly engaged it as they came to a halt. They jerked off again with the tyres scrabbling for traction on the slope and their speed reduced to a snail's pace by the low ratio gear. The top of the pass was drawing slowly but steadily closer and they finally crested the brow. Far below them lay the harbour of Sfakia. A mole extended out from the rocky shore where two Royal Navy destroyers were birthed. An endless stream of allied soldiers clambered up gangways and spread across the decks. There was just enough lighting to allow the growing numbers to embark. They were barely visible at this distance.

Nikolas was now working with the standard gearbox and they rolled easily down the hills with first gear controlling their descent. The atmosphere in the truck relaxed slightly as they felt, dare they believe it, that they were home and hosed. Suddenly Nikolas pulled over and stopped. He got out and rummaged around in a small pack and came up with a flag with an insignia in blue on it.

"We don't want to be taken out in friendly fire eh?" he said as he lashed the flag to an aerial. He jumped back on and they continued on like a car load of cocky teenagers going for a joyride. Evan even perked up.

"I'll have to find out what the magic ingredients are for that medicine your mother gave me. It could be useful."

"Come back after the war and take a look."

"I'll take you up on that."

Alan's anxieties were shrinking at about the same rate as the distance to the ships. They were only a few miles from their destination when they met the final, ultimately friendly hurdle. Their feeble headlights picked up another vehicle a hundred yards ahead. It was the first evidence of the allied rearguard positioned on the main road leading into Sfakia. The vehicle lights flashed on and two soldiers stood on the road arms at the ready. Nikolas slowed but not smartly enough and a warning shot zinged over their heads. Alan leant out waving his rifle pointing skywards with a large piece of white cloth and Nikolas slowed their vehicle to a walk. They eventually pulled up alongside the parked vehicle. More troops were in quickly formed trenches on either side of the road. Two wide-eyed soldiers weren't taking any risks and stood behind their vehicle with their weapons trained on Alan as he stepped onto the roadway as ordered. The first thing he did was give his name, rank and serial number and identify the others. Evan and Nikolas were ordered from the truck and took to stand alongside Alan with their hands on their vehicle with legs spread. One soldier kept his rifle trained on them while the other did a standard frisk search finding and seizing Nikolas's pistol, knife and cosh.

"Right, what the hell are you lot doing here? In particular, what the hell are you doing here with this vehicle, and don't leave anything out?" said the loud one of the two.

Alan gave the full account of the last twenty-four hours and produced identity papers for him and Evan. They listened to Nikolas and appeared convinced but chose to keep his weapons for the time being. They were both Kiwis and carried on a casual conversation with Alan and Evan about home life, New Zealand places, their favourite beer and who the All Black fullback was before the war and what he did for a job.

They listened carefully to the answer but still kept all weapons and continued dropping in the occasional question about New Zealand when least expected. After a brief discussion, the two soldiers decided that they would leave the German vehicle parked up and take the three detainees to Sfakia and report in to their commanding officer. They all climbed aboard their vehicle and headed off towards the port with the non-driving soldier keeping up a light-hearted banter that was part conversation and part 'good cop' questioning, still probing their account for any weaknesses.

The few lights of Sfakia came towards them and the driver swerved into the bay area where the allied command was headquartered in the shelter of a long ravine. They got out and followed one soldier with one behind towards headquarters.

A figure studying several maps looked up as they approached. It was General Freyberg the allied commander who had been given mission impossible to defend Crete with no field artillery, a limited supply of small arms and little or no food for his men. He was short of resources and short on patience.

The two soldiers saluted and gave an account of their interception of Alan, Evan and Nikolas. The General listened intently, decided the story stacked up, then turned to Nikolas and questioned him on his background and involvement in the partisan forces. He then walked over to another officer and returned after a short discussion.

"My colleague agrees with me that we should take further advantage of your friend's experience and knowledge and send him with you two over to Alexandria for further debriefing and then return him with supporting special force personnel at a later date. Do you agree with this plan?" he said turning to Nikolas.

"Yes, I will go to Alexandria and I will provide whatever assistance I can," he replied after a moment's hesitation.

The General then turned and addressed the escorting soldiers.

"You two men will now arrange for these men to have priority transport on the first ship leaving tonight and you will return whatever weapons they were holding when detained."

He sat down and scratched out a few sentences on a pad with an official NZ Army logo at the top, signed the paper, ripped it from the pad and folded it into a sealed envelope. He wrote a name and address on the outside then handed it to one of the soldiers who had escorted them onto the base.

"Sergeant, you will accompany these men to Alexandria and escort them to army headquarters. There you will find Captain Davin. Deliver the orders to him and these men into his care. He will ensure their medical needs are met and they will be repatriated into the forces."

He scratched out another message, signed and folded it and handed it to the sergeant. "This will ensure cooperation with whoever you have to deal with getting to Cairo. That is all," he said and returned to his maps.

"Right, I'll grab a bit of kit and we'll be getting on HMS Glengyle. Next stop Alexandria," he said grinning at his mate and barely able to conceal his glee at the thought of them both getting back to North Africa.

Alan and Nikolas were returned their weapons and followed their escorting soldiers across rubble-strewn ground towards the mole and the dark, sinister silhouette of their transport back to Alexandria. As they approached they came under one of three lights rigged from the destroyer, casting pale patches over weary and war-worn soldiers, exhausted from the retreat over the White Mountains to Sfakia. As they drew closer to their ship the elation of getting off Crete was tempered by the fact that it was a defeat and retreat that found them here.

A slow-burning resentment of this war was turning Alan from an easygoing country boy with a long fuse into man on a mission. A big part of him was now looking forward to getting back to North Africa, getting some medical attention, having a bit of R & R while taking on board good food, clean water and some more of the local brew that he was acclimatised to. He would then look forward to another crack at an enemy that had shown little or no mercy to a people whose only crime was the desperate defence of their strategically important homeland. As they headed up the gangway Alan stopped and looked back at the rugged little island with its brave, unique people. He then turned and climbed quickly up the gangway and onto the ship with his mates.

Chapter 13

The three men sat back sculling cold ale under a large canopy at the coolest bar they could find in Alexandria. They shared a packed courtyard with some fifty ANZAC soldiers who couldn't fit inside. Bar staff with pitchers of beer dodged and weaved their way through the noisy crowd, filling the glasses of men who'd seen it all and were letting off steam on a few weeks of R & R. Nikolas stood out amongst these men of the antipodes and attracted a few challenging stares. An easy command of English, a powerful physique and a dark-eyed stare that didn't backdown was enough for pretenders to find somewhere else to look.

Alan, Evan and Nikolas had now been in Alexandria for two weeks. There was a week of medical treatment including a couple of days in hospital to tidy up wounds, remove shrapnel and get on top of the dysentery. The second week was devoted to some R & R, which for the first few days was tinged with guilt given the mates captured or lying dead in the fields in Crete and along the road to Sfakia. In the meantime, Nikolas had been inducted into a small commando force of three Brits, plus one Kiwi who'd had experience with Crete partisans. Together they would be returned to Crete to make contact with homegrown partisan groups. The intention was to add a measure of sophistication to partisan resistance using Cretan born Nikolas's proven intelligence and special force training to smooth the way. While Nikolas came from a family held in high esteem in the White Mountain community, this fact would only take him so far. His trainers in Alexandria however were confident he was up to the task of handling the hard men he would be leading.

Alan and Evan were coming to the end of the second week and were due to return to their unit the next day. After two weeks of orientation and familiarisation with military matters New Zealand style, Nikolas and his team were to go into a virtual lockdown in a special area of the base to ensure the utmost secrecy around their insertion into Crete. There were plenty of potential spies around with any number of locals prepared to back whoever looked like winning and make some money in the process. He had been granted a day's leave to arrange his affairs and say his goodbyes before leaving on a mission with huge risk.

Although Alan had managed to tempt the serious young man out for a few beers, he instantly sensed a tension about him not present before. Alan thought of his short life, a father killed recently, probably executed in front of him. Priceless breeding livestock seized by a meat hungry enemy and intimidation and bullying from an invading force that had met a fierce resistance they hadn't expected. Nikolas didn't hesitate to end the German officer's life and did it with a dispassionate efficiency that suggested revenge was not part of his agenda. Alan thought of his own interest in boxing and of the fighter who never loses his temper. That fighter is more often the one who prevails. A gut feeling was that Nikolas would prevail and Alan hoped his gut was right.

On the table next to them was a group of rowdy Aussies. There were a few light hearted Kiwi versus Aussie jibes exchanged which had Nikolas puzzled, that Alan explained by drawing a comparison of the rivalry between mainland Greece and the island of Crete.

"Hey Kiwis, want to come for a feed?" asked one of the noisiest.

Alan looked over to Evan and Nikolas, first translating 'feed' into 'meal' for Nikolas. After a bit of persuasion from Alan, Nikolas nodded slowly, his serious side no doubt stewing over the impending mission. The Aussies were standing up and hurriedly downing their remaining beers. Alan and his mates followed suit. The loud one called Steve came over.

"We've got a jeep outside, we'll fit alright if we all breathe out, the place is only a few minutes. Mind you I wouldn't have fitted a year ago on civvy food."

"Yeah I know," replied Alan who was now weighing in at a skinny eight stone, three stone less than his weight back home.

They trooped out behind the Aussies and climbed into the jeep Steve had promised. The sun was now a golden globe low over a horizon of squared up buildings with the occasional minaret spearing skywards. A sunburnt jumble of shops, bazaars and markets lined each side of the street, like a disorderly crowd leaning forward to watch the bunch of Kiwis and Aussies as they headed out on the town. The noisy vehicle shot off down the still crowded street, swerving around locals who all seemed oblivious to the risk of ending up across the bonnet like a prize stag back in New Zealand or an 'old man roo' in Australia.

"Where are we heading?"

"There's a bar that does good food that doesn't have you on the dunny next day"…he paused for dramatic effect… "and mate, they have belly dancers that will make you go AWOL."

Within a few minutes, they had pulled up in a cloud of dust beside a most unlikely looking nightspot. Steve spotted a youth hanging around the entrance.

"Hey Ahab, here's twenty dirham that says you and your mates are going to look after this wreck, not steal the wheels or petrol and remember just like last night there's another twenty when we come out and find it still in one piece."

"Sure Boss." The skinny youth whistled loudly and within seconds the jeep had a guard of several streetwise kids around it.

"Even when they divide that up it will be still ten times more than they can earn in a month," Steve said to no one in particular.

Now that the noisy jeep was silent Alan could hear through the bar doorway the magnetic pulse of music that seemed to sashay up and whisper in his ear, "We know you haven't had a woman in three months." They entered and looked around while they were greeted by a doorman. As their eyes grew accustomed to the low light they took in the interior. Eastern men lounged back on piles of cushions with several sharing a hookah. Some looked up, showed a mild interest in the visitors and then went back to the low murmur of conversation in Arabic.

In the middle of the floor was an area clear of tables and it was here that a dark, exotic woman was performing the sensual undulations of traditional belly dancing. Layers of flimsy silk drifted around her allowing some hint of what lay hidden. Her almond shaped eyes flashed across the room from a small gap in her veil, fastening for an instant on one male before moving on to the next, then the next. The beat and pulse of the music seemed to have captured her body in a soft, velvet grip she happily submitted to.

Alan thought again about the fact that more than three months had passed since he'd had any sort of intimate connection with a woman. Spending several weeks in Greece and Crete in battles that could have seen him killed and had killed plenty of close mates had somehow sharpened the edge of his sexual desires. Death or injury had been at his shoulder and this cold reality contrasted with the hot, urgent throb of the music and the strong sexual message of the dance was throwing petrol on the flame. The group sat back on chairs around an ancient wooden table. A waiter came up and the loud Aussie put his money where his mouth was and stood the first round.

"Like that, Kiwi? Just wait 'till you see the next one!" he said without waiting for a reply.

Evan, quiet and reserved sat taking it all in while Nikolas was enjoying something he'd seen only a few times before. Some British troops came in followed by a short, middle-aged man with a well-trimmed moustache. He sat by himself in a darker part of the room with a double whiskey and water. The bar was now filling with more people including a stunningly beautiful blonde woman dressed in a sleek teal blue dress. She pulled a stool up at the bar and ordered a Bloody Mary.

Nikolas noticed the woman and promptly went up to order an ouzo. He stood nearby, collected his ouzo then covered payment of the woman's cocktail. He returned to his seat and sat back to watch the reaction. The woman turned slowly and ventured the slightest hint of a smile and a nod at Nikolas. The present act ended and the room began to hum with the low drone of a largely male crowd. Nikolas downed his ouzo and headed up for another. He stood at the bar and turned towards the woman.

"Thank you, gentlemen are rare around here," she said in an accent that Nikolas couldn't place.

"My pleasure," he replied.

"Why don't you sit here for a while," she said. Nikolas didn't reply but pulled a bar stool over and sat down.

"What are you doing here apart from fighting Germans."

"Well, being at war with Germans is about all I can lay claim to at the moment, I don't enjoy it, but I believe it's a noble cause."

"Do you know I heard a twenty year-old German say those very same words about fighting you."

"When were you to talking to a German?"

"Oh, this was just before the war started. He was travelling through the Middle East looking for contacts in the oil equipment business for his father's company in Berlin. Well, it's nice talking to you, but I have work to do," she added.

"And what is that?"

"Stay where you are and you'll find out."

Nikolas, looking puzzled, turned and watched her slide smoothly from the stool and without saying another word head towards a door behind the bar. As she walked, stage lights threw a bright sheen of colour and sparkles over a dress that was as good as a second skin. Nikolas couldn't help but smile but what he didn't see was the girl with as yet no name smiling quietly as well. She knew his eyes would be following every movement of her body under the form hugging dress.

There were several minutes during which nothing much seemed to be happening. The sound of the crowd stayed, as a low-pitched murmur interrupted by the occasional guffaw. Nikolas returned to his seat beside Alan and the rest of the ANZAC soldiers while the locals kept puffing on their hookahs.

A low hum of expectation started to spread through the crowd, led largely by those who had been here before. Alan, Nikolas and the rest started to pick up on it and leant forward on their seats in anticipation. The lights were slowly dimmed until the room was pitch black. At the same time, a single instrument from the band started on one long, low, soulful note, gradually increasing in strength and soon joined by the other instruments. The music was reaching a crescendo when suddenly a single spot hit the dance area, illuminating the form of a woman lying as if shot. She had the same layers of silk as the previous dancers but also wore a black textured robe that sparked with flames of gold and jewel inlays.

The music stopped dead and returned to the single instrument as before. The woman writhed and twisted to the drift and surge of the music, gradually rising then falling only to rise again. Alan suddenly grasped the theme. She was a snake being charmed, coerced, tempted and teased into an exhibition that was erotic to its core.

The mouth of every male gaped open as she bumped and ground, twisted and turned as the music increased inexorably in tempo and intensity. With their eyes wide and unblinking, the audience licked dry lips and lent forward to catch every movement. In a frantic gesture as if escaping capture, the woman yanked the robe off and threw it across the floor towards an assistant standing out of the light. In another movement, she tossed a length of silk that fluttered up into the smoky beam of the spotlight and then seemed to ride it softly to the floor.

She was now removing another garment as the tempo of the music increased even more. By now, her veil had gone and she was stripped to a loose wisp of teal coloured silk that formed the barest suggestion of a tiny G-string. The movements of the dance had no longer any pretence of decorum or modesty. Short but sweet glimpses of all the parts that made her a woman and the men watching remember they were men, were there to see as was the evidence of a body completely clean-shaven. Erotic, shocking and extremely arousing.

It was now that Nikolas realised who the woman in the teal blue dress was. She was the nightclub's star dancer, one that more than half of the men of Alexandria had come to see at least once in their lives. The performance ended seconds after the final gesture with the removal of her last garment as she threw herself on the floor in a state of careless abandon. The spot was quickly doused and the room fell into total darkness. The management understood that for the finale, less is always more and almost always guarantees a return visit. The stunned crowd realised they were party to a virtuoso performance that aside from its erotic content was a supreme display of artistry in its own right. To a man they stood and clapped loudly and shouted for more of the same.

Nikolas was mesmerised. Tough and worldly as he was, it had been a long time between drinks in the sexual arena. The time he left Athens as a graduate was when the drought began. The war and the invasion of Crete only added to his deficit. He went back to the bar on the assumption that she would return to her spot. He was right. Within ten minutes, she had returned to sit beside him. He glanced at her reflection in the mirror behind the bar.

Naturally her face was flushed and her eyes that were previously guarded and careful were now bright and dancing. Exciting men in this way was even more exciting for her and if Nikolas knew her better he would know she regarded them all as slightly foolish, naughty boys, silly enough to pay a large cover charge to watch her take all her clothes off for two or three seconds every night and make herself a handsome living by doing so.

But Nikolas didn't know her better and a few minutes later in the 'gentleman's' the middle-aged man that had watched from the dark corner of the room was standing beside him. The man looked around to make sure they were alone and then introduced himself as Captain Westbury of Army Intelligence.

"I need to tell you something right now that is vitally important for your safety and the success of your mission."

"What are you talking about…what mission?" Nikolas replied tersely.

"Very good response. I know about you and your mission because as I have already stated I am a captain in Army Intelligence in this region," he said as he reached into his breast pocket and pulled out a crisp ID card. "If you doubt my authenticity I can tell you virtually every detail you gave at your briefing sessions. I have read your file thoroughly. I know the village you came from and I know you studied anthropology at Athens University from 1933 to 1936. I even know the name of your first lover when you were there. But this is not the place where I wish to conduct a full briefing on what the army now requires of you. The only point I want to make right now is that I have evidence that gives me reason to believe the woman you fancy in the teal dress is not what she seems and is in fact a freelance spy. The department wants you to cultivate a relationship with her and find out if our suspicions are correct. It is unfortunate I've had to make contact in these circumstances but I was forced to act quickly in case you left with her. Wherever you go and whatever you do tonight in her company you must be vigilant and extremely careful of what you say.

For her information at this point, you are just an ordinary infantry soldier with a Kiwi battalion. If pressed further, just say you had a Kiwi father and that allowed you to join their ranks. Tomorrow at eleven hundred hours you are to report to your commanding officer at headquarters and a full briefing on our plans will be given. I will be there and presenting the bulk of the briefing. I want to make the most of this opportunity to nail her. She has the potential to do a lot of damage. Your life, the lives of the other commandos and the lives of your countrymen could be in grave danger. I am asking if you will take on this additional task. If you decide you don't wish to, the whole mission to Crete will be cancelled and you will be left to your own devices. Thank you for your time."

With that, the strange little man abruptly turned on his heel and slipped out a side entrance that avoided going back through the bar. Nikolas was slightly bemused but also excited and now even more interested in this dangerous and intriguing woman whose name he still didn't know. He ran some water through his hair with his hands, checked out the reflection in the mirror, took a deep breath then stepped back into the bar.

The woman was engrossed in a serious discussion with the bar owner/manager that seemed to be over money owed. With Nikolas's newly acquired knowledge, he pondered that although she was clearly a star, in the seedy world of nightclubs and the adult industry things often went awry with payment of money due. Another consideration was what hold the owner may have over her in other ways – drugs, family connections or favours granted – any number of scenarios entered Nikolas's imagination that was now running wild.

But the one thing he noted was that in spite of the certainty she would be well rewarded at the club there appeared to be a shortage of money in her life. This could be all the reason she needed to be indulging in a spot of well-paid espionage and it seemed as if it was going to fall on Nikolas to prove the little man from intelligence right or wrong. He sat drinking his ouzo and contemplating the next few days. He looked up from his drink to find his dark eyes staring back at him from the bar mirror. His own reflection raised the same question the little man had posed. The answer he got back was that all this excited him hugely and was something he was eager to grapple with. The whiff of danger with a sexual undertone reminded him of the smell of cordite drifting around after a gun is fired and he already knew his drug of choice was his own adrenalin.

The argument had distracted her from taking any particular note of Nikolas's lengthy absence and she greeted him warmly when he sat down.

"I've seen more of you then I have of most woman I've known but still don't know your name."

"Stage name, Arabic name or English name?"

"How about we go with the stage name? After all it's where I first met you. So the name is…?"

"Aiesha, in Arabic it means living, something I plan to do plenty of for some time yet." She was interrupted by Alan and Evan who appeared at Nikolas's shoulder.

"We're off mate, I guess you're sorted for the night. Be careful out there," he said with a slight wink.

Nikolas stood and shook both Alan and Evan's hands, each man knew that this could be the last time they would see each other in this world.

"Thanks for everything mate," said Alan which was echoed by Evan.

Nikolas went to embrace both men which still threw Alan a little but they were now getting accustomed to the European ways of greeting or farewelling and with that Alan and Evan moved on to catch up with their Aussie mates and a free ride back to their camp.

"I have a car coming in ten minutes, why don't you come for a night cap."

Nikolas knew that he had an open pass to find out whatever he could about this woman called Aiesha. They sat making small talk over 'one for the road' then picked up their jackets and called it a night when the blast of a horn sounded from outside. Nikolas followed her out to a Humber Super Snipe, the poor man's 'Rolls'. They climbed into a vehicle that smelt and felt like the British Empire all rolled up into one large, lumbering, underpowered car complete with worn leather seats, faded woodwork and stale pipe tobacco.

Nikolas sat back thinking and without panicking, he knew he needed to think fast. The body language from Aiesha told him that there was an agenda behind the perfect face and beautiful smile and he was sure he wasn't just here for sex.

Her driver answered her comments in an English public school accent and a manner that showed he was considerably more than just a driver/servant come 'man Friday'.

"So where are we going Aiesha?" sounding the name slowly to make sure he got it right and mask any hint of nervous apprehension.

"To my home, or our home," she said gesturing towards the driver who she then introduced as Thomas Edlington.

"We'll have a few more drinks and get to know each other."

It was obvious they were driving towards some of the better neighbourhoods of Alexandria. Large houses with imposing walls, owned or rented by business people, high-level government servants or embassy staff sat primly along the street in a polite, well-spaced order. The big car turned in at one of the best and waited as a uniformed man in a gatehouse opened the gates and nodded as the old dowager gathered up her skirts and swept past. They parked out front and Nikolas followed the odd couple – as he now regarded them, into a time capsule of past glories. Walls three feet thick preserved a comfortable temperature in spite of the daytime heat of forty-five degrees and when the temperature plunged at night the interior temperature fell only a few degrees. Ceiling fans moved a gentle airflow around the room. Large indoor plants were visible in a conservatory bigger than most homes.

The trouble was nothing added up. Why was this well-heeled English snob connected to a beautiful woman that every night stripped to next to nothing for the pleasure of turning on fifty or so sex-starved soldiers and a few Arabs not rich enough to have their own harem? Nikolas wasn't confident he was going to find all the answers over another round of drinks but he knew the ball was now in their court and all he could do was wait and see how and where they would return it.

"Gin and tonics all around?" Thomas asked the room while he busied himself fixing his drink.

"Thanks," replied Nikolas. He was still struggling to put a defining frame around the pair and instead decided to give up, sit back in a huge well-stuffed armchair and wait for things to unfold.

Thomas sat opposite Nikolas and while he sipped his gin and tonic stared at him over his glasses for at least half a minute. He then glanced at Aiesha who replied with a small nod of her head. Thomas put his drink down then sat back smiling as if he was about to generously share a valuable confidence.

"We know all about you, we know where you are from and we know why you are here. We also know you had a short meeting in the 'gentleman's' at the club with our friend with the 'Uncle Adolf' moustache. Amazing isn't it that a double agent working for our enemy and yours couldn't resist cultivating such a strong and obvious brand," he grimaced slightly as if coming across something distasteful in his drink then carried on. "I would imagine all this would come as a bit of a surprise."

"Why should I believe you instead of him?"

"Tomorrow you will go to a different address one hour earlier than your meeting with 'Adolf'. There you will meet a person who will provide irrefutable evidence that we are speaking the truth. For now, I shall explain what we are about. We are here to 'manage' your friend. He was cleverly inserted into army intelligence on behalf of the British Nazi Party who believed they had found someone in the British Army with no previous connections to their little band. They identified their man, briefed him at a secret meeting place and then told him to keep right away from their meetings, rallies and party contacts. In fact, he was told to join the 'Backing Britain' mob. It worked a treat. They already had someone on the inside with a bit of pull and before you could say 'Seig Heil' he was on board, eating in the cafeteria and getting a copy of The Times. The trouble was with the cafeteria and I'm not talking about the food, I'm talking about a woman who worked there. She knew of him and fortunately for us he didn't know her. She had a quiet chat to the people that matter and MI5 took over. From now on, for your own safety we will only tell you what you need to know. What we want you to do is to help us 'run him'. We will give you directions and information that we want him to pass on. Unfortunately some of it will have to have some slight basis in fact, otherwise the enemy could catch on to our fiendish plan."

"What is Aiesha's purpose here?"

"There is little on this planet more distracting to a healthy, heterosexual male trying to be a good spy than a beautiful woman. The stress and dangers of wartime, homesickness, strange food and strange people contrive to put all but the strongest man at a disadvantage. A warm, responsive woman is a welcome balm to a lonely and feverish brow and it is amazing what can be coaxed out of some of the most loyal targets. Some refer to it as pillow talk or the honey trap."

"Alexandria and Cairo are like humid, well-watered hothouses for spies, double agents and freelance operatives as well as black marketeers who are just as likely to dabble in selling secrets as they are in selling cigarettes. All have a price and nearly all will be trying to pick a winner in this war, the greatest horse race of all time. Aiesha is fluent in several languages and holds an honours degree in linguistics. She is here to seduce and exploit whatever vulnerable male – or female that has something we need – information, leverage or contacts. She also enjoys sex and has none of the moral inhibitions that would handicap many other women. In addition, she has a deep hatred of the enemy as defined by their Nazi ideology and will use whatever gifts God gave her to help defeat them. This was born out of a personal experience I will leave her to enlarge on if she wishes."

"Only if you wish." Nikolas said looking over to Aiesha.

"I am German by birth. but I married a Jewish man. We had two children. I was studying in America when war broke out and for a time became marooned there. My husband was very fiery and crossed paths with some of Hitler's Nazi thugs in the early days of the fascist movement. He beat one of the leaders in a fair fight, permanently damaging the man's sight in one eye. He was never forgiven. A gang of fascists came one night to our house and barred all the doors, then threw petrol bombs and incendiaries through the windows. My husband and two children were burned to death. Naturally the murderers were never brought to justice. My parents both died several years previously. I was an only child and have a few relatives I never see. I no longer hold any loyalty to a Germany under Adolf Hitler and his crimes against humanity are also ultimately crimes against Germany, the country I still love."

"My father was executed in front of me and my family. Then they charged us for the bullets by taking a milking goat," Nikolas said bluntly.

"Right," said Thomas just slightly impatient to get on with the evening. "I suggest that you stay the night here and I'll arrange a car in the morning to get you to your 'real' briefing. Our operating cover is that I represent a private investment company involved in oil exploration and that I am here to protect our interests in the region."

"How do you explain Aiesha?"

"She is cast as my exhibitionistic girlfriend who gets away with what she does at the club by being thousands of miles from her real home. We have a plutonic relationship. Let's just say my sexual interests lie elsewhere."

"How did you know that I met with Westbury?"

"The bar owner has primitive but effective surveillance where you would least expect it. He is on the payroll funded through us by MI5 who have a critical interest in this region. Medium term it's all about oil and the Suez Canal. Short-term the worry is that Rommel's lot will blow right through here and carry on through Palestine, Syria and into the Balkans. Can't see it myself. Our navy and air force are sinking at least half the ships coming from Italy carrying fuel, replacement tanks and artillery. The sheer distance alone will stretch their supply lines too far to be sustainable. As long as we get our act together militarily we can harass them enough to bring them to a halt or a very slow walk. It is also quite obvious that at least half the Italian army are only lukewarm about being roped into all this."

"And the mission to Crete?"

"Oh yes, well that is on the backburner until we sort this little prick out. We need to create a diversion to take the attention off Crete. Then we'll get on with it. The weather has to be right anyway. You will be going in a rather small boat."

I'll run with this Nikolas thought to himself and just see how well it stacks up tomorrow. "Remember, tomorrow all will be revealed!" Thomas said dramatically, sensing Nikolas's cautious reservation.

Nikolas was shown upstairs and after the rare luxury of a hot shower disappeared into his room to a standard bed that he had last enjoyed back in his student days in Athens. He lay back on a bed that to him, accustomed to more basic sleeping facilities, felt as soft as a cloud. With the combination of having too much comfort and too many things on his mind, he was still wide awake at 2 am. He got up, poured a glass of red wine from a bottle and went over to the window. He pulled the curtains back and opened the set of French doors onto a small terrace.

From a lounger, he looked out on the Mediterranean with a full moon sitting over a calm sea. Just the sort of peaceful and idyllic scene that says to those who are easily convinced, that all is well. But Nikolas knew all was not well. He'd now heard two different versions of the situation here in Alexandria. Choice is the agony of humans all over the world. Far better to be an animal. You eat grass or other animals that eat grass, or other animals eat you, no decisions to make, no swaying this way, or that.

He tried to guess the direction back to Crete, then looked up at the moon and wondered how many full moons had looked down on his father before he was shot. There was a slight movement of the curtains by his bare shoulder. He instinctively ducked and turned at the same time bringing his right hand up and over to grab or fend off who or whatever was behind him. His hand clamped tightly around the smooth slim wrist of Aiesha standing naked and smiling back at him.

"You'll have to learn to watch your back a lot better if you want to be a really good spy," she said softly.

"Christ, don't ever do that again," he replied tersely.

"And what would you do Mr Tough Guy? I'll have you know I passed with flying colours in unarmed combat at the Special Service Operations."

He was still annoyed, more with himself for letting his guard down. He turned fully around and took in all of her. She smiled, bathing in the pleasure of his full, unwavering gaze. She reached her hands up to a full stretch she held for several seconds then brought them slowly down to her shoulders and then even more slowly over her breasts, inching across her stomach to the smooth 'v' between her legs.

"Do you like me, because I do, why don't you do this for me. I can see you really want to," she whispered looking down at the growing bulge in his shorts. Several months of forced abstinence caught up with him like an express train. He stood, scooped her up in his arms and stepping through the door, took two paces and dumped her on the bed.

"Oh Nikolas, please don't be too rough. I hope you're not still angry with me for giving you such a big fright. I was only trying to be friendly. Oh, you are allowed to be just a little bit rough," she teased.

Nikolas left the games to her. He stripped off his shorts and his penis sprang free. Her eyes were eager and glowing as if she had never seen one before. It was way past foreplay. He knelt between her legs and opening her with her help drove into her. She knew she would have more time to savour the next one and let him set the pace his desperation demanded. Afterwards she lay back quietly smoking a pink Sobranie and watching the smoke curl slowly towards the ceiling.

"Your father, my husband, my children like plants ripped out of the ground and thrown on a heap. Are we both damaged goods?" she asked suddenly.

"If we are we've got plenty of good company."

"I don't think I could start again as a wife or a mother, I need to pay them back, the Nazis that is for what they did to my husband and my children. I wasn't there, I was indulging myself in my career in the United States."

"What could you have done? You hadn't done the unarmed combat course by then," he said gently.

"Yes I know, but I would have been able to calm him down, keep him out of trouble. I know I could have done something, I had some influence then, but not now."

"Marry me when this is all over, we'll go to New Zealand and buy a farm."

"Be careful what you say. I might take you up on it. You'll get through this, I can sense it, but I'm not sure I will."

As she said this she sat up, dropped the cigarette into the wine glass, poked her tongue at his protest and headed towards the door.

"This bed's too small for both of us so I'm off to my own little nest. See you tomorrow big boy," she said as she closed the door.

Nikolas lay staring at the door she had just exited through. Her scent still lingered in the room and he shook his head to try and clear her from his mind. He remembered his short course with the British Military in Athens on running a resistance operation behind enemy lines, and the instructor telling him there were more reasons to distrust people than stars in the sky. It was therefore important he develop an instinct for detecting hidden agendas of anyone looking to gain his trust.

He was told of body language, the subtle unconscious messages given out that can be a better indicator of intent than the spoken word. Then there were the typical human weaknesses such as a serious drug or alcohol dependency or gambling. At an advanced stage, anyone of these issues could enslave a man or woman to a tyrannical master and they would already be living a life of lies. Lastly, are they being pressured to betray you through the imprisonment of family members, friends or lovers, along with the additional threats of torture or execution?

After rummaging fretfully through these thoughts, he decided sleep was the better option. With his physical desires finally sated, he turned over, closed his eyes and drifted off.

Chapter 14

While he had arrived the night before in one of British motoring's icons, he was now in the crisp, cool hours of the morning heading towards his rendezvous with the truth in a vehicle from the other end of the spectrum. It was a beaten-up, decrepit Morris Oxford taxicab owned and driven by a local on the payroll of British Intelligence. Thomas had badgered London to fund his man and it had proved a worthy investment. The local, Bashir Mustafa – probably not his real name, was now worth every bit of what to him was a generous allowance – providing tips, gossip, rumours and stories that helped fill the bag of local intelligence from a street level source. Of course most of it was worthless, but an occasional gem when combined with what was already known could help join the dots and create an 'Aha got it,' effect that might change the course of a battle and ultimately the war. His loyalty was assured by the fact that he had so inserted himself into the British cause that Thomas felt duty bound to guarantee that Bashir and his family would be delivered to safety if Rommel ever threatened Alexandria. He also knew too much so there was admittedly a self-serving agenda in Thomas's gesture.

Nikolas bumped and rattled towards headquarters. Bashir, apart from a short greeting, paid him no attention and instead concentrated on swerving in and around pedestrians, donkeys, carts and cars, firing off a furious blitz of insults every few yards at other road users who routinely ignored him. He stopped suddenly by a busy market selling spices, goat meat and vegetables, pots, pans and clothing.

"My instructions are to let you out here, you are to stand by the last table at the fish market. A man looking just like myself will arrive. He will ask the vendor for exactly 2.25 kg of Sultan Ibrahim or red mullet. The vendor will reply that he can only sell him 2 kg or 2.5 kg. The man will elect to purchase 2.5 kg. He is the man who will lead you to the backstreet entrance of the meeting place.

Follow my instructions exactly. By the way, he is my identical twin which we use to our advantage sometimes." Without another word he wrenched at the wheel and pulled out into the traffic firing off a volley of threats and curses at a man leading a donkey carrying two large sacks.

Nikolas was a little amused at all the cloak and dagger stuff and could tell that Bashir was very proud of his association with the British. He had noticed a small picture of the face of Winston Churchill as a young man hanging from the internal mirror. Bashir, a native of Alexandria, and a dedicated Anglophile. Nikolas could only wonder how that came about. His thoughts were quickly cut short when a man, as promised, looking very much like his guide, appeared at the rough bench that served as a counter.

"2.25 kg of red mullet or Sultan Ibrahim please."

They went through the little pantomime exactly as per the script. Nikolas glanced quickly at him, then looked away. Did he see the fish vendor offer him the faintest nod? Just how big is the cast in this melodrama? He stopped wondering and started walking quickly to catch up with the man who took his fish, paid and headed off without so much as a backward glance at Nikolas. The man was about thirty feet ahead when he suddenly ducked round a corner and into a narrow alley. Nikolas followed only to find that the man and his fish had vanished. Nikolas walked warily forward. He was about to pass a deeply inset doorway when he found him standing in the recess.

"We will stay here a few minutes to see if anyone is tailing us," he said, motioning Nikolas towards the back of the recess. They stood with Nikolas feeling slightly ridiculous. Finally the man poked his head round the corner, flashed Nikolas a conspiratorial grin, then beckoned him to follow. They walked about a hundred yards down the slightly curving alley until they came to a heavy gate. His guide went several more paces and stopped, looked up and down the alley then returned to the gate and after one last look around, pushed the buzzer. Eventually a small viewing door opened and a man with a large nose fixed like an afterthought on a sad, serious face looked out, nodded, then quickly opened the gate.

His job done the guide disappeared leaving Nikolas stranded in the entrance way. He looked carefully around, with the gateman poised in midstride waiting for him. After a few tense moments, Nikolas decided elaborate entrapment or not he couldn't resist satisfying his curiosity. What lay in front of him was a short underpass opening into an exquisitely tiled courtyard with a perimeter of ornate arches. In the middle was a pond with a small fountain. Large tubs sprouted palms and lush broadleaf plants. A fine mist sprayed over the plants had left beaded droplets of water and early morning sunlight, from a circular leadlight, fired up the droplets with a rainbow of colours.

The temperature outside this cool green oasis was now climbing towards its normally oppressive thirty-eight to forty degrees, but here Nikolas felt was a place he would never want to leave. He followed the gateman through the courtyard where they paused before two fierce looking guards armed with submachine guns. One slung his gun over his shoulder and conducted a fast but expert frisking while his companion kept Nikolas covered under a piercing gaze. Satisfied that Nikolas was concealing no weapons he was waved on through a door that led into a reception area and then into a large drawing room. In the corner was a desk surrounded by several armchairs. These chairs held two British Army Officers. The chair at the desk was empty. One of the officers looked up and motioned to Nikolas to sit down.

"We're just waiting for Mr Churchill. He won't be a minute," he spoke as if referring to the middle manager of a local council.

Nikolas was stunned. He couldn't believe that the officer was talking about Winston Churchill, the leader of Great Britain and First Lord of the Admiralty. His mouth was still agape but closed quickly when the man himself walked through the door buttoning his shirt.

"Sorry I'm late. This won't take long. I understand you need some reassurance on who's on our team and who's not?" he said as he pulled up the high-backed chair behind his desk and sat down.

"Yes," replied Nikolas.

"Good. I like a man who can give a short answer. Long answers are my domain. The short answer is this; Westbury is a British Nazi. Now the long answer is he got himself into MI5 which we discovered due to some great work from a tea lady in the cafeteria. We played along with him for a while and then one of our bright young chaps suggested he be posted out here. It appealed to his short man ego. It gets him further from Germany and further from other misguided British Fascists. Thomas and the dancer woman are very smart operators and they feed him just enough low-grade intelligence to keep him happy.

"Sadly for little Adolf, coming across you means we now need to totally mislead him on your mission to Crete and through that process he will quickly become redundant. You will then be presented with the job of getting rid of him, which must appear to be an unfortunate accident. There will be a full burial with military honours plus a posthumous gong or two. These bloody Nazis love medals even more than we do. Going on some of the detail in your report you shouldn't find it too onerous. You handled the German patrol in Crete with great aplomb.

"In an hour or so you will go to your briefing with Westbury. He's not the sharpest pencil in the pack – no imagination – but he is thorough and has a good memory. Don't underestimate him, for all we know he may be onto us as much as we are onto him. Remember we want you and your team in Crete causing havoc and we don't want Westbury fucking it up for you. Now I'm turning you over to these two officers. They will continue with the detail part of the briefing and then arrange for you to be driven to headquarters to be reacquainted with Westbury. Take your cue from Captain Simmock and Lieutenant Cunningham. That is all gentlemen." With that last comment, Winston Churchill left the room and there was an unconscious exhaling of air from everyone.

"We'll continue now with all the bits that Winston has left out. Over to you lieutenant," Simmock said looking at Lieutenant Cunningham.

"Righto, firstly we are going to let Westbury run the show or at least let him think that he is. We have control of his radio communications and when he thinks he is talking to his German contact he is in fact talking to a very convincing stand in, a German-Jew defector who came to England just before the war when he was able to see what was coming up. He responds with whatever our clever young dons from Oxford and Cambridge think best suits our purposes. Any questions so far?"

"What do you want me to say?"

"Just agree with most of what he says. He's a bloody little egotist who obviously thinks Hitler walks on water. Mind you he manages to hide his feelings very well. And therein lies his weakness. Massage his ego, praise his thoughts and he'll think you're great stuff and back you to the hilt. We'll let some info through but in the end we'll do something totally different in the way of timing and where we land and the Jerrys will be grasping at thin air. I think we'll make it out to be a lot bigger than it is and we'll pick a place that will drag a lot of their troops in totally the wrong direction. Might even be able to poke a sub in somewhere and get them all excited. I'll provide a bit of subtle guidance to make this meeting indefinite and vague to keep him guessing and we'll see what he's got to say to our German stand-in. A decision will have to be made very carefully on when Westbury will be taken out of the picture. All you need to do is listen and nod. Let us run it and he will be impressed."

Nikolas sat through the briefing at headquarters that was an elaborate concoction of lies, half-truths and smoke and mirrors. He sat mainly silent, taking as much in as he could, then left in a mufti staff vehicle to return to his temporary home feeling that reality was now some sort of space-time warp. There was no longer any solid ground to stand on and know where exactly in the world he was. He arrived to find Aiesha sitting in a kitchen drinking a tiny cup of strong black Turkish coffee and eating yoghurt and fruit from a bowl.

He ignored her and went straight up to his room. He needed time to think and get his head around what was happening. Aiesha wasn't being totally candid. Everything was too neat, too pat and he wasn't convinced that it was just his irresistible attraction that saw her naked in his room last night. They had talked about the honey trap and he wondered if he already had one foot in it. "There are as many reasons to distrust people as there are stars in the sky." The quotation now sat on his mind like a stone in a shoe.

The other thing that gnawed at him was that in spite of the bad rap from everyone about Westbury, watching and listening to him during the briefing session had Nikolas surprised to find there were things about him he couldn't help but like. This didn't prove or disprove anything, but coming from a people who prised a living from the barren mountains of Crete by relying on their wit and gut feelings fitted with what his instructor in Athens spoke of when talking about body language.

There were more questions than answers and there was now something big in the room that no one was talking to him about. He was sure Aiesha was hiding something and he felt like a pawn on a chess board with no say in the moves. Torn by doubt and self-doubt he lay on the bed in an angry mood, frustrated he'd been shifted from decision to the indecision in the space of an hour or two. He drifted into an uneasy sleep then woke suddenly to find Aiesha sitting in an easy chair opposite, looking at him with a flirty half-smile.

"You didn't come and see me when you came back," she said shifting forward in the chair so that her short skirt had shifted to reveal the long well-shaped thighs of a natural dancer.

"You have told me everything and told me nothing," he replied simply.

"Well, I suppose I could expose a bit more of myself," she said, sliding the skirt up her thigh. Nikolas could see she hadn't bothered with underwear and decided it was time to call her bluff. The honey trap could work two ways. His desire for sex was still urgent but it was obvious there was more to her need than just pure sexual desire.

He stood up, walked slowly towards her and knelt between her legs. He put his hands on her knees and parted her legs as wide as the arms of the chair would allow and slowly moved them up the inside of her thighs. His face followed the progress of his hands so that he was only inches away from her centre. He pursed his lips and blew on hers.

The effect of this was to send shudders of deep and desperate breaths through her body. She arched her back and neck as she strived to meet his teasing mouth but his strong hands held her where she was. Her breathing became panting bursts of pleas for him to close the last two inches to her. Given the frustrated intensity of her desire he could have just as easily been two miles away.

"Tell me everything and you will get what you want," his words coming roughly through gritted teeth.

"I've told you all I know," she gasped, her body screaming for the final contact.

"Well, I don't fucking believe you," he fired back, then suddenly stood up and walking casually over to the bed, sat down and stared back at her.

"You total bastard," she spat out. "Come back or I'll kill you."

"You'll be killing no one…you know what the deal is."

"It's not you being killed. It's you doing the killing. You're being kept here on ice to get rid of someone."

"That's old news…I'm here to get rid of Westbury."

"That's what you think big boy…now come back here, be really nice to me and I might tell you who isn't being killed."

He decided he had probably most of what he was going to get today but giving her the benefit of the doubt he stood up, dropped his shorts and approached her spreadeagled body. He knelt again between her legs but this time clasped his lips roughly to her. She opened her mouth and let out a long, stifled scream of relief and release.

"You bastard. Don't you ever leave me hanging like that again."

"If you don't give me the rest, I will have to."

"Shut up, keep doing what you're doing and you'll hear soon enough," she said squirming and writhing against his powerful grip and searching mouth. She then let go one long wail and slumped in the chair, eyes closed, mouth wide open, panting in short rapid bursts.

Aiesha obviously never went on any romantic escapade without her Sobranies and lay back recovering on the large chair gently blowing smoke rings towards a ceiling fan that vanquished each, one by one.

"It's not me or you," she began. "It's not our secret taxi driver Bashir Mustafa or his twin brother, or the man who owns the bar, or Simmock, or Cunningham." She paused contemplating the pink cigarette as if she was holding a favourite pet. "And that is all you're going to hear until the time is right. So take it or leave it."

Nikolas got up and headed for the shower. Aiesha stubbed out the remnants of the cigarette and reached for her skirt and top, pulled them on and let herself out. He stood and let the hot water run over his back for ten minutes as he digested what he'd just heard. It left only one person, but Aiesha had neither confirmed nor denied who that was. Nikolas couldn't comprehend that Thomas, the one name she didn't mention, was the target. Again she'd told him everything and nothing. He heard the door close and the place fell quiet but for the distant sounds of the city and the water splashing over himself and running through the ancient plumbing.

He stepped out of the shower and wandered naked through the bedroom to the small balcony where the sun and warm breeze dried him. Wrapping himself in a large white towel he lay back on the lounger, staring out across a sparkling Mediterranean and wondered just what sort of mess he was getting into, then remembered his weakness for adrenalin.

Nikolas locked the door and decided to fill in the afternoon by grabbing a bit more sleep. The mission was on hold and the fact he wasn't required on base was puzzling but he suspected he was exactly where HQ wanted him to be.

He woke a couple of hours later and spotted a piece of paper folded around a pencil protruding through the door. He opened it to read, "What are you doing for a meal tonight? I suggest you stay in and eat here, with a couple of additions. I'm expecting it will make for an interesting evening. I suggest 7 pm. We have a chef who as you would imagine specialises in the best of Arab cuisine. Please tick the YES or NO and put back under the door. By the way, I have left a range of clothes that you can wear for the rest of your stay in the large wardrobe in your room. Regards, Thomas."

Nikolas checked the wardrobe and found all was as Thomas had described. He picked out what he needed that night and laid out a pair of slacks, one pair of boxer shorts, a shirt, a pair of socks and shoes, then suddenly remembered to tick YES and place it back under the door.

It was only six o'clock so he sat back out on the balcony and watched the sun heading towards the horizon. He'd stopped trying to second-guess what was in front of him and relaxed with his mind cleared of complications and self-doubt, the best way he knew of facing anything. At five thirty, he reluctantly left a spectacular sunset and headed to the bathroom. He stretched his muscles out then dropped to the floor with his feet on the bath and performed incline press-ups until his shoulders and triceps were screaming. A few more stretches, a splash of cold water on his face to freshen up followed by a comb through his jet black hair and he felt ready for anything fate might have up its sleeve.

He bounced lightly down the stairs and entered the combination lounge, dining room through two ornate leadlight doors. The additional guest had already arrived and stood up to cross the room and shake his hand on Thomas's introduction. The male guest was an English man named Conrad Mitchell. He was tall and athletic and when he spoke Nikolas was struck immediately by his clone-like similarity to Thomas. He had the same public school accent and Nikolas pondered Thomas's admission that his relationship with Aiesha was plutonic and that his sexual interest lay elsewhere.

Back with the body language again Nikolas thought to himself as he subtly observed the obvious close friendship of Thomas and Conrad.

"Conrad and I go back a long way. We were both at Eton together from a young age and then onto Sandhurst," Thomas said reading the unasked questions on Nikolas's mind. "Always had a lot in common. Our parents own adjacent estates in Herefordshire and share an interest in local and national affairs."

Aiesha who had met Conrad before sat in stony silence. Nikolas glanced her way, puzzled at her reticence. His thoughts were interrupted by the entrance of the chef carrying a serving platter of kebabs, fuul, falafel and sea bass, while Thomas cruised around topping up drinks.

"This is my good friend Basri Al-Bariqi, the best Arab cuisine chef in the whole of the Middle East."

"It is most unfortunate for Basri as he attends my little soirees in two roles, one as a guest and the other as our chef. He insists that is the way he likes it, but I think he's just paranoid that some interloper chef might take his place." Thomas said poking some gentle humour at his friend.

"Now, my apologies but I must leave you to amuse yourselves for a moment while I get some more wine from the cellar."

Thomas opened a door and his footstep echoed back to the room as he descended the steep flagstone stairs.

"And how is my little German friend?" asked Conrad turning to Aiesha with a thin smile.

"Much the better for finding a new home here," she replied.

"Oh but you must surely miss your old country? If we had kept out of this war Adolf Hitler would have knocked the Bolsheviks and the Communist Jews on their backsides by now and the world would be a lot better place."

"Well, that's a matter of opinion, and opinions that don't fit the National Socialist template aren't free to hold in my 'Old Country' as you put it."

"Well, I think you don't appreciate what you have given up. National Socialism is the only answer to Bolshevism and the conspiracy of international Jewry."

Aiesha had coloured slightly under Conrad's prodding inquisition and Nikolas was becoming aware of a level of antagonism that lay hidden just below the surface of good manners and etiquette.

"You are aware that I was married to a Jewish man and bore his two children and that the children and he were killed in a cowardly attack by Nazis in the middle of the night."

"Yes, a most unfortunate incident, but you can't make an omelette without breaking an egg and Jews have had it coming for a long time. They are infiltrating the financial markets in London. They are becoming a force in the conservative party with their new money and their parasitic habits are what brought Germany to its knees, until Herr Hitler came on the scene."

Thomas had come back and was listening anxiously to the tense exchange.

At that point, Basri came in with several more platters of food with aromas that promised a tempting diversion from the escalating tension between Aiesha and Conrad. A relieved Thomas seized the moment and hurried everyone to the table.

The evening concluded late without any further dramas but the confrontation had alerted Nikolas to what might just be the big question no one was talking about. He kept to small talk but also kept his ears and eyes open to what was and was not being said.

Chapter 15

Nikolas retired as soon as he got back to his room. He lay awake dwelling on the evening then consigned it to his subconscious, turned over and went to sleep. He woke at daybreak and lay for a while thinking about the previous evening and watching the early light skim the elaborate ornamental detail of the ceiling. It was now time for Aiesha to come clean on what was going on. Of course it was likely she was on someone else's timetable, someone from headquarters or further up the chain. He had to consider that possibility. As if to answer his thoughts he heard a faint rustle from the direction of the door and in the half-light he could see yet another written communication. This time it was in a sealed envelope and pushed completely through under the locked door. The deliverer of the note obviously didn't want any opportunist swooping on obviously important information.

Nickolas rolled out of bed and by the time he was halfway to the door he knew the hand that delivered it and quite likely the hand that wrote it. Aiesha's perfume reached out to him like a signaller's flag. He picked the letter up and opened the door onto the balcony. He sat down and impatiently ripped it open. I want to meet you away from this house. I suggest we go to a small café over the road from the club. It is owned by friends of mine and is quite safe. Time is pressing so I need to see you today at 10 am. Stay in your room until you are ready to go. You won't have to see or talk to Thomas. He will be at Army HQ. "I've arranged for him to go there on a fool's errand. It will seem important to him. I have covered my absence with a plausible story. A taxi will pick you up from the rear entrance of the house at 9.30 am. The driver has been instructed to take you to the entrance of a local market. When you arrive, pay him then walk north through the market until you come to the last stall selling copper pots and pans. From here, you will see the café called Wahat Albahar which means Oasis of the Seas, 50 metres away. Go straight in, sit down and the owner will escort you into a private area where I will be waiting. Avoid talking to anyone from the moment you finish reading this letter which I ask you to rip into very small pieces, burn and flush down the toilet. Exciting, Yes? Love as always, Aiesha."

Nikolas reread the note a few times as if hoping he might somehow wring something extra out of it. He then obeyed the instructions to the letter and flushed the small pile of ashes down the toilet. Relieved he didn't have long to wait for the taxi, he quickly showered, dressed and at 9.25 am, headed down the stairs of the empty house and through an obscure rear entrance.

He stood just inside the gate and exited quickly when he heard the taxi pull up and give a light tap on the horn. Entering into the spirit set by Aiesha he got in quickly and slouched back out of sight, taking little interest in the passing cityscape. Within twenty minutes, they were at the drop-off point at the entrance to the market. Nikolas paid the driver, got out and set off for the far end, ignoring owners standing at their frontages hawking their wares. He came to the copper pots and pans shop and stopped. He looked inside at a large rotund owner with the inevitable moustache who after looking at him gave him a nod and turned back to his business of hanging up new stock. A short distance ahead on the opposite side of the intersection Nikolas spotted the café.

He crossed the road and keeping his head down stepped inside and closed the door. No sooner had he entered than the owner appeared and directed him through to the backroom. Nikolas stepped into a dimly lit part storage, part office. The door was closed behind him while Nikolas stood waiting for his eyes to adjust to the gloom after the outside glare. The scene before him was both expected and unexpected. Aiesha sat at a table looking back at him with the hint of a smile. It was no surprise to Nikolas that she was here but the short man with the moustache sitting beside her was.

"Pleased to meet you again Nikolas," said Captain Westbury, extending his hand.

Nikolas took his hand and sat slowly down on the nearest seat, turned and stared open-mouthed at Aiesha.

"The time has come to as they say to put all the cards on the table, but first I shall make sure we have no unexpected surprises." She got up, went to the door and locked it, gave the handle a rattle, then returned to her seat.

"I shall start from the beginning. As you already know I received advanced training in running an espionage operation, more then what you may imagine. My German nationality and my multilinguistic skills made me a highly desired recruit. But probably the most important part was the provable fact that my husband and children were killed by Nazis. That alone was enough for the MI5 to trust me to do anything to assist the allied cause. It was convenient I was in America at the time and that from the age of eighteen I spent more time living out of Germany than in, hence Germany saw very little of me as an adult.

"Aside from a distant relative my family are all dead. In short, I was about as good as it gets when recruiting from the enemy. The killing of my husband and children also meant my motives were more likely to be genuine, rather than being just some opportunistic turncoat who's smart enough to see the writing on the wall for Germany. I'll now pass over to Captain Westbury for him to explain his part."

"My role as Captain Westbury was created as a bogus British Nazi plant in MI5. It was then decided I should come to Alexandria to play the part of a double agent. The purpose of this was to provide a false target or placebo around which all sorts of drama would be played out using Mr Churchill and HQ staff to give plenty of credibility. An infiltrator invented to lull our real target into a false sense of security. You must have guessed who the real target is by now."

"Conrad, the nasty prick who hates Aiesha for jumping ship," said Nikolas.

"Exactly. But he isn't one of your ordinary run-of-the-mill British Union of Fascists from Mosley's lot who parade around in black shirts and stand out like sore thumbs. He's part of a highly secretive organisation formed around Scottish MP Archibald Ramsay called the Right Club. Very few know of its existence, let's keep it that way and we may tempt them to drop their guard. It's a sort of cosy bolthole for a number of rich or once rich, landed aristocracy, military and ex-military personnel, authors, aviators, Earls, Dukes and other titled and entitled types all disaffected in one way or another with social changes in Britain since the end of the first World War.

"They see Russian Bolsheviks fermenting unrest within British trade unions and they are probably right, and as he mentioned at dinner last night they particularly don't like the way Jews have an increasing influence in the Conservative Party. They hate them for their new money and believe it is an international Jewish conspiracy that has Britain at war with Germany. Their view is that we should have supported the Nazis or at least left them alone to sort out Russian Bolshevism and what they call the 'Jewish' problem," replied Westbury.

"Hard evidence of Nazi violence and repression against Jewish civilians in Europe leading up to the war had little or no effect on the views of their more rabid supporters as Conrad said last night, after glossing over the murder of my family, you can't make an omelette without breaking an egg," Aiesha added.

There was a short silence while everyone digested this last sobering statement.

"And you want me to do what?" asked Nikolas looking for solid confirmation as to exactly what was expected.

"Conrad is potentially the most dangerous of all the British fascists. He has contacts critical to the outcome of the war and we believe took a top-level briefing from Berlin to provide intelligence on any efforts to upset the German occupation of Crete. Their occupation is vitally important to the security of their oil supply from the Balkans which as you would know has a direct bearing on their ability to keep fighting this war. In short, he will sooner or later be on your tail meaning the success of your mission in Crete is dependent on getting rid of him as soon as possible.

"Be warned he is very bright with an exceptionally high IQ. He is also physically able having been an amateur gymnast, boxer and athlete, skills I understand he hasn't let lapse. Don't underestimate him simply because he doesn't share your sexual preference. By the way, you may be interested in the many reasons you were selected," said Captain Westbury.

"Which are?" asked Nikolas.

"You have proven experience in this sort of work with your involvement in the partisan movement in Crete. You performed exceptionally well in the advanced training with our special forces team in Athens during the early stages of the war. Very soon after the task is completed you and your team along with Conrad will be covertly transferred to Crete as per the original plan. Conrad will disappear over the side during your voyage. Exactly how will be discussed later. You will have conveniently disappeared and will not be around to face questioning by the police or anyone else. The last reason and always the one that is the clincher in these decisions and to use a little barrack room language, you have the balls for it and probably had them even before they dropped."

"What about Thomas, Conrad's close friend?"

"I'll take over here. I know Thomas very well and one of the things I know is that he has another even 'closer' friend marooned in Germany trying desperately to get out. Their relationship and the fact this friend is Jewish is something Thomas has carefully hidden from his parents and colleagues since schooldays. These two very damning facts put him in serious danger. If the

Gestapo got wind of him, he would simply disappear with the snap of a Hauptscharfuhrer's fingers. MI5 know about him so are helping him escape capture and certain death which is highly likely if he stays much longer in Berlin. This is a very compelling incentive for Thomas to 'do his bit for Britain' and MI5 will hopefully do the rest." Aiesha said.

"So where from here?" asked Nikolas.

"You will act as if nothing has changed. HQ will be looking at an operation plan and I suggest you give it some thought yourself. I propose we have a meeting in two days. We will use a different place and time. You can't be too careful," replied Westbury.

Conrad hated Jews. He also, while carefully concealing his own sexuality, was a loud and vociferous homophobic. Thomas's initial attraction was waning as he began to find Conrad's strong views increasingly abhorrent. Aiesha sensed this and armed with knowledge from MI5 about Thomas's Jewish friend in Berlin, convinced Thomas that they would do all they could to get his friend to safety, providing he maintained his normal friendship with Conrad and cooperated fully with MI5.

She promised to explain all as soon as she was able. It was a strain on Thomas to maintain the pretence but he was now beginning to see Conrad's cynical and vindictive side in an ever more damning light. The reward for his diligence and dedication to the cause would be the delivery of his Jewish friend to the safety of British shores and this was all the motivation he needed to play the double role and step into the shoes of a traitor to his 'best' friend.

Aiesha had to choose the right time to include Thomas in just exactly what their plans entailed. At the next meeting, it was decided Conrad would meet his end eventually in the middle of the Mediterranean after first being overcome with chloroform, then injected with a powerful sedative and put to sleep for eight to ten hours. Once subdued he would be secured with hand cuffs, collected by a couple of brawny Army personal and taken to HQ.

There he would be placed in a special holding cell separated from general staff, interrogated at length and when it was decided they had all the information they could get, he would make his last sea voyage with Nikolas and his group when they set off for Crete, the date of which had been set approximately two weeks hence. Coincidentally these plans were similar to what Nikolas had in mind. It didn't surprise anyone that given the grudge he held against Germany for what was done to his family, people and country, that he wanted to take ownership of the situation. He didn't want to get angry, just even.

Like all good plans it was simple. Thomas was to casually invite Conrad around to try some German wine he had managed to get on the black market. Thomas was to make sure he poured generously and frequently. After an hour or so, Thomas was to invite Aiesha and Nikolas to join the party. A bottle of chloroform was to be hidden in a space behind the toilet cistern and Nikolas would simply bring a clean handkerchief and Aiesha a pair of hand cuffs and a syringe of sedative. After thirty minutes, Nikolas would excuse himself to visit the bathroom which was through a door directly behind where Conrad would be sitting.

Thomas was torn by feelings of guilt and pre-emptive regret at what he was about to be party to. Nevertheless his resolve stiffened when he reminded himself of his friend in Berlin's likely fate if he wasn't rescued soon and MI5 through Aiesha spared no detail on what was happening to 'enemies of the state' in Germany.

The evening came and Thomas was like a cat on hot bricks waiting for Conrad to arrive, but arrive he soon did and sat back talking wine, with German wines the feature. Conrad was a genuine wine expert who was usually focused on Germany, no doubt expecting the inevitable German takeover of most European countries plus dear old, soft, had its day Britain. The 'nation of shopkeepers', as his hero Adolf Hitler once proclaimed.

It was going well. Conrad appeared to be getting more intoxicated and Thomas was even starting to relax, convinced that he'd done his bit and that the evening was moving forward to one conclusion he would have little to do with. There was a light tap on the door and Aiesha and Nikolas walked in carrying a bottle each.

Thomas poured two glasses and they sat and listened to Conrad proclaiming the superiority of the best German wines produced from Riesling grapes, planted back in the Roman era along the Rhine and its tributaries. Aiesha with her homegrown knowledge found herself often agreeing with Conrad that the very best were as good or often superior to all others. The conversation proceeded on an amiable, superficial level, nevertheless there was underlying tension and Thomas's demeanour was starting to concern Aiesha. She worried he'd crack under the pressure and let it all out. Time for action, any delay could mean the moment was lost. She glanced over towards Nikolas. He nodded slightly then stood up and headed towards the bathroom.

As he passed Conrad he noticed he didn't miss a beat in his ramble on German wines and Germany in general. Nikolas stepped through the door and closed it with his pulse racing. He stood still and counted to ten while he waited for his heart rate and breathing to slow down. Was there a shadow of suspicion crossing Conrad's eyes as left the room? Forget it, the time is here and now.

With carefully controlled movements, he reached behind the cistern for the bottle of chloroform. He opened it slowly and tipped a generous amount onto a large handkerchief, adding another shot for luck. With three inches left, he started screwing the top back on but cursed as it slipped out of a nervous hand, dropped to the floor and rolled out of reach behind the vanity. Cursing again through gritted teeth he stood with his eyes closed and counted slowly to five, then dismissing the missing top, placed the bottle back behind the cistern and flushed the toilet. In the room, Aiesha and Thomas heard the plumbing groan and both knew that it would soon be over.

Nikolas appeared at the door. It was now or never. He took one step towards the back of Conrad's head with the chloroform soaked handkerchief. Sixth sense or fighter's instinct flicked a warning to Conrad. His head suddenly jerked around, just as Nikolas whipped the chloroform soaked handkerchief onto his face. The fast half-turn gave Conrad the millisecond he needed to dodge the full dose, while in the same movement he grabbed Nikolas's hand holding the handkerchief. Nikolas saw Conrad was wearing a shirt with the collar done to the top button.

This was where he now went with his free hand. Grabbing the collar, he twisted hard, creating a makeshift tourniquet that got ever tighter as Conrad struggled. Conrad let fly with strangled threats and curses while Nikolas held on with all he had. Conrad tipped the couch over trying to get free and they both rolled around on the floor knocking over furniture and lamps, each desperate to get the upper hand. The tourniquet was no longer working and Conrad was lucky to be first on his feet. He kicked out hard, catching Nikolas with powerful kicks to his chest, shoulder and solar plexus. Winded and gasping for breath Nikolas stood up, buying time as he backed slowly around the upset couch. He knew he was going to have to fight this out close up, knowing he didn't stand much chance beating an ex-boxer with his fists.

Sucking in a deep breath he suddenly charged at Conrad, hitting him square in the midriff with his good shoulder in a tackle any All Black would be proud of. They both crashed to the floor where Nikolas sensed he had an advantage with his wrestler's shorter, more powerful frame. It was a short-lived advantage when he found he was suddenly facing an enemy now armed. Conrad had grabbed a short, flat-handled knife he carried strapped to his lower leg, for this sort of moment. From the floor, he slashed upwards at Nikolas's throat. Nikolas leapt back to his feet with adrenalin assisted speed.

Conrad was up soon after and stepped aggressively forward slashing and stabbing at him, forcing him backwards towards Aiesha. Nikolas realised Conrad was trying to get close to Aiesha to take her hostage. Before he could warn her, Conrad was beside her with his knife. He pinned her up against the wall, pressing the knife to her throat and seizing her arm in a powerful ex-gymnasts grip. He held this position for several seconds regaining his breath, then looked over his shoulder at Nikolas and Thomas and spoke calmly in short, measured sentences,

"Listen carefully. I want total cooperation from everyone or I will start cutting Aiesha into small pieces starting with her ear. If you want to see your apology for a German woman again, don't try anything stupid," he said glancing at Nikolas. Nikolas didn't answer but just glared coldly back at him. Conrad stood silently for a moment then appeared to make a decision and turned to Thomas.

"Thomas, search Aiesha's bag for a pair of handcuffs. You lot wouldn't expect to hold me here with verbal threats alone. Tip the bag out near my feet and don't forget that this knife, is sharp enough to shave with and is very close to Aiesha's jugular. Once you've done that give me the keys and take the handcuffs over to Nikolas. Put one on his right wrist (he'd noticed Nikolas was right handed), ...tighten, then take yourself and Nikolas over to the metal banister, thread the free end through one of the gaps and put the other handcuff on your wrist and tighten... After you've done that your German friend and I will be going on a journey. Aiesha will be my insurance policy, something you have probably already guessed."

While Conrad still had her arm in a tight grip and held the knife at her throat, Aiesha was desperately thinking through what actions were possible. She knew he wouldn't hesitate to kill any of them and wondered why he hadn't. It occurred to her that with the evidence mounting of the war slowly turning against Germany, Conrad, with cover blown, may have convinced himself that he had information valuable to the Allies. Information that could give him a passport back over to the Allies side as a double agent, feeding Berlin 'information' created by MI5. Naturally such an outcome would be less likely if he left a room full of bodies.

Conrad saw that Thomas and Nikolas were now 'self' secured to the heavy wrought iron banister. He turned Aiesha about, changing his grip swiftly to her wrist which he then deftly flicked up her back. Positioning himself behind her he pushed her ahead with a gruff, 'Forward march, slowly.' Aiesha, with an arm pinned up her back and a knife at her throat, was steered carefully to where Nikolas and Thomas were attached to the banister. She glanced at Nikolas but he looked away ashamed he had been so easily beaten. Conrad checked the handcuffs, giving them a quick rattle with the hand holding the knife. It was awkward, but necessary. Satisfied they would be going nowhere for some time he quickly shifted Aiesha and himself away from the restrained but still potentially dangerous Nikolas.

Conrad then nudged Aiesha towards a window looking out over the quiet street. By carefully positioning them both, he was able to keep control of Aiesha and still gain a view without being seen. He soon found what he was looking for. As his eyes adjusted to the poor light, he could just make out the shape of a military vehicle minus its number, containing the two soldiers hunched down, waiting for the prearranged signal to come and pick up their prisoner Conrad.

Bad luck boys, he thought, thanking them for the red pinpricks of light from the glow of their cigarettes that made it easier for Conrad to get a fix on the vehicle parked in the deep shadow of a nearby building.

Chapter 16

Conrad stood thinking, then suddenly marched Aiesha over to a writing desk. He had an idea and a hunch. He wanted to get the vehicle off the two army boys and his idea was to duplicate the signal that would have them leaving the vehicle and heading to the house to pick him up. It was a slim chance but he knew Thomas well and his hunch was that Thomas being a nervous Nellie would never rely on his memory to retain any important instructions. It was difficult but he stood by the desk and still holding the knife at her throat quickly rifled through Thomas's mess. Soon he found what he was looking for, a folded piece of paper with Thomas's careful, pedantic writing.

A sort of morse code for house lights, he thought to himself as he read, "long…short…short…long…short…long…long."

Thomas had no idea what was going on but Nikolas did and he silently cursed Thomas's slack security. Conrad moved Aiesha over to the light switch and trusting his memory performed the morse code signal with the lights. He then moved Aiesha quickly back to the window. Sure enough the two army boys bored stiff from a two-hour wait on hard army seats, leapt from the vehicle and moved at the double towards the house. They had about three hundred metres to cover but there was one more thing Conrad had to do. He headed for the bathroom, opened the door and went straight to the cistern knowing it was the only place to hide what was left of the chloroform. He would be going out the back entrance while the army boys would be coming in the front so he had to move fast as Thomas and Nikolas would start bellowing a warning as soon as he was out of the room.

First he had to neutralise Aiesha and he regarded it as poetic justice he would use the very weapon aimed at him earlier. Still holding the knife at her throat he grabbed the bottle and finding it without a top, sat it on the vanity. He took a handkerchief from his pocket, placed it on top of the bottle and tipped it upside down so half the contents soaked the material.

Aiesha knew what was about to happen, but the knife was still at her throat. Conrad stood behind her and wrapped the cloth over her face. Aiesha struggled furiously but eventually succumbed to the effects of the chloroform. To make sure, Conrad bent down to Aiesha now collapsed on the floor and applied the rest of the bottle's contents. He stood over her for a few more seconds to make sure she was fully unconscious.

Time was running out. The army boys would be approaching the front door any second now. He knew the door was locked and knew he had a built-in delay while they got their combined shoulders onto it forcing an entrance. He grabbed Aiesha in a fireman's lift and quickly headed out of the bathroom and along the hallway to a door with stairs leading down to a backdoor exit. He negotiated the stairs with Aiesha draped over his shoulder and as he closed the exit door behind him he could hear Nikolas shouting threats of retribution to come.

"Only if you can catch me big boy," he whispered to himself as he swung the door closed and locked it, then threw the key into a nearby fishpond.

If Conrad was anything, he was thorough. He had taken the trouble to explore the neighbourhood for just this eventuality. He knew just two strides from the door would take him to a gate that opened into a back alley. He also knew this led to a 'T' intersection with another alley which in turn led to the street where the army vehicle was parked. Thanking Aiesha's trim figure and light weight, he was at the intersection in thirty seconds. The few people still about looked questioningly at him but he simply made a drinking action with his free hand and the locals shook their heads at the overindulgence of westerners and returned to their lives. He arrived at the intersection, turned right and in another thirty seconds was only a few paces from the army vehicle.

"Now let's pray the eagerness of youth won over thoroughness and I'll find a key in the ignition." He leaned in groping in the dark, then sprang back. "Presto we have transport," he said and with boyish glee plucked the key out and held it up in triumph.

Conrad lifted Aiesha into the passenger seat where she slumped back seemingly lifeless. Then he quickly jumped in behind the wheel. He had to put a lot of distance between him and the house. He'd always had a broad-brush plan in case things turned bad and his priority now was to get to the bolthole already carefully organised. The Abwehr, Germany's version of MI5, in briefing him had set up a meeting in Alexandria with an individual of German origins and sympathies who operated a shell company under a false name.

The name chosen was Frederik Maier. Frederik diligently maintained a low profile throughout Egypt and was known locally to only a handful of people. One such person was his English lawyer also with strong Nazi sympathies and business interests in Germany who now kept a close watch on what had become his largest client. Frederick, by using a middleman, had developed a lucrative trade in the secret export of Egyptian antiquities.

The operation's survival and profitability was enhanced and secured by the Abwehr's generous backhanders that Frederik regularly slipped into the pockets of key Egyptian authorities to keep them looking the other way. Before hostilities began and tanks and field artillery started filling the holds of German shipping, there was a small trickle of luxury Daimler and Mercedes Benz cars left in the driveways of individuals with power and influence. Everyone from Frederik down were on the payroll of the Abwehr who with their conviction that North Africa was there for the taking decided it was money well spent. It was towards this organisation that Conrad sped, conscious that although more mufti than official, the vehicle needed to be off the street as soon as possible.

Eventually he pulled up alongside the large walled property that hosted his first and only meeting with Frederik and turned in to an entrance with a heavily barred gate. He sat and flashed his lights a couple of times towards the house. Frederik kept an around the clock watchman who after a short delay came forward slowly with side arm at the ready. Conrad gave his name and added a code prearranged to change on the first of each month. The code was the first sentence of a nominated chapter in an obscure eighteenth century German novel.

The watchman with hand on pistol examined him closely for several seconds, then stepped into the watch house, picked up a phone and dialled a short number. It had been a long difficult night and a nervous tremor ran through Conrad's body as he waited impatiently at the entrance to his safe sanctuary. He gripped the steering wheel tight and clenched his jaw, his way of spilling off excess tension while stuck in no man's land. Finally the watchman had the answer he needed and opened the gate.

Conrad let out a long breath and drove through following a curved drive to the front of the house. Another armed guard stepped out of the shadows and opened the car door. Conrad got out and found Frederik himself standing in a pool of light from the front entrance. He hesitated, then stepping forward, snapped his heels and executed a Nazi stiff arm salute that Frederik returned.

Conrad was visibly moved and from the strength of Frederik's handshake he knew for now and the foreseeable future he was on friendly ground and safe.

Frederik put his arm on Conrad's shoulder and went to lead him into the house. Conrad suddenly remembered Aiesha asleep in the car. He stopped, turned around and opened the passenger door. Frederik stood beside him as Conrad put his arms under Aiesha and lifted her from the car.

"Meet my one beautiful hostage. Her name is Aiesha who believe it or not is German, but a little misguided."

Frederik stopped and stared at Aiesha with open-mouthed astonishment. Then finally gesturing towards the door, turned and Conrad followed him into the house. He could see she certainly had all the approved Aryan features. He led Conrad into a comfortable lounge with a large couch on which Aiesha was carefully placed.

"I need to be able to give her something to keep her asleep for at least another five hours," Conrad said.

Frederik stood in silent thought for a moment then went over to a phone mounted on a nearby wall. He dialled a number and waited. Eventually the call was answered. He made a short, coded comment about the weather, heard a reply that satisfied him and began speaking rapidly in German. Conrad sat trying to translate but the schoolboy German that had fired his interest and affection for everything German couldn't keep up. Instead he sat back and relaxed while keeping an eye on Aiesha. Finally Frederik hung up and turned to Conrad with a satisfied smile.

"My contact is German and a close ally absolutely dedicated to our cause. He is also a medical doctor who worked in Germany and was recently transferred out here. He will be here in a few minutes to administer a long-term sedative that will keep our friend asleep or very subdued for several days. He is available at just about any time for any other medical matters and is completely trustworthy."

With the last twelve hours starting to catch up with him, Conrad lay back on the couch staring blankly at the ceiling deep in thought.

"I had to leave in a hurry. My cover is blown," he finally said.

"You are safe enough here. As you know from our one previous meeting I have friends in high places who receive generous payments from the Abwehr. However they can only be trusted for as long as they remain convinced that Germany is going to win. The moment that confidence is lost, they, like all traitors who are only in it for the money, will turn to Britain and their Allies.

"I will show you your room. There is a full set of clothes although I suggest you stay housebound for several days. My two men will dismember the vehicle and bury the parts in the desert. There will be no trace of you being here. Your friend will have to be secured in a room that is soundproof and without windows. It is in fact a comfortable 'jail'. We have more than adequate food supplies, another benefit of the 'generous payments'."

There was a knock on the door and Frederik opened it to a slight balding man carrying a medical bag. Frederik introduced him to Conrad as Dr Heinrich. After shaking Conrad's hand, he reached inside his bag and produced a hypodermic syringe. He approached Aiesha, primed the syringe and after pulling up a loose fitting sleeve injected the contents into her shoulder.

"She will sleep for another fifteen to twenty hours and wake up hungry and slightly dehydrated. I suggest you put her in a comfortable bed and keep a watch on her and call me if there are any complications…that is assuming you wish her to remain healthy and well."

"Yes we wish that. She is more valuable to us alive than dead," Conrad said bluntly.

Aiesha slept for a further twenty hours and finally woke in a dark room, ravenously hungry and totally at a loss as to where she was or what time it was. She struggled to her feet and groped her way along a wall until she found a light switch. She turned it on and found herself in a small room with no windows. The light showing under her door alerted those in the rest of the house and eventually a small door at the base of the main door was opened and a plate of food with a glass of water was pushed through. She started to say something but her mouth was dry and her brain unable to form the words. However she was able to sit beside the plate of food by sliding down the wall in slow motion. The one thing she was conscious of was her intense hunger and thirst. She began to carefully eat a small amount of the plain meal as if it was gourmet fare. It was hunger and thirst that had dragged her from the depths of drugged sleep but having satisfied her demands for food and water, her body now only wanted sleep. She made her way slowly back to the bed and ignoring the light lay down and closed her eyes, but in the few moments before drifting off she relived a glimpse of her own private nightmare – the two terrified faces of her children, pressed against a window pane surrounded by flames and then the face of Carmo – her husband and first love. She embraced the escape sleep offered.

Aiesha slept for another day and a half and started regaining consciousness late on the second day. As if on cue the door opened and Dr Heinrich entered the room. He closed the door and sat beside Aiesha on the small bed. She looked up at the doctor she was seeing for the first time with eyes that could barely focus. He reached out and put his hand on hers.

"I'm here to help you," he said quietly.

Still finding coherent speech difficult she gave a slight nod of her head then lay back in silence. "Are you able to read this?" he asked holding a piece of paper with just a few words close to her eyes. Aiesha stared at it as the spidery writing swam on the page.

"Yes," she said finally.

The message said…Aiesha, I am your friend and I'm going to get you out of here. He then followed with a full verbal explanation.

"What I am proposing is to give you an injection that will put you into a state that mimics death. I will return in four hours, examine you again and declare that you are dead. I will give a diagnosis of death from cardiac arrest caused most likely by an unknown heart condition aggravated by the sedatives administered previously. This way I have a very good chance of getting you out of here without Conrad and Frederik knowing that the British are onto them. Conrad's cover is blown but no one knows Conrad is here. We want them to feel secure and oblivious to the fact that we know all about Frederik.

"They are now discussing a change of plans for you and believe me, it is very likely you are going to die at their hands and end up buried in the desert if you stay much longer. I will convince them you have already died and that I will take over the problem of disposing of your body. They have total faith in me and are unaware of my change of allegiance. I trained in medicine with a Dr Mengle and had become aware of the so-called research projects he was conducting on prisoners, practices that I certainly didn't sign up for when I elected to study medicine. In short, I became convinced I was morally on a very wrong track. I won't tire you by telling you how I ended up here. Finally I must warn you there is an element of risk in this procedure but as I said your life is at risk here anyway. Aiesha, do you understand all I have told you?"

"Yes, and you must go ahead," Aiesha replied weakly.

He ripped the paper into tiny pieces and swallowed each one.

Dr Heinrich made the critical injection then left the room, locking the door and pocketing the key. He took a deep breath and walked into the lounge where Frederik and Conrad were studying a table full of reports looking for good news on the progress of the Afrika Korps fighting the desert war a few hundred kilometres away. He put his bag on the table, briefly tidied the contents then closed and locked it. He told them he would be returning in three to four hours, bade them farewell and picking up the bag headed for the door. They both nodded to him as he left engrossed in their reports. This slow and methodical procedure was deliberate and he took this trouble with every visit. Consistently following the same habits gave the two men less reason to be suspicious.

The good doctor walked the five hundred metres to his modest dwelling. He unlocked the door and went into a tiny room that served as a makeshift surgery. There he hung up his jacket, then reaching up took down a large volume containing the dosage notes for the sedative he was administering. He read and reread the text, paying particular attention to adverse reactions and side effects, aware as he was of treading a fine line between life and the real possibility of the genuine death of his 'patient'. He was also aware that in a normal life he could be accused of deliberately putting Aiesha at risk but as he reminded himself, there was nothing normal about this situation.

It was now early evening and he sat looking over the late orange and gold light hanging over the desert landscape in the distance. Whatever the outcome, he at least knew he could now return his own gaze while shaving in the morning, something he hadn't been able to do for a long time. Dr Heinrich prepared himself a small meal and finished off with a strong coffee. He picked up his medical bag, opening it on a bench and checking all the things he needed to carry off what would be an audacious confidence trick. He would have to be careful to stifle any hint of nervousness, for as a doctor having overseen countless deaths he would be expected to act calmly and professionally. The smallest hint of something odd could finish them both.

The last card he decided to play was to call up a favour from an old acquaintance he had once helped. He would put it to Conrad and Frederik that to make their hostage disappear without trace he would need the services of a someone he knew who would assist only on the condition that the deed was done in the middle of the night with no witnesses. They would be required to be elsewhere on the night, leaving the task totally to them. A situation that absolved them of any involvement or risk and should hold instant appeal to Conrad and Frederik who still had no reason to doubt the doctor or his loyalty.

The hours rolled slowly on until finally his surgery clock showed 9 pm. He'd already contacted his friend and briefed him on the situation. Once given the go ahead from the doctor he was to turn up at the address at 10.30 pm equipped with a suitable vehicle. Dr Heinrich checked his medical bag for the umpteenth time then left the house and strode purposefully down the road. He arrived, showed his face to the gatekeeper and walked quickly towards the house. He knocked and was led in by Frederik who was upbeat and smiling. Some good news in the reports the doctor surmised. Dr Heinrich had his own key and after a cursory nod to Conrad sitting over his maps and battlefield reports, went through the lounge door and along a short passage to Aiesha's room. He took another deep breath and turned the key in the lock. The doctor blessed the maps and reports that were holding Conrad and Frederik's absolute attention as if they themselves were fighting the war in absentia.

He quietly opened the door and just as quietly locked it. His heart was now racing and a tight knot gripped his stomach. He lent over Aiesha and he could see that to any layman she appeared to be dead. He sat and observed her for twenty minutes, a period of time that he could claim was spent trying to revive her. He knew that Frederik and Conrad would be relieved when he broke the 'news' that Aiesha had passed away.

Now or never, he opened and locked the door and went into the lounge.

"I've something to tell you that I imagine from your conversations in my hearing will please you both. I can no longer find a pulse on Aiesha and all my other checks tell me that your hostage has in fact died. My conclusion is that this outcome was caused by a respiratory arrest from the effects of the sedatives in her system. She also shows signs of an allergic reaction to the large dosages of sedatives administered by myself on top of the earlier application of chloroform." He relayed this in a tone and manner that brooked no argument. He was precise, authoritative and professional.

The two men sat back from their maps and reports and looked up at the little man standing before them. He returned their gaze without a tremor. He could also see relief enter their eyes because although both were self-proclaimed Nazis, neither seemed to possess the mind of a genuine psychopath, someone who could kill without blinking an eye and carry on as if nothing had happened.

"I must now tell you how I propose dealing with this 'accident'. I will make a call to an associate who will be here within the hour. He has assisted me in the past, but I must insist that the two of you leave the property as he demands complete anonymity. The timetable is that we will act at 10.30 pm tonight. At 11 pm, we will be gone and all traces of your hostage will disappear with her. As you would realise this reduces the risks of betrayal of either of you."

It was part reasonable argument and part charade. A second-year medical student could have easily contested his conclusions. Dr Heinrich knew this and thanked the local Egyptian Gods that neither Conrad nor Frederik had any medical knowledge or interest in medicine.

"I insist that your gateman is briefed on the situation and makes himself scarce. Please leave the gates unlocked after all we will only be here thirty minutes at the most and you will need to provide me with a key, which I will return later. Remember, all matters will be attended to and no trace will be found of your hostage. There will be a modest fee, most of which will be for my 'associate'. Thank you for your time."

Conrad and Frederik exchanged glances then Frederik, owner of the house, spoke first, "I can't see any problems and as we've decided that any further uses or value of the woman to us are outweighed by the risk of discovery, do your job and we will stand aside."

Conrad stared coldly at the doctor for a few moments then nodded slowly in agreement.

Doctor Heinrich excused himself and went back to the room where Aiesha lay. He closed the door, locked it then sat on the bed beside her. The time was 9.45 pm. He heard the door slam as Conrad and Frederik left the house. His accomplice in this 'white crime' was due at 10.30 and was bringing with him a canvas body bag to conceal Aiesha and a stretcher to carry her on the short trip to his surgery. The bag was an added insurance against an onlooker being at the wrong place at the wrong time. At 10.15 pm, he left the room and went to check the coast was clear for his friend's arrival. He took a coffee with him and sat to contemplate what might be in store. At 10.25 he stood up, ditched the remaining coffee and headed off to open the gates. As he approached, a flash of headlights shone through the bars casting long shadows on the driveway. He opened them quickly and closed them just as quickly as his friend drove through heading straight towards the house. His haste was to make sure the vehicle was well off the road and out of sight. Dr Heinrich strode up to the parked ex-ambulance already backed up for the easy access for his unconscious passenger. The stretcher sat ready. No words were spoken but Dr Heinrich shook his friend's hand, then each taking an end, stepped onto the veranda and into the house. Time mattered, his friend understood this as they manoeuvred the stretcher quickly through to Aiesha's room. Lying ready on the stretcher was a canvas bag with zipper opened full length. Dr Heinrich performed a quick visual check of Aiesha then lifted her by her shoulders while his friend held her legs. They carefully laid her in the bag and zipped it up. There were plenty of ventilation holes in the canvas and as the trip was only a matter of minutes there was no additional danger to Aiesha.

The stretcher was again manoeuvred back through the house and slid into the waiting ex-ambulance. Dr Heinrich closed the rear doors, walked quickly to the gates and stood while the ambulance drove through. He closed the gates, opened the rear doors and climbed into the back to secure the stretcher for the short trip to his surgery. Within a few minutes, Aiesha was unloaded and lying on the surgery bed. Dr Heinrich was able to begin the process of bringing her out of her unconscious state. To aid the process he administered IV fluids and naloxone, then left her to sleep it off through the rest of the night. He prayed that he had judged the dosage and timing of the last sedative just right, so she would have stood a good chance of passing any check that Conrad or Frederik may have decided to make, but once clear of them recover as soon as possible.

He then took a call from another 'patient'. The contact was from a person impressed with what he assumed was the doctor's determined loyalty to the Fatherland. He was also a person with information and influence that Doctor Heinrich used covertly to assist the allied cause, a cause he decided some time ago was right and just. The call was for an important meeting which meant a fifteen to twenty minute walk, approximately half an hour return plus meeting time. He looked in at Aiesha who appeared as well as could be expected. He bent over and lifting her hand felt for a pulse, it was faint and barely registering but marginally better and slowly growing stronger. He stood up and reached for his bag.

It was necessary to leave her alone in order to make a meeting that could provide important material for his allied contacts. He snapped the bag closed, stepped through the door and closed it behind him. Within forty-five minutes, Aiesha started opening her eyes a few seconds at a time.

Something told her she needed to climb out of her semi-conscious state as soon as possible. The fact the doctor wasn't there gradually dawned on her, it worried her and she was unable to explain why. Maybe while unconscious she had sensed his reassuring presence while also trying desperately to hold on to their plan to get her away from Conrad and Frederik.

Chapter 17

She lay back swimming in and out of consciousness, focusing and refocusing on the pattern of moonlight coming through a skylight in the ceiling, her eyes trying to get the alternate bars of moonlight and shade to stay still and sharp. Suddenly a blurred silhouette of a face appeared in the skylight, then disappeared just as quickly, was it real or imagined? She lay very still, her mind scrambling to make sense of something she was certain she had caught a glimpse of, or had she? She lay with her eyes closed but the face re-emerged, seemingly to swim up from the depths of her recently unconscious mind as she desperately tried to pick real image from imagined.

Abruptly Aiesha opened her eyes wide at the realisation the face belonged to Conrad. She also knew she didn't have long to live if she didn't move quickly to find a weapon and a place to hide. Looking around she reached for a pair of long sharp surgical grade scissors and, barely able to move, crept towards a wardrobe where several white and grey lab coats hung on a rack. It was as good as it was going to get. She saw a row of bottles standing on a bench. She was attracted to one labelled POISON. Without knowing whether it would advantage her or not, she still wanted all the chances she could get. She opened the lid and dipped the long scissors into the bottle. Then knowing time was against her, stepped into the wardrobe, pulled the doors closed and waited for the inevitable. Within minutes, the door of the surgery slowly creaked open. Adrenalin was now coursing through her. She held the handles of the scissors in both hands with the lethal end pointing to where the threat would come. She could hear the slow, careful tread of feet going towards the bed she had just vacated. The owner of the feet stood in the semi-dark room absorbing the fact she was no longer on the bed. A faint sound of shallow, nervous breathing was now approaching the cupboard, only to diminish as it moved on towards the surgery exit. The door opened and closed, but there was no sense of the person exiting through the door.

She soon realised he was still in the room, playing a game of nerves, hoping she would blink first and panic and rush from her hiding place. Minutes went by, each trying to outwait the other. Finally Conrad lost patience and moved quietly over to the wardrobe doors. She could see his midriff through the slim gap. Moving sideways to a different angle she could see he held a small automatic pistol. He's going to play it safe and shoot through the door she decided. She had to act now. She set herself, took a couple of deep breaths and using all the adrenalin fuelled energy she could muster, burst through the doors leading with the scissors.

Conrad, even with his nerves on edge was caught totally by surprise from the attack. He fired off a reflex shot but his aim was spoilt by the door shoving his gun arm away. She drove forward sinking the 20 cm scissors into his torso just below his ribs. Conrad sucked in a big breath, his eyes wide with shock and fear as he tried to repel the next thrust aimed at his throat. Although deflected, the blade still cut a jagged tear in his jugular which started pulsing blood onto the floor.

Another wild shot rang out and Aiesha felt a burning pain in her thigh as Conrad slumped to the floor.

Conrad was in serious trouble and more concerned with his survival than getting the better of this feral cat named Aiesha. If Conrad thought that Aiesha might intervene to save his life he was wasting his time. Aiesha could now see only the faces of her husband and children and Conrad's glib line about making an omelette.

Conrad had tossed his lot in with the devil and for her there was only one way this was going to end. She stabbed again with force and accuracy, this time straight into his heart. Aiesha stood looking at Conrad slumped on the floor as his life slowly ebbed away. The pistol was lying beside him forgotten. She kicked it away. Using the few breaths he had left, he gasped out his final words.

"You bitch. I knew you were up to something."

Aiesha slumped forward with her hands on her knees gasping for breath. With the adrenalin fading fast, she started feeling intense pain where Conrad's second shot had ploughed a groove through the flesh of her upper thigh as he fell to the floor. Blood started oozing from the wound as she lay back on the bed in shock and exhaustion. Sheer terror, adrenalin and the furious action of the moment had somehow overridden the high-level of sedatives still in her body, but there was now a price to pay. Her mind went blank and her world quickly turned black as her body shut down under a huge energy deficit. She lay on the bed totally unconscious with Conrad dead on the floor in a pool of arterial blood. This was the scene Dr Heinrich faced when he opened the door ten minutes later.

The doctor stared in disbelief for a short few seconds, then noting the three critical wounds on Conrad, quickly checked and finding no pulse switched his attention to Aiesha. He dressed her wound to stop the blood flow. Then he checked her pulse and blood pressure and listened to her breathing and heart rate. Cautiously optimistic that Aiesha would pull through, he slumped into a chair and started to address the fact that he now had the problem of a real dead body to deal with. He needed to contact his handler again.

It was inconceivable that Frederik was not aware of Conrad's night-time sortie but maybe he wasn't, maybe Conrad had another agenda, one that involved switching allegiances and swerving around Frederik. The latest reports on the progress of the Afrika Korps were not making for good reading. The Americans had entered the war and it would take only a person of the most fanatical devotion to remain optimistic about Germany's long-term future. Add the fact that unlike Frederik, Conrad was not German born and had observed Germany rapidly evolve into a fascist state from a position of privilege, safety and comfort from across the channel. It was not the same level of indoctrination absorbed by Frederik.

Dr Heinrich hoped that Conrad's mission was one of aiming to have a foot in both camps and keeping his options open. Assuming that was Conrad's aim, then the only other question related to the danger he had posed to Aiesha. It suddenly occurred to the doctor that Conrad still regarded Aiesha as a threat, a person who knew the real Conrad and a person who if left alive would surely kill off any attempt by Conrad to 'jump ship'. Conrad had turned up that night to clean up this 'loose end' and used his ex-gymnast's agility to climb on the roof and look through the skylight, the only way to see into the windowless room and confirm his suspicions.

The doctor then made a coded call to his handler. Frederik still appeared convinced of the authenticity of his 'German' contact supplied by MI5 and so continued to supply him with information and intelligence. It was therefore logical to assume Frederik would pass on information if he knew how and why Conrad had disappeared. There was nothing from Frederik relating to Conrad other than that he had simply vanished.

He finished the coded call that arranged a meeting with his handler for 9 pm the next day, to be held in the backroom of the café across the road from the nightclub. He rechecked Aiesha, then returned to his library and reached for the large book of dosage notes that guided his hand in causing Aiesha's 'death'. He was interested in the section relating to antidotes recommended for treating accidental overdoses. His concern was leaving Aiesha to attend the meeting with his handler and needed to expedite her recovery, so he could go to his meeting with an easy mind. He found the relevant information and turned to his locked cabinet of drugs. He was relieved to find the antidote quoted. Charging a syringe he returned to his 'patient'. Aiesha was improving, but slowly.

Dr Heinrich wanted greater certainty, so didn't hesitate to inject the recommended dosage. He would check her in the morning and repeat the treatment if necessary.

At 8 am, he rose from his simple cot and stepped into the surgery to find Aiesha still asleep. The rug he had found for her was cast off and lying on the floor. He picked it up and draped it over her. He stood looking at the young woman who shared both his nationality and political stance. He knew plenty of like-minded country men and woman with similar views and felt sorry for them having to toe the line under the threat of exposure and certain death. The doctor had soon caught on to the reality of industrial scale annihilation of Jews, Gypsies, homosexuals and others categorised as sub-human, including Germans sufficiently brave to object to Nazi policies. Since he had changed allegiance he had never lost a night's sleep and still considered himself a loyal German. He regarded Nazis as the ones disloyal to Germany and its people.

Several times during the day Dr Heinrich would, after carefully checking Aiesha, lock the door and make house calls to his elderly patients. The patients were well resourced and unwittingly aided the doctor in maintaining his life as a double agent. Towards the evening, on returning to his surgery he found Aiesha awake, but drowsy. He prepared soup which she drank slowly. At 8.30 pm, he entered the surgery and told her he was going to a meeting at which her future at a safe house would be discussed. He advised her to open the door to no one and promised to return within two hours.

At 8.45 pm, he closed and locked the door and walked the short distance to the café. On arrival, Dr Heinrich was escorted into the backroom by the owner and given a coffee. Five minutes later the door opened and the owner showed in a short man with a moustache. It was the first time the doctor had met his handler in person and as per MI5 operating procedure in the field, the doctor knew none of his handlers' contacts upline until Aiesha arrived in his life.

"I understand you have someone in your care who might interest us," the short man said after sitting and staring at the doctor for several seconds.

"Yes, Aiesha was unfortunate to have come up against Conrad and Frederik," Dr Heinrich replied.

"Naturally we want to retain Frederik as an unwitting informant to our 'German' plant which could put you at risk. I will monitor what he passes on to our 'German' contact and give you a warning if he seems to have caught on to what really happened to Conrad. In the meantime I will arrange to have Conrad's remains picked up and disposed of."

He took a long drink of his coffee then carried on.

"I'm convinced Frederik will be very nervous at the unexplained disappearance of Conrad and will therefore keep his head down in case he thinks he is the next on the list to 'disappear'. When Aiesha has recovered, make the usual coded contact and I will organise to pick her up and cause her to 'disappear' also, naturally in much better health than Conrad."

With that he drained his coffee, stood up and moved towards the door. He paused as if he'd forgotten something then turned, reached out and shook the doctor's hand.

"Wait here for at least twenty minutes before leaving. I don't want anyone to connect my arrival and departure with you. The owner will give you the all-clear. Best of luck and as always be careful and watch your back."

With that the little man left the room, closing the door behind him.

Two days later at 2 am on a moonless night, an unmarked army vehicle pulled up beside Dr Heinrich's surgery. Aiesha, with her bullet wound now stitched up, was quickly led to the vehicle. She was far from one hundred percent but the nervous doctor had attached some urgency to her transfer. The longer she stayed the greater the risk to everyone, Aiesha included. With Aiesha slumped out of sight, the vehicle sped through the dark streets and after following a convoluted route to check on tails, eventually pulled into army HQ. The fortified gates swung shut and Aiesha was now as safe as she could expect to be. She was assigned a spartan but comfortable room and advised to get more sleep by an army medic, who gave her a quick check over. In the morning, when ready, she would receive a debriefing to see what could be added to the report filed by the short man with the moustache.

Next morning she woke to a knock on her door from a canteen orderly delivering a large cup of regulation army tea of a strength designed to fortify the resolve of troops preparing for battle. She washed down a couple of pieces of toast and felt better for it. So much so, she was soon dressed in the fatigues left folded by the bed and ready to go, when an officer tapped on her door ten minutes later.

"I'm Captain James Simmock and I will take you through to our debriefing room. It's not very flash I'm afraid. We just want to hear your side of the encounter with Conrad Mitchell and Frederik Maier and then it's on to a secure location where you will be accommodated with two other people who I believe you know, while we work out what Frederik is up to, if anything. By the way, this new location comes with two armed army personal to ensure your security. You won't encounter them but they are nearby."

The debriefing was a non-event as the doctor had already covered most of what Aiesha was able to provide. She was returned to her room where she was to remain until night provided its security blanket over the transfer to her new address. She spent the time alternately sleeping, wondering what had become of Nikolas and contemplating what she suspected might be a seismic shift in her life.

Her new address was a poor version of her former one but the black hooded eyes of Nikolas that met her at the entrance more than made up for the rough and ready accommodation. They both stood and looked at each other for a few seconds until Nikolas stepped aside, letting Aiesha through. She walked into a large lounge and without saying a word slumped onto a couch and closed her eyes. She wasn't as recovered from the last ten days as she thought. Nikolas pulled up a chair and sat watching her. He was not completely comfortable with her arrival. The problem was that his culture and upbringing had raised him to protect, or die protecting any woman in his care.

The fact that Conrad had turned the tables on him only increased the shame and sense of failure he felt. The advantage Conrad had over him with the knife made no difference. He had failed plain and simple to protect the woman he realised he now loved.

Thomas was in his room where he remained most of the time. He knew of Conrad's demise but knew no details of how or why he had died. Having had a close relationship with Conrad he inevitably carried conflicting feelings of guilt and remorse about his part in the whole affair. He accepted that Conrad got what he deserved but still remained in his room, withdrawn and uncommunicative.

Aiesha remained asleep for two more hours before slowly opening her eyes to the face of Nikolas still seated on the chair in front of her.

"Tell me what happened," he said.

Aiesha related the whole story while she sipped a mug of tea.

"Well, you've made it back just in time. I'm going to Crete tomorrow," he said.

Nikolas went to the couch, took the half-finished mug of tea and put it on the floor. He then reached under her and lifted her easily into the air. Her head hung over his arm and he carried her into a bedroom with a large bed with a canopy. She smiled at the incongruity. It was her first smile for a long time and she smiled again when Nikolas folded his arms around her in the outrageous bed. She drifted off into a long sleep, waking eventually to the early morning light of the sunrise. She turned over and lifted her head to find he was no longer beside her but standing naked staring out towards the new day. She lay on her side looking at him while he stood as still as a statue in the pale light. Then he crouched down, picked up the clothes from the floor and began to dress. He came over to the bed, leaned over and kissed her on the lips.

"I'm being picked up in thirty minutes. I guess I won't be back until I'm either dead or the war is over, whichever comes first," he said.

She reached up as he lifted his head and pulled him back onto the bed beside her. "You'll be back, and I'll be here when you get back," she said.

She drifted off into another sleep and when she awoke he was no longer there.

Chapter 18

They were right on time as he knew they would be. He stood quietly at the window until the anonymous unmarked car pulled up. He threw a pack over his shoulder and headed for the door. His mouth was dry. Fear had crept on board until he closed his eyes and saw his father executed in front of him. A father removed so casually, he was owed and his fear vanished like mist at sunrise. Nikolas walked up to the car door and waited for the codeword, 'OCTOPUS' to come from the driver, then followed after a pause by 'EIGHT'. He replied with the Greek word for 'ARMS'. The driver gestured to the front door and Nikolas climbed in. An armed guard in the back watched every move while they drove in silence through the deserted streets as the driver continually checked his rearview mirror. After a circuitous route, they pulled up at Army Headquarters. Another armed guard opened the gate and the car accelerated through. The gate slammed shut and as far as the rest of the world was concerned they were nowhere to be found. Nikolas knew tight security measures were necessary in a community that was not over-friendly to the British and their Allies and full of spies looking for favour or fortune. They pulled up at the office complex and driver and guard got out and stood waiting for him. He opened his door, grabbed his pack and walked ahead of them into the dull green building.

Nikolas was taken to a room that contained three British soldiers and a Kiwi. They were introduced to each other using bogus names. The three Brits were to be known as Ben, Don and Len. The Kiwi was to be called Sam. Nikolas retained his own name to avoid confusion when linking up with the Crete greeting party. The Brits' insignias were of a recently formed Commando Squadron. They all shook hands and sat down waiting for events to unfold.

Ten minutes went by before an officer hurried into the room with copies of charts and papers. He dropped them on the desk and then handed a briefing paper and chart to Nikolas, and Sam and each of the commandos.

It was short and sharp. Their departure to Crete was dependent on two factors. One, the timely arrival in the seas off Alexandria of a Royal Navy submarine and two, a settled weather pattern over the next five to seven days. Nikolas, Sam the Kiwi and three Brits would shortly start on a course designed to give them the best chance of inflicting maximum damage and still come back alive. Nikolas was already a graduate of a similar course while studying in Athens but it wouldn't hurt to have a refresher. A briefing was delivered on the current situation in Crete and instruction on the use of any German weaponry likely to fall into their hands. They were then supplied with the familiar British Sten guns, two Bren guns, automatic pistols, grenades and plastic explosives. Given they were going where the invaders had seized most of the available food, they were fed well over the next two days against the near starvation conditions they would find on Crete. A final briefing regarded their passage to Crete. They were to be taken at night, dressed as local fishermen by boat to a rendezvous point approximately fifteen nautical miles off Alexandria. Here they would be picked up by a Royal Navy submarine and dropped off close to the coast of Crete where they would go ashore in two inflatable dinghies.

The next two days passed quickly. Nikolas was used nonstop to provide local knowledge, safe houses if on the run and a collection of phrases to help communicate with the native Cretans. They would be vulnerable so 'Be prepared' was the message for each day. He knew that beyond this homily it was only luck that would see all, some, or none home alive.

The last lecture was a twenty minute talk from those who knew the details of the abuse dished out to anyone bold enough to challenge the fascist cause. No quarter had been given or was being given to man, woman or child. He was unsure why this message was delivered, but he suspected the army wanted to make sure the team were taking all instructions seriously.

The weather experts at headquarters had picked a date for the trip. It was predicted to be a calm night with no moon. The fishing boat 'borrowed' from a sympathetic local well rewarded for his generosity was now commanded by a Naval Officer and rating, both experienced in small boat handling. This measure removed the owner from being privy to what was afoot. It was equipped with radio so that shore could communicate with both sub and boat. The trouble was with who else might be listening. For this reason, the commander of the submarine and the 'fishing boat' were both familiar with the codes used to update those involved.

The night arrived and the team assembled in their 'fishing' garb. An old truck smelling of fish was used to transfer all personnel plus their gear. In the half-light, the appearance on the wharf of a ragtag band of fishermen was reasonably convincing. They smartly and silently loaded the gear on the boat, then quickly climbed on board as if worried they might change their mind about a trip that was tantamount to putting their heads in a noose.

The first mate let off fore and aft mooring lines while the naval officer started the engine, selected forward and began threading through a dozen or so fishing boats and assorted craft, then finally into open sea. Nikolas sat back and watched the shore lights steadily recede as they settled back into the relaxing beat of the diesel engine.

Once the boat was a kilometre offshore, a figure crouching in a shadowed recess near the wharf, stood up, yawned and stretched then began walking quickly towards his dwelling a short distance away. He inserted a key in a modern lock, opened the door then closed and locked it behind him. Once inside he went through another door to a bedroom. Moving a floor mat aside he knelt down and began unscrewing two floor boards. He placed the screws carefully to one side then paused, listening intently. Nervous and anxious, he suddenly put the rug back in place and went to the main door, opened it and stepped outside. He looked up and down the empty road for several minutes, then went back, relocked the door and returned to the bedroom. He removed the rug again, then working quickly lifted the floor boards to reveal an attaché case. He placed the case on his bed and waited beside it while his breathing returned to normal. He knew the next operation called for a cool head and steady hand. He was preparing to send a morse code signal. The signal was intended for the Nazi occupiers of Crete.

The fishing boat was making solid progress towards the rendezvous point. The naval officer picked up the radio mike and sent out a coded signal to the submarine he expected to be submerged a few kilometres away with radio antenna and periscope breaking the surface. A few minutes passed before Nikolas heard the crackle of the coded response. It meant nothing to Nikolas or the rest of the team and they settled back to the last minutes of relative safety and comfort.

A few minutes later the officer throttled back and the modest little bow wave changed to a mere ripple in a calm sea state. That they were now only a short distance from the rendezvous became evident when the submarine rose slowly out of the water fifty metres away. Nikolas couldn't believe his eyes. The great mass of the hull lifted upwards onto the surface to sit eight to ten feet above the water line. With water washing off its black flanks, it looked ominous and threatening. Nikolas had wondered how they were going to get their gear and themselves onto it. He now found out. One end of a line was attached to the mast and the other to a fitting on the conning tower. Their captain now powered up the boat stretching the line taut. A pair of pulleys were sent across to the boat and their gear bags winched across by crew of the submarine. All that was needed now was for Nikolas and his mates to follow suit. Two harnesses were attached to the pulleys and the five were pulled two at a time over the short gap. Nikolas was the last to cross and in less than a minute he was standing topside on the submarine. He watched as a naval rating released the line from the mast, then he turned and climbed through the hatch, down a ladder and into the submarine. He found himself standing by his companions. An officer quickly shepherded them out of the way into crew quarters. They were told to each take a bunk and relax while the Royal Navy delivered them to Crete. ETA, 5 am.

Nikolas could sense the sub was readying to dive, a claxon sounded for five second intervals followed by the metallic voice of the captain telling crew to prepare to dive. The submarine dived to forty feet then levelled out. Two diesel/electric engines were brought up to speed and the craft was on its way to Crete at four to five knots. Nikolas looked over at the Brits. They looked calm and relaxed, as commandos they'd seen it all before.

Ahmed Basri waited for his message to be acknowledged and when he'd heard the correct response he repacked the radio and morse code equipment into the attaché case and slipped it back under the floorboards. Then he screwed both boards in place, rubbed some dirt on the screw heads, then placed the mat back in the correct position. Ahmed lay down on the bed and closed his eyes to the reality of his life as the plaything of a smart and sophisticated German agent. He prayed every night to Allah that this would be the last time he'd be called on to serve his German controllers. He now hated them only slightly less than the British who'd jailed his elder brother for a minor theft three years ago.

The German agent with an immaculate Oxford accent had covertly researched the occupants of the local jail and then patiently tracked down Ahmed. The deal he had ready was that when the Third Reich had swept all before it in North Africa, his brother would be freed and rewarded with a fishing boat in good condition. He'd made regular contact with the Nazis over several months but had now lost all enthusiasm for the arrangement. His agony was that the German agent, convincingly posing as a bona fide British subject with cover to match, had Ahmed in the palm of his hand. The German had high-ranking connections and strings to pull. If Ahmed dobbed him in, the British would raid Ahmed's house, find the radio and execute him as a spy.

The soothing hum of the large electric motors soon had Nikolas asleep as the submarine nosed its way ever closer to Crete. At 4 am, Nikolas was shaken awake by a rating with a large cup of tea in his hand. "Thirty minutes from your destination sir," he said.

Nikolas sat up, grabbed the navy's version of tea and gulped it down, his heart suddenly beating hard. He stood up and looked over at the other members of the team. They were awake and lying back getting the last rest for what was expected to be a long time. The rating who brought the tea returned with a large plate of sandwiches and they all ate hungrily for such an early hour, each knowing it could be the last food for weeks.

Nikolas followed the three commandoes and the Kiwi along the tight passage to where the commander of the submarine was staring intently at an array of dials. He turned to face Nikolas.

"We are five hundred metres off your destination. As the bottom rises steeply to shallow waters we will surface and take you to approximately one hundred metres off shore. Once on the surface my men will prepare the inflatable dinghies that will get you and your gear ashore. Stand easy here and I'll let you know when it's time to move."

The commander went back to the periscope, turning left and right as he scoped the shore. "One hundred metres, captain," the rating said, looking up from his screens and dials.

"That means you're all go," said the captain and fired out the command to surface.

Nikolas steadied himself as he felt the submarine change its angle and slow almost to a halt.

The captain nodded to them and one by one the group began climbing up the ladder to the hatch.

On deck, their gear was stacked by the inflatables. Two ratings took them both to the stern where the water lapped up onto the sloping deck and secured them to a couple of cleats. Sam and Nikolas followed with their gear bags, dumped them in one of the inflatables and climbed in. A signaller on the bridge picked up a torch light from the shore that flashed 'All Go' to Nikolas. On that short signal, Nikolas and the Kiwi reached up and shook the hand of the captain who'd come to see them off.

Picking up the paddles they set off towards the beach where they could just see the white foam of small breaking waves. Nikolas looked back to see the three commandos load up their inflatable and climb in. He calculated they would be about fifty metres behind by the time he and the Kiwi hit the beach. The pinprick of light repeated from the beach signalled their prearranged reception. They paddled hard and in five minutes the inflatable was grounding in the shallows with the small waves lifting and bumping it further up the beach.

They both got out and pulled the craft up well clear of high tide, then carried their gear bags into a small cave in the cliff face. Taking a handle each of the inflatable they jammed it high into the narrowing cave. Nikolas stood watching as the Brits paddled towards them. The submarine was now one thousand metres offshore and almost submerged. The shore crew manning the torch was in fact a young boy no more than twelve years old. He came up to Nikolas and shyly offered a greeting. The cliff face towered above, with a pronounced overhang, which proved fortunate.

Suddenly a powerful light from the clifftop switched on, illuminating the sea and the three Brits now fifty metres out from shore. Seconds later a burst from a large calibre machine gun ripped across the water and into the inflatable and its crew. One man appeared to be still alive and struggling in the water. Another short burst from above and the struggling stopped. Nikolas was stunned and dragged the boy back into the cave and stood beside Sam, looking at the area where the three commandos and their craft had been. The inflatable was nothing more than a shredded yellow mass of rubberised canvas, the men now lifeless bodies floating face down on the sea.

In the silence that followed Nikolas, Sam the Kiwi and the boy stood frozen to the spot.

"They must have only just arrived. I don't think they know we're here," Nikolas whispered finally, craning his head back to look upwards.

There was no sign of life out on the water and any attempt to recover three dead men would mean there would be five dead. Nikolas swallowed hard on a dry throat, closed his eyes and forced himself to think forward. They agreed to wait it out to see if there was any more action from the clifftop. Hardly daring to breathe and listening quietly they heard a cough followed by a short exchange in

German. Then silence. There were more voices, then the light was doused and they heard the sounds of gear being packed up. There was another exchange in what seemed to be an argument as to whether they should climb down to the beach to check if anyone else had survived. Then another louder voice sounding like the machine gunner defending the accuracy of his shooting.

Nikolas turned to Sam, "This is going to be our first bit of action. We're going to climb up and get those bastards."

He looked at the young boy, "You'd better be getting back to where you came from, but first show me the best way up to the top where the machine gun is."

The boy leaned slightly out from the cliff face and pointed to a fissure little wider than a man's body, then turned, and hugging the cliff jogged off along the narrow beach and disappeared around a headland. Nikolas watched him go then bent over and opened his gear bag. He handed a Sten gun, a few grenades and an automatic pistol to Sam, then grabbed the same for himself. They both slung the Sten guns over their shoulders, put a couple of magazines and grenades in a small pack and holstered the automatic pistols. Then they shoved the gear bags high into the cave.

With Nikolas leading, they walked the few metres to the fissure. It was steep with boulders jammed at intervals. It was going to be a tough climb until Nikolas realised there was a rope with knots every metre. The rope was new and had obviously been recently fitted. Using the rocks as steps they started off, feeling in the dark for their footing and resting every few metres so they weren't breathing too loud. After ten minutes, Nikolas, looking up, could see a small area of stars in a clear night sky. They rested again and listened. A low murmur of conversation wafted down the fissure. Nikolas looked back at Sam with a wicked grin and gestured upwards. They pressed on, the voices and occasional laughter growing louder as they got nearer to the top. They were now only three or four metres from the opening. Nikolas motioned to stop.

He edged forward another metre then stopped and listened again. He heard what sounded like water splashing on the rocks above, then he detected the unmistakeable smell of urine. Someone was relieving themselves, using the fissure as a latrine.

He pulled his knife out of a hip scabbard and gripping it between his teeth, crept slowly forward with Sam close behind. The urinating soldier let out a long sigh of relief followed by the now familiar hacking cough. Nikolas blessed him quietly, the cough gave him a good fix on where he was. The soldier stood fumbling with his fly and began another long coughing fit. The time was now. He looked back at Sam and nodded. He responded with a thumbs up and shifted his Sten gun around to his chest. Nikolas crept on.

The pitch of the track had lessened. Nikolas was now very close to him. He could see his dark shape only a couple of strides away and shifted the knife into his right hand. The soldier was back on, bending over with his hands on his knees, still coughing. Two quiet steps and Nikolas was right behind him. A large bush immediately in front hid them both.

He leant forward and grabbing the soldier by the collar, jerked his head back, exposing his throat. In the same motion, he reached around with his knife and delivered one swift stroke that finished him mid-cough. Nikolas dropped the knife then quickly covered the man's mouth with his hand and pushed his knee into his back, guiding him slowly to the ground. Still holding his hand tight on his mouth he knelt down beside him and hoarsely whispered in his ear as his life ebbed away…

"Alexis Katrakis is the name of my dead father – and they are the last words you will hear in this world – you Nazi bastard."

"Hey Hans, sounds like you really are dying from that cough," joked one of his companions.

"Get moving. I want out of this cold hole," came another voice.

Sam crouched beside him with one hand on the fallen soldier's neck, checking he was dead.

Nikolas picked up his knife, wiped it on his trousers and returned it to its scabbard. He loosened a grenade from his bag and closed in on the bush. Twenty metres away he could see a group of four soldiers sitting and passing around a bottle of wine.

"We'll toss a grenade each and then use the Sten guns, but have another grenade ready," Nikolas whispered.

Then the words came they didn't want to hear. "I'd better take a look at Hans, he's probably dead by now."

"Let's go now," Nikolas hissed as he pulled the pin on one short fuse grenade, and stepping out from the bush, tossed it in a high arc towards the group. Sam moved past him and did the same. Nikolas's grenade rolled to a stop and exploded instantly, blowing the standing soldier back into his friends. Nikolas pulled the Sten gun off his shoulder and fired a five second blast into the group.

Sam did the same, then they tossed another grenade each for good measure and watched the result.

There was no movement. They didn't want to waste ammunition so stopped firing and crept forward, Sten guns ready.

They walked amongst the mangled remains of their enemy. All lay dead or not quite, the arm of one soldier lying on his back slowly lifted from his side, his hand was only inches off the ground and gripping a Luger aimed at Nikolas's back. Sam saw it and stamped out suddenly with his foot, pinning both fist and pistol to the ground. He looked down into the hard eyes of a German stunned but otherwise uninjured. Sam stood over him and finished him with one bullet to his forehead.

"That's for the Brits," he said, adding to Nikolas, "You need eyes in the back of your head or you'll have a bullet instead."

Behind an outcrop of rocks and scrub five figures had crouched in shadow witnessing the execution of people rated as the most hated of all the invaders who'd arrived over thousands of years to their island. Their leader Christos, knew one of the pair as a young Cretan named Nikolas Katrakis, the person they were to make contact with. Christos and his group had arrived at the meeting point to find an elite squad of five German soldiers setting up a heavy machine gun. Luckily they'd seen the Germans arrive first on three motorcycles with side cars, the only way to travel on the narrow goat track. But they also saw they were totally outgunned, so could only keep their heads down as the machine gunner fired the ten second burst that killed the three British commandos. Unaware of the commandos or that Nikolas and Sam had already landed on the beach, the four watched and waited to see what eventuated.

Nikolas and Sam scouted around the dead soldiers collecting weapons and ammunition. Behind the scrub and rocks, Christos held a whispered discussion. After the agreement of his comrades, he stood in full view and called out a greeting in Cretan. Nikolas swung around knowing from his accent and language the man was bona fide. Nikolas answered in their own language and stood watching as Christos and his band walked warily over to greet them.

"You have struck a great blow for us and avenged the death of your father," Christos said as he embraced Nikolas who in turn introduced him to Sam. Nikolas then told him the short burst from the machine gun had accounted for three British commandos from his group. There were more introductions then Christos broke off and went to the machine gun. He ran his hand over the still warm metal. It was undamaged from the grenade and still carried the smell of cordite.

"This is a great prize. We'll take it to our village and get our people ready to fight the Germans and die from their own bullets."

The group quickly got into action. They detached the machine gun, folded the tripod and loaded it all into one of the side cars. The four men climbed two each into two of the sidecars, leaving one for Nikolas, Christos and Sam. They then returned and looked expectantly at Christos.

"Leave now for the village. You must come with us as you have quickly become a severely depleted force. I fear there must have been a security lapse," he said referencing the opportunist killing of the commandos before they'd put a foot on Crete soil.

"First Sam and I need to go down and pick up the packs we hid when we landed. " Nikolas said to Christos.

"I will escort you a quicker way down, then lead you to our village. My men here will head back with the captured machine gun, ammunition and tripod and whatever other weapons they can manage. Any surplus we will throw in the sea," he said. The four partisans got the message and immediately began stripping the dead soldiers of weapons. Those they couldn't carry they picked up and made for the cliff face.

"Wait, don't act in haste. I suggest we hide these weapons and send someone back for them." Christos nodded his head slowly. It did not come as a surprise that Nikolas, the firstborn son of Alexis Katrakis would deem it his place to speak wisely to an older man. The men looked over to Christos who merely nodded to them. They took the surplus weapons and pushed them under the low-lying scrub they had hid behind when observing the German machine gun crew. They then returned and kicking the motorcycles into life, slowly started off on their way back to the village.

"Come my friends. I will now show you the quick way to the beach where you landed."

With that, he marched off along the edge of the cliff and soon found what he was looking for. It was the entrance to a track heavily disguised by scrub. He stood at the entrance until Nikolas and Sam had caught up.

"We'll have to move quickly. I must return to my village as soon as possible," he said over his shoulder.

The men walked quickly down the track and located the stashed gear.

Each took a pack and set off back up the track. They loaded the gear in the remaining motorcycle and road slowly off. With Christos driving, they eventually could see the rest of the group a couple of hundred yards ahead, slowed by rocks on the track and loaded down with the precious spoils of battle. They were all heading for a village of half a dozen small cottages, remote and inaccessible, perched near the rugged coast with steep drop-offs to the Mediterranean. This aspect provided the best part of a tough deal to defend. After an hour negotiating the narrow track they found themselves closing in on the cottages. Nikolas was pleased by the difficult access and absence of roading beyond the narrow donkey tracks and the fact that the area was surrounded by rocky bluffs riddled with caves.

Chapter 19

The four men had arrived and unloaded the machine gun, ammunition and tripod and carried it all to a cave situated high overlooking the village. The men scrambled down the hill and joined Christos and his new allies in front of his house, the largest in the village.

"They may send planes to punish us and we may see troops if they aren't needed elsewhere," Christos addressed the group in front of his house. A few women dressed in black appeared and dished out some food and wine.

"We will have to be ready to take cover in the caves. We are doomed if we stay here too long."

Several other members of the village gathered around, more food arrived which embarrassed Nikolas as he knew from his own life in Crete that good food was scarce, none more so than since the Germans arrived and seized nearly all available. Nevertheless they sat in a circle as three woman dished up small helpings of a mix of herbs, lamb and goat. Christos finished his plate and stood and made a short speech in which he thanked Nikolas for returning to the fray and lavished appreciative words on Sam, the Kiwi from the other side of the world, risking life and limb in a fight that wasn't his. When he finished, the three woman stood and sang an ancient Cretan song familiar to Nikolas. The song spoke of heroism, love and loss from other times and other battles fought for their beloved island. The women cleared the few plates from the simple meal and the men gathered for a meeting called by Christos who stood in the centre of the group and began to speak.

"I have decided we need a change in strategy. The Germans have shown they can only think in straight lines, their assumption will be that the placement of the machine guns will be immediately above the village, the easiest position to accomplish. I say we place one Bren gun in the cave system on the eastern side of the village. Every man here knows and we can assume the Germans don't, that the cave system extends through multiple tunnels, some manmade but most formed by thousands of years of water erosion. We also know there is a spring-fed reservoir deep underground that will sustain us. This position will give us a chance to attack unexpectedly from the other side of the village. We will leave lamps on and cooking fires burning to lead them to believe we are at home. I have sent a runner to our neighbours in the south to see if they are able to provide reinforcements. They owe us a favour."

Christos stopped and looked expectantly at the group.

Nikolas stood up and looked silently at each of the men. Then he spoke, "I am Nikolas Katrakis, my father Alexis Katrakis was executed before me in the first wave of the German invasion. I agree with Christos, we will be outnumbered and in that situation must do what is not expected. I see in your leader a man of vision. He would not be your leader if he wasn't."

After another period of silence Christos spoke, "Alexis Katrakis was a respected man and loyal Cretan. We are fortunate you were spared Nikolas. Now they shoot the whole family and their neighbours if they are nearby," Christos said, then sat down.

An older man stood and began to speak, "My name is Adrianos. I am the oldest man in the village and four of my sons were killed by the evil invaders. You will need someone to attract them to the village that will expose them to your fire from the caves. I wish to be that person and have the opportunity to avenge the deaths of my sons. I will die, so be it. I will not die a happy man, but I will die satisfied being able to take many of these sons of Satan with me."

Christos stood again and asked for a volunteer to return to the coast and retrieve the weapons left behind. A man who rode one of the motorcycles to the village got up and headed over to the motorcycle. He kickstarted it, gave a wave and headed off along the narrow trail.

Christos beckoned to his second in command, a man called Sakis. Both went and squatted down beside Nikolas and Sam where they began a stocktake of all the weaponry available. Nikolas and Sam listed off their weapons, including plastic explosives and ammunition. Christos added this to the weapons known to be held by his men, plus whatever he thought might arrive back from the hidden stash.

Christos fell silent for a few minutes, "We need something extra, " he said and sat deep in thought, then with a smile, he turned to Nikolas, "We will use the plastic explosives you have and the expertise of one of our best men to even up the odds."

He turned and gave a short instruction in Cretan to Sakis who rose and walked over to a young man smoking a cigarette. The man listened to Sakis, and after finishing his cigarette went and joined Christos, Nikolas and Sam.

Christos introduced him as Kostas and explained that he had been trained in the use of explosives and small arms in covert, 'dirty tricks' operations by British Army personal in Athens just before they were kicked out of Greece by Hitler's troops sent to save Mussolini's reputation.

"Here's what I'm thinking. Kostas will place the plastic explosive in positions of his choosing in the rock face above the village. Adrianos will draw enemy fire for a short time, then we will pull him out. The enemy will approach the house assuming that Adrianos is dead. Bottles of wine and food will be left lying around as if we were surprised by their arrival. When a sufficient number of the enemy are in or around the house Kostas will explode the charges bringing down part of the rock face on the house and surrounding ground. We will be ready to mop up any survivors. Whether it works perfectly or not it will throw some heavy projectiles at them that should cause huge shock and plenty of panic. I will probably lose my house, but if the operation is successful we live to fight another day. I am now going to address the rest of the village."

Christos stepped up onto the front doorstep of his house. He raised both hands in the air to quieten the low murmur of the two dozen or so people gathered to be part of the biggest thing to happen in their lives.

"Here is what I believe will happen starting at dawn tomorrow. The enemy will probably send two or three fighter aircraft to strafe and bomb our village. I propose we defend against this attack with the captured heavy machine gun located in the caves up the hill behind my house. I don't want to give away our intentions of mounting a defence against their infantry from the eastern cave system. I want that to be a surprise. We need to be ready early tomorrow for that event." He turned to Kostas and grasped him by the shoulders.

"Kostas, you are young but this is your chance to show what you learned from the British in Athens. Go with Nikolas and Sam up behind the village and using Nikolas's plastic explosive place it in positions that will create large rock fragments to rain down on the enemy. It will be our heavy artillery bombardment."

He turned to Sakis, "Sakis, I want you to organise the German machine gun and two men to fire it to greet the aircraft we are expecting at dawn tomorrow. Also move supplies into the eastern caves to sustain all for two to three days."

The tiny village became a hive of activity as the total population of twenty people; men, women and children ferried food, clothing and basic cooking utensils up the steep hillside track to the eastern cave complex. Christos sat at his table, watching proceedings. In less than an hour Nikolas, Sam and Kostas had returned from planting the plastic explosive. Christos beckoned them over and the three sat down at the table. A young woman in black appeared at Christos's shoulder. She was carrying a bottle of wine and four glasses and set them down in front of the men, then went and stood near Nikolas. Christos looked up and spoke.

"Ah. I want you to meet Agapi, my daughter. She has recently become a widow."

Christos introduced her to Nikolas and Sam. He then pointed out the growing shortage of young males due to the high mortality rate of defending their homeland. Christos and his daughter looked directly at Nikolas, who now found himself returning the unwavering gaze of a young and beautiful Cretan woman. The point was blunt and not lost on Nikolas.

Christos returned to the present, "We must now finish this wine, our last bottle and possibly the last for some of us in this world, although I am sure there will be fruit of the vine in the next world. It would be a raw deal if there wasn't. And then, I strongly suggest we retire for the night to build strength and resolve for what tomorrow holds."

The four men drank the rest of their wine and went their own ways. Christos disappeared into his house and Nikolas and Sam headed towards a small unused cottage with two cots made up for them. Nikolas suddenly found the warm presence of Agapi beside him. She reached out and touched his arm. The touch turned into a firm grip and then an insistent pull to follow her. She led him past two houses and onto a worn track that wound its way up the hillside. Nikolas had no answer to her determination. Events of the last twenty four hours including the savage and sudden deaths of the British commandos and the deaths of their killers, all that, after several glasses of wine, had left him drained of any resistance to the female wiles of Agapi.

He followed her along the path for several minutes until they came to two large rocks that were part of the hillside and towered several metres above them. The path continued on but Agapi paused and turning sideways squeezed herself into the tight space between the rocks. She stood and waited. Nikolas halted at the narrow opening. A weak half-moon hanging over the nearby hills lit her face in a soft light. Her eyes glowed and beckoned him to follow. He followed. It was a squeeze for him too, but curiosity and desire drew him in. The gap opened into a small cave. Happily the moon shone a band of light that picked out a straw mattress and pillows plus a fat tallow candle that Agapi lit with a worn cigarette lighter that she returned to a nearby ledge.

Agapi lay back on the bed and looked at him. He realised they were in a 'lovers retreat' patronised by courting couples hiding away from snooping mothers or irate fathers. It is very likely that she and her late husband frequently slipped away to this scruffy but cosy cavern.

She maintained her unblinking stare as he stood beside her.

"I'll get straight to the point. I need a new husband. Crete needs new husbands to make new children ready for the day we are liberated."

He didn't have the words to respond but knelt beside her and put his hand on her head, stroking her thick black hair. She reached up and grasping his wrist pressed his hand onto her chest, then pushed it under her loose smock. He didn't resist and kept it there absorbing the warmth of the bare skin of her breast. After what felt like an eternity, Nikolas took his hand away and leant back against the wall of the cavern. He needed time to think. He looked back down at Agapi and cleared his throat.

"I need to tell you something. I'm already with someone who lives in Alexandria. She is waiting for me to return."

"Who is this someone?"

"A woman called Aiesha."

"Aiesha is an Arab name. You have taken up with an Arab woman?"

"She is not Arab, she is German."

"You're telling me you have committed yourself to an enemy of my people, your people, an enemy that killed my husband before we could even have children, and killed your father."

Agapi was now red faced and angry, with tears flowing down her cheeks.

Nikolas sat stunned and silent. He knew the reason he'd ended up in a tight spot in a little cave was the dangerous mix of his own desire and curiosity and the obvious sexual hunger of Agapi. The words he searched for weren't there until the obvious became obvious. He would simply tell her of the sad reality of Aiesha's life.

Agapi lay silent and listened to the story of Aiesha. While he spoke, Nikolas avoided her gaze by looking out at the half-moon, still sending soft light into the cave. He fell silent, then turned to Agapi. Her dark moist eyes looked back at him.

"Just hold me as tight as you can. That is all I want now." She reached up and pulled him back onto the rough bed.

Nikolas woke an hour later. Agapi stirred as he carefully released himself from her arms. He sat for a moment looking back at a beautiful face framed by long black hair and knew it was a choice that belonged to a different time and circumstance. He shook his head and rubbed his eyes.

The moon had moved on and was no longer lighting the cavern. He reached out and with one hand touching the wall he carefully made his way to the entrance. He looked back one more time then squeezed himself through the tight gap and out onto the path. He found the moon higher and brighter and showing the way back to the village. Time was getting short. He needed to get back to the cottage and catch another couple of hours sleep before they were hit with whatever the Nazis had in store. Sam was asleep when he opened the door to the disused cottage and he fell, still fully dressed, onto the bed and was soon sound asleep.

A panic attack nightmare with the sky full of ME 109 fighters and the village infested by scores of German infantry, caused Nikolas to sit bolt upright with sweat covering his face. In fact, he opened his eyes to early light of a beautiful day and the face of Christos with a wry half-smile poking through the door.

"Fortunately I can rely on my men and women of the village to be up and ready for what's coming."

Nikolas sheepishly stood up and gave Sam's shoulder a wakeup shake. They both grabbed their kit and followed Christos out onto what passed for a village square. By now, nearly all of the twenty or so men, women and children had vacated the village and were armed and hiding in the caves. That left Adrianos, who was holed up in the house closest to the only possible direction of the attack and armed with a Bren Gun and several grenades, courtesy of Nikolas and Sam. Agapi arrived on the scene and immediately confronted her father.

"I'm not letting you leave Adrianos alone to face the enemy."

"You have no say in the matter," he replied bluntly.

"We'll see about that."

On that note, she turned and strode off in the direction of the eastern cave complex.

With all their assets in place, Christos and Nikolas headed off to their vantage point in one of several caves between the eastern complex and the village. Sam climbed up behind the village, rejoining Kostas in getting ready to set off the charges intended to blow large fragments of rock onto the German troops once they were within range.

Two men manned the heavy machine gun seized from the coastal attack on the commandos. Their task was to try their damnedest to take down any aircraft approaching the village with murderous intent. Christos had calculated that their position in a cave directly above the village would be at approximately the same height as an aircraft intent on a bombing or strafing attack.

With a Bren gun in the house and one in the eastern cave complex, Christos was confident of success but unsure how many would survive. He also had the thought that putting up a fierce fight might discourage the Germans from spending more time, men and ammunition on such a small prize.

They all sat or stood in their positions waiting for what they knew was inevitable. The keenest ear heard it first before any eye saw it. A young man put his two fingers to his mouth and sent out a piercing high-pitched whistle. The sound bounced around the rocky bluffs and everyone from the youngest to the oldest heard several seconds later the raspy drone of the powerful V12 engines of two ME 109s. The men with the heavy machine gun visibly stiffened and began breathing deeply to alleviate tension. Within another thirty seconds, they could both see the large dots looking and sounding like angry bees, heading towards them at maximum speed. Both were confident of at least one kill given the aircraft were flying at a similar altitude to their position. The planes would not be a target that would shift greatly in their sights until the last second, when on releasing their payload, they would lift up into a steep climb to clear the bluffs above the village.

The men knew if they could get a lucky strike in the right place – a fuel line or tank – the outcome would be catastrophic for the enemy airmen. An automatic weapon not visible and situated at a similar height to them would be a total surprise to the two pilots. The men both knew they would only get one chance. If they missed, the pilots would circle back around and direct cannon fire at their position.

Christos and Nikolas were both armed with Sten guns plus an automatic pistol. Each sported a small pack which carried six short-fuse grenades. They were ready and confident. Nikolas produced a pair of binoculars and began scanning the ground forward of the village. They both agreed that the troops would hang back and wait and see if the aircover could do the job for them. And sure enough, Nikolas sighted the helmets of German troops with heads down, ducking behind rocky outcrops or anything else that would stop a bullet. He handed the binoculars to Christos who counted twenty enemy that he could see with probably another ten that he couldn't. At approximately eight hundred metres away, they were out of range of anything except a sharp shooter with a sniper rifle.

By now, the two aircraft had settled at an altitude that with minor adjustment would take them on a course to blow the village and their occupants into oblivion, if they were there. At a range of four hundred metres, the two pilots were preparing to release their bombs. Christos and Nikolas had briefed the machine gun crews on the correct time to fire. Within five seconds, they were right on cue. As the pilot of the leading aircraft reached for the release lever, the big machine gun hidden in the cave opened up. It wasn't point blank but with the aircraft locked in the sights and the pilot unwittingly looking straight down the barrel of Germany's biggest and best it was as good as.

By the time the pilot had a hand hovering over the lever, the aircraft had taken ten rounds of the twenty fired. Two rounds had smashed through the cockpit, killing him instantly. The aircraft continued on at four hundred kilometres per hour towards the cave. The two men had a second and a half to decide they'd done their bit and they both leapt backwards as one, just before the aircraft hit the cliff face. The impact bounced both men off the ceiling and they fell bloodied but alive on the cave floor. The unreleased bomb blew on impact sending a further shockwave and rock laden blast into the aircraft following. With engine screaming at full throttle, the pilot fought to control his runaway machine and clear the rocky crags.

He was successful but was trying to gain control of a heavily damaged aircraft that wasn't responding to the controls. The plane was now over the sea and heading down. With no way of changing the outcome, his only option was to bail out. Miraculously he did and watched wide-eyed in shock as he followed his beautiful aeroplane down into the sea.

Christos, Nikolas and the rest of the village that had a view of the action were stunned, excited and pleased all at the same time. To retain the element of surprise Christos had cautioned everyone to remain hidden as long as possible. Obviously the German troops who witnessed the demise of one of their aircraft and the probable demise of the other would now know that the job was theirs alone.

"Planes are scarce and are needed elsewhere so it's unlikely more will turn up. We are a small prize for them to lose two aircraft. They will seek their revenge with their troops who are far more expendable than aircraft," Christos said as he checked troop movements with the binoculars. He glanced back at Nikolas who simply nodded in agreement.

"Better take a look," Christos said and handed the binoculars over to Nikolas.

The score sheet was looking good for the early skirmish but both men knew that the troops would be angry but careful about falling into any more deadly traps. The binoculars showed troops were on the move, using whatever cover and protection they could find.

"Stay here. I'm going up to Sam and Kostas. With a bit of good luck hitting them with half a cliff face might be the winning blow," Christos said and headed off through the back of the cave and an exit that delivered him close to Sam and Kostas's position.

Nikolas watched him go then went back to observing with the binoculars. He could now hear Adrianos firing from the house to attract the German troops towards the village. Nikolas was sweeping the binoculars over the scene and suddenly stopped and let fly with an expletive. He could see a young woman carrying a Sten gun, making a crouching run towards the back of the house, the house that held Adrianos, the decoy. Nikolas squinted through the binoculars again and confirmed the woman was Agapi and watched as she arrived at the door, opened it and stepped inside.

Nikolas looked again praying that Agapi would suddenly appear. He was met only by the image of the closed door. Nikolas looked around hoping Christos would return. He realised there was no answer other than the one right in front of him. He grabbed a Sten gun and the pack with several grenades inside. The last thing he did was shove his automatic pistol in his belt. He was now ready for the rescue. A quick recce of the situation showed German troops steadily and carefully making ground on the house. He had to move now, right now if he was going to be any help. He rechecked the approach to the back of the house and calculated he needed about ten minutes to get where he wanted to be before any troops were in position to pose a threat.

He slung the Sten gun over his shoulder and exited the cave. A rough track with a naturally formed wall augmented by a stretch that was man-made, led steeply down to an area of flat ground near the back of the house. He moved fast, bending over to avoid being spotted and arriving at ground level, stopped behind a large rock to make sure he wasn't a target of an early arriving German. The ground was clear so he sprinted the last twenty metres to the recessed door. His pulse raced as he stood with Sten gun ready while he checked no enemy was about to grab an opportunity to rush the door as he opened it. Not wanting to be a victim of friendly fire, he sent out the familiar short sharp whistle then slowly and carefully opened the door. Agapi and Adrianos both heard it, but were standing, guns ready, in case any smart German had caught onto the ruse. When they saw who it was, their faces showed relief.

Agapi was partially obscured by a freestanding wardrobe, crouching below window height with her Sten gun. Adrianos stood behind a heavy table loaded with sand bags. The window had been smashed out and the Bren gun sat neatly between the two piles of bags. He was facing towards an enemy more content to wait him out rather than die pointlessly. The destruction of the aircraft told them that people were here that included skilled and experienced soldiers. The elimination of the machinegun crew at the coast showed they wouldn't be a pushover. He kept looking out the window and fired a volley to keep them interested. He then turned to Nikolas.

"Why are you here? No, don't answer. You are here to drag this nuisance of a girl back to where she belongs by her father's side. He must be furious and very worried."

"Yes, you're right but I think time is short for getting out of here."

They both stood staring at each other until they were suddenly interrupted by the door smashing open and a huge German soldier bursting in. He swung his gun around towards Nikolas, but Agapi was quicker. She dived sideways and sprayed the soldier with a short burst from her Sten gun. He fell backwards firing into the ceiling and then lurched forward. Nikolas struggled to get his weapon quickly off his shoulder but was too late to save Agapi who took two shots from the German who was on his knees and dying. Nikolas fired a burst into his chest and head to make sure then raced to help Agapi, lying face down on the floor. He knelt beside her and lifted her up. Her face was white and her breathing coming in short gasps. She struggled to speak and finally choked out one sentence.

"I pray your German woman is a good person, …you owe me. She and you must return to Crete and help rebuild lives here for me and the child I never had."

Agapi drifted into a coma moments later and lay in his arms while Adrianos was having to concentrate on keeping German troops from trying to kill anyone else. Nikolas laid her on the floor and searched for the wounds that were leaving a growing pool of blood on the floor. He had to make a quick decision. Medical supplies were at the cave. There was nothing Nikolas could do but get her back up to the cave fast. He went to Adrianos and stood shouting at him above the racket of the Bren gun.

"I'm getting Agapi back to the cave, you need to get out as soon as you can. The whole cliff face is going to come down."

"I know. Christos has told me to leave when I'd heard three rifle shots and then one shot. I don't plan to stay and die under a heap of rubble if I don't have to."

"I wish Agapi had known that."

"If Agapi dies, Christos will be sad for the rest of his days," was all Adrianos could say.

"Agapi is losing blood, she needs attention urgently. I'm taking her now. Give me covering fire while I'm getting her to the big rocks, then you follow."

Nikolas went over to Agapi and lifted her onto his left shoulder. He then picked up his Sten gun and headed for the door. He opened it and looked back at Adrianos who waved impatiently for him to go. Nikolas stuck his head through the door. He looked back once more at the staunch figure of the old man, then made a bolt for the cover of the rocks near the cliff face. He could hear a nonstop volley from Adrianos and muttered a short prayer for his survival. The covering fire kept German heads down and with adrenaline running hot and legs pumping he carried Agapi as quickly as he could up the walled track to the cave he'd left only fifteen minutes ago. At the entrance, he stopped then staggered inside, legs burning from the stiff climb. He put her carefully down on a blanket and stood up. He opened a pack and pulled out a length of bandage. Agapi was bleeding heavily from flesh wounds to her shoulder and arm. He bound both wounds tightly and saw that the bleeding had stopped.

Chapter 20

Christos was still with Sam and Kostas overseeing the operation to drop the cliff face onto the German soldiers. He went to the mouth of the cave and took a quick look with the binoculars. Adrianos had stopped firing his Bren gun and all Nikolas could hope for was that he had made it out. The binoculars showed that the Germans were now well advanced on the houses.

Nikolas turned and checked Agapi then returned to the mouth of the cave with his binoculars. He heard the three rifle shots then a pause followed by a single shot. He watched and waited for five minutes then felt a rumble roll through the cave like a powerful earthquake he'd once experienced in Greece. It was followed by a deafening roar and he watched as the hillside to his left erupted up and outwards, breaking into large fragments that fell onto the houses scattering the German troops in all directions. Many had been hit and injured and lay where they fell. The Bren gun from the other cave opened up from an angle the German soldiers weren't expecting, dropping several as they ran. Those still mobile were reduced to a chaotic retreat. Five blasts were staggered individually so the enemy never knew when or where the next would come from.

Nikolas was undecided as what to do next. The first priority was Agapi. He would wait here until Christos returned and explain what happened. Christos would be furious that she almost ruined everything. He would stay and smooth things over. He went back to the front of the cave and looked out at an operation that was going surprisingly well. He was learning that the German soldier, fit, well trained and equipped with the very best weaponry had one flaw. Many had fervently believed Hitler's declaration they were a race superior to all others and therefore expected all resistance to crumble when faced by German aggression. As a modern invader of an island set upon by countless foes over the centuries German soldiers were told they would be welcomed as liberating heroes. The relentless determination to resist aided by British, Australian and New Zealand troops including the fearsome Māori Battalion was not what they expected.

The German troops were now in a full, ragged retreat. The 'bombardment' by rocks, big and small had shocked and unnerved them and they were unsure whether it was all over. The Bren gun attack from the eastern caves had exposed them from an unexpected quarter and they could no longer rely on air support.

A firm hand lay on his shoulder and Nikolas turned to find Christos's face inches away from him. Nikolas started to say something but Christos put his hand up.

"Don't say anything. I know what happened. Adrianos made it back to us just before we made the sky fall on the Germans, he told me everything. As soon as we are sure the last of the Germans have gone we'll put a small party in to check the village and look for booby traps, although I don't believe they would have had time to lay any. The women and children will have to stay a few more nights in the caves. Now about Agapi, while you were looking at the routing of the Germans I had my medical man take a look at her. I am told that her upper arm is broken by the impact of the bullet and that she needs to be taken off the island to Alexandria for treatment, with you."

"Me?"

"Yes, a fishing boat will pick you and Agapi up and take you to Alexandria. She will get the best treatment with you going along. You had the misfortune to lose three of your party before they set foot on Crete. You've done enough here. We believe the Germans know you are here and have worked out who you are. They recognise you as the son of an important man that they executed and they are keen to do the same to you. You are a heroic figure and that is a problem to them and now for us. There is a price on your head and you are too dangerous to have around any longer. They will be back to even up the score. I'm not asking you to go. I'm telling you as head of this village, go back to Alexandria. The Germans will know when you are back by the same way they knew when you arrived. Sam will stay here in your place."

"How am I and Agapi going to get all the way to Alexandria by fishing boat?"

"My radio operator has made contact with the Royal Navy and the same submarine under the same commander that brought you here, will take you back. The fishing boat will pick you and Agapi up from the beach you were landed on and take you both to meet it tonight, which is not a moment too soon. You will go to the coast as soon as it is dark on one of the motorcycle sidecars. We kept both in a secure hiding place away from where the rockfall was happening. You have about one hour to get ready. By the way, the man taking you is the person who retrieved the arms from the coast."

Nikolas and Agapi, carrying with her a large pack of painkillers, made it to the coast in one of the sidecars. The rider helped Nikolas manoeuvre Agapi down the track and onto the beach. Nikolas found the narrow cave where the inflatable was hidden and dragged it out. It was still buoyant having lost only a small amount of air. The rider had now done all he could so bade them farewell and good luck.

Nikolas sat on the round side of the inflatable with Agapi lying inside it semi-conscious under a heavy dose of painkillers. After half an hour, the fishing boat they were expecting chugged slowly around the northern headland and glided up towards their torchlight. It came to a reluctant halt when the Captain put the diesel motor into reverse and it sat rocking back and forth on its own wash. Nikolas gently tapped Agapi on her good arm and lifted her out of the inflatable. He pushed it into the water and held it while she climbed awkwardly onboard the fishing boat.

There was no moon so the master of the boat had to rely on compass bearings to arrive where the submarine was expected to surface. After ten minutes of steady progress from Crete, he throttled back to a slow crawl. The exhaust burbled and spluttered as the craft lifted and dropped on gentle swells. A sea mist arrived and with it the worry they were not going to make the connection. The master turned the motor off and they drifted slowly to a stop and sat in total silence.

"We may hear them before we see them," he said quietly and everyone sat straining ears and eyes through the mist.

"Aha," he said suddenly…he had picked up the light metal on metal sound of someone tapping a wrench on the conning tower. They then spotted a small prick of light filtered by the mist. The Master pushed start and the little boat crept forward towards it and the now familiar black hull of the submarine suddenly loomed up out of the mist. A large torch was played on them from the conning tower and several crewmen climbed onto the deck and stepped carefully towards the stern. A crewman from the fishing boat threw a line towards the submarine. A seaman grabbed it and looped it around a mooring cleat. Once secured the fishing boat crewman threw another line secured to their stern. The boat was now pulled around parallel to the submarine and secured.

It was the best that could be done given the problem of transferring Agapi onto the submarine. Three able seamen stood nearby while Nikolas lifted Agapi over the side and into the strong arms of the Royal Navy.

The last Nikolas saw of Agapi was when both were delivered to Army Headquarters in Alexandria and he watched as she was wheeled out through the door and taken by army ambulance to the local hospital. Nikolas sat both exhausted and relieved at the same time. The army wanted to debrief him as soon as possible but decided he would be better value after a good night's sleep. They would let him talk until he seemed to have nothing left to offer. Then questions would be asked that they already had answers to. Their aim was to see if he was accurate or could be prodded into revealing something he'd forgotten.

Nikolas woke finally to a late morning sun shining through a poky window speckled with fly dirt. He closed his eyes again while collecting his thoughts. He was not focused on the upcoming debrief, just Aiesha. He had been in survival mode in Crete and found thinking about her was a distraction and a possible threat to his survival. The fact he remained faithful in the cave with Agapi…with the moon lighting a beautiful face, was persuasively making her case… meant he could restart a new life guilt free, with Aiesha.

There was a knock on the door and an orderly brought in a cup of tea. He set it down and left with the message that Nikolas was expected at a debriefing at ten am, in thirty minutes time. The place was the meeting room where the pre-mission briefing happened a few days ago.

Nikolas sat and talked for thirty minutes solid in detail. He was then questioned closely regarding the early deaths of the British Commandos. HQ staff expected hard questions from the British on the disastrous start that cost the lives of three highly trained and valuable soldiers. There was already a discreet probe into just who or what was responsible for such a damaging lapse in security. One lone officer was asking the questions and Nikolas wondered if the investigation was focusing on headquarters staff. Maybe there had been the old 'honey trap' or a bit of loose pillow talk.

His job was done for the time being. He was being returned to the safe house and Aiesha. Before he left, the debriefing officer advised him to keep his ears open and his mouth shut and stick around as he might be needed for more questions.

"Oh, one last thing." He reached into his pocket and took out a fat envelope and slid it over the desk to him. "Just a little back pay." He picked it up and slipped it into his back pocket. The army had obviously appreciated the damage done on their behalf.

He picked up his gear bag and walked out to the waiting staff car. He'd been away less than a week but was surprised to feel uneasy returning to Aiesha. He suddenly realised the near miss he'd had with Agapi who put a small grain of doubt in his mind about the wisdom of his relationship with Aiesha. The easy familiarity with a person of the same nationality edged into his thinking about Aiesha and himself.

With this occupying him, he decided he would sit, enjoy the ride and let the future happen. The car pulled up in front of the safe house and Nikolas swung his gear bag out and walked up to the door. Aiesha had seen him arrive and loss of her family fifteen months ago had left her raw to the threat of another loss. Relief surged through her as she opened the door to a face that seemed to have aged six years, not just six days. Death and injury had come to comrades as well as the enemy in his gunsight and the arc of his army issue knife and throwing arm. Aiesha, now recovered from the stress of her deadly conflict with Conrad, turned her focus to Nikolas that somehow she felt was carrying a burden that was too heavy.

He followed her into the house and they sat opposite each other. Nikolas leant his head back in the large easy chair, staring at the ceiling in a sombre mood. Aiesha sat for a while going with the flow, then abruptly rose and went to the door of her room. She stood for a few seconds then opened it and went inside. She lay on the bed looking out at the last of the sun touching the roofs of Alexandria and sparkling off the Mediterranean in the distance, then slowly drifted off to sleep. She felt the bed move a little and then the warm weight of his body sink it further as he lowered himself down beside her.

"I didn't hear you come in," she said.

"I took my shoes off."

"So you are just wearing socks?"

"Yes."

"Well, take those off as well. It's bad form to wear socks in bed. How many died?" She asked suddenly.

"Three British commandoes, and two, maybe three villagers."

They both lay back watching the sun surrender the roofs to shadows deepening over the city.

It was at three in the morning that Aiesha stumbled on the ghost that was haunting Nikolas. He was asleep but suddenly sat up in bed, speaking incoherently. His eyes were closed and sweat beaded on his forehead. After ten minutes, he went quiet and just as suddenly fell back on the bed. The only words she recognised were, 'don't kneel, don't kneel down'. The words were obviously significant but she couldn't understand why and lay awake for a long time staring at the ornate ceiling as if it held some clue.

The next morning Aiesha was up before Nikolas. She went into the kitchen and fixed real coffee and a favourite Arab dish of fava beans cooked with onion, garlic, tomato and spices, then garnished with spring onion and parsley and seasoned with salt and pepper. The final touch was aish baladi bread pockets, the 'people's bread,' a staple of every Arab meal and freshly baked locally in the early hours of the morning. She carried it to the bedroom on a tray that she set on a table near the large window. Nikolas finally woke to the combined aromas of fresh coffee and the mouth-watering breakfast. He climbed out of bed, stretched once and yawned. He gave Aiesha a little smile, then sitting down, poured himself a coffee and set to work on the exotic, but simple meal. Aiesha watched him carefully. She didn't want to spoil it for him but she was desperately curious about his nocturnal outburst. She had finished eating so went and sat by the window. When he'd finished, he came and sat beside her.

"Don't kneel, don't kneel down." Aiesha said looking at him as she repeated what she'd heard the night before. Nikolas looked up and stared at her.

"What are you talking about?"

"I'm telling you what you said in your sleep last night. I spent a long time lying awake trying to figure it out."

Nikolas sat with his coffee in hand, staring into it. He finally took a mouthful then finished the lot in one gulp.

"I know what it was about, but I need to give it some thought before I tell you about it."

"Why can't you tell me now?"

"Alright, I'll tell you what happened. A German platoon came to our village looking for men who were part of an attack on soldiers celebrating with wine and food taken from local Cretans. A group of five men, including my father, planned and executed a successful raid, killing several soldiers including a high ranking officer. Their orders were to detain, interrogate and execute any man unable to prove they were not present at the attack. The commanding officer went through this process which was largely a charade. They were there to execute someone anyway. It was decided that my father was complicit and would be shot and was ordered to kneel with his back to the officer. He said to them, 'I refuse to kneel before illegal invaders of my country.'"

"Refuse to kneel and I will have your eldest son shot as well."

"My father stared at me then turned around and slowly put one knee on the ground. I couldn't stand the sight of my father kneeling for those bastards and jumped forward to stop him. Two soldiers put my arms up my back and one grabbed me around my neck and pulled me away. I was beaten and kicked and left lying where I fell. I turned my head to see him with both knees on the ground. I looked away and as I did I heard one shot and then another. They must have decided he was worth two bullets."

"Oh my God," she said behind both hands cupped in front of her face. She turned to look at him with tears welling up and running down her cheeks.

"Well, you lost your husband and your children as well," he said so softly she could barely hear him.

"I know. I know it was the way your father died that made me think of it."

Unable to stand the pain on his face any longer, she took her coffee to the seat by the window and sat staring across the Mediterranean. She sat for almost a quarter of an hour with the now empty cup beside her on the floor. Nikolas came to her from behind and put his warm hands on her neck, slowly moving both to her shoulders and then down along her bare arms. He returned to where he started and repeated the soothing massage until the sun had left the rooftops and climbed high in the sky.

Nikolas was left for a week to his own devices by Army Headquarters while he and Aiesha spent the time planning a future. Nikolas was still intrigued by the thoughts of going to New Zealand, whereas Alan had told him a strong, energetic and ambitious man could own some land and spend a lifetime working it and making a good living. The army broke their silence when one day an officer dropped by to say, 'Thank you very much for your services and by the way the war was now in its final stages'. He told them that New Zealand troops were closing on Trieste and the German presence in Italy was being reduced by a steady drain of deserters with only the hardest and most dedicated remaining.

Next morning Nikolas lay alongside Aiesha, daydreaming about New Zealand while trying to visualise a place with less than two million people, where nearly the whole country was lush green and with friendly, big brother Australia, just across the Tasman. Aiesha was not entirely with Nikolas on all this and Nikolas was puzzled that her early warmth to the idea seemed to have cooled a little. He pushed the question but she became irritated and clammed up.

Several weeks later, the same officer reappeared bringing good news. The first was that aside from the Japanese, the war was as good as over. Isolated pockets were still resisting the inevitable in Italy but most troops from Australia and New Zealand were moving eagerly towards their nearest embarkation point to head for home. Nikolas was told that the war in Crete was also over. The novel and exciting pull of New Zealand was strong, but not as much as the sudden need to get home to Crete, see his family and help where he could, given there was no man in the house.

The next day Nikolas tidied himself up, kissed Aiesha on the cheek then set off for Army Headquarters to speak to staff charged with the movement of troops returning to their home countries. He fronted up to the gates and handed his pass through the portal to the sentry. After a minute, the pass was returned and the small pedestrian gate opened to let him in. He presented at reception and his request was passed on to a short, harassed looking officer who bustled up to the counter. He greeted Nikolas with one simple sentence, "So you want to return to Crete?"

"Yes," Nikolas replied.

"Right, with the cessation of hostilities we now have various people going to Crete tidying things up, tracking missing people, checking for booby traps and land mines. In fact, large areas need to be totally rebuilt now that those bloody Germans have gone." He paused, took a deep breath and continued, "Where do you want to go?"

"Safika, my mother, if she is still alive, lives in a cottage in the White Mountains which is where my father was executed."

The officer's attitude softened slightly.

"You can go on the next sailing. It departs Alexandria in two days' time, at seven o'clock in the morning. If you will please take a seat, I will have the documents prepared to allow you on board."

Nikolas returned to the safe house with his documentation and told Aiesha the news. She looked serious then spoke slowly and carefully.

"You have made your decision on your future so here is mine, I am returning to Germany to try and find what relatives I have left and whether any of my husband's relatives are still alive."

Two days later, Nikolas rose at six o'clock and folded the few garments he owned then packed them into a small bag. He went into the bedroom and looked down at the sleeping form of Aiesha. A portion of hair lay over her eyes. He moved it carefully to reveal the face of the person he knew he would love for the rest of his life. He bent over and kissed her softly, then stood up and turned to go. She half opened sleepy eyes and turned her head to look up at him.

"I said you'd come back, what I didn't say was that you would leave. That was something I didn't know." She watched him go through the door then closed her eyes and drifted back to sleep. The last memory of Aiesha that Nikolas took with him was the perfume she always wore.

Chapter 21

Nikolas found his way to Crete and was reunited with his family. He was quietly relieved to greet his mother and sat in the small cottage telling her of the last months of his life. She spoke of his father and his quiet courage. There were long silences which seemed to communicate as much as the words spoken. He spent several months at the cottage where he worked on repairs and on the small plot of land.

He was in the middle of rebuilding a drystone wall for keeping sheep and stood up to take a drink of water. He was tipping cool water down his throat when he heard the sound of heavy boots approaching on the narrow road. He put the water bottle down and looked up. A short distance away a small group of young men and women were heading up a steep section of the road towards him. He leaned back against the wall and watched as they approached. A few minutes later they were standing in front of him. A young woman produced a piece of typed paper with an official logo at the top. She handed it to him and stepped back. It was a message written in Cretan and English. Nikolas read both.

The note introduced the group and explained that they were young Germans who had come to Crete to help rebuild the damage created by their army. When she could see he had read the message, the young woman asked if there was work they could do here. Still slightly astonished at their boldness showing up in Crete so soon after the war was over, he gestured to the stone wall lying in pieces. They immediately put down their packs and began working. Nikolas went back to the house and told his mother.

"If they are staying they can sleep in the small barn," was all she said and went on with cooking the evening meal. She added some extra precious smoked lamb and some herbs and plants she gathered from the hills around the cottage. The young people stayed for three days keeping a respectful distance from Nikolas's mother, then moved on.

The show was over and his mates gave him a whistle as they were leaving. He slammed his empty down and hurried after them. He didn't want a long walk back to base and end up on a charge.

After their R & R Alan and his old mate Evan were back in their 22nd Battalion and seeing patches of action more frustrating than anything else. Evan was a medic and joined Alan on several weeks of manoeuvres, thrusts and counter thrusts that ceded then regained ground only to lose it again to the desert fox, Field Marshal Rommel.

This changed when the 22nd Battalion along with the 18th, 19th and 20th Battalions were involved in a night attack on Ruweisat Ridge, a forty foot high escarpment held by the enemy, looking out over the Alamein battle field.

The Kiwi Battalions caught the German defences napping with the speed and ferocity of their attack and forced a retreat. Alan's 22nd Battalion reached their designated position at the base of the ridge and dug in as best they could to wait the next couple of hours until daybreak and the tank support promised.

Alan stood and searched in vain but the beautiful glow of predawn light brought only an ugly and brutal truth. The tanks promised to the infantry once they had established their positions failed to show. Instead German tanks were clanking and rattling towards them with machine guns flicking off rounds at anyone silly enough to stick their head up. The result was the capture of virtually the whole of the 22nd Battalion. Having nothing to worry a full size tank with other than standard issue rifles, the soldiers could do little else but surrender. Alan, making sure no one had the rash desire to be a dead hero, stood up, put his hands in the air and the others in his platoon followed suit. They were rounded up, searched for arms and were then sent on a twenty four kilometre march that started out under a fierce midday sun. After reaching a plateau, they were left to stand in baking heat without food or water. Alan knew the purpose of this was to take the fight or flight out of them, making them easier to handle and easier to keep where they were meant to be.

After several days, a German supply column of lorries arrived to transfer the prisoners en masse to an ex British prisoner of war cage at Daba. Here Alan and other officers endured rough handling and threats of execution while being questioned by German interrogators, payback for what the Germans regarded as an excessive use of force by New Zealand troops encircled at Minqar Qaim near Mersa Matruh. There, New Zealanders had fixed bayonets and escaped during a surprise night attack through German lines. In the process, many German troops were shot or bayoneted.

As payback New Zealand troops were regularly subjected to ill-treatment and their supply of food and water reduced to starvation levels. Alan and his troops sweated during the day and froze at night when the furnace-like daytime temperature plunged to near freezing and spent several days in the cage before being loaded onto trucks and driven to the Port of Benghazi. They then boarded a cargo ship recently converted for troops and then assigned to prisoner transport.

Destined ultimately to arrive at the Port of Taranto in Italy, the rusting vessel eventually eased out of Benghazi Port, tightly packed with prisoners, and set a course to take them first to the Port of Piraeus in Greece through the Corinth Canal to Patras, and then across the Adriatic to the Port of Taranto in the boot of Italy. Alan and his troops were still being routinely starved of even the most basic provisions of food and water, a continuation of the strategy to take away whatever fight or flight the Kiwi troops still possessed. Alan wondered what Polish civilians would feel about the German's sensitivity to 'unfair tactics', but he kept this to himself and instead tried to negotiate for his troops the best possible treatment from their German and Italian captors.

The less direct course to Taranto was designed to reduce exposure to attack from allied aircraft and being sunk by friendly fire. The troops had now settled into the stifling heat and cramped conditions of the ship's hold containing a stomach-turning stench of ancient bilge water and engine oil. The voyage was gross but uneventful and after briefly stopping over at Piraeus they negotiated the Corinth Canal, bypassed Patras and then birthed at Taranto four days later. All troops on board were unloaded down one gangway and directed into a holding pen by a couple of loud obnoxious guards. They were stripped naked, deloused by chemical spray followed by a washdown with high pressure hoses, then dressed in prison fatigues. They lined up for a meal of leftover scraps that surprisingly included meat and vegetables boiled up into thick grey soup. It was the first food that faintly resembled a normal meal and was eagerly eaten as if it was a gourmet meal. Alan, accustomed to large meals on the farm even managed to get a second helping.

Alan's medic friend Evan was soon aware there was something wrong with Alan that was beyond what the other troops were suffering. Evan checked him out as well as he could and decided it was likely Alan had a condition he had some awareness of but was not widely known to the general medical community.

Evan in his last year of medical school in Dunedin, New Zealand, had spent a two week holiday on a sheep farm in North Otago with his uncle, Bruce Radcliff, who owned the farm and lived there with his family. His uncle had his own medical studies cut short by call up for the First World War where he served as a medic.

As a once aspiring doctor he was naturally interested in Evan's career and one night after supper began relating some of the medical problems he encountered of soldiers being confined for long periods on extremely low rations. He told Evan that at the end of the war there had been many cases of unexplained illnesses when severely malnourished prisoners were fed large amounts of food by well-meaning people eager to provide the necessities the men had been missing. Several deaths had been documented.

His uncle went on to say that he intervened and took charge of the treatment of a group of ex-prisoners. He told Evan that without knowing the medical reasons why, it was apparent that the sudden ingestion of large amounts of food was causing much more serious health issues than a little indigestion. This adverse reaction was common to nearly all ex-prisoners. Common sense suggested much smaller portions or even a weak soup option was preferable. This meant that Evan was going to have to watch Alan's back through the slow train journey to Campo 51 transit prison camp, a few kilometres northwest of Altamura, approximately seventy kilometres north of Taranto.

Alan was in a confused state, slow moving, breathless and weak. Evan knew he would need to work hard to camouflage Alan's illness in case German authorities decided he was more a liability than an asset for the labour camp they were destined for, a conclusion that in a fascist state could mean one thing, a quick and brutal end for Alan.

With these thoughts, Evan manoeuvred Alan into a quiet part of a big group of men sitting around having a smoke and a yarn. He sat down beside Alan and began in a serious tone to address the issue he saw in front of them both.

"Alan, listen very carefully to what I am saying. You are quite ill and suffering from the effects of eating too much food, too quickly after a long period of starvation. You must from now on eat only thin watery soup and clean water. When they load us onto the train, I will mix you in with a mob of men and help you get on board. Don't look at any of the guards. Although fortunately these ones seem a more affable bunch." Alan nodded slowly.

After the meal, the troops were lined up for the short march across marshalling yards to a waiting prison train. Alan's platoon were now part of a body of one hundred plus men in the bag as a result of bad communication of the allied commanders and quick actions on the part of the Afrika Corps. A mix of German and Italian guards marched alongside them, rifles and automatic weapons at the ready. The pace was a slow stumble over the several dozen railway tracks, but fifteen minutes later they were standing beside a line of eight boxcars. A couple of railway workers walked beside the train, pulling back the sliding doors. Evan and a slow moving Alan waited until half of his platoon were on board and inserted themselves into the crowd. A couple of their men quickly pulled a weak Alan up while avoiding the eyes of the guards.

Alan and Evan grabbed a corner and gratefully lay back on several inches of hay. After an hour of loud German and Italian commands to hurry up, all prisoners were on board. A period of silence was followed by a loud whistle, a blast of steam and the train slowly chugged away, jolting and rattling over tracks and points, destined to arrive after many delays and stoppages at Campo 51, the transit camp near Altamura.

Several hours at the same steady plod and Evan had no idea where they were but worked out that they were probably due for a food and water stop. This did happen eventually but with Alan now lying in a barely conscious state. Evan stood up as the train, with brakes squealing, came to a halt.

After a few minutes, the door was drawn carefully back a couple of feet by the guards. A large container of water was heaved up single-handed by the biggest man Evan had ever seen. The water was followed by a wooden crate of two day-old bread. The same Italian guard looked up at Evan and shot him a huge wink and even bigger smile. Evan's heart lifted.

Obviously not all Italians were inevitably on side with their German allies. Evan took over dealing out the water and bread to the troops. Their exhaustion from limited food supply had the one advantage of minimising what would have otherwise been a mad scramble and fight for bread and water. He eventually took a mug of water over to Alan who was lying propped up against the wall. He put the mug to Alan's lips and tipped it carefully back. When Alan had swallowed a small amount, Evan handed him a piece of bread. Alan took one bite and swallowed it down with a mouthful of water.

"That's all you're getting for now mate," Evan said.

They settled back, a guard slid the door closed, and after a short spell the train gave a jolt forward, a blast on the whistle and they were on their way. Evan and Alan both slept fitfully and woke an hour later to realise the train had stopped. They remained that way for an hour and could hear the voices of guards and railway staff. Evan had picked up a little Italian and gathered that they were waiting on a siding for another train to pass. Another hour passed and then the rumble and noise of the other train passing filled the boxcar. Silence followed until their train started moving forward and clattered over the points, then back onto the main line to resume the journey on to Campo 51.

Campo 51 was a new camp five kilometres northwest of Altamura. When the prisoners arrived, they found the camp in a semi-advanced stage of completion. It sat on a large area of flat, stony and dry ground. Almond trees grew in one small area. Accommodation consisted of simple bivouacs that were common to transit camps throughout Italy and the only option for more than a thousand men.

Food provided was vastly better than what they had experienced so far as prisoners of war. Vegetables, cheese, bread and clean drinking water were routinely provided. However, under Evan's careful watch, Alan was prevented from eating anything more substantial than a very thin and watery soup made from the vegetables. Evan made himself known to the authorities who gladly accepted his offer to provide medical care to any prisoner or guard who cared to turn up at his tent.

To Evan's eyes, Alan was ever so slowly improving. He was still weak and carrying a leg injury that Evan was able to dress and clean so that after two weeks Alan was venturing short distances to neighbouring tents with long rests between. Life was far from ideal but infinitely better than the two months at Benghazi and idled along at an easy pace that in Alan's mind threatened to deceive. And so it was proved at a roll-call the camp commandant announced that as this camp was transitional, the time had come for half the camp to be moved on to Grupigano in northern Italy.

The time for this was virtually immediate. Tomorrow at 5.30 am all prisoners in the southern section of the camp were to assemble ready to march the two kilometres to the railhead. They would then be transported over the following three days to Grupigano in the Cividale del Friuli region.

The commandant snapped his heels together and marched off with his staff of two for his evening meal of roast beef accompanied by a good red from a local vineyard.

Chapter 22

Ersilia Abelli wasn't home when the militia called but arrived a few hours later to find her mother and father lying face down on their kitchen floor with a bullet hole each in the back of their heads. Her father's right arm was flung towards, but not quite reaching the hand of his wife of twenty years. A printed circular with ACHTUNG! set in bold, above a swastika, and a threat of random reprisals for damage to property of the Axis powers were pinned to each of their backs. Ersilia had half expected it and sank slowly into a chair with her head in her hands, eyes closed to the cold, hard evidence of great loss.

After a minute that felt like an hour, her shoulders started shaking in silent sobs. She drew in a long shuddering breath and stood up. Her parents were past any help in this world and she had to decide now on a course of action. There was high risk of a revisit by the militia. They were aware her sympathies lay with communist resistance groups in the area and she knew they would be disappointed they were unable to scoop her up in their last visit. Ersilia knew she had escaped a certain death that would have been preceded by hours of torture to try and prise lists of names from her.

She avoided looking at her parents and tears now streamed freely from her eyes, while she quickly put some food and a goatskin wine bag into a pack. She then went to the timber mantelpiece above the fireplace and pushed it sideways on its stone mounts. A few minutes of effort and a cavity was revealed in the rock wall. Ersilia reached in and pulled out a revolver wrapped in oil cloth, standard army issue given to her father prior to the first world war. She put the package on the table and reached further in to pull out a wooden box. She slid the top open, tipping out three dozen cartridges, then unwrapped the revolver. She broke it open and loaded the six cartridges into the empty chambers. The spare cartridges were wrapped in the oily rag and put along with the revolver in the bottom of the pack. She pushed the heavy timber mantelpiece back into position. Ersilia knew her cargo meant instant death if a patrol discovered the weapon, but anger sharpened by the brutal murder of her parents and the fascist's presence in Italy had made it an easy decision and if challenged she would take as many with her as she could.

She went to pull on a heavy coat, but was attracted by shards of broken glass in a corner of the room. She went to it and found a picture frame lying behind a chair. She picked up the frame and carefully extracted a drawing of a small bird, one of many she'd done as a young girl. She held the drawing up to the late light coming through the small window, then quickly rolled it up and put it in a side pocket of the pack. Ersilia's drawings of birds had found places on the walls of several neighbours and friends. The militia had added one extra shot of spite to the casual destruction of her parents.

She pulled on her coat, shouldered the pack and looked for the last time at her mother and father, before closing the door on the first twenty years of her life. After looking carefully about, she skirted around to the back of the house and then began climbing the well-formed steps cut into the steep hillside. She could feel the reassuring heaviness of the gun in the bottom of the pack bumping against her as she climbed off the last step and onto a rough track cutting across the steep slope. For an hour, she followed the track as it zigzagged up an easy gradient back and forth across the hill, steadily taking her higher and further from the valley and her home.

A woodcutter's hut appeared ahead in a clearing roughly where she had expected it to be. She stood beside the door taking deep breaths, then gave the rudimentary handle a twist and stepped inside. She leant back on the edge of a table and looked through a small window back down the hill towards the distant cottage and further on to the valley and plains. There were no tears, just a heavy wooden feeling of inevitability. Her mother and father had paid the price of the partisans' success.

She shrugged the pack onto the table, opened it up and stood eating bread and cheese and swallowing mouthfuls of rough red wine. The sun was now low in the sky as she watched for any signs of the militia returning as they often did if others on their lists weren't around when they first called. She was also worried over the whereabouts of her brother and found herself praying for his safety before she stopped suddenly. Ersilia, raised a catholic, was now a committed communist and determined to adhere to standard Marxist doctrine regarding religion.

She would stay overnight and leave early next day, and stood looking down the hillside before she began setting a fire in the grate. Now the sun had set any smoke would be surely covered by the growing darkness.

Tomorrow she would look to connect up with an Italian partisan group that had been stiffened by two brothers who were Slav communists from over the border. She had met one of them while at a covert meeting of communists and sympathisers in a safe house several kilometres from her own cottage. The younger Yugoslav sought her out after the meeting, urging her to join their group.

Ersilia's interest was piqued for more than just political reasons. Her admirer's name was Adrijan Markovic who spoke excellent Italian and reasonable English. He was a qualified engineer and spent a year in England on further studies before the war. The attraction of the two communists and the execution of her parents gave her all the motivation needed to extend her role from being an occasional courier or 'staffette' to becoming armed and dangerous. Ersilia leant back on an old chair, staring into the flickering and hissing little fire. When it had died to just embers, she lay on a mattress stuffed with straw. Although her eyes were closed, she was wide awake to the thought of her parents growing cold on the kitchen floor. Providing a burial was difficult and dangerous and she knew from a 'plant' in the militia they were aware of her contact with the communists. She would be next on their list. Ersilia soon fell into a sleep of those who have made a decision that feels totally right.

At 5.30 in the morning, Ersilia slowly opened her eyes to the early sun picking its way through the little hut. She lay back gradually reabsorbing the blunt fact of her parents' death. She also thought of her father and if he were alive, what would he be saying to her right now. She knew the hardness underlying his easy manner would emerge. He would suggest strongly that if given the opportunity she should take maximum revenge on the enemy for their lives taken and the many civilians killed in retribution for partisan successes.

Ersilia struggled to her feet, aching from a night on a mattress that was way short of even the basic bedding she was used to. She scrabbled around in her pack and found the remaining food and also a map of the area, including the locality favoured by the partisan group and its two Yugoslav members.

She stood in front of the window eating the lean rations and studying her map. Her friend Adrijan had given carefully edited information as to where they might be found and she realised that all she could do was to simply set off and hope they would meet up. One thing she knew from the militia plant was their reluctance to extend patrols too far from base without backup, and becoming exposed to partisans who could readily multiply their numbers by calling in nearby groups.

With this in mind, she knew the further from her home she got the less likely she was to encounter patrols. She also knew a family located right on the border with Slovakia. The father, Alonza Mancini, had been a comrade of her father in the Italian army during the First World War. She decided to try and find them. They would be saddened by the loss of her parents and would be ready to help with shelter, food and information.

Ersilia took a last bite of the hard, peasant-baked bread and washed it down with a mouthful of wine. She stowed the small amounts left over in the pack and swung it over her shoulders. In the half-light, she stood and looked back down the valley at her home of twenty years. She closed the door then turned and started back on the track that had taken her this far. The track went through a short flat area of stubby grass and rocks then headed steeply up the side of a ridge. She aimed to follow the track to the pass at the top where she could take a break after the hard climb and have a view that with the map would give her a direction to follow. It would also let her see if any patrols were following up the hillside.

Halfway to her goal she stopped at a small spring. She knelt on a flat stone worn smooth by centuries of travellers, and bending forward, submerged her father's army issue flask in the cold clear pool. The air from the flask bubbled up to the surface and when it stopped she lifted it out and screwed the cap back in place. Next she took the matching cup and drank four refills in quick succession.

A feeling of peace and serenity came over her which surprised her, until she realised what she was doing was what she had done every day as a child, fetching water for her family. Only now it was only for herself. Thinking of family strengthened her resolve. Live or die she was in this fight not just for some abstract notion of country or nation or political beliefs, but for her family and the honour and memory of her parents and a brother she still held fears for.

Fortified and refreshed by the water she shouldered the pack again and set off. As she climbed the steep track she thought about the young Yugoslav, Adrijan Markovic. He was intense and took an engineer's slide rule precision to everything in life including his communist ideals. She found his absolute focus appealing as it filled in some of the vague areas in her own thoughts. She put it all to the back of her mind as she was now reaching the pass from where she could get a good view of the country ahead. She stepped onto a large flat rock, dumped the pack on the ground and pulled out the map. It was topographical so she was able to sight and identify some of the high points and landmarks. She found a stream and traced it to a point she confidently predicted was near to the location of the house of her father's army friend, Alonza Mancini. She now knew from her map that following a little stream nearby would lead onto a bigger stream. This bigger stream runs near to the home of the Mancini family. Get there and she would then be with old friends and comrades.

Her thoughts were confirmed by the reappearance of the track which followed the stream along its left bank. Ersilia made easy work crossing on boulders that kept her feet dry. She set off again watching her step and working hard on the steep pitch to slow her momentum. A few more paces and the slope eased and she lifted her eyes to find she was looking directly into the face of Adrijan Markovic leaning nonchalantly against a tree twenty metres away. He stood up and walked slowly towards her. They stood facing each other a few feet apart. He slowly reached forward and took her hand in both of his. He looked for what felt like an eternity into her eyes.

He knows about my mother and father, she thought to herself.

"I know what the militia did and I know how to make them pay," he said, squeezing her hand in a strong grip.

"Now you must come with me. We have work to do," he said and lifted the pack off her back, adjusted the straps and slung it on his own back.

"I guess you are here to join our group?" he suddenly asked as a last minute afterthought as they turned to start down the hill.

"Yes, but I was going first to the family of my father's friend, Alonza Mancini." Adrijan slowed to stop in front of her. He turned and faced her.

"I know to who you are referring, they are no longer. Their youngest son was killed in a gun battle that cost the militia many men. They traced him back to his family and came and killed them all."

Ersilia turned her head away with tears brimming in her eyes. She sat down by a tree. Adrijan stood mutely beside her looking up at the sky. After a minute or so she stood up, took a long deep breath, then brushing the leaves and twigs off the seat of her pants, she started walking slowly down the track. Adrijan watched her for a few seconds then shrugged his shoulders and strode off to catch her up. Adrijan kept up a fast pace in silence for fifteen minutes which took them well away from the pass area. He slowed up and finally spoke.

"We needed to keep off high ground. We are too easily seen by reconnaissance aircraft," he paused, then went on. "I am taking you to our encampment...our group are resting up waiting for a supplies and weapons drop from the Allies."

They kept heading along the same track that now cut through a forested area and gave good cover. "We are now going to follow the stream and in the process get ourselves a bit wet," he said and started carefully picking his way down the sloping bank and onto the shingle bed of the stream. He then stepped into the shallow water at the edge and waded downstream for twenty metres before stopping and turning to check her progress. She had followed but was now ten or so metres back. He turned and saw her looking worried. He stopped and waited for her to catch up.

"We are going to have to wade for about another fifty metres, then we climb onto the other side and follow another route which will take us to the encampment. Please don't touch or brush anything on the way. We are trying to make it difficult for tracking dogs that might come looking."

She agreed and focused on keeping her footing in the shallow water. Soon Adrijan picked a shallow part where the stream widened. He stopped, turned towards the opposite bank then looked back at Ersilia four to five metres behind. When she came up beside him, he put his arm across her shoulder. She followed suit and they both waded slowly through knee deep water to the opposite bank.

They climbed onto dry land with water dripping from pants wet to their knees. They were still locked in their side-on embrace. She self-consciously removed her arm but he kept a hand on her shoulder. He reached for her other arm and pulled her gently towards him. She was worried, being brought up a devout Catholic until she swapped God and Jesus Christ for Karl Marx and Comrade Stalin, meant sex and a relationship with a male was totally forbidden. The fact both her parents were dead was irrelevant given the constant drilling of behaviour befitting a good Catholic girl. She let him hold her close for a few moments then gently but firmly pushed him away. She had to admit that it felt quite strange, but quite special.

Adrijan was unperturbed and after checking she was ready to go set off on what was now a less defined track. After fifteen minutes, they came to a wide shingle scree slope. He stopped for a minute or so looking and listening. Then with Ersilia following close by headed diagonally up the slope towards a series of large limestone rocks propped one upon the other like some juxtaposed supersized puzzle.

He stopped beside the nearest, motioning her to move out of sight of any aircraft that might come roaring over the hills with no warning. He then put his fingers to his lips and sent out a convincing bird call and followed a minute later with another three in quick succession. She knew the bird he was mimicking and was impressed. Within a minute, an answer came back. She noticed the answer had four calls after the first one, which was probably a simple pre-agreed code.

Adrijan stood looking towards the largest rock and waited. Eventually a giant bearded figure stepped into view with a submachine gun pointing vaguely in their direction. No one totally trusted anyone. The enemy could be holding a family member, lover or child as hostage and manipulating the situation to their advantage. Nevertheless, the man waved them on but maintained his position in the shadow of the enormous rock. When they stood in front of him, he lowered the machine gun and reached his arms forward and engulfed the slim Adrijan in a huge embrace.

"This is Branko, my friend and comrade," Adrijan said, turning with difficulty towards Ersilia. The friend let him go then stood facing uphill and made the same bird call. He repeated it again and waited. Minutes went by until an answer came from up the hill.

"And this is Ersilia," Adrijan said to Branko when he was satisfied with the response from up the hill.

"Yes, I know of her and I know her family. I also know of her great loss," he said and then beckoning them both to follow, he started threading his way through the rocks that towered two or three times their height above them.

"We have good cover and good firing positions against an enemy that have to traverse two hundred metres across open scree and there is no other way to get to us. Fifty metres that way there is a deep ravine with near vertical sides," Adrijan said pointing in the opposite direction.

The track became steeper and conversation was replaced by deep breathing in the cold still air. They rounded another large rock and Ersilia was suddenly standing in front of a twenty metre square area of hillside covered in camouflage netting and leafy branches. From a gap at one side, a man stepped out with a submachine gun slung from his shoulder. He said something rapidly to Branko, then turned and held the netting aside for the group to enter a large cave that cut at least twenty metres into the hillside. Above a stone fireplace a blackened cooking pot produced endless stews that kept stomachs full. Ersilia guessed that a few of the four men and three women that were sitting around would have been adept poachers and would keep the pot full of rabbit, wild pig and the occasional domestic chicken.

They looked up and acknowledged Ersilia. The men rose and formally greeted her and the three women, all Italian, seemed to warm to the addition of another female. Adrijan introduced them using first names only, as Aurora, Sofia, and Greta. One got up and began ladling stew out of the pot and silently handed it to Ersilia. She then filled another for Adrijan. They sat on some handy rocks and ate in silence while the rest of the group talked in a low voice. When he'd finished eating, Adrijan joined the group now seated in a circle on an assortment of crates, rocks and one wobbly chair. They became engrossed in an animated discussion that Ersilia barely understood.

Tonight was to be the much anticipated supply and weapons drop. The group was organised into three female torch lighters [plus Ersilia] for the drop zone, and two armed sentries and two porters to locate the supplies and start ferrying it to the encampment. The group had seen no action for several weeks and the imminent delivery created a buzz of excitement.

Adrijan moved back from the group and joined Ersilia at the cave entrance. He put his arm around her shoulders and they stepped through the opening just in time to catch the last glow of the sun before it vanished. He leant back against a rock and pulled her close. Her head tilted back and she smiled up at him. She decided she enjoyed it. They stood quietly for several minutes. He could feel the sun-warmed rock against his back and turned her around gently so she could see what he could see…the stars that blinked slowly on one by one as the night grew around them.

"We should rest up until the time is right to go to the drop zone," he said.

"Where is—"

"Half a kilometre over the scree slope there is a clearing," he said, reading her mind. "We have been enlarging it to make it easier for the pilot, it is still a difficult drop. We have had to retrieve packages from trees and streams on the first one, but I'm sure your father would think it worth it."

"I know that."

"We're expecting the RAF to drop at 11 pm tonight. The moon will be full and will be a help to the navigation officer. You are included as one of the torch bearers. Take your instructions from the other women. Tonight's drop will give us what we need to score a major victory against the Axis powers. There will be retribution but it's a dark blessing that at least you now have nothing more to lose," he said.

They were joined by another man who Adrijan introduced as his brother Dejan.

Ersilia looked up at Dejan. He was smoking a pungent, self-rolled cigarette that had Ersilia stepping away. He was a heavier, fleshier version of his brother. Where Adrijan had an open, friendly face Dejan was closed and secretive like a shut door. He held Ersilia's gaze for a few seconds then looked away. She stood looking at him then turned and followed Adrijan back into the cave. Adrijan had a sleeping pad made from two sacks stitched roughly together and filled with assorted leaves and straw. Two threadbare blankets lay on top. He pulled the top one back and lay his long frame under it keeping the cover open. He looked up at Ersilia. She was acutely aware of the other women watching. Finally she made a decision and bending down flicked the cover back over Adrijan, conceding only to lie on the top cover. She looked over at the other woman who turned their heads back to what they had been doing. Ersilia picked up that the worldly Adrijan with his study time in England and a university degree in engineering, carried a lot of weight in a group of largely peasant farmers and would shield her from moral censure. She wasn't totally comfortable with special treatment but had no other solution than to go with it. She knew that with Dejan in the mix it was better that she was spoken for by the quiet one – Adrijan, the one that carried authority easily on a tall, rangy frame.

They both lay back with the ancient blanket keeping them apart and proper in the eyes of the three Italian women. Time drifted slowly towards 9.30 pm, the departure time necessary for them to get to the drop zone and be ready to light flares for the proposed 11 pm drop. Adrijan looked at his watch for the third time then suddenly sprang off the bed.

"It's time," he said to the dark form of Ersilia.

Others were beginning to stir, the three women picked up bundles of sticks wrapped in oil-soaked rags, while the men were pulling on dark heavy jackets. The man appointed as guard picked up his rifle, put a spare magazine in his pocket and after checking the bolt slung it over his shoulder. A man with one of the two torches led the way out of the cave with the others trailing behind. They walked in silence with a weak moon showing enough of the way forward. A vague track took them downhill, skirting the shingle scree for a while, then abruptly turned across it and into the forest on the other side. They followed it, hurrying over the open ground of the scree until they stepped into the sparse cover of the forest. Dejan carried one torch at the rear and the other torch in front, which provided just enough light to get them along the rough track. Adrijan frequently checked his watch. Another five minutes at a good clip and they were soon standing on a bare ridge with a good view of what lay ahead, a small plateau, the drop zone. Even Ersilia who'd never seen it before knew they were near where they were meant to be.

"OK, it's unlikely the militia would get a significant force up here without us hearing from our friends but don't assume anything. Dejan and I will do a forward scout and when sure it is all clear we'll give the signal. Stay quiet and keep awake," Adrijan said, his voice tight with tension and fear. Dejan started moving slowly off, splashing the light from his torch onto the track. Before he followed, Adrijan glanced at Ersilia, gave her an encouraging smile and turned to catch up with Dejan. They continued down a gentle gradient until on level ground where both stopped dead, listening and watching for several minutes. Then following the same procedure as for previous drops, they started walking quietly and carefully in opposite directions, stopping frequently to see if their presence had anyone interested. Within five minutes, they met back where they started from.

"I think we're safe, I think we're safe," Adrijan repeated as if trying to convince himself. He looked again at his watch.

"If they are on time, they should be overhead in 25 minutes. Give the signal to the others and we'll start setting up." Dejan pointed the torch up the hill and flashed a short morse code for SAFE followed by a three digit numerical code. A reply came promptly so there was nothing to do but wait for the rest to arrive. Within five minutes, the group were back together. The three women, each carrying a flare, headed off to each corner of the drop zone. Ersilia held her flare and had been instructed to stay with Adrijan.

Adrijan listened intently, rechecked his watch and knew they were late. A minute or two went by then he heard the deep thrum of a piston engine aircraft flying fast and low. He gestured to Ersilia to hold the torch up and, pulling a zippo cigarette lighter out of his pocket, touched it to the oily rag. It spluttered into life, growing from the base until it had enveloped the whole of the torch with a cherry glow. The other three women followed the cue and lit their torches.

Adrijan knew once he was able to hear the sound of the approaching aircraft that it would be only a minute or two away. He was right. Abruptly the twin engine aircraft appeared, following the line of the nearby river. Half a mile away it spotted the flares and banked hard heading straight for the group standing in the drop zone. The plane then throttled back, until approaching stall speed. At two hundred metres from the group, it suddenly jetsoned its cargo of arms, ammunition and provisions. The pilot opened the throttle wide and the plane, suddenly relieved of its load, roared up into a steep climb, banked hard and set off for home. The three large packages, each attached to a parachute drifted towards the drop zone. Two hit the ground tumbling over several times to end up in handy positions. They were not so lucky with the third. It ended in an area of low trees and scrub. Not a disaster, just a little short of a perfect drop.

Two men raced in the direction of the third package. They scrambled through the low scrub and were soon standing under the errant delivery. It was a well-oiled operation. The tallest man, Branko, had the task of releasing the parachute lines snared in the low branches of a tree. Five minutes of furious action with a knife and the package slowly descended one severed cord at a time to the ground. His companion, Marko, grabbed a rope handle and started dragging the package through the scrub and out into the clearing. Branko stayed to clear up the tangle of cord and branches. Anything left behind was a dead giveaway to patrols that might venture this far from base. After several minutes of hard work, Branko finally appeared with the tangled remnants of the drop. He joined his companion who'd made fifty metres of progress, grabbed the other rope handle and together they half-dragged and half-carried their valuable cargo towards the rest of the group who were beginning the lung bursting struggle up the steep track with their packages.

The group were now seriously armed. They had a Sten gun and an automatic pistol for each member. Two Bren guns and ammunition for all weapons plus a box of twenty grenades completed the arsenal. Adrijan considered the Bren guns to be intended for a last ditch stand among the giant boulders…a situation he hoped wouldn't eventuate. Last and most important was explosives for the demolition of rail bridges and tracks. This was Adrijan's area. All members of the group apart from Ersilia were trained in weaponry but nevertheless stripped, cleaned and practice fired all weapons they'd received.

Chapter 23

Adrijan and Ersilia took up the same sleeping arrangement as before. Adrijan had an early start next day for a meeting with a local informant. At daybreak, he woke and bending over the sleeping form of Ersilia, kissed her lightly on the cheek. She murmured something in response and brushed her hand over her face in irritation. He stood looking at her face and her long, beautiful hair, then after taking a deep breath, slowly and carefully threaded his way between the sleeping forms.

Dejan was the only one awake and he watched his brother with eyes half-closed as he stepped past him then out through the cave entrance.

With the aid of a torch and a smudge of daylight showing on nearby hills, he negotiated his way past the towering rocks standing guard over their underground hideout. He arrived at the track and paused for a few seconds, checked his watch then marched off at a fast pace. He had to be on the pass summit by 6 am. In half an hour of fast walking, he'd made good progress to arrive a few hundred metres from the meeting place and on time. He spotted the pinprick glow of a cigarette and stepped behind a rock. Adrijan had to make sure his contact hadn't been compromised. Putting his fingers to his lips he made the call of a local night bird and waited. The cigarette glowed brighter as his man sucked in one last breath, then the light dipped downwards and disappeared. A minute later the response came to his bird call. Adrijan waited, then crept cautiously from the cover of the rock and, keeping to the shadows, made his way over the last hundred metres.

His contact was standing in the shadow of a tree. He had rescued the cigarette he'd extinguished with a pinch of labour toughened fingers and was now trying to relight it. His furious drags sucked in the leathery cheeks of a face way older than his time. The cigarette spluttered into life and the man who was agitated and jumpy turned and faced Adrijan.

"Comrade, I cannot stay for long. The militia are everywhere and I need to go back to my house before the sun has fully risen."

"OK, so what have you got for me?"

"A prison train is on its way to one of the prison camps in the north, or it may be going all the way to Germany. It will be through here in two days, we will have a more exact time tomorrow. I will send my son with information this time, this place tomorrow," he replied.

He gave a hacking cough then turned and strode off back down the track.

Adrijan didn't hang about and set off to get back to base as soon as possible. As he came up to the rocks guarding the approach he could smell breakfast cooking. He knew the plentiful supply of good food was critical to maintaining fitness, strength and most importantly morale. If an army fights on its stomach, then so does a partisan group. Adrijan followed his nose that followed the gamey fragrances of a rabbit stew drifting down the hillside.

He stopped and gave his bird call sign and got an immediate answer. He met the large, formidable Branko proudly bearing his new Sten gun twenty metres from the cave entrance. Adrijan demanded the group remain totally alert by rotating sentries at all times. If they were discovered, they would stand and fight it out and if all were killed they would have died knowing they'd taken their share of a fascist enemy they detested, whether they be German or Italian.

He stepped into the cave and found Ersilia working with the other women on breakfast. He was handed a metal plate of rabbit stew with a chunk of camp bread. Hungry from his early morning sprint up to the pass and back he sat and ate everything on the plate. Everyone else had eaten so he quickly polished off a second helping. The group all sat expectantly waiting for him to finish. He wiped the plate clean with his bread then stood up and looked around the group who were for once totally silent. He bolted down the last portion of bread and cleared his throat.

"We now have a significant target to attack. As we expected, a prison train is due to come through the valley on its way north to the camp in Grupigano or it may even be destined for Germany. It is full of Allied prisoners captured in North Africa. These men who came from countries far away deserve their freedom and may well bolster our own ranks. And, as we all know, any damage to the war effort of the Axis powers will drag more of their troops away from the rest of the fray. There is no one here tonight that hasn't suffered personal losses in this cruel and tyrannical occupation.

"Tomorrow I have to return to the same meeting place to be given the exact time the train will come through our territory. Be strong. Be ruthless. Take revenge for your family, your parents, your friends in this war against those who give no quarter and deserve no quarter."

He glanced down at Ersilia and saw a tear on her cheek. He looked quickly in the opposite direction. He didn't seek her company but reached into a pack at his feet and pulled out a rolled up map. He nodded at Branko and Marko. They both stood and followed him out through the cave exit.

He unrolled the map on a flat rock and placed a small stone on each corner, then reached down for a handy stick long enough to use as a pointer, and while he talked he traced the path of the main northern railway to where it crossed a river.

"To make this operation a success we have to create a diversion and this is where I think it should happen," he said pointing at the bridge. "We all know that the best place to attack the railway is where it runs through the cutting right here," he said and dragged the pointer slowly down the track and stopped at the cutting.

"There is a long incline that slows all trains down to a fast walk. We know that, our enemy knows that, and this is why I want you and Marko to create a big diversion on the bridge three kilometres north," he said, shifting the stick back to the bridge.

"Use two charges, timed to go off two minutes apart, one at each end of the bridge. I want you to set both off when you see and hear the train on the straight five kilometres below the cutting. I suggest Branko keeps watch for the train from the rocks that are directly above the bridge. Branko will signal Marko to ignite the charges. Once the fuses are lit Marko is to head quickly over to assist in our operation. Branko will set up the Bren gun on the forest edge among the rocks that will give you plenty of cover. You will be looking down on the bridge so remember to adjust your sights to allow for the angle. One in five rounds will be tracer that will help you find your range. I suggest when the troops arrive, shoot off a magazine, then shift twenty or so metres and fire off another. Carry four grenades each, let them have a few."

Adrijan stood deep in thought and then carried on.

"Branko, I want you to hold your ground with the Bren as long as you can. Take as much ammunition as you can carry. I want them to think there are five or more up there."

He stopped abruptly and looked at both men. He knew he could be sending them on a suicide mission, but he also knew that any one of them or more could be dead or captured inside a week.

Branko and Marko stood up, stretched, then quietly went off to recheck their weapons. Both were dedicated communists and had lost family in the fascist occupation. Their motivation was inspired by their belief in two contrasting forces, one, a new-world political order; the other, the ancient ties of old-world families.

Adrijan was now totally preoccupied with the preparation of the attack. He compared notes with Branko and Marko and when he was convinced they and he were as prepared as they could be, he called a meeting of the group. The group that hadn't been involved in planning so far were Ersilia, the three women and Dejan. Adrijan had taken the easy route ignoring Dejan in the planning. He had virtually none of the fighting experience of Branko or Marko and was inclined to take over the discussion.

He was damned either way. Involve him and it would end in a counterproductive argument, leave him out and he would smoulder away. Dejan decided on the latter and instead directed his anger at the enemy. His redeeming features were that he was a superb marksman, had the fitness of an athlete who had competed at national level before the war, and had spent two years training in field medicine as a medic with the Yugoslav Army.

Adrijan took his usual speech-making position and began an outline of the plan he, Branko and Marko had come up with.

"I will be responsible for setting the three charges. One I will place under the tracks. The other two will be placed in shallow holes I have pre-dug under two very large rocks. These rocks are situated on the edge of the cutting above the track. My plan is to place a charge that will blast one rock that will land twenty or thirty metres ahead of the charge placed to destroy the track. The other rock is situated three hundred metres back down the track and will be timed to be blasted onto the track once the last wagon has gone past. If this plan is successful it will, due to the difficult access into the cutting, delay repairs to the track and the removal of the rocks and debris. Timing is critical. I have observed a train passing through and know exactly where it will be when each of the fuses are lit. I have calculated the length of each fuse to achieve the outcome we are after. The train has to be in view and committed to getting its cargo up the incline. Too early and the driver will see the charge go off, and given the walking pace speed, will have time to brake and reverse out of our trap. Get the timing right and a train full of prisoners, our Allies, will be stuck between two huge rocks and a destroyed section of track. Luckily the wagons open on our side of the track. We will access the track by a narrow set of steps, the location of which I will show you all at the time. Then form into pairs with one carrying a Sten gun. We will head south alongside the wagons. The unarmed person will open each door while the person armed stands guard. Ersilia and myself will move north doing the same. Marko will come back as soon as he can from the diversion attack on the bridge and will take up a position where he sees fit on the edge of the cutting, providing added cover fire. The prisoners are to be directed back to the steps. We will have a piece of white to show the position of the steps. My thoughts are that the guards will not put up much of a fight with all the drama, the diversion blasts and the blasts in the cutting. I like to think they'll be inclined to wait for the local militia to come and sort it out. With a bit of luck and quick work, we might be able to get most of it over by the time the locals arrive."

Adrijan stood and watched the reaction of the group. He had reconnoitred the area several weeks ago. Over this time he formulated and refined a plan from broad-brush to the finished product that he had kept to himself. He was suspicious and wary of his brother. He knew that he was envious of him and had a big mouth that Adrijan didn't trust. He turned to Dejan and sat down beside him.

"Dejan, you are our best marksman by far. I want you to take a firing position on a piece of high ground. I will show you where it is. This is a position that should cover most of the action. There are several large rocks on the highest point that will give plenty of protection. You will be armed with the closest thing we've got to a sniper rifle. You are critical to this operation and are responsible for eliminating as many of the enemy as possible while the prisoners are being released. To help you recognise friend from foe each of the group, including me, will wear a white scarf knotted around their necks."

Early next day Adrijan repeated his rendezvous with his informant's teenage son and got the message he was waiting for. The day after the train was due to pull into a minor station fifteen kilometres south of the cutting. It was a food stop scheduled for 5 pm where the prisoners and guards would receive basic food and water for the next two days travel as they headed north to their destination.

Adrijan knew from past observation that the train would be in the cutting by approximately 7 pm. Darkness would be upon them. Darkness that would be part curse, part blessing. Ultimately a blessing, at least they knew where they are going and what they are doing. The enemy, until the diversion attack and then the real attack unfolds, are none the wiser. Even then Adrijan prays that a state of chaos and confusion reigns. He knows there is conflict between the Italian fascists and their German mentors. Conflict that is stoked by the false information and rumours carefully fed to the Italian Secret Service by turned agents working for MI5.

Adrijan provides the latest update to his small army and briefs them to check and recheck their arms, rest up and mentally prepare for tomorrow in what might be the best day or worst day of their life. The group got little sleep that night and spent the next morning of D-Day eating whatever food they could keep down, all aware it could be their last meal on earth or their best meal for a long time if captured. The departure time agreed on was twelve noon and important. Their exposure to daylight had to be as short as possible, but still have enough time to get where they needed to be and get set up. Adrijan also knew that they would have to deal with any chance encounter with an enemy patrol with lethal force, or the attack would not happen.

The morning came and with it brought low mist and cloud. Exactly what Adrijan wanted – limited visibility didn't matter to them – they knew where they were going and what they were doing.

Conversely poor visibility limited an enemy striving to be all-seeing and all-knowing. At noon, the group stood with arms draped around each other's shoulders and sang L'Internationale, the song written by Eugène Pottier, a Parisian transport worker uniting all communists wherever they hailed from. At the end, Adrijan slung his pack loaded with the explosives and coiled fuses on his back and headed for the exit. The rest of the group picked up their weapons and ammunition and followed Adrijan out of the relative security and warmth of the cave towards whatever God or fate had in store.

Branko and Marko had a longer journey to make so departed an hour earlier than the others. Conversation was minimal and rapid progress soon had them at the pass. The group remained concealed by low bush and scrub while Adrijan and Dejan scaled a vantage point that gave a view of the whole valley including the railway cutting. Adrijan scoped it with his powerful field binoculars, then handed them to Dejan. Nothing seemed amiss or out of the ordinary. So far so good.

Adrijan and Dejan rejoined the group and they all followed each other out from cover, then onto the track and on their way. Adrijan knew of a little known basin concealed from the track and close to the scene of the action to come. It would fulfil the role of a temporary hideaway for the group while Adrijan packed the charges into their readymade holes and ran out the required lengths of fuse. Each fuse would be lit at the same time, the sequence of the detonations governed by the length of each of the fuses. The signal for the group to close on the attack scene would be the sound and sight of the diversion detonations on the bridge. If the diversion didn't happen, the main attack wouldn't happen.

As they made their way down to the track Adrijan pondered the decision he'd made to keep most of the plans to himself until the last few hours. This decision was taken to avoid the group stewing over details and ending up in arguments and internal strife that would be disruptive and affect morale. He modelled his approach on a standard army procedure that was applied to planning of campaigns the army wanted it's enemy to be totally oblivious of, achieved by the maintenance of absolute secrecy, and critical details shared with only a small number of the most senior officers. Adrijan's equivalent were Branko and Marko. The few issues they raised were answered and they backed Adrijan to the hilt. His other consideration was that Dejan had sibling rivalry problems because of this growing attraction to Ersilia. Anything Adrijan had, Dejan desired.

They had by now reached the location of the basin. One of the Italian women knew the access route so Adrijan instructed her to lead the way for the rest of the group. Adrijan embraced them all and told them as soon as they heard the train to leave the basin and make their way quietly to the cutting. Although they had not gone with Adrijan on his reconnaissance missions, the territory was familiar to both Italian women who came from the area. Adrijan headed off, his pulse leaping in anticipation of what he knew was coming. It suddenly occurred to him that in spite of all the planning, thinking and visualising he'd put into it, the outcome was no more predictable than what the weather would be on a particular day in six months' time. There would be weather of some description either good, bad, mild, or stormy. Any result was possible. While his logical engineer's brain could sit smugly, and satisfied in his head, and do all the calculations it liked, it was his emotions, normally carefully controlled, that were being cajoled and jostled by fear and trepidation that were demanding attention and scaring the hell out of him.

He stopped for a minute, acutely aware he alone was personally responsible for the people and events of the next two or three days. This fact suddenly terrified him. His continual interaction with the group camouflaged the reality of the task he had set himself. Feeling like he was looking for an escape he looked up towards a gap in the cloud and mist that revealed deepening blue. Why did he always look to the sky when stressed? It only served to remind him of the big task ahead and the limited amount of daylight to achieve it. He counted out ten controlled breaths while gradually collecting his thoughts. What was the worst thing that could happen? He could die, Ersilia could die or all or some of the group. He didn't ask for the war, that was in the hands of others. He was in it now and reminded himself of the commitment he made to the communist cause and the determination to put right the wrongs dealt to common working men and women by the rich and powerful. The rich and powerful that were invariably friends and allies of the Italian Fascist Party, together with large landowners and businesses reminded him of what he was fighting against. His breathing slowed and the rapid thump of his heart subsided. Restored and fortified Adrijan was now convinced more than ever of his own direction and that of his partisan group.

Adrijan shifted the pack to a more comfortable position and set off with new purpose. He had only three or four kilometres to cover to reach the cutting. It was now just approaching dusk. While it was making it difficult to see what he was doing, it also made him difficult to spot. He was nearing the cutting, and once reaching it followed the edge until he came upon the narrow steps leading down to the track. He paused and looked around. There was no one around so he began carefully descending the steps and arrived at the two perfect lines of the track reaching north and south in the dark. It seemed an offence to his engineers' sensitivity to destroy something that looked so right. Nevertheless, he stepped out an exact hundred paces north from the steps to a point where already he had removed rocks to create a small space under the rail on the steep side of the cutting. He was now moving quickly, shifting the few remaining rocks to create the ideal container for the charge. He attached the detonator and placed the package into the hole. Some of the spare rocks he placed on top and the remainder he threw into the drainage ditch on the side of the track. He then backtracked to the steps, laying the fuse cable as he went. He ran the cable up the steps and left it beside the entrance.

He was sure that the enemy would be most concerned with the security of the bridge two kilometres north and, after a quick look around, he walked north beside the mist now lying in the cold air of the cutting like a purpose-built blanket. He soon found what he was looking for. The large boulder suddenly appeared out of the gloom. He stood with his hand on it like it was the shoulder of an old friend. Again he looked around and listened for a few seconds then got to work. At the base, he quickly re-excavated the pre-dug hole and placed the next charge. He connected the detonator and replaced the fill. He now walked south laying the fuse back to the entrance of the steps. He dropped it there with the other coil and then went and found the second boulder. He buried the last charge in the prepared hole and then returned with the fuse back to the steps, his base point for igniting all three fuses. He now pulled firmly on each of the fuses to take out the slack, then located each of the markers taped to each fuse. He then cut each at their marker and joined them together as one. He wrapped a length of tape around the bundle and placed it on the ground. He folded his knife and put it back in his pocket, then stood up and looked and listened one more time. When satisfied, he was on his own, he turned and walked off towards a large rock with a depression behind it.

This was where he was going to hole up, collect his thoughts and get ready for whatever was coming his way. His first task was to get the Sten gun from the pack and fit one of the four magazines he had brought with him. He put one in his pocket and the rest back into the pack, now empty of the explosives. He also carried a Beretta M1934 automatic pistol, standard issue to the Italian Army. He put it into a holster he retrieved from the pack and buckled it around his waist. Three spare bullet clips for the pistol were stuffed into a jacket pocket. He now finally decided he had done all he could to pull off a small but significant victory for communism against its arch enemies, the fascist states of Italy and Germany. He lay back against the boulder, closed his eyes and drifted into a short but refreshing sleep. He woke with a start ten minutes later and checked his watch. If the time was right, the train should be leaving the station in the south about now. One drawback to the mist was that the sound of its approach would be muffled. He agonised over this, then realised that he would get a better warning doing the oldest trick in the book, of lying on the track with one ear pressed to it. He didn't have to worry about the group holed up in the basin. They would hear the explosions of the diversion attack. That was their signal it was all on and to head to the cutting at double time.

Adrijan stood up and checked it was all clear, then walked quickly to the steps and down to the track. He lay down and pressed his ear to the cold metal.

For ten minutes he maintained his vigil, then there it was, the tiny vibrations of sound through the rail barely detectable, but there was no mistake. It meant only one thing, heavy metal wheels rolling on metal track. He waited another minute then the realisation they had got noticeably stronger in that short time scared the daylights out of him. He jumped up and quickly retraced his steps to the stairway up from the cutting and raced up two at a time. Slow down, slow down, take your time he told himself. One trip on the steps could mean a sprained ankle or broken leg and it would be all over. He craned his head above the rough ground, trying to get an early sighting of a headlight masked to hide it from enemies like himself, or RAF raiders. He took out his zippo lighter and checked and rechecked that it worked. He should have had another for backup. It would be bloody ridiculous if the outcome of tonight came down to the performance of one five dollar lighter.

He kept looking and could see the faint glow of a big headlight creating a funnel of yellow for twenty metres or so in the mist. As he watched, trying to gauge the distance the muffled sound of two huge explosions, only seconds apart, came to him from the north. The sound of the diversion charges might have been reduced because of the mist but he still felt as if the pressure wave had passed through him. There was now no turning back. His pulse lifted again but he was strangely relieved because he now knew that do or die it was all on. He turned his attention back to the train while holding the bunched fuses in one hand and the zippo in the other. He had a marker in the form of a tall signal light post he could just see. When the train's headlamp went past the signal light, he would light all the fuses and retire back to the depression and his friendly boulder. He waited, waited and watched. The head lamp seemed to inch towards the signal light in slow motion. He watched, seemingly mesmerised by the intensity of the situation, so much so that the light had reached it and inched past before he woke from his reverie. Furious with himself, he grabbed the lighter, flicked it on, and with the flame adjusted to full, he waved it over the fuse ends. One by one the fuses spluttered into life. He stood and watched for half a minute as the miniature little flares fizzed and spat as they moved steadily along each of the wires. He waited another half minute and then moved back to the safe spot behind his rock. As he expected the group were all gathered ready and waiting. He acknowledged each in turn. They all looked north as one when Branko's Bren gun stuttered into life and was in turn answered by enemy troops who had turned up as planned.

This part was working, so far. An image of Branko the jovial giant sprang into his mind. No longer religious, now a committed communist, Adrijan nevertheless looked at the few stars that were out. The cloud cover had lifted a little. Adrijan, a communist and atheist, still crossed himself while he kept looking up for another twenty seconds. He hated to acknowledge it, but couldn't help wishing that Branko was his brother and not Dejan.

He could see the whole length of the train had now passed the signal light, albeit in a soft focus created by the mist still clinging stubbornly to the ground. Adrijan looked at his watch. The train seemed a little ahead of where he would expect it to be. By now, the individual boxcars carrying their human cargo were just visible. Something worried him. He carefully counted them out in the low light. One, two, three, four, five, six he whispered to himself. Six, six, he repeated out loud. There was going to be at least ten. That explained how it was fifty metres or so ahead of where he had calculated. The train with the lighter load was going faster, not by much but enough to upset the careful calculations he had planned around. He was powerless to change anything and could only watch and wait. The rest of the group were oblivious to any problem.

"Be ready for anything," he said without looking around. There was no point in giving them anything more to worry about on top of the real possibility of dying in the next three or four hours.

He turned and found the face of Dejan in the group.

"Dejan, now is the time for you to head up to the high ground," he said quietly and turned back to the train.

Dejan picked up his rifle and ammunition belt and walked off.

The train, now clearly visible, was tackling the incline with a methodical trudging gait and the puffs of steam and smoke that punched into the air underlined the difficulty of the climb, in spite of pulling a lesser load. It entered the cutting where the funnel was all that showed above ground. The situation had now reached the eleventh hour and every person watching in the partisan group started taking short nervous breaths through dry mouths.

The funnel was now almost directly opposite them and nothing had happened. Will Branko be risking death for nothing? These thoughts were plaguing Adrijan when suddenly a huge tremor rolled through the ground and on past the group. The locomotive seemed to rear upward in slow motion as the full force of the charge, contained and concentrated by the cutting walls, acted on the hundred ton locomotive, heaving it into the air like a super heavyweight shot putter. A flash of a thousand suns and the pressure wave had come first, followed by the sound that ripped across the space between them. The locomotive ploughed forward, pushed for another fifty metres by the boxcars until the squeal of metal against metal finally brought it to a halt. Adrijan could see the fire box door gaping open and the red hot coals spilling out. In the midst of the chaos of sound and sight, he thought he heard a scream. Water streamed out of a large gash in the boiler, and turned instantly into clouds of scolding steam on contact with the hot coals that were still pouring out, a likely cause of the scream. A moment later the explosion further up the line rocked them as it punched its huge burden of rock high in the air, and then down onto the track. Then several seconds later he heard the downline blast follow suit.

It worked, not the way Adrijan had planned, but it had worked. Miraculously, due to the slow speed, all the boxcars were largely intact. The boulders were roughly where he wanted. The locomotive had landed partly astride the track and had then lurched over until it was held by the near side of the cutting. Adrijan was about to set off when he heard the whine of high velocity bullets passing overhead, quickly followed by the crack of Dejan's rifle directing fire from his elevated vantage point at the end wagon, where the guards were holed up. Adrijan knew that now was about as good as it was going to get. Dejan's laying down of accurate fire would give the guards good cause to lie low. Right now there was time and space to get to the train, knock the bolts off the wagons and release the prisoners.

"Let's go, let's go," he shouted as he turned and looked at the band of partisans. They were all as excited and shocked as he was. He grabbed Ersilia by the arm and, both keeping low, ran towards the steps with the rest of the group following. A couple of bullets sang well over their heads from the guards' van. It was followed by a burst of gunfire from Dejan. The enemy fire stopped abruptly. An advantage of the cutting was the steep sides that limited the angle the enemy had to return fire, while Dejan, from his elevated position, was able to direct fire onto the top half of the guards' van. Adrijan arrived at the steps first, where he waited for Ersilia to catch up. Both descended the steps, relieved to be in the temporary shelter of the cutting. The rest of the group were a few metres behind and turned left at the track to do their work on the wagon doors.

Chapter 24

Adrijan arrived at the first wagon and released the door latch more easily than he expected. Ersilia stood guard with her Sten gun as he opened the next three wagons. Slowly the prisoners started to emerge, stunned and blinking at the surprise rescue. Adrijan directed them towards the steps as he continued towards the engine. He remembered the scream of pain and the picture in his mind of an Italian railway engine driver and his stoker, critically injured from the impact of the explosion, and possibly suffering burns from the superhot steam. He regarded them as comrades; innocent working men who deserved to be rescued from a situation not of their making. He skirted around the coal tender and climbed over the coupling that had twisted but was still holding on. He waited while Ersilia joined him with her Sten gun. Both rounded the back of the engine and could see the driver lying propped against the cutting wall. His uniform was ripped open. In the light of the burning coals, they could see his left arm and face were badly burnt. As they moved forward, what they didn't see was his right hand reach into his jacket and pull out a Luger pistol. There was a flash, followed instantly by a loud bang. Adrijan let out a short yelp of intense pain as he felt the burn of a bullet tear into his neck. As he fell Ersilia was given a clear line of fire and her Sten gun rattled off a short burst. The railway man slumped forward onto the ground. He rolled over and Ersilia caught sight of a small Fascist insignia on his jacket. She opened her mouth in a long silent scream and fell forward onto her knees beside Adrijan. She cradled his head in her arms and found the entry point of the bullet in his neck. They needed Dejan and his field medical experience. Ersilia was going to have to do whatever she could to save the man she loved, but with whom had never in their short time, made love. She grabbed her white bandana and tied it as tightly as she dared around his neck, pressing it hard against the wound.

Adrijan was in a bad way. In fact, he was on the way out as the bullet had severed a critical artery and he was losing blood at a dangerous rate. With her limited medical knowledge, Ersilia did not know she was losing him. But Adrijan knew and he turned towards her.

"I know I'm finished, it's over for me. You'll have to take charge with Marko and Branko, but watch out for Dejan," he gasped. His head felt heavy and it slowly rolled to one side as he lay taking his last few breaths. Ersilia felt for his pulse. It was weak and erratic, but she held on, desperately pressing the bandana to the wound. Adrijan was now at a stage of needing critical attention that was beyond Ersilia's ability or expertise. She was in the middle of an agony of indecision. Stay and he would probably die from loss of blood, go for help and he would most certainly die, with Ersilia no longer there to apply the pressure to the tourniquet. She started sobbing when her voice returned, while she tried to contain the blood flow from the wound. She began to appreciate the full extent of the injury and that her efforts were not working. She felt again for his pulse and found it becoming weaker. He gave several long gasps, then death came to him.

Ersilia determinably held the bandana around the wound, until after checking the non-existent pulse, reluctantly released the tourniquet. Numbed and shocked at the suddenness of his death, she awoke suddenly to the memory of the stoker. What would Adrijan have done? She needed to find and neutralise him so she didn't end up an easy target like Adrijan and make his death pointless. She rested Adrijan carefully onto the embankment and still shaking but with Sten gun ready, moved quietly forward. A few metres away she saw what could only be the dark shape of the stoker lying motionless in the shallow ditch beside the track. With the Sten gun levelled a metre from him she gave him a hard push, then a harder one with no reaction. She couldn't bring herself to shoot him in cold blood, so trusting her instincts he was dead, gave him a quick frisk, pulling out the same Luger pistol that the driver carried. She rechecked Adrijan and kissed him one last time on the forehead.

She closed both his eyes, crossed herself, then made her way back around the engine.

Ersilia climbed back over the coupling and stuck her head around the corner of the first wagon. She could hear sporadic gunfire from the direction of the guards' van and hung back in the shadows trying to assess what was happening. She could see a few dark figures that were moving towards the steps. The cloud cover was lifting and a half-moon had appeared. When they passed through a patch of moonlight, she could see from what they were wearing, that they were the allied prisoners. They were taking some half-hearted fire from the Italian guards from the end of the train, but they were more interested in avoiding Dejan's accurate fire from his perfect vantage point. Losing Adrijan so suddenly made it doubly important she stay alive to see the operation through. She also had to get back to the group and find Marko and Branko, if Branko was still alive. She took a few paces along the side of the first wagon and looked through the open door. A man was sitting back against the wall looking ill and totally spent, apart from eyes that stared back at her, seeming to see everything and know everything. She checked along the train again, then put the Sten gun on the floor and heaved herself up and crawled over to him.

"What's your name?" she asked. He didn't reply.

"Can't you walk?"

"It's my leg," was all he said, then made a frustrated gesture of both hands that had held a part of his leg wrapped with a dirty bandage.

"Where are you from?"

"New Zealand," he replied.

Ersilia was none the wiser. Her sketchy knowledge of English and his accent made him difficult to understand. She looked at his leg wound that seemed infected. Not for the first time in the night she regretted her lack of field medical knowledge and the absence of Dejan. She found herself again staring at his eyes.

"I'm getting you out of here," she said suddenly, with a force that surprised her and him. "Best of luck luv," he replied.

She remembered the tourniquet around Adrijan's neck and quickly lowered herself onto the track to retrieve it. She was back in less than a minute and began wrapping it tightly around the existing bandage. He swore under his breath, then when she had finished leaned forward and started dragging himself over to the door. Ersilia beat him to it and lowered herself onto the track, then turned to support him as best as she could. He sank into a rough embrace that she converted into a supporting carry with his arm around her neck. His weight after weeks of near starvation was less than fifty kgs. Thirty-five kgs under his weight recorded on enlisting. If she had known that she would have been relieved that at least capture and its privations had made him more portable. She was about to step forward then remembered the Sten gun. She leaned back against the wagon floor then managed to grab it in her right hand. A big hand from the man from New Zealand reached back and took it from her.

"You've got enough on your plate luv," he said.

Ersilia wondered why he was talking about plates at this time. Of course he's sure to be hungry. She felt oddly comfortable with this strange man from a faraway place, and after a moment's concern about him grabbing the Sten gun realised there was no way she was able to handle him and the gun. They stumbled along in the shadow of the wagons, inching slowly closer to the steps. The moon shone a path to their target and Dejan's regular volleys had the guards keeping their heads down out of harm's way. They will be waiting for reinforcements that are still coping with Branko's diversionary action she thought to herself, and in the middle of her own problems allowed herself a quiet smile at the amiable and large lump of a man called Branko. She hoped his size and strength had enabled him to carry plenty of extra ammunition for the Bren gun. They were now opposite the steps and had to move from the shadow of the train and cross a ten metre patch of moonlight, exposing themselves to whatever fire the guards at the end of the train could muster up.

She looked up at her new mate whose six foot three inch frame towered over her by nearly a foot and met those eyes again. He stood up straight, gingerly putting weight on his bad leg.

"Let's get cracking," he said and promptly set off, hobbling unaided across the deadly patch of moonlight. Seconds later he was standing bent over, favouring his knee in the shelter of the steps and looking back at her. There was a renewed volley from Dejan. Ersilia knew this was when she had to go. Sure enough, Dejan's trigger finger did the trick and crouching low she scampered over the ten metres of no-man's-land to fall unintentionally into his arms. In that instant, she felt shame and guilt. Shame that as a girl brought up as a strict Catholic was in close physical contact with a male she had known less than an hour. Guilt that also less than hour ago she was on the way to becoming the soul mate of Adrijan whose body still lay beside the railway track, less than fifty metres away.

Warfare has a habit of overtaking people's ability to keep up. She was, by accident and only for a moment, physically close to a man she could barely understand, whose name she didn't know and whose country of origin she'd never heard of. Ersilia's Catholic upbringing from birth was like a rugged and rocky coastline of beliefs, customs, and faith that remained solid and unmoved, immune to the tide of recent indoctrination in communist theories and teachings that had washed over, but could never quite remove, the underlying bedrock of faith and belief.

She stood up and gestured towards the steps. He lifted his head and his eyes followed the thirty closely spaced steps to the top. He nodded, then slowly lifted his good leg onto the first step and then dragged the bad one up beside it. Changing the Sten gun over to his left hand he used his right to grip handfuls of the rough grass as an aid. Methodically repeating this process and with Ersilia following closely they made their way up to the last step. He stopped, and turned to look at her concerned face.

"Keeping up?" he grunted back to her with a wry smile on his face.

"Of course I'm keeping up," she said crossly, thinking, how could I not keep up with a lame, half-starved idiot who talks in riddles.

They both stood together in the moonlight. He looked carefully around with his trained soldier's eyes. The moon had conveniently disappeared behind clouds helping mask their presence from the enemy.

"Follow me," she said and started walking towards the large rock that was their assembly point. She stopped after twenty paces or so and waited for him to catch up. He was soon standing beside her.

"You haven't told me your name yet," she prodded.

"Alan Marshall at your service," he replied and raised his eyebrows expectantly.

"And I am Ersilia Abelli," she said and turned and started walking towards the same large rock the partisan group had assembled behind one hour ago. It was visible in the half light of a cloud covered moon. Again she stopped for him to catch up. While she waited, she stood facing the rock and put out the current bird call used to alert their group. She stood listening carefully for twenty seconds or so and then heard the reply. Alan also heard it as he arrived beside her and together they set off slowly, towards the rock. So far so good, but Ersilia knew that they were living in their enemy's time frame. Dejan still had the nervous guards pinned in their van, but his shots were now fewer as he tried to make his ammunition last.

The other enemy forces at the diversion action at the bridge would have caught on by now that they were there because of an elaborate bluff and realised they were fighting only one man. A few would stay to try and finish off Branko while the rest would be heading to the real action of the night at the railway track through the cutting. These were the thoughts that made her frustrated with her new charge as she kept getting too far ahead of him. She slowed down again but was surprised to find him soon beside her. Although injured, the long journey, crammed into a boxcar, had caused his legs to stiffen up. The enemy weren't interested in keeping prisoners in good physical condition as that would serve only to make them more difficult to contain. He was now making better progress as his legs were loosening up. They were now approaching the rock and she could see a dark figure standing beside it with a rifle levelled at them. It was Dejan taking guard duty. He'd decided he had achieved all he could and had descended from his firing position. He knew who was approaching but wasn't taking any chances.

Ersilia and Alan drew up to the large rock and stopped in front of Dejan. "Where is Adrijan?" It was the question she had been dreading.

"Come with me," she said.

They walked a few paces away from the rock and stopped. Dejan knew without asking that he was now the only one of his family left alive. He sat down and took in several deep breaths, then sat with his head bent over, staring at the ground.

"He went to attend to the driver and stoker but the driver was a Nazi. He pulled a pistol out and shot your brother in the throat. He fell down. I had a clear shot at the driver and I killed him. I tried to stop the bleeding from Adrijan's throat but I couldn't, I couldn't get it to stop."

"Who's he?" Dejan asked in a voice that was a hoarse whisper and pointed at Alan.

"A soldier from New Zealand," she replied.

Dejan pulled a pre-rolled cigarette from his pocket and lit it. He drew in one big lungful of smoke, then leant back on the rock staring up at a moon filtered by scattered clouds. Ersilia left him to it and stepped back behind the rock. She found the rest of the partisan group including Sofia, Greta and Aurora plus Marko who had made it back from the bridge. There was another allied soldier and he was standing beside Alan who had his arm around his shoulder.

"This is my old mate Evan Jeffries. He's a qualified doctor and trained medic, just the handy sort of bloke you need in a war eh?"

Ersilia stood and looked at the new addition, then turned and addressed the group.

"We must move as soon as we can. The enemy will have noticed that Dejan is no longer at his post with the rifle. Most of the force from the bridge will be heading fast towards the train and from there they will be on our trail." She turned to Evan. "Can you do anything for your friend? We have to be quick."

Ersilia was taking control. Amazingly the partisan group had all survived the operation. The remaining allied soldiers released had all scattered into the countryside. The partisans had achieved what they set out to do with one major loss, their leader Adrijan. Ersilia knew she had inherited a big job from Adrijan. She remembered Adrijan's warning about Dejan, but so far Dejan hadn't put a foot wrong. His accurate covering fire had been a major factor in the success of the mission, though Ersilia knew that it wasn't military matters that Adrijan's warning was about. It was about the sibling rivalry for her attention that bubbled just below the surface. Dejan was dark, still waters.

With Adrijan no longer alive to act as the controlling older brother, she worried about what might lie ahead. Occasionally she would look up to find him staring at her. She couldn't help not liking him and would quickly direct her attention to matters at hand. The operational part of the attack was over and the task now was to leave the area quickly and go back into hiding. The war was slowly drifting from the grasp of the Axis forces and Ersilia knew this. She also knew that the average Italian, dragged into it by a strutting Mussolini and his Fascist Party was likely to quietly disappear one by one or in twos or threes at the first opportunity to get back to home and family.

She turned and checked on Alan's leg. There wasn't a lot that could be done here and the best course of action was to get back to the cave as fast as possible where there was a more complete first aid kit delivered in the airdrop. Also they now had Evan, their own newly qualified doctor, fresh from New Zealand. Dejan stood up and started towards the track. The rest of the group followed with Ersilia, Alan and Evan, bringing up the rear.

Ersilia hoped that Branko would make it across country and follow them up the track and on to their underground hideout. They were keeping the pace as fast as they could with the injured Alan limping gamely along. Ersilia noticed a small branch stuck oddly into the ground just off the track. She told the others to keep moving and walked over to investigate. There was a mound of leaves and branches and she lifted them away to find a cache of several Bren gun magazines. She knew this would be Branko's stash hidden to provide a 'tail-gunner' resistance to anyone on their trail. That of course would depend on him surviving his mission at the bridge. She put the leaves and branches back and hurried on to catch the others.

It was slow going with Alan holding up the back three. Though she was growing impatient Ersilia had to admit there was something about the tall rangy soldier from New Zealand that caught her eye, already half opened by her short relationship with Adrijan. However these thoughts also held open the internal door to guilt. Guilt that she had been unable to stifle feelings of attraction she was reluctant to admit to. With Adrijan dead less than a day, a nagging serpent of guilt was now entangled with the magnetic appeal of the most penetrating pair of eyes she'd ever returned a gaze to. Though as they trudged on she more easily admitted to being impressed by the physical stamina of a man carrying an injury.

They came soon to the ancient spring of clear, clean water. Splashes made by Dejan and the others still darkened the large flat smoothly worn rock. Ersilia guessed they were about ten minutes behind them. Each of the three took a turn at gulping down cold mouthfuls of the water and splashing some over their faces. While she waited Ersilia turned and looked back down the track, listening for any signs of pursuit. There was no sign or sound, but a vacuum of silence was no comfort to Ersilia and she hurried impatiently on when they'd all had their fill from the bubbling spring. They covered the next five kilometres to the pass alone with their thoughts. Alan concentrated on keeping up and Evan focused on helping him as best he could. They stopped when Ersilia heard the birdcall signal. They were now approaching the pass and she waited for a few minutes until the caller showed himself. Eventually a figure sidled out from behind a tree and raised his arm in a tentative wave. It was Marko and he was carrying a Bren gun as insurance against any militia troops on their tails.

Ersilia approached him and asked for an update on Branko.

"He was holding out fine. Half the troops left to go over to the cutting when they realised that was where the real action was. I am heading down the track to meet him, if he's made it. We'll have two Bren's and plenty of ammunition to discourage the militia. We'll do a covered retreat. I'll cover him then and he'll cover me."

"Yeah. I saw his stash of magazines," Ersilia said.

Marko only nodded, then said goodbye and turned on his heel and headed off to meet his friend Branko. They battled on with Alan noticeably slowing up. At the top of the pass, Ersilia stopped and motioned them to sit down out of sight. She then climbed up a short side track leading to a rocky crag. Here she stood on the highest point of the pass looking back down the hillside to the valley now far below. She was listening for the sound of gunfire. In particular, the characteristic sound of the two Bren guns and the responding sound of German and Italian automatics. She was about to step down and return to the others, then she heard it. One Bren opening up followed a few seconds later by the other. This was followed by the different sound of the German and Italian automatics. She stood motionless, taking several deep breaths while she listened. We can't help them from here, she suddenly realised, and wiping a damp eye, she moved quickly off the rock and rejoined the group.

"We need to get back to the cave as soon as we can."

"You go on at your pace. Evan and I will follow," Alan said to her.

She knew he was right. She thought for a moment then reached into her pack and pulled out a dog-eared map.

"I will tear off four pieces that aren't needed for this area and spear one of them into the ground with a stick at the point where you depart from this track. Where I leave it you will find nearby a barely visible track. There will be another stick beside a stream you will come to. Step into the stream and follow it down for approximately one hundred metres. Keep checking the far side of the stream and you will find the third stuck on the opposite bank near a large tree, partly in the water, partly on the bank. From there walk across until you come to a shingle scree slope. Stand facing across the slope. Then turn your head to two o'clock. You will see some large rocks, some twenty metres high. The fourth piece of map will be stuck in the ground in front of the rocks. Head towards it. We will post a sentry. When he sees you, he will whistle four times with a birdcall. Your reply will be three whistles, count to five, then one whistle, count to five and then two whistles. Any whistle sound will do, just get the right number. Throw the sticks away but keep each of the pieces of map and bring them with you. I will do this now, while you two start making progress down the track.

This will not take long so I'll catch up to you in a few minutes."

Alan and Evan both nodded and headed slowly down the track. Ersilia picked up four sticks, quickly sharpening all to a point with her pocket knife, then pushed them through each piece of map. She set off again with half her attention on the way ahead and half on the battle still happening on the lower part of the track over the pass. Within a few minutes, she had caught up to Alan and Evan. As she passed them she told them the side track was only a hundred metres on, but to keep an eye out for the map on the stick. She came to the faint track cutting across the slope of the land and poked her first stick into the soft forest floor. She could see them coming and they could just see her. Secure they would find the marker, she pressed on. She was soon at the stream and pushed the second marker into the bank in a prominent place. She stepped tentatively into the stream and waded down until she reached the log marker lying partly submerged, partly up on the bank. She put the third into the bank. From here, it would be plain sailing. They only had to keep on a reasonably level course through the remaining forest and they would find themselves on the edge of the scree slope. And this was where after twenty minutes Ersilia found herself. She tested her two o'clock instruction and found it to be near enough. The tall rocks were approximately where she said they would be. She headed across the scree slope and at halfway stopped and gave the bird call. She waited impatiently and then got a response. A figure appeared from behind one of the rocks and held up a hand in greeting when they recognised her. It was Dejan.

Ersilia was not looking forward to this meeting but made her way quickly over the three hundred metres of open ground and followed him through the maze of rocks she hoped would provide an impregnable barrier to enemy troops if they ever got this far. They came to the cave entrance and pulled the camouflage flap back and went inside. The three Italian women, Sophia, Greta and Aurora had been busy setting a fire and boiling water that might be needed for the medical treatment of Alan when he arrived, or Branko or Marko if they returned alive, but wounded. There was also food in the form of a soup made from snared rabbit and local leaves and herbs the women were familiar with.

Ersilia turned and looked over at Dejan.

"I need you to go and man the sentry post by the rocks soon. Alan and Evan will be here in about half an hour. When they arrive, I want you to make all the medical supplies available to Evan, who is a doctor," she added after reading the negative expression on Dejan's face.

She sat down exhausted and hungry. She held out a plate and Sophia, who was looking after the cooking pot, ladled some food onto her plate. No one spoke and the absence of Adrijan hung heavy and unanswered. So far Ersilia had handled everything as best as could be expected but she knew Adrijan's presence was missed.

"We need more ammunition for the Bren guns, rifles and Sten guns," she said to no one in particular. With no radio, any airdrop request had to go to a contact known only to Greta. Ersilia looked at her and Greta nodded that she'd got the message. She knew there was just enough daylight to get to her contact over the Yugoslav border. She served herself a plate of stew, pulled on a jacket, and after a glance at her companions, now her close friends, stepped through the opening and into the late afternoon sun.

Ersilia sat deep in thought while she finished her plate of stew. She put the plate down and stood up and looked around at the others.

"Dejan, I want you to stay and set up the defence of our base. The two soldiers will be here soon. Make sure they have all the medical supplies they need. My place is down on the track beside Branko and Marko." She picked up the Sten gun and several magazines, then pulling the camouflage flap aside, stepped through the opening and headed off to join with Branko and Marko in the battle, or what remained of it.

She paused outside the cave, slung the Sten gun and a pack containing the magazines over her shoulder, and set off at a fast walk/jog. Within twenty minutes, she was over the stream and heading up to the pass. At the pass, she climbed onto the crag to get a view of what she might be getting into. In the distance, she could make out the figures of Marko and Branko behind their barricade of rocks. There was no sight or sound yet of the militia but they wouldn't be far away. They would have scoped out the terrain and realised what advantages lay with the partisans. She knew they would have called up more troops and would be lying low waiting for their arrival. They had time on their side and they knew it.

Chapter 25

Branko had found the perfect position to cover the track and its approaches with the Bren gun. Using his great strength, he rolled two boulders and several smaller rocks onto the track to form a wall, that together with the advantage of a natural depression, would provide some protection from militia troops. He knew the troops would be coming soon, but before he got behind his gun he opened a shoulder pack and pulled out a stick of dynamite and fifty metres of fuse wire held back from the bridge mission. He found what he was looking for, a deep fissure at ground level in the rock wall. He carefully pushed the stick of dynamite in, then covered the fuse with rocks and debris as he walked up the track feeding out the coil. He secured the end under a rock, but stood up quickly when hearing footsteps from further up the track. His Bren gun was fifty metres away but he still had an automatic pistol in a jacket pocket. The track disappeared around a curve so the owner of the footsteps was hidden from view. Branko didn't have long to wait. Marko, his comrade in arms, came swinging around the bend with a Bren gun over one shoulder and two belts of ammunition over the other. Branko was both happy and annoyed at the same time.

"Welcome to the fight brother, but you shouldn't be here," he said but wrapped his arms around him all the same.

"I am privileged to join my comrade. I believe we are hugely advantaged here," Marko replied, looking at the narrow track and the steep drop down to the valley.

"Besides, two Bren guns are better than one," he added.

"I want to see what cover we can build here. Then I will go down to man the lower position. We need to move fast," said Branko.

Marko and Branko struggled with another couple of boulders that had come down off the cliff face. They rolled them into position along with other smaller rocks. Then stood and surveyed their work while a satisfied Branko filled Marko in on his strategy.

"You probably know what I'm up to," he said.

"You are having one of us provide cover from this barricade while the man at the lower one retreats back up here when he needs to."

"That's it. But I also have a little extra surprise waiting for them." He walked over and held up the fuse that ran fifty metres back to the rock fissure.

"You are a clever man," Marko said.

"You are going to stay here. I will be at the lower barricade and when I detect any sign of the enemy, I will lay down heavy fire to keep their heads down. Then I will quickly come back to join you at the top barricade. I'll keep close to the cliff while you provide cover. When we're both behind the top barricade, we wait until they check why there is no more fire coming from the first position. They may think I've been hit. We'll keep our heads down here and wait while they bring troops up and use that position as cover. When there is enough fascist bastards there, I will light the fuse and the hillside will come down on as many of them as possible. It will also block access up to the pass. If anything happens to me, I want you to light the fuse."

Ersilia still hadn't heard anything that sounded like a firefight, but she hurried on down the track she now knew well. She estimated she was now about fifteen minutes away from the scene of Branko and Marko spotted from the crag on the pass. She broke into a slow jog, hindered by the pack and Sten gun. She reckoned she was now only five or six minutes away and then she heard the first shots. Most seemed to be coming from the Bren guns. She was still convinced that the nature of the situation would see the militia adopting a conservative strategy. They had a supply line of food, water, men and ammunition. So the scene that confronted her when she rounded the corner in the track shocked her.

Branko was sitting on the track beside the lower barricade. He had several militia surrounding him with more heading up the track. She saw instantly that Branko was a hostage or human shield preventing Marko from doing anything except watch in anguish as he was being given a beating at gun point. He wasn't telling them what they wanted to hear, which was the names and hiding place of the partisan group they accused him of being a part of. The troops also knew that holding a hostage gave them time to deal with Marko or anything else that may come their way.

Ersilia arrived at the top barricade and quickly crouched down beside Marko. "What has happened?" Ersilia asked the obvious question.

"Branko was about to retreat back up here but got hit by a speculative shot that ricocheted off the wall right next to him. Coming off the wall the bullet made a big hole in his leg. He fell on the ground and the troops that were there grabbed him and pulled him back behind the barricade."

Ersilia swore under her breath. She knew from the casual dispatch of her mother and father that Branko was doomed. She stared down the track at the enemy that now numbered about twenty.

"What is that?" she said pointing to the fuse held under a rock.

"Branko has planted a stick of dynamite in the cliff face. The fuse is hidden out of sight for most of the distance back here. The militia haven't seen it yet. But they soon will when they finish with Branko."

They both looked at each other and knew what the other was thinking. "We can't do this," Ersilia said.

"We have to do this," Marko replied.

The militia had dragged Branko to his feet. His bloodied face looked towards his partisan comrades. He lifted his right hand and drew his thumb across his throat. His message was clear. Marko picked up the fuse and handed Ersilia the lighter that Adrijan used to blow up the train. He held the fuse up in front of Ersilia. She looked back at Branko who was hanging his head while being harangued by an officer. Ersilia saw his bloodied head turn slightly towards her. He mouthed one word. She sensed the word rather than hearing it. It was Yugoslav for yes. She flicked the lighter three times. It suddenly burst into life on the fourth try. She touched the fuse and watched it ignite with a splutter and race towards the barricade, with its gloating militia standing over Branko, Ersilia's hero of the moment and for the rest of her life.

Marko and Ersilia crouched low behind their small barricade. Thirty, forty, fifty seconds ticked by. Ersilia couldn't stand it. She lifted her head an inch above the wall to see the cliff face expanding outwards, seemingly in slow motion. She watched as the huge mass lurched up and out, breaking into smaller pieces as it went. An instant later the sound of the blast had their ears ringing, followed by a tidal wave of air that fired smaller rocks against their wall. They huddled together while pebbles blown skyward rained down. They lay low for another five minutes then slowly lifted their heads above the wall of the barricade.

A large cloud of dust was still climbing to the heavens. Ersilia could see just enough to know the track was gone. A hole thirty metres wide was now where the track had once been. They were safe but Branko was dead, and as much as she tried to convince herself there was no other way, tears fell from eyes that stared blankly at a hole, that only seconds earlier twenty enemy troops and Branko had stood.

"Let us be gone," Marko said and pulled her away from the scene.

Both walked in the silence of their own thoughts. At the pass, they stopped and looked back. A few troops that had been on their way to the battle stood looking at the hole in the hillside. Ersilia was suddenly tired of conflict. Her mind was closing around the fact she had to spend the life of a close friend to achieve victory. Suddenly communist theory was no more than dry words on a page, and Catholicism she grew up with as a child, seemed a warm and familiar refuge.

They walked to the stream, waded down to the half-submerged log and climbed onto the opposite bank. In half an hour, they were on the scree slope heading towards the familiar towering rocks guarding the entrance to the cave. Dejan appeared at the side of the largest rock and greeted them as they approached.

"So Branko is dead?" he said.

"Yes, he was captured and died in the same trap he had set for the enemy."

Ersilia became silent and followed Dejan up to the cave entrance. Dejan went back to his sentry post at the rocks. Ersilia and Marko entered the cave. Their body language and the fact that Branko wasn't with them told the others as clearly as words that Branko was dead. Ersilia stood inside the entrance and spoke to the group.

"By taking advantage of our comrade Branko's clever tactics, we have inflicted heavy casualties on the enemy. We have also damaged thirty metres of the track, so in the short term it is no longer able to be used by the enemy to pursue us. That won't stop them sending reconnaissance aircraft over this area so everyone must be alert. As far as I'm concerned our operations here are finished. It is up to you to make your own way out of here. The war is turning in favour of the Allies but you would be safer to remain here until the situation is clearer. There will still be armed fascists in Italy."

Ersilia was suddenly deathly tired. They were now relatively safe for at least the next two to three days. She helped herself to the stew then lay down on her mattress of leaves and fell asleep. She woke four hours later to filtered light of early morning and could hear the sound of birds she realised she hadn't heard for days. Ersilia lay back stretching out in the luxury of there being no immediate threat or need for action. She looked around in the half-light of the cave and saw that Alan was still asleep. She looked at him and was surprised by feeling a sudden surge of desire. This is ridiculous she thought, but then realised the deaths of Adrijan and Branko had ripped two valued males out of her life in quick succession and she suddenly felt a blunt and urgent desire to create life amidst all the death and destruction.

She also realised that while her eyes were on Alan, Dejan, who had just returned from sentry duty, noted and measured the feelings Ersilia obviously had for Alan. Ersilia, glancing nervously back at Dejan, saw eyes of sullen malevolence. Feelings would have to be hidden more carefully. She had a desperate need to visit the group's latrine and got up and headed out through the entrance. Coming back on the narrow path she looked up to find Dejan blocking her way.

"I will not permit you to have a relationship with a person not in the people's army. He is a landowner in his own country and exploits labourers that work for him. He is not part of a collective and profits personally from the sale of his farm produce. I am the correct choice to be the husband of a committed communist."

Ersilia could see he was angry that she preferred a landowning capitalist farmer from New Zealand, who owed his rescue from a German prison camp, to his dead brother Adrijan.

She attempted to go around him but he stepped across the track and wrapped her in two big arms. She struggled to free herself but couldn't overcome his size and strength. Suddenly he lifted her onto his shoulder and carried her back down the narrow track ignoring her struggles and screams.

When he reached a small clearing, he dumped her on a patch of leaves then fell on top of her. Stifling further screams with his left hand he roughly pushed his right hand under her top. She felt him groping for her breasts. Feeling totally helpless with his weight pinning her to the forest floor, his other hand pushed under the band of her trousers, searching lower. She closed her eyes.

Suddenly she heard a shout and the crushing weight was pulled up and off her. Her eyes opened to see Alan with a grip on Dejan's jacket, holding him at arm's length. Dejan swung wildly, missing Alan, who threw a short, hard punch to Dejan's jaw. He took another wild swing. Alan let go of the jacket and connected with another good punch to his solar plexus. A winded Dejan crumpled to the ground. Alan had used all of the little strength he'd built over the last two days of food and rest. He bent over, dragging in deep breaths and thanking his lucky stars for landing two good punches on a bigger man in better condition.

"You all right luv?" He asked bending over Ersilia.

She didn't answer but just looked with gratitude up at the lanky Kiwi. "I don't think I can carry you back, that scrap just about finished me."

"I am alright," she said.

"What will we do with him?" Alan asked.

"I'll send Marko back from the cave," she replied. "How did you know?"

"I've got very sharp hearing and you've got a loud scream," he shot back.

Alan wasn't being totally truthful. He also wasn't asleep as she'd thought. He'd watched her get up and leave the cave, then noticed Dejan following thirty seconds later. Back at the cave Ersilia spoke to Marko who nodded and went off in search of Dejan. He returned half an hour later to tell them Dejan was nowhere to be found. Good riddance to bad rubbish thought Alan. Marko confided in Ersilia that it might be the last time he'd be seen. He'd suffered a big loss of face at the hands of Alan and had lost the woman he'd decided he should have inherited from his brother. The heavy sleeping Evan was now up and about, catching up on what had happened.

"Do you need any medical attention?" he asked Ersilia. "No, I'm alright thanks to Alan."

The three Italian women, Greta, Sophia, and Aurora were in a group talking in low tones. Greta stood and spoke to Ersilia and Alan.

"We three are leaving, we have done our duty for a free Italy and will now, God willing, make our way back to our homes."

With that, they stood and began packing their few belongings into sacks with cord tied to each. All embraced Ersilia and Alan passionately, then left the cave and partisan group and went off in search of their previous lives.

"Now our rabbiters have left I'd better see if we have anything in the traps," Marko said.

"I'll come with you," Evan said, eager to be useful, having slept through the Dejan disturbance. The two men grabbed a sack each and walked out to the low sun of the beautiful morning.

Alone with Alan, Ersilia lay back on her sleeping pad of assorted leaves and started weeping. The action that cost Branko his life and the assault and attempted rape had hit home. Alan lay beside her cradling her head on his chest. Her weeping gradually subsided, she closed her eyes and drifted off to sleep.

Alan lay back staring at the ceiling of the cave. He was now thinking of the next two weeks rather than just two days, two hours or two minutes. He needed to get hold of Ersilia's map and see how they could get themselves out of here. He started formulating a rough plan. They would hang out here for three to four days then look to find the best way across country to Trieste. From information picked up on the train, he knew the Allies were slowly pushing German troops further and further north. Towns and cities of southern Italy had been freed of Axis control and many Italians had by now accepted the reality of defeat in a war they were bullied into by Mussolini's fascists. A different fate awaited their countrymen who'd embraced the fascist cause. He looked down at Ersilia, suppressing his desire to wake her, then he too slowly closed his eyes and drifted into a deep sleep.

They both woke an hour later to the sound of voices from outside of Marko and Evan returning with their catch and they both came in with two furry prizes. Evan, who had shot, skinned and cleaned plenty of rabbits on his parents' farm back home, started that chore while Marko grabbed some twigs and restarted the smouldering embers of the cooking fire. He then put on some bigger wood, added more twigs and small branches then sat beside it waiting for it to take hold. Once satisfied, he placed the blackened pot on a ring of rocks, then poured in some water from a couple of wine bottles, followed by a handful of edible leaves and herbs gathered while clearing the traps.

Evan finished gutting and skinning two healthy rabbits and dropped them in the pot. He stood staring at the brew, lost in thought. Finally he turned to Alan and cleared his throat.

"I have decided to head off with Marko. We are crossing into Yugoslavia and staying for a while with Marko's family. Doctors are in high demand so I guess I can make myself useful over there." He looked at Marko who nodded in agreement.

"We'll have a bit of this once it's ready then take off. Marko knows of a hut about three hours away so we'll kip there tonight and be at Marko's place late tomorrow," he said. The others sat glumly absorbing the news.

"Well this show's just about over," Alan said and looked at Ersilia who seemed sad. "Buck up luv it's not all bad news. At least, you're still alive and kicking."

"It was so…" She searched for the right words, then fell silent. She tried again. "I had a hand in the death of Branko, but then through him we killed many of our enemies, some who probably had a hand in my parents' death. I also lost my friend, Adrijan, but now I have you." She turned and put her arms around him and felt her eyes drawn to his. He hugged her tightly, swaying gently back and forth.

Evan and Marko, who had kept their heads down, quietly eating some of the rabbit, wiped their mouths on their sleeves and stood up.

"We're off," Marko said which ended any further conversation. They picked up their bags and shook hands with Ersilia and Alan. But before they left, Ersilia told them of their plans to get to her Uncle Artemio's home near Monfalcone. On that note Evan and Marko marched out of their home and refuge of several weeks into the early afternoon sun.

"We're on our own luv," Alan said.

"I can see that myself luv." She giggled, adding a heavily accented tease and staring up into his intense, see everything eyes. Eyes that seemed to drag her bodily to him. Like when she found him in the boxcar, two days ago.

"Our meal is ready for tonight, so why don't we walk to the top of the hill?" He asked. "How far…How long…?"

"Not much more than five minutes I reckon."

"Ok…but I'll be keeping time."

"Don't worry. I can't handle any more than that."

He picked up the cover from the bed and she followed him into the daylight. The track to the latrine forked right then headed up an easy climb through forest that thinned out as they gained altitude. The sun was heading down making silhouettes of the hills he thought lay just inside the Yugoslav border. Small columns of smoke rose from a few scattered cottages, bending over with the drift of a slight breeze. They picked a spot and he lay back on the cover. Ersilia propped herself on her elbow, looking towards the hills and cottages.

The scene reminded her of her parents. Cottages alive with people, aromas of simple food cooking and the clatter of dishes and utensils. A modest evening meal at a heavy wooden table, muted talk fitting the serious times. Ersilia sat silent, thoughts of a family at the meal table drifted into a mind no longer preoccupied with fighting a war or just staying alive. She lay back and closed her eyes and the scene of her parents lying on their kitchen floor came to her, then Adrijan and Branko. She opened her eyes and looked at Alan, suddenly hating him for being so attractive to her. Adrijan had only been dead two days and she felt the knife of guilt cut into her, exposing shame and regret.

His hand reached out and touched her bare arm. The effect was electric, but not of pleasure. She felt repelled and turned her body away. Alan, although coming from the back blocks of rural New Zealand, knew something was wrong and decided to keep his hands to himself. His father had died when he was twelve years old and his youth was ruled by an articulate and intelligent mother plus two older sisters.

"You OK?"

"Don't talk."

"OK."

There was a moment of silence while Ersilia, choosing to ignore the scene that opened raw memories, lay back with her eyes closed. Stillborn tears welled up and sat where they were as she lay locked in her thoughts.

The sun was now only a sliver of deep orange. Alan stood and looked down at her still form. Like a young child falling asleep away from its bed, she had drifted off. He was loathe to wake her. Knowing they had to move while it was still light he bent down, reached under her prone form and lifted her up. He was still well short of full strength and fitness, but Ersilia's war rations' weight was not going to be a problem descending the track to the cave.

In the cave, he laid her on the bed still asleep, then sat down beside her. Someone had left a near full bottle of merlot. He pulled the cork and consoled himself with a couple of mouthfuls. He was developing a likeness for something not often drunk by the ordinary men of the land in New Zealand. Another mouthful and the warm glow of the wine was making him wonder at his fondness of beer since he was a teenager.

"Don't drink all that," Ersilia said with put-on sharpness. "So…awake at last."

She sat up and reached for the bottle.

"I'm starting to like this, got any more?" he said handing it to her.

"One bottle, I think we should keep for tomorrow night. Both bottles came from my parents' cellar." She paused as she swallowed a mouthful. "Even peasant farmers have wine cellars, the Germans took most of ours but missed two hidden behind a loose stone. If they'd found them, my parents could have been shot there and then instead of having another three months of life."

She sat staring at the empty bottle as if her parents might materialise from something that had always been part of the evening meal. She put the bottle down and leant her head back against his lean frame. Her right hand reached over and pushed his shirt back. She walked her fingers across his chest, still showing signs of the long days clearing scrub on the family farm.

"You don't feel like you've spent much time sitting around," she said.

"I've done my share."

"But you own a large farm. Why don't you have labourers to do all the hard work like our big landowners?"

"It doesn't work like that in New Zealand. Most farmers do their own work, but some workers come and shear sheep or build fences."

"How much land do you own?"

"About two hundred and fifty acres in one farm and one hundred and fifty acres in another. They are owned jointly by my parents and myself. I will probably take them over when I get back."

Ersilia felt she had asked enough questions and lay back turning the answers over in her mind. It was a different world in this sliver of land called New Zealand, tucked away in the southern reaches of the Pacific Ocean. The warmth of the wine and the gentle drift of the conversation had her back asleep, dreaming of a fantasy land of palm trees and sheep. He had told her there were plenty of sheep and quite a few dairy cows, but not a lot of palm trees, at least not those fringing beautiful islands with white sandy beaches.

Half an hour later she woke with her head lying across his chest. She sat up and turned to catch his eyes looking straight into hers.

"I'm hungry and tired of rabbit but it's all we have." She slowly stood up and scooped two portions out of the pot that still had embers glowing around its base. She handed him the plate with a bent fork. They ate in a comfortable silence, more typical of couples who had spent years in each other's company, not just a few days. She finished and lay back again. Her head turned and looked at him, thinking about the next sentence.

"What are we going to do and when?"

"I say we bed down for the night. Tomorrow we should start looking for the best way to Trieste."

They slept the sleep not of innocence, but of total exhaustion and woke in the morning to the scattered rays of the new sun pricking the camouflage over the cave entrance. She rose early and stood for a few seconds looking at his face. Different to Italian males, he was quieter and not given to quick flashes of emotion or mood. It was taking her a while to change down a gear to a more measured and steady pace that was the quiet style of this man. She liked it.

She stepped quietly away towards the back of the cave, where after a few minutes searching in the lowlight, found what she was looking for, a short length of cord poking out between loose rocks. She pulled at it, at the same time she pulled backwards on the largest rock. Kneeling down she reached into the gap and got hold of what she was after, a green army issue satchel.

"Thank you Adrijan," she whispered to herself.

"Who's Adrijan?" asked a voice behind her.

She jumped up to find Alan looking over her shoulder.

"This was going to be a surprise. Here, make yourself useful," she said handing him the heavy bag.

She followed him through the entrance and into the sunlight. He put the bag on a handy rock and opened it. Inside were several cans of bully beef, two can openers, a sealed tin of coffee and two cans of condensed milk.

"But who is Adrijan?" He repeated.

"A comrade who was shot dead when we blew up the train you were on."

"So he left this little gift and you were the only one who knew about it."

"That's right. Now we have enough food to get us some of the way to Trieste." They stood looking at each other.

"Get the map and show me just how we're going to do that."

She reappeared and spread the map across the flattest rock she could find. After a few seconds, she pointed her finger at their present location.

"Our position is roughly halfway between two towns, Cividale del Friuli and Gorizia, and very close to the Yugoslav border. My father had a brother living near Monfalcone about a couple of days walk from here. I say we head for that and the sooner we start the better."

They finished what rabbit was left in the pot and gathered up their few belongings. Ersilia had her pack and Alan used the green army satchel. They knew the larger weapons left lying around were more a liability then an asset, and decided to each keep a more easily hidden automatic pistol, plus twenty rounds of ammunition. They disposed of a Bren gun and three Sten guns down a short drop at the far end of the cave. They were now packed up and ready to go. One last check saw other evidence of their occupation following the Bren and Sten guns into the short drop. They hefted their packs on their backs and stood at the entrance for several seconds looking back, then set off.

They weaved their way through the now familiar jumble of limestone rocks and after carefully looking around stepped out onto the scree slope. The need was to move quickly as this would be the only point of exposure to any aircraft out hunting partisans. No aircraft were around and they soon entered the forest on the other side. They stopped under the cover of the trees and looked back across the slope to their palisade of limestone rocks that had given security and protection. They knew they wouldn't come this way again and moved on knowing they were parting from comrades in arms, both alive and dead.

They were still on familiar ground and could hear the stream ahead. Alan got to it first and held back waiting for Ersilia, but he was also holding back to make sure there were no nasty surprises waiting. Alan was suspicious. Everything seemed to be going so well, maybe too well. Ersilia joined him and they slowly entered the ice-cold water. Following normal procedure they waded fifty metres downstream and then climbed onto the opposite bank. They planned to follow the track down to within ten kilometres of the border, then head south on old tracks used by peasant farmers making their way to the market towns of Manzano, Cormons, Gorizia and Cervignano del Friuli. This, Ersilia told Alan, would get them well on the way to Trieste. She also calculated they would be close to her uncle living near Gorizia by nightfall and avoid having to sleep out.

The track was all downhill so they made good time and reached the turnoff point that would take them south in ninety minutes. As they were not up to date with the latest war news they chose to stay clear of well used roads to dodge possible enemy patrols and instead made use of the old tracks and lanes that interlaced the countryside. Their progress was being slowed by the hilly terrain. They had been walking now for three hours so found a small clearing off the track to have a break for food and rest. They both drifted into a light sleep and woke up half an hour later to the realisation they weren't going to make it to Ersilia's uncle by nightfall. Alan stood up and looked around. He began to realise there was signs of people having been around the area. He skirted around the edge of the clearing and found an overgrown trail leading away. He pushed through the grass and low scrub and followed the trail for twenty metres, then turned back and called for Ersilia. She came and together they continued along the old trail. The trail took a sharp turn and there they found what they were hoping for, a small, abandoned goat herders' hut, similar to the one Ersilia spent her first night on the run from the militia.

"This will do us," Alan said and gave the door a shove.

The door fell in held on by one rusted hinge. They went in and pushed it back in place. They could spend the night here, get a good sleep and make an early start tomorrow. A surprisingly good mattress lay on a hand fashioned frame. The sun was disappearing behind a hill so they made the most of the remaining light and fixed a scratch meal of bully beef washed down with a mouthful of leftover Merlot. They turned in early and Ersilia was soon asleep. Alan lay awake mulling over the last two days. Something nagged at him that he couldn't put a finger on. He had a sense of déjà vu that made no sense. He looked at his watch, it was ten o'clock. Abruptly something did make sense. A faint but definite aroma was part of the little hut and it was the same smell of the cigarettes that Dejan smoked. Yugoslavian tobacco that had a distinctive and pungent odour. Dejan must have been here recently, maybe today, or an hour or two before they arrived.

He was worried. Dejan was nasty piece of work and bitter about the events of the previous day. Alan knew that Dejan was capable of anything and also knew he would want his head on a stick. He was very aware he'd got a lucky punch in on a bigger man in better nick than himself. He mightn't be so lucky next time. Ersilia turned over in her sleep, then suddenly got out of the bed, and before he could react, opened the door and went around the back of the hut to relieve herself. He lay waiting for her to return. Suddenly the door bashed half-open but instead of Ersilia it was Dejan. He stepped around the half-open door and took one long stride to the bed and stood over Alan pointing a revolver at his head.

"It's the end for you my friend," Dejan said coldly.

There was a loud explosion from the doorway. Ersilia had come back and saw Dejan with the revolver. Fearing wild pigs Alan had talked about, she'd taken her automatic with her and without hesitation pointed and fired it at point blank range into his back, a second before he was about to snuff out Alan. Dejan pitched forward and fell on the floor. Alan jumped up and grabbed the revolver from Dejan's hand. He rolled his body over. Dejan was alive but only just. He looked up at Ersilia with eyes that condemned her. He opened his mouth to speak then reached up with his right hand. No words came out and the hand dropped to the floor. His eyes closed for the last time.

"God. What have I done? I've murdered someone!" Ersilia screamed. Alan's mouth was dry and his voice a hoarse whisper.

"You haven't murdered anyone. You've killed someone that was about to murder me. It's self-defence on my behalf. We've got to get him out and into the forest. We'll stay until first light then get the hell out of here. There's wild pigs around. They'll take care of him."

"Oh God. Oh God forgive me," and she closed her eyes, and silently, with her lips moving in a short prayer, crossed herself.

Alan stepped over to the body and grabbed the front of Dejan's jacket…adrenalin adding to near panic gave him the strength to drag the heavy body to the door.

"Open the door wider for me. Stop praying and just open the door," he said through gritted teeth.

Her eyes opened from the trance-like state she was in and turned and dragged the sagging door back into the room. Then she grabbed an arm and together they pulled the body through the door and onto the ground outside. They stood with hands on knees, gasping in the cold air, and after a few seconds restarted their efforts. It was a little easier on the slick, dew soaked grass and they managed to pull Dejan's body into low scrub that obscured it from anyone going by.

"The pigs will take care of him," Alan repeated. He pushed his hand into each of Dejan's pockets and pulled out an ID card and some papers, then he grabbed a numbered neck tag and yanked hard. It came off in his hand. These articles will be disposed of away from the scene. He put his arm around a stunned Ersilia and together they walked back to the little hut.

"He must have been stalking us and staked out the hut. He knew we'd be coming this way."

They lay now in each other's arms. Ersilia fell silent, brooding over the knowledge she'd now had a hand in several deaths. Dejan's death was more than just a hand. Hers was the only hand. Alan knew what was going through her mind.

"Hey, remember that while you caused Dejan's death, you caused my life. I was a goner. He caused his own death by trying to cause mine. It was something he chose."

She turned and looked at him. She knew what he said was true, spoken in a simple, straight, uncomplicated way. He returned her gaze with the most honest eyes she'd ever seen. She reached out and put her arms around him, squeezing his body into hers. She could feel all of him against her, his hardness pressing into her stomach. Her fear and sense of guilt had now somersaulted into a desperate need for life and love. She parted her legs and pushed herself against him. He responded and reached down, freeing himself and her from the garments they still wore. She'd never had full sex but understood all she needed to. Ersilia rolled onto her back and opened her legs. He rolled on top of her and she opened herself for him.

"Yes," she said in his ear and bit into it as he pushed forward. "Oh yes. Oh God. Yes. It hurts but don't stop. Please don't ever stop." They both kept going oblivious to anything else in the world.

Chapter 26

Alan woke first and realised he'd just had the best sleep for days. This in spite of the killing of Dejan and his body lying no more than fifty metres away. He realised he'd been unconsciously worried about Dejan and what he was doing and where he was going. The threat had haunted him since he dealt to him in the clearing by the track from the cave. Ersilia woke, stretched and opened her eyes. She looked at him differently now. He was lying still, thinking and staring into the distance. Maybe he regretted last night. Then it occurred to her that if they like you, most men don't make a habit of regretting sex. She looked at his face for another few seconds. She liked his chin and nose. Clearly defined on an already strong face...and there were his eyes. Steady and seeing everything. Slowly he turned his head to her and looked into her face.

"So what are you looking at mate?" She said using the colloquial Kiwi label. He smiled back at her, the first time for a while.

"Don't ask me what I'm looking at. You were looking at me."

"No. You were looking at me," she said.

"Anyway, you're not allowed to call me mate. Mates are people I drink beer with, shear sheep with, go duck shooting and fencing with, and, I don't sleep in the same bed as mates."

And so the word game went on until the lowlight in the hut became shards of sunlight coming over nearby hills and through the one smudgy cobwebbed window.

The conversation gradually ebbed into a sleepy silence. Later, and still half asleep, Alan suddenly sat up shaking his head, trying to exit a nightmare of a wild pig and a dead body. He turned half opened eyes towards Ersilia and at the same time last night's events came rushing back into his life. He was soon very wide awake.

"Ersilia, we've got to get the hell out of here. Let's grab some food and the map and find the quickest way to your uncle's place and we need to go soon, very soon."

This was the most animated Ersilia had seen Alan. She pushed her feet out of bed and stood on the rough planked floor. Minutes later and both ravenously hungry, they were bolting down another can of bully beef. They had no heat, so they mixed condensed milk with ersatz coffee and water from the army flask and drank it cold. Alan put empty cans and anything else incriminating in his pack. No clue was going to be left that could link them to a dead body or its skeletal remains.

Once more they said goodbye to a shelter that served them well and was lucky for them both. "It was a lucky little hut, " she said.

"It was a very lucky little hut," Alan replied with a faint smile.

Alan led her quickly down the half-formed track that soon turned left onto the main track. An ancient stone marker with Gorizia and an engraved arrow showed they were heading in the right direction. They walked in silence, both thinking about the previous night. Ersilia stopped and pulled out the map.

"My uncle's home is on this side of Monfalcone. We must avoid towns on the way in case German troops are still about." Alan just nodded. They continued on, following the tracks and trails that served Italian peasantry for centuries. Ersilia walked with the map in hand, stopping occasionally to confirm they were still on course. A meeting of five tracks converged into an ancient intersection. She stopped and turned the map around until she had it orientated to the lie of the land.

"We need to change direction so we don't go through Gorizia," she said holding up the map. Alan didn't say much. It was Ersilia's home, her country and she had a working knowledge of the local geography. He nodded and looked at her. "So let's go, what are we waiting for?"

They walked past another stone marker pointing to Gorizia. Ersilia stopped and took another look at the map.

"We need to follow this one," she said pointing at a rough, unpromising track that wasn't going to Gorizia. Alan was starting to flag. The starvation diet of captivity, intended to make prisoners tame and easy to keep under control was taking its toll. They had now slowed to a shuffle and finally a halt. They sat down and Ersilia dug another can of beef out of her pack. She opened it and they shared the contents like it was a gourmet meal. Alan lay back and drifted into a fitful sleep. He could soon hear the soft, tinkling of bells. Then he felt Ersilia shaking him.

"Someone's coming," she said. He sat bolt upright and looked around. She was now standing, pulling on his arm to get up. He stood and followed her into a patch of scrub. They didn't have long to wait. Around a corner came a farmer, a dog and a small goat herd.

"The dog's going to find us," Alan hissed in her ear. Sure enough within thirty seconds the dog had sniffed them out and came and stood a couple of metres away, wagging its tail and whining.

It was a border collie, a dog that Alan was used to working with, but no amount of kidding was going to convince the dog to go about its business. The stalemate was broken by the arrival of a middle-aged peasant farmer. He stopped opposite them cradling a shot gun, carried no doubt to bag any rabbit he came across.

"Chiunque tu sia, tichiedo di mostrarti," he called out. "He has demanded we show ourselves," Ersilia translated and replied, "Siamo disarmati veniamo in pace. I have told him we are unarmed and come in peace."

They both stepped out onto the track with the dog happily following new friends. The man immediately snapped the shot gun closed and aimed in their direction.

Ersilia and Alan stood looking into the man's eyes. They had to decide if he was a well-disguised fascist or just as he appeared, a kindly, gentle and hopefully a friend to those fighting German and Italian fascism. Ersilia engaged in a slow, careful conversation with the man in her own dialect. Alan could understand no more than one or two words, so concentrated on his face. After a few minutes, the conversation concluded and Ersilia turned to Alan.

"Our new friend accepts what I have told him and has offered us shelter in one of his farm buildings. German presence is less in this area. Their troops are moving south to face the American forces advancing to the north. But there are spies around and a few local Italians still loyal or obligated to the Nazis. We have to be careful and treat everyone as an enemy. We will follow him two hundred metres behind. That way he won't be compromised if he meets a patrol and we will have some warning. He knows of my uncle and where he lives."

The man understood what she said to Alan so turned around with his dog and goats and headed off as if they'd never met. Alan and Ersilia waited while the little group rounded the next corner, then set off following the goat bells tinkling in the distance. Alan felt a big lift in his spirit and an even bigger lift in his step. Ersilia was given a description of the farm building lying well away from the farmer's house with a grove of walnut trees nearby. They could eat as many walnuts as they liked, stay the night and be away early in the morning.

They trudged on in silence making steady progress. A late start, the rest stop and the meeting with the old man meant early dusk was approaching as they were getting close to their destination. The barn lay well off the road near a grove of walnut trees as the old man described. They both looked up and down the deserted road then headed quickly towards their next place of shelter.

Alan approached the door and gave it a careful push. A couple of pigeons scared the daylights out of them as they shot past through a door that had been shut for several months. They stopped, took a couple of deep breaths, then walked through the door into the warm smell of farm animals both were familiar with. Hay and other winter stock feed lay around the floor and a pile of clean hay filled one corner. This was the obvious place to spend the night. Alan went back to the door, checked outside, then closed it. A barn cat kept to control mice wound itself around his leg. He suddenly felt he was on familiar ground. It brought back memories a world away, about home in New Zealand and a life that was so different yet at the same time not so different.

They ate more of their shrinking store of bully beef, grabbed some water from a rain barrel outside the door, mixed some ersatz coffee and condensed milk and swigged it down cold. It was still light so they decided to risk being sighted and went outside to the walnut grove and quickly scooped up as many walnuts as they could. They hurried back inside and spent half an hour cracking open walnuts for a welcome change to their diet. A hole in the floor took the shells. The food was getting less and less so they still went to bed hungry with rumbling stomachs.

Alan woke at three am with the farmer standing over them. He carried a masked off lantern and was speaking urgently in Italian to Ersilia. He finished, saluted them both and left as quickly as he'd arrived.

"We have to leave now. He has been warned the Germans that are still here are planning a dawn raid through the valley. If we are found, we will be shot as partisans along with his family. Their house and farm buildings will be burnt to the ground. We must go now. We must get rid of any walnuts, just throw them down the hole in the floor. If we were caught with them, the Germans will know where they came from, their walnut grove would be well known in the district.

He doesn't think we were betrayed by anyone but the militia have to show they are doing their job."

Alan didn't say anything, but stood up, grabbed his gear, then went and emptied two handfuls of walnuts down the hole. He turned to see how Ersilia was going. She was dressed and shouldering her pack. They looked around then headed for the door and stepped out into the night. There was no moon and a heavy mist lay over the ground. A mixed blessing, they couldn't see the enemy but then neither could the enemy see them.

They pressed on through mist that wet their faces and swirled around them like a bow wave. Every ten minutes they stopped and listened, mindful that although invisible from more than a few metres, the mist also muffled the sound of enemy troop vehicles approaching. They walked nervously on, ready to dive off the road if a vehicle suddenly loomed up.

"You can't always trust the information you get. They might try and surprise us with an early pre-dawn call," Ersilia said.

Alan merely grunted as they trudged on through the early hours.

They were now well past the farmer's home and could just make out the faint glow of sunrise.

"The mist will burn off soon and we'll be sticking out like the proverbial"

"Proverbial what?" Ersilia asked.

"Never mind. I'll explain later," Alan replied.

A rumble coming up from behind froze them in their tracks. They dodged in behind a handy rock and waited to see what turned up. They didn't have long to wait. A noisy Fiat truck suddenly appeared out of the gloom and clattered to a halt opposite their hideout. A young man opened the door, got out and stood beside the truck. He spoke urgently in Italian.

"Sono il figlio del contadino che ti ha permesso di restare nel granaio la scorsa notte, posso portarti entrambi a Trieste."

"He said he is the grandson of the farmer whose barn we stayed in last night and he can take us to Trieste. I believe we should go with him," Ersilia said.

"I agree. I'm bloody sick of walking, so when can we get on?"

The young man walked a few paces and appeared around the side of the rock wearing a big smile. "C'e un pavimento falso nel camion che trasporta un carico di fluido di maiale, che sara pieno e maleodorante, ma l'odore impedisce ai tedeschi di avvicinarsi troppo. Ha funzionato fino ad ora," he said still smiling.

"He has told me there is a false floor in the truck. It will be a crammed journey and also smelly. He carries a load of pig swill. It discourages the Germans from looking further. It also confuses any dogs that may be with them. He says it has worked so far."

"It's probably better than taking our chances on the road with the sun coming up," Alan said.

"Come ci hai trovato?"Ersilia asked the young man.

The young man merely stuck his hand in his pocket and brought out a handful of walnuts.

"Hai lasciato una scia debole," he said still smiling.

"He just followed a trail of walnuts when he found us gone from the barn," Ersilia said.

Alan held up his pack and found a hole in the corner where several he'd forgotten had dropped through. The young driver had merely followed the trail to the rock.

"Mi chiamo Flavio."

"He said his name is Flavio."

He went over to the side of the truck and unscrewed a metal panel running under the tray. There was a space just big enough for two half-starved people like Ersilia and Alan. They shoved their packs on board and slid in after them.

"Niente piu noci ovunque? Any more walnuts?" he asked.

"Assolutamente no," Ersilia replied.

He crouched down and spoke at length to Ersilia who lay next to the opening while Alan lay beside her staring at the boards that formed the false tray inches from his face.

"He told me that it will be crammed and smelly which we already know. He takes the load to a farmer who raises excellent pork that he gives free to a select few in the militia. It compromises a favoured few so they are a little less rigorous in their checking, but are in big trouble if their superiors find out, especially when it's something they are not part of," Ersilia said.

The young Italian then flipped the panel up and quickly replaced the screws. Alan and Ersilia soon found it wasn't only the smell that followed them, on every bump. Juices from the vegetable scraps leaked through the planks onto both of them.

"Are you sure this is better than walking?" Alan whispered.

"You'll get rid of the smell eventually but at least you're more likely to be alive," she whispered back.

The truck bumped and rattled on for what felt like hours until Alan and Ersilia felt it slowing and turning off the road. It continued on another rough track they guessed would be the entrance to the farm. They pulled up in a yard and heard the young man get out and start talking to someone. They froze when the other person replied. Ersilia turned her head and looked through a small gap in the side of the truck. Her hand was holding Alan's arm and he felt her grip tighten. What she saw was a pair of shiny, black jackboots as worn by Nazi officers.

"Germans," she mouthed to Alan who slowly nodded his understanding. She gripped his arm even tighter as she watched the boots walk towards the truck, stop suddenly, then quickly back away.

"My God, it amazes me that something that smells so repulsive, can create pork made in heaven," he said with a perfect Oxford accent.

"It's the walnuts that make the difference," the young man said.

"Oh really? Well, it certainly works," he replied. She let out a long slow breath and watched them walk towards the entrance to the farmhouse kitchen. A few minutes later Ersilia caught a glimpse of him leaving with what she guessed was a large package of meat then disappear from view. She heard a few sentences exchanged in German followed by laughter. A vehicle door slammed shut, the engine started and the vehicle headed off down the drive and onto the road. They both breathed out slowly and lay waiting for the young man to return.

"You can let go of my arm now," Alan said.

They heard the kitchen door closing and the sound of heavy boots coming towards them. The boots halted by the truck. "It is I, Alfonso. I will now take you to your uncle who lives near Monfalcone. I know of this person. He is a good man and trustworthy. My grandson Flavio has told me that is where you wish to go. I am old. I've had my life and I do not wish to risk the life of my grandson any further. I have already lost two sons to those bastards." With that Alfonso climbed into the driver's seat and started the little diesel. He engaged first gear and they were on their way again.

It was a rough ride, but they both fell into the sleep of those who've had very little. Alan woke to singing. It was Alfonso running through his favourite operas loved by all Italians. New territory for Alan but well known to Ersilia who was still asleep. Soon the rural roads were replaced by the smoother surface of main roads. Alfonso had started on Puccini and the moving story of a love forlorn maiden, who, forbidden to return the love of a suiter not favoured by her father, threatens to throw herself into the Arno. Ersilia woke and her eyes turned to look at Alan. She could see that, while unable to understand the words, the emotion of the music had breached his usual control, something she hadn't anticipated. She moved closer to him and in the cramped space wrapped her only free arm over his chest. He stiffened slightly, coughed and turned his head away, then turned back to her and pulled her closer. They stayed like that for several minutes.

They both dozed fitfully as the little truck rolled on. Eventually they heard the engine slowing and the truck pulled onto a short road that took them to the back of a large two-story house.

"Your uncle's house near Monfalcone?" Alan asked as Ersilia peered in the half-light through the tiny gap in side of the truck. The answer came when Alfonso got down from the truck and after carefully checking the surrounding area, removed the side panel. Ersilia put her face out into the clear night air, then climbed down from the truck and looked around. She remembered the house from when she was a young girl. Memories flooded back and she stood motionless, hands clasped in front of her face, and prayed that her uncle, aunty and their family were still alive and living in their home. Alan had joined her beside the truck and both stood, stretching arms and legs stiffened from hours of travel in a tight space.

A light turned on in the house and she caught sight of an anxious male face looking out. The face disappeared and there was no more sign of life for five minutes. Then a door cracked open and a figure appeared with a lantern in one hand and a shot gun in the other. It was Ersilia's uncle, bent over and older then she expected until she realised she hadn't seen him for fifteen years. He moved a few paces and held the lantern up towards them.

"It is I, Ersilia Abelli, Uncle Artemio." The old man shuffled forward. "Ersilia, my dear niece Ersilia. Is it Ersilia I am looking at, my brother's daughter?"

"It is Ersilia," she replied.

"And who are those people with you?"

"This is my friend Alan Marshal from New Zealand and this is Alfonso from near Gorizia. He delivered us to your door."

The old man shook Alfonso's hand, then directed him in Italian to drive the truck around the back of the house, where he would find an implement shed. He followed the truck to the shed, opened the doors and waved him in. He closed and padlocked the doors. "Come inside, come inside," he repeated as he wrapped a strong arm around his niece he hadn't seen for so long. He stood in the doorway and waved the others through to a large lounge with a kitchen attached. Looking discreetly around Alan reflected that Ersilia's uncle was probably at one time, if not any longer, a man of substance.

"Why are you followed by such a strong smell?" He cupped a big hand around his good ear and listened as Ersilia explained the reason for travelling under a tray of pig food.

"Well, here's what I suggest, you fix some food for everyone. There's a little cheese, sausage and bread in the safe. I will light a fire under the washhouse copper. You can use that as a bath, just like you did when you were little. Sadly it is all I can offer you. The fascist bastards came through here and took all the metal away for the war effort, their war effort," he added.

She looked at him as he headed to the door. He stopped and looked back at her. He knew what she was going to ask him.

"Your aunty, my darling Daniella died two years ago when she was arrested and held on suspicion of being a staffette."

"Courier, or message runner," Ersilia explained to Alan.

Ersilia's spirits sank. She realised her family and extended family now amounted to Giuseppe, her brother she hadn't seen for eighteen months, possibly lying dead on a battle field and her ageing uncle Artemio who was heading off to light up the washhouse copper. She went to the wall safe and took out cheese, sausage and bread. She found three plates and set them out on the table. After eating everything, all three sat in exhausted silence with their own thoughts.

Artemio returned to find Alfonso asleep and Alan and Ersilia almost. He went to a moulding on the wall and gave it a sharp pull. Alan's eyes opened wide as a door swung back to reveal a small wine cellar. "You've got to keep something from the thieving buggers," he said, reaching in and pulling out two bottles of Merlot. He held one up to the light.

"Had this one for ten years. Tonight's the night we lay it to rest." He put both bottles on the table and took four glasses off a shelf, putting one in front of each person. Alfonso woke with a start to find a full glass of Merlot in front of him.

"A good reward for a long day's work," he said and quaffed it down.

Artemio followed suit. Ersilia saw everything was running smoothly and giving a little wave to Alan picked up the lantern and went outside to find the washhouse. It was where she remembered…pushing the door open she was hit by a wall of warm air from the expertly lit fire. She put the lantern on a brick ledge and leant over to feel the water. Just warm enough and it would warm up more while she soaked up the heat. She put another three good sized logs on and started stripping off the smelly clothes. She would wash them once the bath was over. Now as naked as she was as a child fifteen years ago, she climbed onto a stool, pushed the wringer attachment aside and stepped into the large family-sized copper, now a makeshift bath. The warm water enveloped her and soothed the aching muscles she had lived with for the last few months of sleeping and living rough.

Meanwhile Alan's mind was dwelling on the thought of Ersilia soaking in the old copper. He could see the wine was taking hold of Alfonso and Artemio was succumbing as well. A few minutes later and both old men were slouched back in their chairs asleep. Alan picked up the new bottle plus a glass off the shelf for Ersilia and quietly headed for the door. He creaked it open and looked back to see Artemio's eyes open briefly at the sound then close again. His head slumped forward and he began snoring loudly. Satisfied now there would be no interruptions from Ersilia's one remaining family member, he stepped outside. Twenty metres away he could see the washhouse with steam wafting from a small window and the glow of Ersilia's lantern. He stepped carefully across the dark yard with the precious cargo.

Holding the neck of the bottle and two glasses in one large hand he quietly turned the ornate door handle. He wasn't sure what reception he was going to get. Granted, Ersilia and he had made love but he was very aware of the modesty and strictures of a Catholic upbringing from his youth in New Zealand. Guessing she would be naked, he stepped quietly into the steam filled room. Ersilia was sitting with her head tilted back and eyes closed, unaware he was there.

As he looked at her the lantern threw a flickering glow over two beautiful breasts with large brown nipples. He stopped, unable to move, transfixed by the scene and a measure of guilt for being a secret witness to it. Ersilia woke from her dreamy state and turned her head to stare shocked and wide-eyed at Alan. No male including her father would have seen her as a mature woman. Her hands flew up to cover her breasts, but then her eyes softened and one hand slipped back into the warmth of the water. Without taking her eyes off his she reached out and picked up a piece of homemade soap from a nearby shelf. Maintaining her steady gaze she held the soap out for him.

Alan put the bottle of wine down with the two glasses and grasped the soap. He knew what he was here for. He stood behind her and after dipping it in the warm water he began gliding the soap over her breasts. Ersilia slowly slid up into a standing position. She bent her head back so her mouth was beside his ear.

"Take your clothes off, all of them. They smell anyway," she whispered. Alan was still just a shy young man from the country with little experience of women, particularly one that wanted him to strip naked in front of her. Needing a bit of courage he put down the soap and reached for the bottle of wine. He popped the cork and poured two glasses. He handed Ersilia one and took a big gulp from his. Ersilia leant back in the old copper and looked on with eager, expectant eyes. Alan, fortified by the wine, began to disrobe. He removed everything down to his shorts which he finally dropped to the floor.

"Well, thank you. After all you did sneak up on me but I think I've got room to squeeze you in out of the cold," she said and moved over to give him space. They had found another piece of soap and took turns cleaning each other as the candle lantern finally spluttered and died away to nothing.

She lay back against his chest with his long legs wrapped around her. A large moon low in the sky glowed orange through the window, replacing the spent candle.

"Another lucky little place," she said.

"Lucky, very lucky," he replied tracing a soapy finger between her breasts and resting at her navel. She placed her hand over his and slowly moved it down until it found a home between her legs. She sighed and stretched out as far as the old copper would let her. She sighed again and again, then stretched her legs and arched her neck back so her head and face crushed hard against his cheek. She pushed harder and harder against his persistent hand and then let out one long last sigh.

They both dozed off for several minutes and woke to find the fire going the same way as the candle. She looked around and saw something she was certain wasn't there before. Two dressing gowns hung on the back of the door. There was only one explanation, Artemio. He must have woken up, noticed Alan missing and realised what was going on. He also knew both arrived with no garments to replace the dirty ones. He came to the rescue and surreptitiously arranged for the two gowns to be hanging on the door probably while they were asleep or otherwise occupied. Also hanging on each hook was a large white towel. They both exchanged glances and Ersilia gave a nervous little giggle at the thought of it.

"You go first," she said to Alan.

"No, ladies first," he replied quickly.

"OK, we both get out together," he agreed, and carefully avoiding eye contact, they climbed out and in the near dark and headed for the robes. Ersilia grabbed the nearest and quickly pulled it on. Alan did the same. Alan's robe barely covered his butt and Ersilia's was several sizes too big. It was a comical situation that should have had them both rolling with laughter on the floor but Ersilia, in spite of her recent communist indoctrination, was still a good Catholic girl at heart who took being naked in front of a man very seriously.

With the matters of modesty now sorted, they closed the washhouse door behind them, and opening the door to the house, crept quietly inside. Artemio was sound asleep in an easy chair with an empty wine glass still held loosely against his chest. Basic garments for each of them were left in two neat piles on the table. They picked them up and Ersilia, with Alan following, headed to a doorway leading to a bedroom. They found themselves standing by two small children's beds.

Forgetting previous modesty, Ersilia took off her robe and pulled on what was her aunt's old nightgown. Alan followed suit with a cast-off from Artemio. Ersilia was only a little too big for her bed, but Alan's feet stuck out at least twenty inches, yet they were both asleep within minutes.

Chapter 27

Alan was the first awake and couldn't believe he wasn't back on the farm in New Zealand. He could smell bacon cooking, something he wondered whether he would ever smell again. He grabbed his dressing gown and followed his nose to the kitchen. Alfonso was already up and well through a breakfast that would see him on his way home. It wasn't a cruel dream. Artemio really was standing at an old wood stove cooking bacon. Alan sidled over and looked into the frying pan to make sure.

"Where did you get that from?" he asked.

"Someone owed me a very big favour, it was the only way he could pay. This is the last of it. We're having a celebratory breakfast to welcome Ersilia back into my life and to welcome you, Alan, our new addition, and to farewell Alfonso. He's off back home when he's finished his breakfast."

Ersilia joined them and they finished off with ersatz coffee. Alfonso put his cup down and pulled on a hat and coat. He wrapped his arms around Alan, then Ersilia. He reluctantly let her go and stepped through the door and climbed into his truck Artemio had parked nearby. Ersilia stood leaning back against Alan as they both watched the little diesel chug off down the drive. Alan and Ersilia retired back to the bedroom to get some extra sleep after months living rough. Ersilia was asleep in minutes and Alan dozing lightly. They had slept an hour when Alan woke to the sound of voices from the kitchen. He could hear Artemio speaking in Italian with two Italian males. He rolled over and gently shook Ersilia's arm. She moved in her sleep, yawned, stretched and gradually woke. She lay back staring blankly at the ceiling, savouring the last few moments of a comfortable bed. By then, she'd become aware of what had Alan's attention.

"They're talking war news," she whispered.

"I guessed that. We'd better get up and listen," Alan said.

"No wait, they're friendly but I think the less people who know we're here the better. Let's just listen a bit longer."

Ersilia lay back catching most of the conversation, then she suddenly slipped from the bed and grabbed a dressing gown.

"I need to be part of this, they're talking about Rome, where my brother is."

She headed to the door and waited while Alan struggled into his dressing gown. He came over and stood beside her as she turned the handle. The door opened to Artemio sitting at the table opposite two men. They both looked in their thirties and stood up as Ersilia and Alan entered. One was almost as tall as Alan and the other was average height. They had a strong resemblance to Artemio who introduced them as relatives, but declined to name them. Alan had the impression they may have been in the Italian army which Artemio more than hinted at when he began describing their recent experiences.

"These men are recent participants in this disastrous war that as you will hear is promising to get a little better every day, better that is for Italians loyal to the idea of a democratically elected government." Artemio paused and looked over to the shorter of the two men.

"My name for our purposes today is Piero. I will give you the latest news about this conflict," he said leaning back in his chair. He was silent for a moment then began speaking quickly.

"Unless you have access to a radio you will probably not know of what I am about to tell you. Beginning on July the ninth and concluding on August the seventeenth this year the Allies successfully invaded Sicily. This caused the surrender of the Italian Government who then switched over to the allied cause. Germany quickly occupied Italy and followed in September with the takeover of Rome. This happened with little or no resistance from the thoroughly intimidated Italian Army stationed there. Mussolini, imprisoned by King Emmanuel III, was rescued by German special forces and re-established a fascist government at Salo in Northern Italy. The major holdup for the Allies was the difficulty of dislodging German troops from the Monte Cassino monastery. Hindsight has shown the bombing of Cassino produced more problems than it solved. Debris hampered tank access and provided perfect cover for the German troops clinging to the now destroyed monastery. I won't go into any more detail other than those that affect Ersilia, who I understand wishes to go to Rome to find her brother, Giuseppe," Piero said looking to Ersilia.

"Yes, apart from Artemio, he is all that is left of my family," she replied.

"Well, what you need to know is that your brother is most likely in the hands of the German occupiers, providing expertise for their vehicle maintenance and if he has black market contacts it is also likely he provides a ready supply of goods and services to his captors. Other information I have is that while German forces still hold Rome, I believe it is a situation that will not last. Polish troops succeeded where others failed. Germany's grip on Monte Cassino was broken by legendary General, Wladyslaw Anders, who skilfully harnessed his troop's hatred for Germany and led them to a heroic victory. The allies are now able to advance and will inevitably take Rome and then Florence not long after. I respectfully suggest you stay here under Artemio's care until the Allies are in control of both cities." With that Piero stood, picked up his cap and with his companion followed Artemio to the door.

He stopped in the doorway and turned to face them. "We will be in this locality for a while. Artemio knows where we are, and I will let him know when the time is right for your journey to Rome." They both shook Artemio's hand then left them with their thoughts.

Six weeks went past before Artemio heard again from the men. The Allies had swept into Rome and while in some degree of control, still faced resistance from pockets of Italian fascists loyal to the cause, and Germans prepared to go down with the ship. Artemio called Ersilia and Alan into his kitchen where they both sat to hear the latest news.

"What we now know is that the Allies have taken Rome and are on their way to take Florence. But be warned. If you go now, you are likely to encounter armed militia still obsessed with Italy staying a fascist, one party state. There are plenty of abandoned weapons lying around. There are also plenty of lunatics bent on revenge who are likely to mistake you as partners in the madness that Mussolini – the original lunatic – started. They suggest that you wait until the Allies have captured Florence, at least by then most of them will be hiding out in Salo praying for a miracle."

Alan and Ersilia decided that this advice made sense and settled into a heads down, low profile life. One uneventful week led to another and another as Alan and Ersilia spent time catching up on sleep and family memories with Artemio.

Alan was lying in bed beginning to feel safe one morning when he woke abruptly to the sound of a vehicle pulling up outside. He heard a door slam shut and booted feet approaching the door. He looked around for a place to hide. There was nowhere except under the bed. Ersilia was also awake now, sitting up wide-eyed and worried. A knock on the door was followed by silence, then another louder, more urgent knock. They both heard Artemio's footsteps followed by the door opening.

There was the sound of Artemio and another male talking. The other voice made Alan's throat go dry. He recognised it as the near faultless English of the German officer who collected a package of pork from the pig farm many days ago. Ersilia also recognised him. She and Alan both knew there was nowhere to go except under the bed and pray. Several minutes passed before Artemio opened the door to their room, stepped inside and closed it.

"Ersilia and Alan, I have something I need to tell you. The German officer who was at the pig farm has arrived. He knows you are both here and wants to make a deal with you that also includes me so you need to come out and hear what he has to say." Several seconds passed until Alan then Ersilia poked their heads out from under the bed.

"There's no way out of this. He is armed and has an armed guard in their vehicle."

Artemio stood at the door and opened it as Alan and Ersilia walked with pulses racing into the lounge. Seated in the best chair was the German officer as Artemio promised.

"Greetings, my name is Hauptmann Einhardt Schmitt. Before I start, I demand you both declare all weapons and bring them here to me. Artemio, your niece will remain here under close guard to ensure you don't do anything rash. As you can see I am armed as is my associate in the vehicle. I warn you we are both desperate men and will be alert to any effort to 'turn the tables' as you English put it. I have explained to your uncle that my comrade and I are both determined to escape the inevitable fate of the German army. In return for not disclosing your whereabouts, your uncle has agreed to obtain two priest's cassocks we will wear to avoid capture. This plan is known to us only and if you do not cooperate I will contact my headquarters and a squad of armed soldiers still dedicated to the fascist cause will come and arrest you."

He turned to Ersilia, "Your soldier friend will be returned to captivity and almost certainly executed for providing assistance to an illegal partisan organisation. You and your uncle will be both shot for the same reason. If you don't comply with these terms, I will conclude this operation in the normal way and take you into custody. Your uncle will be executed instantly for harbouring two partisans responsible for the killing of uniformed German troops. The decision is now in your hands. I will stay here while you have your discussions in the room you have just come from."

Alan, Ersilia and Artemio looked at each other and without any alternative all stood and headed into the bedroom. The officer followed them, gave the room a quick inspection, then offered a caution that any attempt to 'turn the tables' would see an armed squad arrive to subdue whatever resistance was being offered. Satisfied, he looked at his watch and told them they had ten minutes to give him an answer, then closed the door behind him and left them to it.

"How did he find out we were here?" Alan asked, his eyes wide with surprise.

"Information from an informant. The fascists often pick up and hold a spouse on charges real or trumped up, then pressure the target to provide information, in return for the release of their relative. It's possible someone with a relative in captivity connected with the pig farm found out who you were and where you were going," Artemio said bluntly.

"We have no choice, we can't risk calling his bluff. He will just find someone else then have us arrested. Can we trust a German Nazi. Is there an alternative?" Ersilia asked.

"There is no alternative. The only reason he allowed this meeting is for us to be all as one on the decision. It lessens the risk of one of us making a run for it," Artemio added. He stood up and headed for the door. They all filed back into the lounge.

"We have all agreed that we will comply with your wishes. I will go and obtain the priest's cassocks," Artemio said.

"Your niece and her partner will remain here under my guard. You have until 3 pm today to return with the garments. Failure to return will result in them being taken into custody. You have my word on that."

Artemio grabbed a hat and coat and left house. Fortunately he had a brother who was the local priest. His church was an easy fifteen minute walk, but anxiety put haste in his step. On the way, his thoughts were on the situation they were in. The first priority was to minimise the threat to the three of them. His main concern was for Ersilia and Alan. Artemio's future as an aging widower wasn't so precious. The emptiness he'd been feeling had been alleviated by the arrival of Ersilia. She told him of the death of his beloved brother and sister-in-law, Ersilia's parents, casually killed in their kitchen by a fascist patrol.

The fate of his two sons in North Africa, dead or captive was unknown. The fascist cause that dragged Italians into a war they were never going to win, destroyed family and relatives and threatened his own grip on a life that was losing its lustre until Ersilia arrived. He had no choice but to take the German officer at face value, follow through on the mission and to keep all options open, whatever they were.

He turned down a short lane and through the arched gate of his brother's church and approached the door. He loudly knocked three times. There was no answer. He knocked loudly again then stood back and waited. A minute passed until he heard footsteps approaching. The door creaked open and the bespectacled, jowly face of Artemio's brother peered out. After a few seconds of careful examination, his face broke into a smile of recognition. Father Emilio then opened the door fully, embraced his brother and led him inside.

Artemio followed him into the vestry and closed the door. After greeting each other warmly, he quickly related the whole account of the German officer and what he was demanding.

"Please describe this person," his brother said.

"He is sophisticated, educated at Oxford in England with impeccable English. He is of slight build and about 1.75 m tall. His rank and name is Hauptmann Einhardt Schmidt."

"That's about as tall as you. I know of this man and I know that to obtain information he has committed the most heinous crimes, often on children. I will give you the garments you ask for but I want you to consider doing something to reduce his chances of escaping and going on to live a happy and successful life."

The priest got up and left the room. He returned thirty minutes later with two garments. Both were old and worn. "As you can see there are two patches, one stitched to the area around the neck, the other lower down on the front drape. Your story, if asked, is that this work was done by my housekeeper several days ago."

Artemio took both garments, rolled them up, and after embracing his brother, thanked him and left. Artemio had been away an hour and a half. He walked quickly as he was anxious to get back to the house as soon as possible.

Father Emilio walked to the gate and watched Artemio hurrying down the road. When he'd turned the corner and disappeared from sight, Father Emilio went back to his church and selected a large leather-bound Bible. He decanted a small measure of red wine into a glass which he swallowed in one gulp. Now fortified he picked up the heavy Bible and after locking the door, headed down the path to the gate and turned left onto a narrow pathway.

There were few people about but as this was a clandestine mission he kept his head down under a wide brimmed hat and walked quickly. After several changes of direction and checking behind, he selected a narrow alleyway leading to an inn. He looked around then went inside. A waitress approached and he ordered un piccolo biochiere di vino. The drink arrived which he drank quickly. Then with his hand resting on the Bible he asked the waitress to inform Signora Francesca that he was here for their urgent meeting on parish matters.

The waitress returned and beckoned to Father Emilio. With the Father following, she began climbing a narrow stairway that led from the side of the bar. She paused at a door and knocked. A voice answered as Father Emilio climbed the last two steps and stood beside the waitress red-faced and breathing heavily. She opened the door for him and with his Bible under his arm he entered a tiny lounge.

"My dear Father Emilio, please sit down. I am resting after an arduous week."

"Signora Francesca, I am very appreciative that you are able to see me at such short notice. In fact, at no notice," Father Emilio said, and bending over kissed the hand Signora Francesca offered.

"It must be an important mission. Perhaps a little more important than administering pastoral care to an errant soul like myself."

"There is always time for that, but at this time it is other souls I wish to be able to rest more easily, through justice administered here on earth."

Father Emilio described the German officer and what he was about. Without mentioning the role of his brother, he described the patches on the cassocks the officer and his accomplice would be wearing, and how it would provide a reason to apprehend and question any so-called 'priest' who was wearing them.

"I will pass this information on to our operatives. He is one small fish in a big pond, but even the small ones are worth catching. Now, I have news for you that is probably the reason our German deserter is looking to jump off the ship. My operatives tell me that allied forces composed of New Zealand and British troops are making good progress. They will soon cross the Piave River and are then expected to be close to the Isonzo River within about a week. They are encountering strong resistance from parachute regiments but other troops are melting away in the face of the increasing evidence of an inevitable victory for the Allies."

"My brother and his friends will be interested in this information, but before you leave, are there any parish issues you wish to discuss? It always pays to have something bona fide to take back to the church." The two old friends talked parish politics for another half hour while Father Emilio wrote notes on a thin pad he kept in his Bible. When finished, they toasted dead family and friends and to the eventual end of a war that began primarily to burnish the self-inflated egos of fascist thugs.

Artemio, with the two cassocks in a bundle tucked under his arm, turned into the entrance to his house and banged loudly on the front door. Alan opened it and let a relieved Artemio inside. The German officer was sitting back where he'd left him an hour and a half ago, but now held a black Luger pistol resting casually across his chest, a reminder that he still held all the cards. Ersilia and Alan sat on a couch within the arc of fire. Artemio dumped the bundle on the table and the German officer wandered casually over and picked one up on the end of the Luger. He put the pistol down on the table and held the garment up to closer scrutiny. Artemio held his breath momentarily as he stopped and looked closely at the patch. He raised his eyebrows and looked over at Artemio.

"It's a moth hole, a repair to a moth hole," Artemio said.

He picked up the other and held it up for inspection. He turned it around and looked again at Artemio, "Another moth hole?" he asked and casually dropped it on the table without waiting for an answer.

"I have always been impressed with the apparent wealth of the Catholic Church, obviously a little misplaced," he said and picking up the Luger went back to the chair and sat down. He rested his right hand with the gun on the arm of the chair pointing directly at Artemio.

"Well, Artemio, moth holes you say. Please pick up one of the garments, turn it inside out and show me evidence of these hungry moths. Do that with both garments please." Artemio picked up the nearest garment, praying for convincing evidence of moth holes in both cassocks. Holding up the first one, he turned it inside out, masking a sigh of relief when finding what appeared to be a genuine moth hole. He did the same with the other with the same result.

"Please let me see these moth holes," the officer said.

Artemio took both to the officer and held them up for inspection. "Hmm, please put them back on the table."

The officer sat staring and pointing the Luger at Artemio for several seconds, then stood and walked slowly towards him with the pistol aimed at the centre of his forehead. He stopped when the barrel was less than a metre away.

"Pray I'm an excellent shot, or maybe a rotten one, which one are you picking Artemio?"

Alan and Ersilia sat frozen as they watched his finger slowly squeeze the trigger. There was a sharp crack as the Luger fired and a bullet smashed into the wall. Artemio's hand leapt up to clutch his left ear which now had blood pouring from it. The German officer had adjusted his aim to remove the tip of Artemio's ear lobe.

"Just a warning in case you think you can play me. We are leaving you now. I'm not sure why, but I have decided to let you all live. I hope it wasn't against my better judgement."

He picked up the bundle of clothes and the two pistols surrendered by Alan and Ersilia, opened the door and stepped out to his waiting vehicle. As soon as the door slammed shut Ersilia, Alan and Alfonso rushed to the aid of Artemio. The wound was far from life-threatening, but painful and bleeding profusely.

"In the cupboard there are a few bandages that will do to stop the blood," Artemio said.

"It should be stitched as soon as possible," Ersilia said as she returned with the bandages.

"Well, that's a problem. The nearest doctor is a day away but there are suturing needles in the same cupboard. I suggest that you put a few quick stitches in," Artemio said through clenched teeth. The wound was stitched up and doused in brandy, retrieved from a hiding place, then wrapped in the cleanest bandage they could find.

"Waste of a very fine brandy, "Artemio said and before he could say anything else was interrupted by a knock on the door. Ersilia went to the door and opened it cautiously to reveal Father Emilio. She let him in and stood by while Father Emilio listened to the explanation of why his brother sported a large bandage around his head and covering his injured ear. Satisfied that all had been done for his brother he sat down and related the good news from Signora Francesca.

"Tell me what else you know about New Zealand troops and where they are positioned," Alan asked.

"The New Zealand troops are due to cross the Piave River in a week and should be near the Isonzo River in another week or so. When the moment comes I can arrange transport for you to meet up with your people."

"That's the best news I've heard for a while," he replied and went and sat on the couch beside Ersilia.

"You will be going back to your people. I can tell you have someone there. You must go back. You don't belong here." Alan didn't say anything, there was nothing he could say that would sound right.

"I will come back."

There was a long silence. "No you won't," Ersilia whispered.

An obviously embarrassed Father Emilio stood up and cleared his throat. "I will go back to my contact and arrange your eventual transfer to the New Zealand troops. I will put this arrangement in place soon. The situation is changing constantly and mostly for the better. I am not sure how we will make it work but I will have a young man return when the time is right, with the means to get you where you need to go, to be with your people. I can't say when that will be. You just need to stay here and be ready to leave when the moment is right." With that, he turned and headed out the door.

The room was silent apart from the sounds of Ersilia making a scratch meal from a stale loaf of bread, some cheese and sausage. They ate in silence alone with their thoughts. Sensing that something significant was coming to an end, Artemio fetched the last bottle of Merlot from his secret wine cellar and carefully poured a glass for each. Ersilia, however, was occupied with more than just her thoughts. There was something feeling more like a beginning… her period was late, which was unusual and a personal matter she could not discuss with any male in the room, including Alan. Her mother was the only person she could have talked to, but Ersilia had to leave her and her father lying dead on the floor of the family cottage. Alan would soon be going back to New Zealand, a country she barely knew of and further away from northern Italy than she could imagine. She tried to convince herself she wasn't pregnant but knew in her heart that she was. Her heart also told her to not tell Alan. With a bit of luck he'd soon finish unscathed from this war and return home to kith and kin – where Ersilia knew he belonged. Ersilia would be on her own but would turn to Elena Lombardi, the widow of a local Doctor who lived nearby. She'd heard she was friendly and a qualified nurse who'd practiced medicine and birthing children alongside her husband. Ersilia resolved to contact her once Alan was on his way home. Ersilia and Alan sat beside each other, still silent in the fact there was not much more they could say. Artemio kept filling their glasses and carrying a low murmur of conversation.

Two more weeks passed until one evening Artemio answered a cautious knock on the door to find his brother standing in front of him. After a short, whispered conversation, Father Emilio left.

Artemio called Alan and Ersilia into the room. They both sat looking at him.

"Tomorrow night a young man will arrive to take you to meet with your countrymen. He will arrive at 6.30 pm so you will be making the journey at night. He is risking his life to do this but feels it is only right that you are returned to your own country."

The next day arrived with Alan trying to hide his excitement of beginning what he hoped was to be his journey home. Late in the day Artemio, Alan and Ersilia sat eating their last meal together, looking across the fields to the last of the sun on the nearby hills. It was soon dark and Alan and Ersilia looked up at the sound of a motorbike slowly approaching the house. The headlight flashed across the window as it stopped outside. Footsteps approached the house. There was a light tap on the door and Artemio went to open it. A young Italian said a few words that included the name Alan Marshall. He was ushered into the house where he stood and from a piece of paper read a short sentence in Italian. Ersilia translated for Alan. "I am here to pick up Alan Marshall and take him to meet the New Zealand 22nd Battalion on their way to Isonzo River." The young man then said another few words Ersilia translated as, "We must leave now."

Alan had only the clothes donated by Artemio that were a bit light for any distance on the back of a motorbike. Artemio saw this and headed into his room and came back with a sheepskin flying jacket. Alan looked reluctantly at it but then put it on when Artemio said he couldn't see himself on a motorbike anytime soon. The jacket dwarfed the skinny soldier and Artemio handed him a small salami to get him on his way. He turned as Ersilia came close and wrapped her arms around him. Before he returned the favour, he reached into his pocket and pulled out his ID tag with his number 18366556 inscribed on it and pressed it into her hand. "It's all I've got to leave you with. You never know, it might come in handy one day." He wrapped his arms around her as they both kissed each other goodbye.

"I am coming back," he said. Barely perceptively she slowly shook her head. He turned and shook Artemio's hand and then embraced each in the Italian way.

The door closed and the motorbike started up and settled into a reassuring rhythm as the rider engaged first gear and Alan climbed on board. Ersilia stood at the window and listened as the bike accelerated down the road. The sound receded in the distance until she could hear nothing.

Alan had ridden on plenty of motorbikes but none as a pillion rider. They dashed through the dark countryside and past small cottages and large estates. Of course Alan had no idea where he was and only a vague idea where he was going to end up. He had complete trust in the young rider and was convinced the fascist threat had reduced to insignificance. As he told himself, if he was a fascist, German or Italian, he would be keeping his head down or getting out of the country as soon as he could.

They had been travelling for less than an hour on second grade backcountry roads and came to an intersection with a main road. Signage pointed left reading del Friuli 30 km. The young rider stopped and unfurled two small flags the size of handkerchiefs mounted on short metal rods attached to the handle bars. One flag was white and the other was the official Italian flag. He turned and flashed Alan a quick grin, then grabbed first gear and then carefully negotiated the left turn onto the sealed road and accelerated away, with the flags flapping happily in the breeze. He was maintaining a slower speed now and seemed to be looking ahead for something. Soon enough he found what he was looking for, a platoon of soldiers sitting on the roadside having smoko. He slowed down and pulled over. Two soldiers stood up with rifles ready. As soon as Alan saw the Kiwi emblem he knew he was as good as home. He climbed off the bike and the moment he opened his mouth the two guards lowered their weapons.

"What the hell are you doing out here mate?" asked the guard nearest Alan. Alan had rehearsed his reply every day since he was released from the prison train several weeks ago. "I am Alan Marshall. My rank is Lieutenant and my serial number is 18366556. I was taken captive on Ruweisat Ridge in North Africa four months ago. I was freed from a prison train in Northern Italy by a partisan group. I am hungry and need a uniform." The guards seemed to buy his explanation but frisked him nevertheless. One pulled out the salami and jokingly aimed it at his mate and said BANG! They all had a good laugh and the comic handed it back to Alan.

"Ok, stay here with us and you can get a lift on transport that's coming through here in an hour. Johnny, take this cove and give him a good feed and ask him about the size of his salami."

They all roared with laughter again and Alan knew he was home.

The young Italian started the bike, gunned the throttle, did a U-turn and took off back where he came from before Alan could say thanks for the ride.

While Alan was fed, he talked with fellow Kiwi, something he hadn't done for a long time. He finished his food and turned to see the lights of an army transport truck approaching.

"This is our lift and yours," his new mate Johnny said. "Get on board."

Alan didn't need to be asked twice and heaved himself up on the deck. The rest of the platoon followed and they drove off.

"Where are we going?" he asked Johnny.

"About twenty kilometres up the road to Cividale. We man a checkpoint there to weed out any Germans or their Italian mates from sneaking through either way. Some are trying to get out of here through the port at Monfalcone. There's still a few small groups around that don't know the war is just about over. I think you'll be earning your tucker doing a bit of checkpoint duty."

Alan sat back while the noisy low-geared truck whined and bounced along the poorly maintained road. He thought of Ersilia and felt bad, maybe another time and another place, but being in the right time and place now to be heading home soon, was what he was holding tight. He leaned out from the truck and could see arc lights ahead then sat back and looked over at Johnny.

"That'll be home for you mate, for a wee while at least," he said as they pulled into a makeshift yard. Alan jumped off the truck with the others and followed the platoon commander into a large tent set up as headquarters. He stood and waited while the general in command held a meeting with three junior officers. He finished and turned to face the commander. The commander related the background of Alan's last four months since capture at Ruweisat Ridge. The general turned to Alan and outlined what was going to happen over the next three days. First he would receive a health check with the medical staff attached to the battalion and then receive full rations to regain fighting fitness and strength. He would also receive a replacement uniform and a standard issue 303 army rifle. Then he would be assigned to a checkpoint detail and serve out what little was left of the war on those duties.

Alan was absorbed into the life of the temporary camp and scheduled to take up checkpoint duties in two days. He got to know his comrades and took a briefing on how to operate a checkpoint.

The day came for his first stretch of checkpoint duty along with five other soldiers. Chaos resulting from partial surrenders and widespread confusion caused large numbers of civilians and locals to pass through the barriers daily in search for missing relatives, food and other such missions. Alan and his mates marched the five hundred metres to the checkpoint and swapped banter with the troops finishing their shift. A few civilians drifted through in the early morning hours, but as the day wore on numbers grew to a series of large mobs. Alan was feeling out of sorts, bored by the lack of action from standing for long hours, that was more tiring than a forced march.

He looked over at a new group coming through and glanced at a priest wearing a cassock walking towards him in the middle a large group. It was not unusual to have an occasional priest go by. He was tired. He closed his eyes and opened them again. A patch, "The patch," he whispered to himself. He now knew he was staring into the eyes of the fugitive Nazi officer, Einhardt Schmidt.

Schmidt recognised him and looked away, but before he did, he held Alan's eyes, then reaching up, took hold of his ear lobe for no more than an instant. Alan stood rooted to the spot. In one second of wordless communication, Schmidt had reminded Alan he had chosen not to kill them all, three days ago in the tense confrontation in Artemio's lounge. Alan was frozen with indecision and that was enough time for Schmidt to melt into the crowd and escape. Alan knew he would take this to his grave.

Chapter 28

Ersilia was beginning to notice the changes in her body and mind and felt anxious about the situation looming ahead of her. She was a frequent visitor to the widow Elena Lombardi and listened to her calming words about what the future might hold. On the last visit they were interrupted by a knock on the door. The widow checked through a side window, then went and opened the door to a young man who appeared worn out, tired and hungry, but not Italian.

"Buongiorno, my name is Evan Jefferies," he said, then after struggling with a little more Italian he gave up and reverted back to English. The widow dealt with the mangled Italian and managed well enough with English. He asked if Ersilia Abelli was available. The widow left him at the door, turned and went through to the makeshift surgery where Ersilia was waiting. She told Ersilia that a young man named Evan Jefferies was asking for her. If she'd already met someone from New Zealand she would immediately recognise the 'New Zealand way' with words and pronunciation. She went back to the young man and ushered him into the surgery. Ersilia stood up and without saying a word reached out to him. No words came while they rocked back and forth in a never ending embrace. Finally she released him after whispering in his ear that she had thought she was never going to see him again.

Evan sat beside her on an old couch and spoke of his short stay in Yugoslavia treating anyone needing medical attention. The widow smiled to herself with the knowledge there was now another Doctor in the house, albeit from the other side of the world. Although she was barely showing, Evan, ever mindful of the severe food shortages, suspected that the actual cause of her slight weight gain was that she was pregnant.

Evan had found his way from Yugoslavia to Artemio's home. He arrived exhausted and hungry and disappointed he had missed Alan by less than a week. Artemio told him that Ersilia was now spending most of her time with the widow of the local doctor, Elena Lombardi. Artemio wasn't aware Ersilia was pregnant and was fed a falsehood that she was ill, her Catholic upbringing causing Ersilia to conceal her condition from her uncle as long as possible. Evan rested up for a day and ate whatever meagre supplies Artemio could spare. After listening carefully to Artemio's directions he set off on the thirty minute walk to the widow's house, determined not to miss catching up with another friend again.

The widow Elena sat down beside Evan while Ersilia was asleep and in hushed tones spoke rapidly of what she thought would be the best outcome for everyone. As a qualified Doctor, Evan could stay here and fill the gap created when her husband died. She also confided that she believed Ersilia was too mentally fragile to raise a baby. She told Evan that Ersilia often spoke of her part in lethal action that caused her to feel personally responsible for the souls of friends lost in the war and left her dreading the responsibility inherent in raising a child solo. Evan agreed to stay and make a team of two for the duration of Ersilia's pregnancy. He took what Elena said seriously and would be extra vigilant while attending to Ersilia.

Ersilia shifted permanently into Elena's house to remain under the care of Evan and the less qualified but more experienced Elena. Food was a little more plentiful as the regular flow of patients usually paid with vegetables, eggs and the occasional chicken, and Evan always remembered Artemio and regularly dropped small surpluses over to him. Evan also made use of the medical library left by the widow's husband, adding to his existing knowledge on pregnancy and attending to the birth of children. Ersilia lived through an uneventful pregnancy until the eighth month when things started to happen. An underweight girl was born one month early to Ersilia at 7am on the morning of Saturday November the 14th 1945. The birth went smoothly and the name 'Helen' was duly entered into Elena's birth register. Evan and Artemio [who had been updated on Ersilia's situation] provided witness signatures.

Ersilia was surprised how easily she'd coped with the birth but this only caused her to be more suspicious of good outcomes in her life, which included the arrival of baby Helen. In his final year of study, Evan had read the latest research papers on Psychology, the newest branch of medical science. The opinion he formed from his reading was that Ersilia had internalised the part she played in recent lethal conflict that produced the violent deaths of friends and comrades. She was simply unable to take on the responsibility of another person, even her own flesh and blood. It was increasingly obvious to Evan and Elena that Ersilia was conflicted over competing loyalties…'Baby Helen' versus

Guiseppe Abelli, Ersilia's only brother. With that realisation Elena began discreetly taking up the slack caused by Ersilia's lack of enthusiasm for rearing her child.

#

Nikolas had now been at his family's home for nine months when an army vehicle pulled up in front of the cottage. Nikolas was eating a meal and went to the door. He was greeted by an officer, who when he spoke reminded him of Alan Marshall. He was handed an envelope with a New Zealand postmark. The letter was in fact from Alan Marshall, and offered him a roof over his head and work on a farm that now included a large block of rough scrub-covered land, urgently needing a strong back to clear. Nikolas's mother offered the officer a herbal tea which he sat and drank while Nikolas, under the light of a small window, read and re-read the simple message. The letter was short and to the point, but it was all that was needed to fire his imagination. Every word Alan used to describe New Zealand while sitting at the cottage table many months ago came back in vivid detail.

"How do I get to New Zealand?" he asked looking up at the officer.

"Well, it just happens to be where I come from. If you collect your gear, I will take you back to HQ and you can ask the questions there."

"You must go. I can see by your eyes that you must go." His mother stated bluntly when he looked guiltily over at her. Nikolas nodded slowly in reply. He felt the pull from home, but he knew she spoke the truth. He grabbed his kit bag and after rummaging through a couple of drawers pulled some clothing out and soon had the bag filled to capacity. His mother went to a cupboard, and removing a loose board, took out several banknotes. He returned half to his mother then pocketed the rest.

Nikolas stood in front of the house he was born in and said farewell to his mother and two younger brothers.

"It is best you do this for yourself. If you don't, I know you will never be happy. I also know you will be with good people," his mother said. She knew he felt guilt over his decision and wanted to make sure he didn't change his mind. She embraced him, holding him tightly to her for several seconds. She reached down for his right hand and pressed into it a small leather pouch with a drawstring threaded through eyelets around the top.

"You have never seen this before. Inside the pouch is a Minoan figurine that was found on our land by your grandfather. It was passed down to your father and it now goes to you. It is very old and I believe of some value but as we have lost nearly everything through no fault of our own I wish it to remain in our possession. The figurine is a fertility symbol. If you look after it and keep it safe, it will look after you."

Nikolas placed the pouch with its contents in his pocket and fastened the flap firmly. He grabbed his kit bag, then turned and climbed on board the waiting jeep. The engine coughed into life and accelerated down the road. Before the first corner, Nikolas turned for one last look at life as he had known it. His mother had already gone inside the cottage.

#

A guilt-ridden Ersilia was now driven by an all absorbing obsession to find her brother. She told Evan that she planned to return soon to Artemio's house to contact the network of people wanting to help her reconnect with Guiseppe. Evan, although impressed with Ersilia's recovery advised her to wait another week before taking on the thirty minute walk. Ersilia agreed, but insisted that the delay would be only three days. Evan acquiesced, but only on the condition that he would accompany her to Artemio's house. When they arrived she knew instantly that Artemio was not at all impressed that Ersilia had seen fit to 'abandon' her daughter, but grudgingly accepted her decision.

Ersilia chose her moment carefully. She sat down in front of Artemio and was silent for several seconds, gathering her thoughts.

"I've got to find Giuseppe," she said finally.

Artemio cleared his throat and began quietly, "The last thing I knew of Giuseppe was that his mechanical and engineering talent had got him conscripted into the vehicle division of the Italian Army, where he worked long days behind the front line keeping the army mobile. The person in the best position to help is my brother's associate Signora Francesca. She has connections in the resistance and the Italian army."

"Please, let's do it now, right now. I have to find out what's happened to him."

They both stood, and putting on a hat and coat, left the house, heading towards the inn of Signora Francesca. They decided to stop on the way and enrol

Father Emilio into the cause. Father Emilio was out, but close by. They waited several minutes before a surprised Father Emilio opened the door to find his brother waiting. Both greeted each other, then sat as Artemio related the whole story with Ersilia nodding in agreement.

"There's a person I know who could help and that's Signora Francesca," said Father Emilio.

"Exactly what I thought," Artemio replied.

Father Emilio grabbed his hat and coat and together the odd threesome headed off to Signora Francesca's inn. They entered the bar and waited for the bartender to inform her of their arrival. Eventually, they were summoned and plodded slowly up the steep staircase to the Signora's private room. She was seated, tiny and insignificant behind a large ornate desk, that seemed to shrink when her strong voice filled the room.

"I know of the loss of your parents. I met them only once, when your family visited many years ago to stay with Artemio. You were a beautiful young girl then and still beautiful now," she added. Ersilia blushed and looked down at the floor.

"There's a way we can do this. I can provide an escort who was a prominent young resistance fighter against the fascists, a fight I understand you also bravely pursued after the death of your parents. The remaining fascists still loyal to their cause are being pushed further north. That means you and your escort will have, to some degree, a free pass to travel between here and Rome. Be warned though, there are still fascist interests that remain a threat. My information tells me your brother is in Rome and still in the Italian Army, now aligned with Britain. I suggest you go home and pack a small bag, as you need to travel light, as you are going by motorcycle. It is the best and only way to get anywhere fast on bomb damaged roads, clogged with traffic. I note there is urgency so I will instruct your escort to pick you up from Artemio's house at 6 am tomorrow. Is everyone in agreement on this matter?"

Artemio, Ersilia and Father Emilio all nodded, so with no further discussion, the three stood up. The two men kissed the Signora's offered hand, bade her farewell and left her to her quiet sanctuary.

Ersilia was now even more motivated about her mission and made her way quickly back towards Artemio's house, with the two men struggling to keep up.

Ersilia kept herself occupied by filling a small pack with her belongings and reading a stray book she'd found. Evan, Artemio and Maria who had moved in to ease the departure of Ersilia, sat with her and ate a scratch meal of leftover sausage with hard cheese grated over tomatoes. Ersilia retired to her room while the widow Maria put the little girl to bed.

Ersilia woke early and sat in the kitchen drinking ersatz coffee. No longer remembering the taste of real coffee, she drained the mug as if it was the real thing, then carved off a piece of cheese, refilled her coffee and watched the glow of a new day on the distant hills. Gripping the strap of her pack beside her, she glanced nervously at the kitchen clock. The Signora's contact was due in ten minutes. She went to the front door and closing it quietly sat down on a battered couch. She looked along the road, listening with a tight feeling in her stomach. The sound of a motorbike reached her. She stood and walked onto the road. The bike suddenly appeared out of the gloom and pulled up beside her. Attached to each handle bar was a small flag; one, a bold white cross on red representing Savoy, the house of Victor Emmanuel III, and the other, the standard flag of Italy. One glance showed the declaration of loyalty to the new order of monarchist forces known as the Italian Co-belligerent Army fighting for the Allied cause. The rider tipped his helmet in a casual salute and said, "Just call me Diego and it's better that I don't know your name yet," then shifted forward to let her climb on. They accelerated off and Ersilia suddenly felt a great sense of relief. Lost parents had created a gap she needed Giuseppe's presence to help fill up.

It was early and the sun was still not up. They were making good time threading through the small amount of traffic until reaching the first checkpoint. Diego throttled back and idled up to two soldiers manning the barrier. One slung his rifle over his shoulder and walked towards the stationary bike. The other stood looking more purposeful, covering them both with a light machine gun, then suddenly stiffened when Diego reached into his jacket pocket and pulled out a single envelope. He opened it and withdrew a typed letter. The letter was marked by a hastily contrived letterhead with a coat of arms. The text gave Diego full authority to travel unhindered with his co-rider, Ersilia Abelli.

The base of the letter was signed by Victor Emmanuel III and accompanied by his royal seal. As the King of Italy, he had originally supported Mussolini, but the Grand Council of Fascism, tiring of a war that was turning into a monumental failure, voted to limit Mussolini's power and ceded control to the King. The next day, after meeting with Mussolini, the King dismissed him as Prime Minister and had him imprisoned. Victor Emmanuel III and General Pietra

Badoglio were granted full control of Italy. A declaration of a continuing allegiance to Germany was made, while behind their backs, the new Italian government negotiated an armistice and joined with the Allies. The growing knowledge of these manoeuvres added power to the letter and was enough to win the day. Diego returned the letter to his jacket pocket, restarted the bike and accelerated down the road, leaving a couple of guards happy that an armistice was in place and that the Allies were steadily gaining more territory and control.

Diego pressed on, intent on covering as much distance in the lowlight as possible. What he hadn't told Ersilia was that they were to stop at an address in Padua. From there, Diego would drive them by car all the way to Rome. What Ersilia also didn't know was that quiet, mild-mannered Diego was a determined individual who had run the local resistance at the behest of Signora Francesca. His actions against the fascists had come at the expense of his brother and sister who were both executed while he escaped and went into hiding. Diego was haunted by the guilt of escaping the fate of his siblings and eagerly grasped the opportunity to help a young woman who reminded him of his sister and had a similar proud record in partisan action.

With the regular beat of the motor and wrapped in a cosy embrace with Diego, Ersilia drifted into a light sleep. She dreamt of things from a simple childhood with Giuseppe and her parents. She had no other siblings and had understood in her teenage years that her mother's medical condition made it impossible to complete a full-term pregnancy. Ersilia was therefore born to a rare situation in Italy, a family with two children not six, eight or ten.

Ersilia woke slowly to the realisation that the motorbike was gradually slowing down. Diego dropped into a lower gear and the machine lurched to a crawl. Ersilia looked over his shoulder and realised they were now on the outskirts of Padua. It was now light and they were weaving through people pushing carts and walking with bundles of clothing over their shoulders. Abruptly Diego braked, and dodging a family group, pulled into an alleyway. He increased his speed for fifty metres then braked to a walk. Ersilia looked around to find herself in a courtyard. No sooner had they stopped, than a door on the nearest building opened and a woman appeared, peered at Diego, then beckoned them both inside. Ersilia found herself in a kitchen with a thick timber bench. There was ham, prosciutto, salami, olives and pane. The woman took one look at Ersilia, decided she liked her and wrapped both arms around her.

Diego introduced her to Ersilia as Signora Chiara, who unwrapped her arms and bustled off to prepare food and coffee for all.

Signora Chiara was the widow of a leader in the local resistance. He was killed during a firefight with retreating fascists, only weeks before an armistice was signed that promised to bring a degree of peace and stability to the war wrecked country.

The group sat at the heavy table and Ersilia drank real coffee for the first time in months. They ate all the food and finished with a local red. Signora swallowed the last of her wine and stood up. Ersilia and Diego leaned back on their chairs and waited for her to speak.

"We are all blessed by these gifts of food and wine that came to our table as an appreciation of the sacrifice my husband and many others made to rid Italy of fascism. We also have the use of a vehicle from a respected landowner who skilfully maintained a position of neutrality in his dealings with the local fascists. Signora Francesca is the person who has made this all possible. I now propose a toast to Signora Francesca and her God-given mission."

Ersilia stood and looked around the table, "I speak on behalf of my parents taken by the evil disciples of fascism. The black-shirted killers ripped a painful wound through my life and our country. However, though it has hurt us greatly, we must put the past behind us and work for the Italy of tomorrow and the people who suffered through the most unholy alliance that ever existed. I propose a toast to all those who'd suffered and died for Italy."

Ersilia sat and waited while Signora Chiara leant forward in her chair, closed her eyes and wordlessly mouthed a short prayer. She stopped and suddenly sat upright in her chair and looked around at Diego.

"Right, down to business. You are here to drive Ersilia to Rome. This is right?"

"Yes," Diego replied.

"Good, then tomorrow the owner of the car will bring it here with a full tank of petrol so you can make an early start on your journey to Rome. You won't see him. We still have a few enemies in our midst who would like to extract some sort of retribution and revenge for their defeat. He has connections with the new government headed by King Victor Emmanuel and will provide you with papers that will allow you to purchase petrol on the way if you need it. He will also provide you with a sum of money to finance your trip south. I suggest you get an early night and be ready to go at 5 am tomorrow."

Ersilia and Diego followed Signora Chiara up a flight of stairs to a landing with two doors leading off. She opened the first door and directed Ersilia to a single bed. Then she opened the other door for Diego.

"I'll be waking you both at 4.30 am, enough time for a good breakfast," she said from the passageway, then turned and headed back down the stairs.

Ersilia lay in her bed listening to the house quietening down for the night. She carried two burdens, the heavier being the guilt of abandoning her daughter and the lighter regarded the journey to Rome and the uncertainty of finding her brother, Giuseppe. She closed her eyes but held alternatively to the thoughts of her daughter and of Giuseppe as she drifted off to sleep.

Replete with a good breakfast, they drove all day, threading through refugees, locals and soldiers trying to get back home or away from their past. Night was closing in and both agreed they needed to be off the road somewhere soon and having a meal. A light appeared in the distance and as they drew closer the light turned out to be the two windows of a small tavern. Hungry and tired they pulled up outside. Even with the car doors closed they could smell the familiar odours of a country stew cooking over an open fire. They got out and opened the front door to a small bar with wooden wine casks beside smoke stained walls. A middle-aged couple took their order and brought them two plates of stew and two glasses of red wine.

They ate steadily until finished, then sat back and looked around. Diego realised a group of four men were sitting in a corner in quiet conversation. The oldest suddenly lifted his head up and looked over at Ersilia and Diego. He was short, swarthy and tough looking, with dark curly hair and wearing a rough peasant jacket over a quality dress shirt. Diego also saw, when he turned his head into the light, that he wore a black eye patch. The dress shirt didn't fit in but the man continued his examination, particularly of Diego. He turned back to his companions and began an animated conversation with them. Diego noted it all and turned to Ersilia. "We're out of here. I know the one who's staring at me." Downing their wine and not looking back they walked calmly to the door and stepped outside. Holding back panic, they climbed in the car. Diego floored the accelerator, pulled out onto the road, then stopped suddenly beside a parked car. He leapt out and ripped up the bonnet and disappeared under it for a few seconds, then he stood back up, triumphantly holding four spark plug leads. He jumped back in beside Ersilia who was sitting looking at him, mouth wide open.

"I know the man that was staring at me. I also know his car." Diego had left the motor running. He jammed the car into gear and accelerated onto the road. In his rearview mirror, he could see the four men burst out of the tavern and run towards them. He also saw the short man stop and hold up a pistol in both hands. The muzzle flashed three times and two shots whined off into the night, but the third smashed through the rear window and nicked Diego in his right shoulder. He yelped with pain, but kept driving, holding his right arm low and steering with his left. Ersilia let out an expletive, then took off her cotton blouse and with the strength of sheer panic, ripped one of the sleeves into a long bandage. She climbed over to the back seat and wound the improvised tourniquet tightly around the top of his arm. She climbed back into the front and looked at Diego with an ashen face.

"He is a big landowner and a black shirt Nazi. He was one of those who was after me. They caught my brother and sister and shot them both. Now he's trying to kill me," he said through teeth clenched against the pain. They were coming to a small bridge. Diego braked in the middle and grabbing the leads handed them to Ersilia. She knew what he wanted. She jumped from the car and threw them over the railings as far as she could then climbed back in. They accelerated down the road leaving the four men, a kilometre back, trying to start their now useless car.

"We're going to have to get to Bologna tonight. I have another contact there and we will be given a roof over our heads, a meal and beds for the night. He is an old friend. His sister is a nurse and will treat my wound. It is only superficial."

The borrowed car was modern, powerful and fast. The only chance 'the short assassin' had of catching them was to make radio contact with previous comrades in arms. His problem was that, after the signing of the armistice with the Allies, Italian police and army were wary and unlikely to provide the service that was once available to the fascists. Whether they had grudgingly or wholeheartedly served the former fascist state, many were now jumping ship and keeping their heads down, worrying about a hand on their shoulder to answer for war crimes.

Chapter 29

They drove on through the night, negotiating frequent checkpoints with the letter signed by King Victor Emmanuel III to smooth the way. The main fear was ad hoc justice meted out daily to ex-fascists or those suspected of being so. Diego was alert to the threat of revenge seeking partisans.

The issue was that the car was not a 'car of the people'. It was a Lancia and expensive, therefore suspect and likely owned by a wealthy fascist. Diego was relying on an addition to the car's fenders, of the flags from the motorbike, one being the house of Savoy of King Victor Emmanuel III and the other the Italian Co-belligerent Army. Each little flag fluttering on the car, Diego hoped was a convincing declaration of whose side they were on.

As the night wore on traffic diminished and progress became swifter. Diego still nervously checked his rearview mirror. Superficial wound or not, his arm was beginning to throb and he was forced to steer and change gear with one hand, using the damaged one as a temporary prop. Small towns and settlements came and went until they finally drove by a signpost reading MODENA 120 KM. Diego now knew they were closing on Bologna and told Ersilia there was less than an hour to go. They carried on in silence.

A sign reading BOLOGNA 10 KM appeared and Ersilia knew she was more than half way to finding her brother. There was also relief that a dangerous enemy was keeping their heads down in the shadows or had moved north to join remnants of German forces trying to form a rearguard action. To the south, where they were heading, were the Allies, the American and British, New Zealanders and Australians, plus a mix of strays caught in the action. The time was heading towards 3 am and Bologna was now a short distance ahead. They arrived to deserted streets, and when Diego spotted the one he was looking for, Ersilia knew they would soon be in the protective custody of another friend with a safe roof over their heads. Diego turned right into a narrow lane and slowed to a crawl alongside two-storeyed houses with front doors opening directly onto the lane.

One or two had makeshift garages cut into their frontages. There were randomly spaced pockmarks of bullets on many, a reminder of the recent skirmishes between the militia and partisans.

Diego pulled up in front of an ochre coloured building with a makeshift garage. He got out and stood, willing someone to show an interest in their arrival. He kept looking up at windows on the second story and was suddenly rewarded. A curtain was pulled aside and a face that broke into a huge grin showed in the narrow opening, then disappeared. There was the sound of heavy feet descending stairs, then a door creaking open.

A large man with a barrel of a chest and a stomach to match stepped into the dim light of a lone street lamp thirty metres away.

"My friend," he exclaimed in a loud whisper and assaulted Diego with an enveloping hug. He released him only when he realised that Ersilia was standing beside the car like a spare part.

Once Diego had caught his breath he introduced his large friend as Alonzo who promptly went through the same meet and greet with Ersilia. He finally released them and herded them into the house. It was then in the light that he noticed the bandage around his friend's upper arm and shoulder. He let out a long, low whistle and led them through into a kitchen where they found a woman in a dressing gown sitting over a cup of coffee.

"What happened? No, don't tell me. Just sit down and let my sister Elena here take a look. Is it bad? Elena here is a trained nurse," he said to Ersilia by way of introduction. He fell silent and watched as Elena nodded to Ersilia, took a gulp of coffee, then started to methodically unwind the bandage. As she worked she fired short, sharp orders at her nosy brother to fetch boiling water in a basin and a fresh bandage.

Where Alonzo was large and loud, Elena was reserved, slim and quiet. When Alonzo had fetched all she required, he paced the floor while questioning Diego. Diego told him of the encounter with the three Italian fascists belonging to Mussolini's Black Brigades and the fluky shot that winged him with the flesh wound to his shoulder. A shot that was fired by a short, tough man with curly dark hair and an eye patch. He also told Alonzo about disabling the man's car, a black four-cylinder Lancia. At this news, Alonzo stopped pacing and slowly sat down beside Diego.

"My friend, I'm afraid you have bloodied the nose of a very dangerous man but I guess you already know that. He is well known and still maintains a small force of die-hard fascists. They will soon be heading north to Turin where they will join with the militia and Germans fighting a rearguard action. Before that, he may be tempted to throw one last punch in your direction to level the score. By now, you will be well known within their circles."

Diego turned towards Elena to thank her for the first aid. She averted her eyes but before looking away Diego saw her face was flushed and her eyes bright with tears. She suddenly stood up, walked quickly to the door and left the room. Diego looked at Alonzo for an explanation but all he got was raised eyebrows and an open-handed gesture of puzzlement.

"Might have to check this out," Alonzo said and went to the door Elena had just disappeared through. He stood beside it and tapped softly, waited a few moments, then opened it and entered the room. Diego and Ersilia both listened to the low murmur of Elena and Alonzo's voices. Both coffees had gone cold by the time Alonzo reappeared followed by an embarrassed Elena.

"My sister has just disclosed a worrying situation that she is involved in. Before Elena explains what has happened, I must emphasise that for your safety, you must leave here soon, in fact very soon. Everyone turned and looked towards Elena.

Elena wiped tears from her eyes and cleared her throat. "I am under an obligation to a local militia group to provide information in exchange for the life of a man I am betrothed to. He was kidnapped two weeks ago and the group has contacted me with the details of what they require to ensure the safety of my man."

"I have to say that no information has been passed on by Elena although it is likely they have this house under surveillance anyway. We will quickly put together a food package, top up your petrol tank and reluctantly say farewell," Alonzo said tersely.

Alonzo had barely finished speaking when there was a loud crash and the sound of the front door splintering open, followed by footsteps coming up the stairs. Alonzo moved quickly and pulled open a door disguised as one of the wooden panels as part of the wall.

"I put it in for just this sort of moment," he said as he bundled Diego and Ersilia into a small cavity and closed the panel behind them. He looked around and scooped up the incriminating evidence of two extra coffee cups. With nowhere to hide them, he strode quickly to the window, opened it and threw them as far as he could. He slammed the window shut and turned to face whatever was coming. Only two men came through the door. Alonzo was relieved by that and the fact only one appeared armed. They were vaguely familiar and he hoped they were underestimating him as a large, harmless buffoon. He played up to this by making a jokey comment about maybe knocking next time they called. They weren't amused but he sensed a slight relaxation in their attitude. His chance came in the next instant. A stifled sneeze from the dusty cavity hiding Ersilia and Diego startled the gunman who turned towards it. Alonzo, who was still able to put in a solid thirty minutes as a striker in the local football league, lashed out with a lethal left foot that had left plenty of experienced goalkeepers spreadeagled on the ground. The power of one hundred and fifteen kgs smashed the machine gun from the hands of the hapless militiaman and sent it flying across the room. The disarmed man rashly charged Alonzo, who employing more deft footwork, stepped sideways and connected with a big stiff right arm. Grabbing him with one big hand by the seat of his pants and the other by the scruff of his neck, he used his momentum to smash him hard against the window. The man crashed through the glass and ended lying motionless on the roadway below.

Diego and Ersilia moved quickly from the cavity and secured the gun from where it ended up near their hiding place. The other man was clearly not itching for a fight and had relied on his armed sidekick to carry the day. Alonzo, convinced that he needed to send a strong message, grabbed him, escorted him to the door and propelled him down the stairs.

Diego and Ersilia both stood wide-eyed and open-mouthed at the lightning reactions and slick moves of such a large and seemingly ungainly man. Alonzo was aware of their astonishment.

"I am very fast over a very short distance, but enough of that. Elena, please get hold of some of that sausage and bread we still have and put it in a bag. I'll go down and get some petrol for Diego's flash car, although I'm not sure it is his," he said with a sly grin.

"I'd like to think that might be the last we see of them. I believe they will both be heading north with whatever fascist friends they have left but don't worry about us. I've now got another weapon to add to my small arsenal. You both need to be out of here now. As you know Rome was liberated a while ago by American forces, but what you probably don't know is that New Zealand troops have only just liberated Florence."

With a tank full of precious petrol and their stomachs full of food and coffee, Diego and Ersilia drove off fast towards Florence and Rome and Ersilia's brother.

At the mention of 'New Zealand troops', Ersilia's eyes had suddenly moistened. She drew in a few deep breaths and started talking. "I had a friend named Alan Marshall. He was captured in North Africa and held on a prison train heading from Campa 51 to Grupigano. I belonged to a partisan group that blew up the train and released him. He joined the group but now I presume he has returned to New Zealand. He gave me his army ID tag as a memento. It's something that might be a help when we get to Florence."

Ersilia went quiet and they sat in silence as they motored on through what little was left of the night. Diego glanced at her. Maybe Alan Marshall was a bit more than just a friend. The first signs of Florence and its Kiwi conquerors suddenly appeared in the half-light of the new day, when a forward unit of four soldiers manning a roadblock loomed up. Ersilia put her hand in her pocket and felt for the ID tag from Alan. Diego also reached for the envelope containing the letter signed by the King, Victor Emmanuel III and co-signed by General Pietra Badoglio. Although both were aware the unpopular king had recently fled from Italy to Alexandria in Egypt, the letter was still compelling evidence they were siding with the Allies and not a couple of fleeing fascists.

Diego put the car into first gear and crawled slowly up to the two soldiers standing in the road with weapons at the ready. They came to a halt, climbed out of the car and were led to a small tent with a table and chairs inside. After being frisked for weapons, they were sat down. Diego then passed over his letter of introduction to the officer seated at the table. The officer read it and looked up at Diego, who began relating the whole story of where he and Ersilia were from and why they were travelling to Rome. The officer turned to Ersilia who enlarged on Diego's account of why she was here. She then reached into her pocket and pulled out Alan's ID tag. She told the officer of the part she and others had played in fighting fascists, German or Italian, then sat and listened again to the now familiar flat vowels and the slow, deliberate verbal plod of most Kiwi males. She already missed him and imagined it was Alan seated opposite making good ordinary common sense. His message to her was excellent news. Because by her partisan actions she had saved several Kiwi soldiers from doing time in a concentration camp, she was to be rewarded with a safe passage provided by NZ Army for the remainder of the journey to Rome.

The officer, who collected them from their rough and ready accommodation, wised Ersilia up on the peculiarities of living in a country the size of Britain with a total population less than one of its smaller cities. He told Ersilia that he knew Alan Marshall. He told her that back in New Zealand he was also a farmer and came from a district half an hour's drive away from Alan. Ersilia had the distinct feeling that compared with living in Italy everyone in New Zealand must know each other. He didn't know of her brother living in Rome but when told of his position in the Italian Army he was sure he could be tracked down and would likely be filling a valuable role now keeping Allied vehicles on the road.

My orders are to take you to headquarters. They have verified your story but will doublecheck the details you gave. They will also want to debrief you on the last six months and anything else you can tell us about Alan and the others you were with. They drove on in silence and arrived at Florence HQ late in the afternoon. They were both assigned separate rooms and told to be ready for an evening meal at 6 pm. The debriefing would happen after the meal and would likely last approximately an hour and a half. The next day Ersilia, Diego and the officer continued on to Rome with a letter of introduction for their American counterparts. The letter explained who they were and what their mission was. A dilapidated apartment was found a short drive from the mechanical repairs workshop, taken by the Americans from the rapidly retreating German forces, after first being cleared of mines and booby traps.

Ersilia didn't have far to go to the workshop. They pulled up beside a couple of American jeeps with their bonnets up. Ersilia, Diego and the driver walked up to the nearest and stood waiting for the mechanic to lift his head. Eventually the driver coughed and the mechanic stood up slowly with an annoyed expression.

"You wouldn't believe how long I've been trying to finish—" he stopped mid-sentence as his eyes moved from the driver to Diego and halted at Ersilia. A ring spanner he held loosely fell to the ground with a loud clang. The sudden noise broke the silence.

"I, I thought you were dead, killed with our mother and father," he blurted out finally and remained frozen to the spot. Ersilia reached out slowly to the last member of her family still alive. She touched his shoulders with her fingertips then suddenly gripped them tightly and pulled his skinny frame towards her. He wrapped his arms around her and she did the same.

Ersilia moved into the small apartment Giuseppe occupied courtesy of the US Army. She had a bedroom just big enough and began a new life with her brother. Several months later the situation in Italy was slowly and painfully inching towards some semblance of normalcy. Giuseppe retained the garage space and began diversifying into light engineering while employing several mechanics to look after vehicle maintenance and servicing. But Giuseppe also had his fingers deeply into another business, the local black market. Ersilia was critical of this and eventually prevailed on his good sense to quit. Her argument was strengthened by several court cases that saw the bigger players do jail time as the government sought to distance itself from the corruption and malpractice of twenty years of fascism. Giuseppe's engineering business was growing and he expanded his workshop to include the large building next door. His talent was in demand with work coming through the door and money in the bank, a situation Ersilia kept a careful watch on. The end of the war was now more than two years ago.

The Marshall Plan initiated by America, donated aid that totalled one and a half billion US dollars deposited into the central bank of Italy over a period of four years from 1948 to 1952. This measure was intended as a bulwark against any government inclination to accommodate the strong Italian communist party. New Zealand troops had seen off the land grab ambitions of their former Yugoslav communist allies in an armed standoff in Trieste at the war's end. The series of payments with strings attached was America's way of stopping further communist opportunism exploiting the wreckage and devastation of post-war Europe. The final payments overlapped the advent of the Korean War of 1950 to 1953. With a new war to supply, the high demand for light engineering products grew ever bigger and the combination of Giuseppe's talent and Ersilia's business savvy saw their joint enterprise take off in leaps and bounds. With a cash rich government eager to advance money for expansion, Giuseppe and Ersilia were ready to shift from premises that were limiting further growth. A brand new factory was purpose-built at one of the main manufacturing centres in Turin. Further enhancing their success was the advent in 1957 of the European Common Market. As a foundation member Italy was favoured with numerous export and investment opportunities. A public company known as Engineering Specialists was formed that was soon riding the wave of the 'Italian Economic Miracle'.

Life for Ersilia and Giuseppe was better than good. But Ersilia, ever suspicious of what seemed a too easy success when contrasted with her brutal wartime experiences, made sure surpluses were salted away in a basket of wide-ranging investments. By the late sixties, the economic boom had brought an urban society vastly different to the rural life of her childhood. Household consumer goods such as cars, television sets and washing machines had become cheaper and increasingly more available to the masses. Millions of migrants both external and internal had followed the money and jobs. They were accommodated on the outskirts of cities in large tracts of low-cost housing where the bed mates were crime, violence and social unrest. The previous years of growth and high productivity were degrading slowly but surely into a blight of strikes and industrial upheavals.

Ersilia watched all this carefully, then she moved. She knew they'd had their day and held a board meeting where she tabled a motion that didn't surprise anyone. She proposed that the board accept a standing offer to buy the company. The offer was made by Fiat, the largest carmaker in Italy and a long-time purchaser of outsourced auto parts.

The motion was carried, and after settlement, Ersilia and Giuseppe became instant millionaires. Other board members also profited handsomely, none more so than their close friend, confidant and long-time business partner Felicio Milano. Felicio had numerous business interests including major holdings in the fledgling mass tourism industry. The burgeoning middle class of nearby Europe and Great Britain and further afield in America, Asia and the South Pacific were fascinated by the radically different life experience a vacation in Italy could hold. Felicio, in a meeting with Ersilia and Giuseppe, told them he had made a significant deposit on a block of land on the Amalfi Coast, overlooking the Tyrrhenian Sea. The title included a building site approximately eighty metres above the high tide and covered ownership down to the sea level. If they were interested, they could become partners by providing the rest of the funds to secure the deal. He had also commissioned a high-profile architect to provide concept drawings which he would show them.

Ersilia was very interested and wanted to play an active part in the idea. Giuseppe was prepared to put in his share but would remain a sleeping partner. He had already received a very good job offer with Fiat. "My passion is engineering and cars, not overfed tourists with large cameras and larger waistlines." They all shook on the deal and Giuseppe would receive a monthly share of the profit. His lawyer and accountant looked over the arrangement, made their suggestions and ultimately their approval. Papers were signed and after twenty-five years together the brother and sister, now middle-aged, shook hands and went their separate ways.

Ersilia settled in a small flat in nearby Amalfi and for her health walked the short hilly road every day to the now completed resort. The top floor was finished with a penthouse suite that Ersilia paid for personally. She was looking ahead to the time when she would find the daily walk too formidable. Then she would cease letting out the penthouse separately and move in along with a man servant. Ersilia dreamt often of her daughter and always felt the guilt of abandoning her. She wondered how her life had gone in the faraway land of New Zealand and wondered also about the tall quiet man who had entered her life and changed it forever.

Months grew into years and the years grew one on top of the other until at the age of ninety-three Ersilia felt the memories of the tall quiet man and her daughter fading. For a reason she couldn't explain, she still checked the daily guest register, then one day saw a reservation made for Helen Marshall. She took her glasses off, cleaned them carefully, then put them back on. The name was still there. Helen Marshall was arriving from New Zealand in two weeks. Ersilia went back to her penthouse and sat looking out over the sea and the sun sinking below the distant hills.

Before she went to sleep, on her calendar she drew a leafy branch and two little birds on the date of Helen's arrival. If there was one thing she knew, she wasn't going to leave this world before that day.

Helen Marshall arrived on the date marked. The same day exactly four weeks later, Ersilia Abelli died peacefully in her sleep.

Epilogue

Alan watched the familiar hills and distant mountains roll slowly by as one of New Zealand Railways finest chugged along the main trunk line between Wellington and Auckland. The carriage was full of soldiers, some on crutches, some with serious looking head bandages ominously covering an eye or ear. He realised he'd got off lightly as two soldiers limped past. The train gradually slowed as it pulled into the last stop before his. It came to a halt so he stood up and joined the mob of olive green moving along the aisle towards the exit. Some moved with the ease of youth, others holding everyone up ribbing each other as they pushed and jostled for the iconic NZR cuppa. He climbed slowly down behind a soldier on crutches and joined the queue for one of the best cups of tea he'd ever tasted. He could never work out what made it so good. Maybe it was just the temporary relief from the agony of the government owned, tortuously slow service. Ten minutes later he was back onboard and less than twenty miles from home, a farm half an hour's drive from a small town close to the West Coast of New Zealand's North Island.

Alan had now been home a couple of weeks and he was still adjusting to a life of peace and tranquillity. He felt restless after several months of facing life and death daily. He had lost mates and farewelled a beautiful Italian girl he would never see again. His parents had met him at the station and driven him up to the farm. They sat on the porch looking out over pasture and bush-covered hills. He said little but listened while they brought him up to date on local affairs since he left New Zealand. After an awkward silence, he suddenly began talking in no particular order about the last fifteen months. His parents stayed awhile longer then departed knowing he needed to be alone with his thoughts.

But he was lonely and after giving the situation serious thought decided to call Margaret and see if he could resolve their on/off relationship. She agreed to a night out in a nearby town that had a café and picture theatre. They would have a meal and see a film. The short trip would be in the farm truck. Tonight was the night he would give her an ultimatum, marriage yes or marriage no. He drove the old truck to Margaret's address and they both set off in time for the meal and movie.

As they expected in the shortages of post-war New Zealand the meal was average but at least they didn't have to cook it themselves. They made small talk both conscious they were skirting around an issue that wasn't going away. Alan took a deep breath to say something important but Margaret leant over and put a finger across his mouth.

"Leave it until after the picture, I've been waiting to see this one for months. I will tell all then. I promise."

"Ok," Alan replied.

The picture came and went and they stepped into the dark street and walked in silence to the truck. They climbed in and slammed the doors.

"This old dunger is fairly noisy so we better talk before we drive."

"I can't marry you, " she said suddenly.

"Why not?"

"Because tests I've had show that I can't conceive. I can't have a baby. I didn't want to tell you until I had tried all the options. I found out while you were overseas. That's all I can say."

"But I don't mind, " he said lamely.

"Not now, but what about when you take over the farm. You'll want someone to leave it to, you know that as well as I do."

Alan drove in brooding silence, not sure what he thought or how he felt. He dropped her off, gave her a peck on her cheek, and pulled out onto the road and headed for home.

A week later, Alan finished afternoon milking and trudged up the farm track to the cottage where he now lived, just not with Margaret. Bellbirds, tuis, wood pigeons and fantails lived in bush that fringed neat, well-fenced paddocks, but this slice of paradise did nothing to lift the flat feeling he'd lived with since the night at the pictures. He stood on the porch looking down on the gravel road winding through the valley. From here, he watched the local rural delivery man pull up and drop mail in their box. He then pushed the little red flag up and drove off down the valley. Alan walked the fifty yards down to the road, pushed the flag down and picked three letters out. One was from the bank and one from his stock and station agent. The third made his stomach tighten. In the top left corner was the crown emblem of the New Zealand Armed Forces and in the middle was his name and address, tidy and correct. Apart from the Japanese, the war was well over so there was no reason to worry that the envelope held call up papers, he hoped.

Alan decided to sit down to read the contents, so he strode back up the hill and stepped through the French doors left open for the late afternoon sun. He sat back on the couch and opened the envelope. Inside was a letter from a Major Calder from Wellington. It detailed in short sentences that an individual named Evan Jeffries had contacted them seeking the address details of one Alan Marshall, recently a combat soldier who was captured in North Africa and escaped as a result of a partisan action in Northern Italy. The officer went on to say a decision was made to include Evan's letter with their correspondence. Alan folded the army's letter and tucked it in his pocket, then eagerly opened the letter from his old mate.

Evan got quickly to the point.

Hello Alan.

Following is a brief outline of what I've been doing since I left with Marko and travelled to Yugoslavia. I stayed for several weeks and provided basic medical attention for injured Yugoslav partisans. With the eventual cooling of relationships with our previous communist allies, I slipped out of Yugoslavia at night and travelled south towards Monfalcone in an attempt to find you and or Ersilia. I also wanted to be in the right place and time for when Allied troops liberated Italy's northeast. I had a rough idea of her uncle's address and after a few discreet enquiries ended up near Monfalcone where I found Ersilia at her uncle's house. You were long gone, presumably back to New Zealand. Eventually Ersilia admitted what was clearly obvious, she was pregnant. Given the desperate conditions of post-war Italy, with limited medical facilities or reliable food supplies, Ersilia was very pessimistic about having the baby by herself. I convinced her to have the baby and committed to stay at the house and oversee the pregnancy. I was lucky to gain access to a large collection of medical books kept by the widow of a doctor who had lived nearby. His widow happily gave them to me, including all his medical equipment not stolen by the fascists. I set up a makeshift surgery in Artemio's house and burnt the midnight oil trying to fill the gaps in my knowledge. At the time, any knowledge or expertise was better than none. I learned fast, which is often the best way. I had been treating local people for common ailments, but illnesses due to an extremely limited diet are more difficult to deal with.

The baby, a girl, is now four months old. Ersilia is struggling to cope and I am concerned by her mental state and believe she is suffering what I can only describe as some sort of version of shell shock. The violence she experienced, combined with the feeling of responsibility for the loss of her parents, as well as Branko and Adrijan, has dragged her down into long periods of quiet depression. She only just manages to feed her little girl but struggles to relate to her. The widow of the local doctor has stepped into the role of doting stepmother. I believe Ersilia is emotionally overloaded and probably as a result of her parents' deaths, talks incessantly about finding Giuseppe, the brother she hasn't seen for more than a year. She accepts you have another life to live. She bears no grudges but is deeply concerned that her and your daughter, is not getting the best start to a good life. As a result of the deaths and casualties from the war there is a shortage of young able men. Alan, you are a fit, able man. I suggest you come here and adopt the little girl who is as beautiful as her mother and has a little bit of you in her. I recall you telling me that a woman friend you were seeing back home was reluctant to marry you. Her health problems you described sounded like issues that prevented her from being able to bear children. To be quite blunt there is a baby going spare that would find a great home with you and your partner in New Zealand. I look forward to your reply.

Yours faithfully, Dr Evan Jeffries.

PS. By the way, as far as my future is concerned, I am soon to move to Crete, possibly semi-permanently, if they will have me. There is a heavy need of medical expertise and experience which I believe I am slowly accumulating. I will keep in touch as to how that is going.

Alan was stunned and sat back staring through the doors and over the green lawn that stretched off to native bush. The letter dropped from his hand and fluttered to the floor. A breeze from the backdoor lifted it up and shifted it a few feet. He watched it as it moved closer with each puff towards the large double door. The sun was now low over the ridge of bush.

He stood up and in two strides bent down and picked it up. He'd thought long and hard and finally decided Margaret was the woman he wanted to marry. He would simply go around to Margaret's home, give her the letter, then return home and wait for her reaction.

Alan and his new bride accomplished the feat of adopting a baby from Italy with assistance from the re-established Italian embassy in Wellington. They returned to New Zealand five months later with a daughter they named Helen.

Evan Jefferies' letter was carefully folded, then placed in a legal envelope and permanently held by Margaret's lawyer in her personal file.

#

Nikolas arrived in New Zealand and while working on Alan's rough, scrub and bush-covered block, grew to like the land and its people. He lived in the farm cottage and understood that the block would be half-owned by him and half by Alan. He began with a small herd of cows donated by Alan and supplied milk to the local dairy cooperative.

On a wet, drizzly day he was walking his cows in for afternoon milking when Alan drove through the gate and pulled up beside him.

"Something for you mate." He wound down his window and reached out, holding an envelope with a German postmark. Nikolas's dog came up and rubbed against his leg. He took the envelope, but before reading the address, he'd already recognised the perfume. A bead of rainwater from his nose dropped onto the front, spreading the ink of the familiar script that read:

Nikolas Katrakis c/-Alan Marshall RD 1 Manganui, New Zealand.

He didn't open it but just stared at the careful writing, then slowly turned it over to the return address on the back. His other hand opened the domed flap of his back pocket and slid inside to take hold of the leather pouch he always carried.